LETHAL JUSTICE

KATHY LOCKHEART

Editor: Susan F. Staudinger with SS Stylistic Editing
Proofreader: Jovana Shirley, Unforeseen Editing, www.unforeseenediting.com and Judy Zweifel, Judy's Proofreading, www.judysproofreading.com

Cover design © By Hang Le

ISBN 978-1-955017-08-4 e-book
ISBN 978-1-955017-09-1 Paperback
ISBN 978-1-955017-10-7 Hardcover
ISBN 978-1-955017-11-4 Large Print

Published by Rosewood Literary Press

LETHAL JUSTICE

For my mom, my role model in unconditional love.

AUTHOR'S NOTE

Lethal Justice is a tension-filled romance. While the romantic scenes are not extremely graphic, this forbidden love story contains violence and other content that may be triggering for some readers. I prefer you go into a story without spoilers, but if you would like a **list of detailed triggers**, you can find it posted on my website at KathyLockheart dot com.

1

No one ever expects to be held captive by three men who intend to murder them. No. They go about their lives, oblivious to the imminent danger around the corner—even when it's only a few hours away.

Just like I was doing right now while Dad watched the evening news, the anchor's voice piercing through our townhouse.

"Another brazen robbery last night, this one in the River North neighborhood. Where police say two armed men broke into a home and stole over $20,000 worth of valuables."

Twenty grand. Jeez, Louise. *I wish I had that kind of money.* I glared at my latest utilities bill, which had been haunting my countertop for the past five days, as if a contagious plague would sicken me the moment I opened it.

Which was stupid. I'd turned off the air conditioner despite the sweltering summer heat, so I bet it was under a hundred. Maybe even below ninety. It had to be. Anything beyond that, I was screwed, even with my upcoming paycheck.

I tore a tiny corner open with my nail and then slowly ripped a line down the envelope, taking a deep breath before I unfolded the paper and looked at the amount owed.

$154.12.

Ugh.

Maybe by some miracle, another bill hadn't cleared yet, and I could do that magic juggling thing, where this bill got paid while another was in limboland. I opened the banking app on my phone and checked my balance.

Nope. A whopping $25.57 sat in my checking account, pre-grocery shopping. *Pre.*

Deep breath. You made a fantastic case to Michael, and he was supportive of your ask.

For two years, the company I worked for had not given raises to anyone, citing pressures from the economy. While I didn't think I was above others, I'd watched a TED Talk that inspired me to put a business case together and be brave enough to ask for one. To advocate for myself. As a marketing analyst, my work this past year had brought in $1,500,000 in advertising fees to our company, which was $350,000 over my target. I'd worked my butt off to accomplish that, and I was mega proud of it. And yet, when it came time for my performance review? I got a pat on the back instead of a raise.

Again.

This time, I decided to stand up and ask for what I felt was fair—something I did professionally with a lot of financials to back up my request. And the great news? My boss, Michael, was taking it to HR yesterday, who had the final say.

He probably hadn't emailed yet because he was trying stupendously hard to get a yes. Or maybe he was able to secure more than the five percent I'd asked for and wanted to share the good news in person.

I checked my phone anyway.

Holy crap.

There's his email.

My heart spasmed as I opened it.

. . .

Re: Raise request

Zoey,

As discussed, I spoke with HR about your request for a raise. Unfortunately, they will not make exceptions to the company-wide policy of no annual adjustments this year. I'm sorry it wasn't the answer we were hoping for, but please know your hard work is very much valued in this company, and hopefully, next year might be a different answer.

Sincerely,

Michael

Damn.

The company withholding raises for all employees sucked, but what sucked even more was that this put me back to ground zero with solving our financial problems.

My eyes stung.

"Everything okay?" Dad asked.

I cleared my throat and smiled. "Fine," I lied.

Dad hadn't been able to work since his accident, and as it turned out, my marketing job wasn't enough to pay for everything my dad needed. His prescriptions alone were seven hundred dollars a month.

Seven. Hundred. Dollars. My older brother, Anthony—who lived on the other side of the country and was desperate to help after the accident—sent us more money each month than he could probably afford. It covered half of Dad's meds, and I was immensely grateful for that, but there was still the other half. And that didn't include medical bills, physical therapy, and all the other stuff he needed if he had any hope of recovering.

Lesson learned: Don't fall victim to an accident. It could screw you *and* your family.

But I guess that wasn't entirely fair. If it had happened when Dad was still employed with health insurance, our financial situation wouldn't be in a complete tailspin right now.

Whatever. I couldn't let this setback stop me from focusing on my goals: help my father recover and regain his independence, so we could both get our lives back and get justice for him against the son of a bitch who hit Dad with their car and then sped off without even checking if he was alive.

Justice that hadn't come in the eight months since it happened.

Dad resumed staring at the news story and said, "I don't want you going anywhere near that neighborhood." As if I were a teenager and not a twenty-six-year-old woman.

"We have nothing to worry about."

Not as far as robberies went, anyway—those felons only targeted rich people, and we were anything but rich. Our rented townhouse that hugged the outskirts of Chicago was long overdue for a renovation. Its cherry wood doors, cabinets, and trim had suffered so much damage in the forty years since it'd been installed that in some places, baseboards had turned black with water damage, which came with the added bonus of omitting a faint smell of mold. The matching hardwood floors weren't much better, chipped and scratched in more places than it wasn't, and the kitchen and bathroom countertops were police-caution-tape yellow. I'd often wondered if the person who'd picked them was color blind. Point being, we didn't have to worry about burglars.

Money, on the other hand, was another story.

Case in point? I knew what Alex—a family friend and Dad's current physical therapist—was probably coming over to talk to me about, and it had kept me up half the night, worrying about it. That email from my boss? Was basically my nail in the coffin.

What in the world was I going to tell Alex now?

As if my anxiety had summoned him, a knock at the front door came.

"Look through the peephole," Dad said.

I refrained from rolling my eyes. *Armed burglars don't knock.* But whatever. I appeased him, confirming it was Alex before opening the door.

"Hey, Zoey."

With blond hair and green eyes, Alex stood six inches taller than me. He had a lean body with broad shoulders and very thin legs, but the most prominent part of him was the freckles speckled over his nose and cheeks.

I'd first seen those freckles when he and his parents moved into the house across the street from ours right before our high school freshman year. He used to come over for dinners at our house a lot and had been like a brother to me, a friend to our entire family, really. So, after getting his college degree in physical therapy, he'd heard about the accident and offered to help.

Alex nodded a hello to my dad, then returned his gaze to me, shoved his hands into his pockets, and nodded toward the front yard. "Can we talk out here?"

Crap.

I stepped into the summer air, noting the pastel purples drifting through the pinks with the setting sun.

Summer had always been my favorite time in Chicago. I loved the warm weather and how the bright blue skies canopied the skyscrapers with happiness. I loved the tourists who traveled from all around the world, reminding us not to take our remarkable museums, historic architecture, and gorgeous landmarks for granted. And I loved how there was an endless list of things to do.

I'd get to enjoy all of it again. I totally would, just as soon as Dad got back on his feet.

We stood on my front porch, which sat on a street with rows of identical townhouses, many with rusted chain-link fences. The narrow buildings sat so close together that only a few feet separated them, and the two-lane road in front of us was a favorite for teenagers blasting loud music from their cars while the smell of weed wafted out of them.

I stared at the porch's cedar planks, noting a fresh crack splintering near the steps that led to the sidewalk. I bet the board never saw that crack coming, probably thought it would exist forever without problems.

"Listen, I wanted to talk to you about something." Alex wouldn't meet my eyes. He kept his gaze pinned to his shoes, as if they'd give him the courage to say whatever uncomfortable thing he was about to say.

"I'm going to keep helping you guys," he caveated. Which was bad. Caveats were very bad. "But, uh..." Alex grabbed the back of his neck. "The thing is, my landlord just upped my rent, and, uh...well, there's a new client that wants to take your dad's spot."

No. No. No.

After eight months of hell, things were finally on the cusp of turning around. Dad's physical therapy had gotten him from being bedridden to wheelchair-mobile, and last week, Dad had a major breakthrough, standing up and getting a couple of steps in with a walker. He was, as doctors put it, at a precipice in his rehabilitation. A fork in the road. Keep pushing forward? He'd regain his ability to walk and live a normal life. Scale back, and his body would regress.

Physical therapy was the only tool that would make or break the most pivotal point in his recovery, and if Alex stopped giving it to him, it would throw almost all of Dad's progress down the drain.

"I was going to turn him down," Alex said, his tone laced with apology. "But..."

But I owed Alex $2,200 and counting. No matter how good a family friend he was, no matter how much he wanted to help us, that was a lot of freaking money and time to be spending not getting paid. Especially if his rent just went up.

For a long time, Alex had done Dad's PT for free, but when I realized we were in this for a much longer haul than expected, I insisted on paying him *something*. He'd given me a mega discount, and even then, I was behind.

"I can still come at least a couple days a week," Alex offered. "Hopefully more."

But anything less than five wouldn't progress Dad; it might simply slow his regression.

My voice was a near whisper on account of choking back tears; I swallowed them down, so I wouldn't make Alex feel even worse by crying in front of him. I could cry later, alone in my room.

"Please," I said. "You're the only person who's willing to work with us on this, and if Dad doesn't keep his current therapy, he might never get out of that wheelchair or get his independence back."

And I'll never get my life back.

What a selfish thought to have when Dad couldn't even walk and Alex was getting screwed right now. It wasn't fair to ask him this.

I felt like a terrible person, like I was taking advantage of him when he had his own bills to pay. I mean, honestly, how could I ask Alex for an extension when I already owed him for three months of unpaid work? But this wasn't just about me. It was about Dad and his quality of life.

Alex studied my eyes, a crease in his forehead appearing, as if my desperation had caught him off guard. I wondered if Alex wasn't as hopeful as I was that Dad would have more breakthroughs. And fully recover. The thought of him doubting it made a rock drop in my stomach.

"You know what?" Alex offered a smile and waved his hand. Guilt etched through his words as if *he* were the one being selfish for having even entertained the idea of getting paid for his time after eight months of favors. "Never mind. I can figure this out."

"No," I insisted. "I'll get you your money." I'd find a way...

I knew this financial breaking point was coming. It was a juggling act I'd avoided for nearly a year. Robbing Peter to pay Paul—charging groceries on my credit cards, things like that. But now, my credit cards were maxed out, and I had no more financial tricks up my sleeve.

But I did have one option left. A painful option, but I would do anything to keep Dad's rehabilitation going and not take advantage of Alex in the process.

"I have a ring," I said. A special ring Dad had given to me the Christmas before I left for college. "It's worth a lot, and I can pawn it."

I'd have to get it from Dad's old place, but that was totally doable; it hadn't sold yet, and I still had Dad's spare key.

"Zoey." Alex's voice dropped low. "I don't want you to do that."

"I'm doing it whether you like it or not," I decided. Maybe after I paid Alex, I'd have some money left over to put toward other bills.

"Zoey..."

"I don't want other people having to bail us out, and I know what it's like, trying to make ends meet." I didn't want to see Alex struggle the way we had; I didn't want to drag him down like that. "It's no big deal," I claimed.

Alex sighed, the same exacerbated breath he used to do when we were teens. And then his gaze fell across my face, flickering in curiosity. "I don't understand why you're doing so much for him after what he did to you."

I kept my face neutral, as if his words hadn't detonated inside me, blasting shrapnel throughout my chest.

"I can't thank you enough for all that you've done for us," I said. "I'll pawn the ring, and I'll have cash in your hand tomorrow."

Alex looked at the ground and shook his head in frustration. "Your dad had to be making, what, multi-six figures as that corporate strategy executive? He should've had enough money for a lifetime or, at the very least, for any medical crisis. But his negligence becomes your problem? It's bull."

On top of losing his physical health, Dad had lost his money and his old home—a high-end condo, where he'd lived for the past several years. Any day, it would sell, and he wouldn't even profit from it or break even. Not with all the money owed to the banks and hospital bills. No, that money would go to creditors.

Not that I said any of that; I preferred not to feed Alex's resentment toward my father. Truth be told, I hadn't resolved my own frustrations over my dad's financial negligence, but I needed to stay focused on the hurdle before me—securing continuity in Dad's therapy.

Alex put his hands back into his pockets. "You know I'd do anything for you, right?"

"Is that a yes?" I balled up on my tiptoes.

Alex nodded.

I reached up and hugged him, catching him off guard. He wobbled back a couple inches and returned the embrace before I released him.

Selling the ring was a stopgap. One that wouldn't last for long, but these days, my life was so chaotic, I could only focus on one hurdle at a time.

And this was a gigantic hurdle that had moved out of my way.

"I will make this up to you!" I didn't know how, but I would. Someday, I'd pay him interest on all this overdue money, and in the meantime, I could do little things, at least. "Do you want to stay for dinner? I'm making tacos."

Alex looked at his watch. "I'm running late for my last appointment."

I nodded, and when he stepped off my porch, I said, "I'll have your money tomorrow."

He pulled his lips up on one side, sadness still pulsing through his gaze before he began to amble away. "I'll see you later, Zoey."

"Alex?"

He turned around.

"Thank you."

After getting a lopsided smile from Alex, I went back inside, struggling to contain my glee.

"Everything okay?" Dad asked.

"Yeah," I said.

Because now, everything might just be okay. The fear of losing Dad's therapy had been suffocating me for weeks, but I'd been lucky to get this reprieve. And while it didn't solve all of our problems, it was a huge win, and I hadn't felt this light in forever.

I'd go to ten pawn shops if I had to, maybe even jewelry stores, to get the absolute best price for that ring, but by this time tomorrow? So help me, Alex would have that money in his hands.

Thank God.

I hummed as I loaded the dishwasher and cooked tacos, and when they were done, my dad wheeled himself over to the kitchen table.

At six feet tall, Dad once had broad shoulders, thick black hair, and a commanding aura that demanded respect. But now, his shoulder bones poked out of his shirt, his hair had thinned enough to see the scalp, and his legs were like skeletons with skin. It was scary how quickly a human body could go from being healthy to withering away to almost nothing.

Dad glanced at the television, which was on another news station about the robbery—this one focused on the manhunt.

"Speaking of criminals," I said as I sprinkled shredded cheddar onto my taco, "I'm thinking of asking for a new detective to be assigned to your case."

Dad frowned as he picked up his water glass, which was already frosted in condensation, thanks to the ice cubes battling it out with this summer heat. Even with the windows open, a bead of sweat trickled down his temple. "Maybe it's time to let this go."

My jaw almost bounced off the floor. "And let him get away with what he did to you? Fat chance."

"We need to accept that it's improbable the case will get solved at this point. It's not healthy to be this obsessed over it."

"How can you say that?" It would be bad enough if Dad had been jaywalking, but he'd had the pedestrian green light. "A person hit you and drove off like it meant nothing. They left you dying in the street. They took everything from you."

"But not my life."

"And that means you let them off the hook? Because you happened to survive? Seriously?"

"I'm not defending them. I'm just saying you've been fixated on this for too long. I want you to be happy and live your life."

"And I want the lowlife that hit you to rot in prison for the rest of their life."

"You're twenty-six, Zo. You should go out with friends. Date. Not obsess over some cold case."

"Some cold case? It's not a case; it's our life."

"Zo..."

"Let's just drop it," I said. Because I was downright blissful for once, and this was about to burst my bubble.

We finished dinner in silence. I ate and pretended not to notice Dad's troubled glances my way. Honestly, he didn't need to worry about me so much. Did this situation drag on longer than we expected? Yes. But it was temporary. For now, the best thing I could do was ensure Dad made all his appointments and I got Alex his money.

"Will you be okay if I head out after I get you settled tonight?" I asked.

This piqued Dad's interest. Which, I had to admit, was a little pathetic in terms of a twenty-something's social life. I didn't see my friends very often because Dad was home alone all day, every day, and while he *could* be alone, I felt bad, leaving him longer than I needed to. Even though Dad tried many times to get me to go out.

"Where are you going?" he asked.

"To meet up with some friends."

Dad smiled. "Really?"

I hated lying to him, but if he found out that finances were so bad that I needed to pawn my ring, he would try to stop me. And this wasn't up for debate; it needed to get done and get done fast.

"I won't be long," I said.

I cleaned up the kitchen, got Dad situated, made sure he had his phone, water, and the remote control easily within reach, and then headed out to run my secret errand.

I walked several blocks to the "L" station and cringed; I wanted to enjoy my little bliss bubble, but no. When I walked across the platform, three guys locked eyes on me.

"Hellooooooo..."

Here we go.

These guys harassed every woman at this "L" stop, and it was getting old. Didn't they have anything better to do with their time than make people uncomfortable?

Sometimes, they made sexual innuendos about my wavy black hair, chocolate eyes, caramel-colored skin, or thick lips. But most of the time, they were far more explicit than that, reciting what they'd like to do to me if they got me alone.

The taller guy followed me, looking at me up and down like a piece of meat, and then had the audacity to position himself a mere two feet away.

I clenched my hands into balls.

"You have a beautiful mouth," he said, licking his teeth. "Know what would make it prettier?" He grabbed his crotch. "Seeing it wrapped around this."

"How are you out in society right now?" I asked. "Did someone leave your cage open?"

His two buddies let out a burst of laughter, punching each other in the shoulders as I stood on the platform, watching the train approaching.

Unfortunately, my quip didn't shut the guy up.

"You know when I saw you tonight," he said suggestively, "a thought crossed my mind."

"Poor thought. Must have been a long, lonely journey."

His friends let out more laughs as the "L" rounded the final bend with a metallic wail and came to a rest, opening its doors. I stepped onto the train, grateful they didn't follow me. They never had before, but I always worried one of these days, they might escalate their harassment.

In any case, I enjoyed the ride into the heart of the city, where I got off and began walking the rest of the way.

Tonight, Chicago looked mythical. Seventy-story skyscrapers glistened against a thin layer of fog, stretching toward low-hanging clouds that swallowed their top floors. I could taste the hangover from this morning's thunderstorm, the air muggy, causing a bead of sweat to roll down my back. The smell of wet concrete blended with the scent of fried potatoes funneling from nearby restaurants while a rumble of engines echoed off the buildings as vehicles chugged along the roads.

When I reached my dad's old building, I took the elevator up and entered his condo.

As soon as I stepped inside, though, the skin on the back of my neck prickled with an unsettling feeling. I scanned the space, trying to isolate why my sixth sense's alarm bells were sounding, but there was nothing to explain it. The lights were off, and the only sound was the ticking clock above the fireplace.

I flipped the lights on and looked around again. The condo was like entering a time machine, back to when Dad was in the prime of his life. The blue and gray furniture, picked by some decorator, complementing white cabinets in the oversize kitchen—the kind that closed gently and had organizers galore. Wood flooring, high-end artwork, and even higher-end electronics.

But the pride and joy of my dad's old place was his sports memorabilia collection. Two dozen white baseballs with red stitching and black signatures proudly sat in a six-foot-tall mahogany case with custom lighting. Some of them were worth a few hundred. Some a few thousand, maybe more. All were a point of contention in the bankruptcy case.

None of his assets had been sold yet, but they would be soon to pay off Dad's creditors.

With only a couple of exceptions. Like the ring. Since it was a gift to me, I was the legal owner, thus I could sell it. I just needed to retrieve it from the safe in Dad's office.

My dad's ex-wife, Holly, had put it there after I'd thrown it in my dad's face.

But that was a whole other story I didn't need to think about right now.

I went into the office and walked around the L-shaped mahogany desk that sat between shelves stacked with books, organized by height and color. On the far wall, a painting of the Chicago River winding through buildings—its primary color an unnaturally greenish teal—hung in front of the concealed safe. I carefully lifted it up and off its hanger, set it on the ground, and started on the combination Dad had shared with me when I'd become responsible for helping with the sale of this condo. Frankly, I should have cleared the safe of any personal effects we had by now, but other priorities kept delaying me.

When the dial clicked on eighty-eight, my vision went black, something pressed against my mouth, and I was pulled until my back pressed into something hard. It took my brain a fraction of a second to realize my screams were silenced by a leather-gloved hand. My sight blocked with another.

"Don't move," a man's voice growled.

2

My nose's breath whistled against the smoky smell of the leather glove clamping my mouth, and my heart thumped in my ears while needles of adrenaline shot through my fingertips.

"Keep your eyes closed," he said. "Did you hear me? Keep 'em closed."

I nodded, and when he took his hand away, I obeyed, clenching my eyes shut. His chest peeled away from my back, and then something soft draped over my eyes and knotted behind my head. Among the sea of my long black waves, one hair howled in pain, getting plucked out in the process.

"Will you keep quiet? Or do I need to gag you?" he asked.

"I'll be quiet," I whispered.

His cold gloves gripped my upper arms, traced them down to my wrists, and pulled my hands behind my back, wrapping a similar silky fabric around them.

The bondage pinched my skin and tugged three times with each knot formed. Which might as well have been a one-two-three punch, for in this moment, I knew I'd done all the wrong things. I should have run. I should have kicked. I should never have let myself become bound and blindfolded because now, I had no way to fight against whatever horrors this guy might unleash upon me.

My odds of fighting him off might not be great—at five foot four, I was only a hundred and fifteen pounds. But any chance would have been better than none.

"Come here." He took me by the arm and guided me a few steps.

It was disorienting, trying to move without sight, trying to think coherently with fear suffocating the blood flow to my brain. Something pressed into the back of my thighs, and one of his hands pressed down on my shoulder while the other wrapped completely around my bicep as he gently lowered me into the chair.

I opened my eyes, grateful for a small strip of light near the brim of my nose, where the fabric didn't meet my cheek. I could only see a bit of his feet, but it was something, and if I tilted my head, I saw more.

He's wearing black combat boots.

Was he a squatter? Or here to rob the place? Or worse...had he followed me—his real target—in here to...to...

I couldn't even finish the sickening thought.

Through the crack in my blindfold, I saw his knees appear.

He's squatting in front of me.

"What's your name?" he asked.

"Zoey."

"What are you doing here, Zoey?"

It was eerie, hearing my name roll off his tongue, but at least I didn't seem to be his primary target.

That didn't mean I was out of danger, though. Even if I wasn't the original purpose of him being here, he might certainly adapt his agenda. Make me his primary focus...

No. I needed to stop letting fear take control here. I was fine. This was fine. I would absolutely get out of this. I mean, if the guy wanted me dead, he could have done it right away, before I even knew he was here, and the fact that he tied me up? Was probably a good thing, to make him feel like he was in control, so he'd just get the hell out of here.

But evidently, my nerves weren't completely sold on my safety because when I spoke, my voice quivered. "This is my dad's condo. I came tonight to get a ring that I left here."

He was quiet for a moment. "A ring."

I nodded, conscious of the way my body twisted backward, recoiling as far away from him as possible.

"This house has been empty for months."

How does he know that?

I wasn't sure, but I'd file that clue away to tell the police when I got out of here, so the cops could find this guy and put him away forever. Hell, I'd gather as many clues as possible.

"We were waiting to clear it out until it sold," I explained.

"Shit." He stood up and, based on the clunk of his steps along the wooden floors, began to pace. "Why did you have to show up tonight of all nights?"

The anxiety in his voice made my mouth run dry. A hostage expert I was not, but that level of nervousness couldn't be good. There was a reason the expression, *Wrong time, wrong place,* was so widely known.

Focus, Zoey. Focus on information. Tonight of all nights.

That meant he was only here for the night, so he wasn't a homeless squatter. He had to be a burglar, then. *Right?*

"I haven't seen anything," I said. "Just let me go, and I'll never tell anyone."

I held my breath, waiting for an answer as his feet stilled, angled toward me.

He didn't answer my plea for release, though. Instead, notes of confusion braided around his frustrated tone when he finally spoke. "Were you hanging around this building a couple weeks ago?"

Was I...what? "No," I said. "Why?"

I felt his gaze on me. "You look familiar."

I evaluated his voice with a fresh level of scrutiny, trying to match it to anyone I knew. His voice was rough and deep, like something you'd hear from a radio host, but no one in my life sounded like him.

"Do I know you?" I asked.

Nerves prickled my skin.

One Mississippi.

Two Mississippi.

Three Mississippi.

"No," he said.

Which had to be true. If someone in my life was a secret villain, they'd recognize me, not fish around, trying to place me.

Might he know my dad?

Dad...

Oh God, right now, he was home, assuming I'd be there in the morning to cook his breakfast and help with the bill collectors and bankruptcy attorneys and everything else. I was the only person he had, so I couldn't let this guy do something to me.

Who the hell was this guy, anyway?

What if he's a killer? Or a guy who's already served two stints in prison, one strike away from being sent away for life? Prepared to kill any witness that could jeopardize his freedom?

No. That was fear talking. There was no need to blindfold someone you're going to kill; dead people can't rat on you.

But just when hope flickered, another sound extinguished it.

A clomp-clomp echoed down the hallway's planks, yet this guy's shoes remained frozen in place.

"Shit!" A scratchy voice sent ice through my veins.

Through the sliver my blindfold didn't block, I saw his brown boots as he came into the room, followed by a third set, wearing blue Converse.

Brown boots. Blue Converse.

"The hell, Green? *This* was the sound?"

Green must be the original guy's last name. The guy that tied me up.

"She hasn't seen anything," Green said in an authoritative tone.

"You don't know that," Brown Boots snapped in a condescending voice.

When I sensed him walk toward me, my body instinctively shrank into the chair.

"I haven't seen anything, I swear." I hated that my voice sounded high-pitched and wobbly.

"Shut up," the guy in brown boots yelled just before he slapped me.

It stung so badly, a handprint probably reddened on my cheek.

"Brown," Green cautioned in a sharp tone.

The name of the guy that hit me is Brown?

Pathetically, my entire body shook like an animal left in the cold. At least the first guy hadn't been rough with me. This guy was clearly dangerous, but worse, he was irate and flustered, too.

I discreetly yanked at my makeshift handcuffs, the cool fabric assaulting my skin with rug-like burns. But it didn't deter me. I needed to get my wrists free, so I could make a run for it, or fight, or hide, or do something other than just sit here like a caged animal.

"Now, what are we gonna do?" the guy in Converse asked. I hated that he sounded nervous; nervousness couldn't be good right now.

"She didn't see anything, Orange," Green said in a calming voice.

Orange? No way the guy's last name is Orange. It has to be some sort of code name, just like Green and Brown must be, too—each man assigned a color as another layer of protection, just like those criminals in that movie.

When the three guys stepped into the hallway, my hope swelled that they might leave, but they stopped just outside the office and had some sort of huddle. I could only make out part of what they were saying, but I tried to unravel every word.

"...she'll call the cops..."

"...might've seen..."

"...recognize our voices..."

I perched at the edge of my seat, trying to convert my ears into satellite dishes.

"...no other option..."

"...not going to prison for the rest of my life..."

The anxiety in their voices had settled into a resolve that made my palms sweat.

"...no choice..."

"...have to kill her."

And then silence.

A chill cooled the air around me as ice frosted around my lungs, making me tremble.

I wasn't going to make it out of here. I wasn't going to go back to our apartment, slide under my covers, and forget this day ever existed. I wouldn't help Dad regain independence.

I'll never see him again. I'll never have the chance to apologize for what I'd done.

I would give anything to have just five more minutes with everyone I love. To feel their arms around me and tell them I love them one last time. Because suddenly, all the other times I've said it before doesn't feel like enough.

A sequence of events flashed through my mind.

I see my ratty teddy bear's head bobbling in the corner of a cardinal-red wagon as my dad pulls me through the zoo.

I see the black hairs below my dad's knuckles as he grips my bicycle's handlebar while he runs alongside me, cheering, "You're doing it!"

I smell cinnamon cookies while Mom pats her daisy apron with its sunshine-yellow tie, leaving white handprints on her lower tummy.

I smell wet leaves as my brother and I race through a field of red and orange trees sheening with dew.

I'm eight, swaying in Dad's arms in my elementary school's gymnasium at the annual father-daughter dance.

I'm thirteen, picking a piece of food out of my front tooth's braces.

I'm three, running from the front door to my dad's car and jumping into his arms.

I'm twenty-six with my arms tied behind my back, about to experience the moment of death.

I heard two sets of footsteps clomp down the hallway, their sounds getting quieter the farther they got from the office, but the third set took a couple of steps closer and stopped.

I leaned my head, seeing a set of black combat boots standing ominously in the doorway. Green—the original man—stood with his feet slightly apart.

Here to end my life.

3

"You really screwed things up by being here tonight," Green snarled.

Evidently, criminals don't like having to murder people unexpectedly. They must prefer to plan it out.

This wasn't fair, dying just because I'd interrupted a robbery. If these guys thought I was just going to sit here and accept their death sentence, they had it wrong. I might not survive, but I'd go down swinging—that was for damn sure.

Aside from the slice of light near the brim of my nose, blackness extinguished my vision, so my other senses completed an urgent inventory. The faint thumping of footsteps confirmed the other guys were on the far end of my dad's place, and louder steps disclosed only Green was near me.

If I wanted to make a run for it, it was now or never.

Adrenaline surged needles into my legs, and my lungs drew in a large gust of oxygen as my heart thundered in anticipation. I shot up like a missile, blasting my body through the office and into the hallway.

Where I didn't make it far.

My captor's arm shot around my stomach, the other just beneath my breasts as he pulled my back against his iron chest, my feet now dangling in the air. The calmness of his grip screamed of a man in power, his arms a cage around me while my hands remained helpless balls, pressed between my back and his stomach.

Which was rock hard, skin stretched over firm ridges.

Shit. He's built like an athlete with a broad chest and lean body, so it'll be seriously hard to get away from him.

But not impossible...

"Let me go!" I screamed, provoking the leather glove to trap my voice.

He pressed his cheek against my jaw as his lips brushed against my right earlobe. "If you don't stay quiet, I'm going to have to gag you."

He shifted his hand over my belly button and pressed up, lifting me higher off the ground.

He's tall. Though how tall, I couldn't be sure.

I kicked my legs wildly, trying to land a blow to his shin, but missed. Instead, my body spun, and simultaneously, I flew higher off the ground, something slammed into my stomach, and a bar squeezed behind my knees.

He's carrying me in a fireman's hold. My body now draped over a blanket of muscles, covering a gargantuan body.

I jerked my legs, trying to break from his grip, but I didn't feel him flinch.

Or sound fazed, for that matter, when he said, "Calm down."

My belly button squished further into his shoulder with each of his steps as he carried my irritatingly small body.

Once we were back inside the office, he slid his hands up the backs of my legs, and when one reached my thigh and the other my upper back, my body twisted through the air, and something soft slammed into my back and butt. His hand was on my shoulder now —thumb on my collarbone—forcing me to sit while the other reclaimed its position over my mouth.

The leather cool against my lips.

"Are you done?" he asked.

I used his voice as a guide, kicking my foot straight toward the sound, hoping to pulverize his nose, but he captured my ankle in his rigid grip. I threw my other foot forward, but like the first, it missed its mark, and he pinned my thigh down with his knee.

I sensed him hovering over me, the heat of his breath bouncing off my cheek.

His face is only inches from mine.

I jerked my head forward, but my headbutt missed.

"*Now*, are you done?" he asked.

The amusement in his tone made me even more frustrated with my failure.

He isn't even out of breath. I fought with everything I had, and it wasn't even a challenge for him.

After almost a minute, Green released me and walked to some other part of this room.

"Who knows you're here?" he asked. His deep voice drifted through my skin like an arctic blast and sent a shiver down my spine.

Lie. Tell him someone knows you're here.

No, don't lie. If he thinks people are looking for you, he'll kill you faster. As hopeless as this situation feels, you can't give up yet. You have to find another chance to escape.

"No one," I admitted.

"You didn't tell anyone that you were coming here tonight?" he clarified.

"No one else will walk in that door and become a witness. No matter how much I wish they would."

"That's not why I'm asking." His tone was lower, as if he was... unsettled by something.

Which got my attention. If he wasn't vetting potential complications, where was he going with this?

"Why'd you come *tonight*, specifically?" Tension wove through his words.

Beneath the cloth that felt like a silky tie, I blinked, confused by his line of questioning. Wasn't the only relevant fact a potential second witness showing up?

"I owe someone money. Why?"

The clock on my dad's desk ticked four times.

"It doesn't matter."

But it did matter. I could tell. I just couldn't imagine why.

I tilted my head, so I could see through the gap beneath my blindfold, noting he was now blocking the doorway. Facing me, based on the position of his boots.

Holding a knife perhaps. Or a gun.

Desperation flooded my veins like an animal waiting in line at the slaughterhouse, smelling death coming.

It's tragic how confronting your own mortality makes you realize the value of your life isn't exclusively defined by your lost experiences, but also in the devastation your death will have on others.

Like Dad.

Fight and flight had failed, but I had to keep trying, if not physically, verbally.

Maybe I can convince him to let me go. Get him to see me as human, help him to understand what's at stake tonight.

"It's not just my life on the line if you kill me." I felt beads of sweat drip down my back. "My dad's disabled. He lives with me, and I take care of him, and if I don't return—"

The clock in my dad's office ticked on.

Tick. Tock. Tick. Tock.

"Facing your demise and your first thought is about a family member." His low tone made me wonder if this had at least given him pause, if only for a moment.

"He needs me."

Tick. Tock.

"What happened to him?"

"He was in an accident."

Tick, tock.

"What kind of accident?"

The memory of that day made me wince. "A hit-and-run of a pedestrian. He can't live by himself, so he moved in with me."

"And you take care of him." His voice was almost a growl.

"Someone has to help him recover."

Judging by the sounds of his footsteps, Green walked to my right several steps and then stopped. "Who's the woman?"

I blinked. "What?"

"There's a picture on the desk. Of a guy—assume he's your dad, based on the age—and some woman. Who is she?"

"She *was* my stepmom." Lord, I hated that term, even when she'd made my dad happy.

"And she can't help him?"

My animosity for Holly billowed in my chest. Could she? Yes. Would she? No. She was too busy, being an awful excuse of a human.

"She won't even return his calls."

How do you go from marrying someone to not caring about them?

"I'm all he has," I repeated. "So, please. I haven't seen anything. You came at me from behind and immediately blindfolded me."

"Maybe you saw something before that happened."

I tightened my fists behind my back.

Maybe this was some sort of game to him. Foreplay that he got off on before the actual murder. I wanted to tell him off, tell him to go screw himself. But as he paced on the other side of the room, I forced myself to remain calm. To refrain from antagonizing my captor and would-be killer.

"Please, just let me go."

"Afraid that ship has sailed."

I clamped my jaw shut. How could he be so callous? Especially after everything I'd told him. "I won't tell anyone what happened."

"Can't take that chance."

I scraped my nail into my palm, and this time, when I spoke, I couldn't suppress the anger from my tone. "You *know* I didn't see anything. You know I can't identify you or your friends even if I wanted to."

"I don't know that," he said in a monotone voice, like he didn't care about having to end my life.

"You do. So, you have nothing to lose by letting me go. But if you don't? And you do something to me? You'll be running from the police forever. There's no statute of limitations on murder. You want that chasing you every day for the rest of your life?"

"Stop talking."

"Think about that. A month from now. A year from now. Five years from now. Twenty-five years from now. You could be caught and get life with no parole."

"Stop. Talking."

"I. Haven't. Seen. Anything. I have no clue what you look like. Who you are. You'd be killing me for absolutely no reason."

I waited for him to say something, to give me any indication I was getting through to him, but as the seconds passed, despair dumped a rock into my stomach.

"There's nothing I can say to convince you to let me go"—my shoulders sank—"is there?"

Tick.

Tock.

"Afraid not."

Afraid not. Two words that, strung together, never created a more sinister meaning. Will you help rehabilitate Dad until he's finally back on his feet? *Afraid not.* Will you live past the age of twenty-six, have the chance of finding love again? *Afraid not.*

He was going to kill me. No matter what I did or said, he was going to kill me.

It's crazy how, in a single moment, your entire life can change. That summarized my life as of late. Every time I turned around, the landscape of my future repainted into something darker.

Almost three years ago, my boyfriend died. It was shocking. Violent. And tragic.

He was murdered.

There one day, gone the next. Not because of some accident or unfortunate illness. Because some vile human being willingly and purposely ended his life. As if it meant nothing.

And one of the things that had gutted me the most? Was that when my boyfriend was being brutally killed... when he was suffering unimaginable pain and terror, I was mad at him. I was mad because he wasn't answering my calls. I was mad that he hadn't come home yet and didn't have the courtesy to at least text me back. I was mad because I'd jumped to the conclusion that someone who claimed to love me hadn't made me their priority.

As my boyfriend fought for his life, as he took his last breath, I'd been angry with him.

I don't know anyone who can come back from that kind of guilt.

And I don't know anyone who could stop the torturous questions that came next. How scared did he feel? How long, exactly, did he know he was going to die? What were his final moments on this earth like? How badly did he suffer? The questions had infected my mind like a disease.

Now, facing a similar fate, I knew the answers to some of those questions. And that knowledge was unbearable.

I tried to combat those thoughts by forcing myself to think about the good memories I'd had with him.

One memory in particular flashed through my heart.

"Tell me something you've always wanted to do, but haven't done yet," my boyfriend says.

I'm lying with my head on his lap while he looks down at me, running his fingers delicately through my hair. Each stroke concludes with his fingertips dancing along the skin on my neck, warming my chest.

I feel so peaceful in his arms.

"I've had a dream since I was a little girl to watch the sun set over the Grand Canyon. To see its 270-mile-wide rock formations, while the blue water of the Colorado River snakes along its bottom." I smile. "I want to hike to the South Rim, take off my socks, and feel the red rock beneath my

feet while I watch the clouds turn pastel purple as the sun dips below the canyon. Casting birds into silhouettes."

His tone is soft. "Why haven't you done it yet?"

I shrug. "It's expensive, I guess? Spending money on that when I have so many other bills seems irresponsible."

His eyes turn reflective. "When my parents were suffering through the grief of my sister's death, they let years pass without doing the things that made them happy." He brushes his knuckles along my temple. "Life is short, Zoey. No matter what happens, you have to prioritize living."

This is something I absolutely love about him. He's full of wisdom far beyond his years.

"I want you to promise me something," he says. "Promise me that you'll go there. Soon. And that you'll never let anything stop you from being happy."

This had to be hard for him—witnessing his parents' grief had manifested into worry for those closest to him. I want to make him feel as good as he makes me.

So I bring his palm to my cheek and say, "I promise."

With our future stretched out in front of us, it was an easy promise to make.

Until he died a week later.

At first, his death didn't feel real. I kept expecting him to call me or walk through the door. One night I'd even woken up, and texted him, **I love you and can't wait to see you tomorrow**. And then the brutal reality came crashing back and shattered me once again.

It was shocking to know he'd never be at Thanksgiving dinner again, skimping on the mashed potatoes to save room for his mother's homemade apple pie. Heartbreaking to picture his chair empty, uncaring that its void would suck all the happiness from every celebration.

It wasn't fair that he had to die. If life had to take someone, why did it have to be him? Why couldn't it be someone else? Which was an insensitive thought, but that's what grief does to your mind.

The finality of him being gone hit me like a dial on the radio, turning up slowly, and as it did, I no longer wanted to be happy.

Pain was the only thing I had left of him, and I held onto it like a toxic security blanket, scared that once the pain left, it would mean he was gone. For good.

But then I'd feel ashamed of myself, because I was breaking my promise to him, and he'd be devastated if I let this destroy my life.

So eventually, for his sake, I put myself back out there. I tried to construct some semblance of normalcy. But even when I thought I was starting to make progress, grief would hit me out of nowhere. I'd see someone that looked like him. I'd see apple pie on a menu. Or a song would come on the radio, and my heart would rip in half again, spilling carnage everywhere.

And in the rare times I caught myself having fun or smiling, guilt would immediately shock me like a dog's electric collar as it ran from the yard. How dare I smile. How dare I feel happy when my boyfriend never would.

And thus began my seesaw of guilt. Guilt for allowing the pain to swallow me, which felt disrespectful to his life. Guilt for having any moments of joy when he was dead.

Every day felt more exhausting than the last.

Losing someone you love is like being sliced in half with a chainsaw. Your body will never go back to the way it was before the chainsaw cut it. Your tissue will regrow differently, and you must learn to live with the scar tissue left in its wake.

Instead of fighting the grief, I finally surrendered to it. Accepting that I couldn't make it go away. I needed to learn how to wrap my life around it and weave in happy times wherever possible.

Praying that one day the happy moments would begin to outweigh the sad ones.

So, after a tremendous amount of counseling, I finally started living my life again. I spent time with my friends, took long walks in the fresh air, and began to welcome joy back into my life. And you know what? It felt good.

Did Dad's accident disrupt that a bit? Of course. And of course it brought back some pangs of grief after almost losing my father, but I was proud of how far I'd come. It was like I'd sunken to the bottom of a lake and had swum all the way to the surface. And I knew that my boyfriend would be proud of me, too.

The stresses I now coped with were the stresses of life, not the grief of losing him.

But as proud as I was that I'd overcome grief—as much as anyone can, that is—I still hadn't fulfilled my promise to him. So even though I didn't have the money yet, I'd started planning the Grand Canyon trip.

But I would never see the sunset at the Grand Canyon or anything else because this thief was about to rob me of my future.

And for who knew what reason, he was dragging it out, torturing me by waiting for the reality to slowly sink in.

"I heard what you were planning in the hallway. Why haven't you done it already?"

No answer, but when I peeked through the sliver of sight below my blindfold, I saw his feet still there. Doing nothing. Was he having second thoughts? Could he be getting cold feet?

But as quickly as hope came, sorrow snatched it away when I realized what must be going on.

"You're going to wait," I deduced in a sick voice. "You guys are going to wait to kill me until you're done robbing the place, in case the cops show."

One one thousand.

Two one thousand.

Three one thousand.

"Yes," he said in a near whisper.

4

Of course they'd wait to kill me until the robbery was done. Who'd want to risk having a freshly murdered body on their hands if the cops showed?

Why was I upset about this? I should have been elated since it afforded me more time to try to get away, but I was praying he'd change his mind. That today wasn't really my last day.

"And you have to stay here and babysit me, so I don't get away."

He didn't answer.

Which wasn't just unsettling; it was unacceptable. This guy viewed my life as a disposable inconvenience. A complication of his criminal acts, stealing from hardworking people. People who spent *their* entire life working their ass off to pay their bills, pay their taxes, and be a contributing member of society.

"Shit, this night is spinning out of control." Green's tone rose in pitch, and he started pacing again. "Why couldn't you get your damn ring yesterday? Or wear it like a normal rich chick?"

How dare he. Break into our home, tie me up, vow to murder me, and then, on top of that, try to *blame* me? *Me* for having interrupted his burglary?

This guy has some balls.

Maybe the smart thing to do was play nice, but it was getting harder to bite my tongue, and that was what he expected, wasn't it? For me to sit here and keep quiet until they killed me. I was not about to do that; I'd make another run for it, and the only realistic chance to succeed was if this guy left the room or lost his focus. Keeping quiet wouldn't achieve either of those things, but maybe if I irritated him and got under his skin, he'd want to take a break and leave the hostage alone. Or at the very least, take his eyes off me long enough, so I could bolt out of this room.

I raised my chin. "Listen, you moronic waste of space."

Green stopped pacing. "Did you just call me a *moronic waste of space*?" His casual tone didn't sound irritated yet; if anything, it was surprise, mixed with enjoyment.

"I'm the opposite of rich," I said.

"Swear you did, but that can't be the case."

"This house isn't ours; it belongs to the bank."

"Because you seem halfway intelligent."

"I sold our only car to pay for food and medicine."

"So, I'd expect you not to anger someone in my position."

Speaking of position, I leaned my head back to confirm what the sound of his voice made me suspect—he was now standing only a couple feet in front of me.

I kicked my foot toward him, hoping to slam the heel of my foot into his dick. But he blocked that one, too. I tried to yank away from his grip, but doing so rocked the chair and tilted one side of it into the air. Before I could correct the center of gravity, the chair tipped over, sending me into a free fall, my nose on a collision course with the wooden planks.

But he grabbed me before I hit—one arm around my stomach, his other hand gripping my upper arm.

He pulled me into a standing position as if I weighed nothing and set me back on my feet.

"Careful," he said, a blend of irritation and enjoyment seeping from his tone. "I'd hate to see you hurt that beautiful face of yours."

"Because you prefer to do it yourself?"

I heard him huff a laugh-breath.

Why isn't he letting go of me?

He stood there, his hands on my body, doing what? Staring at me? Smelling like burnt sugar.

Strange. I'd have expected him to smell like chemically rotting feet, not delicious and inviting.

"So, this is what you do?" I said, heat pooling beneath my cheeks. "Break into people's homes and then murder them if they happen to come inside?"

No answer.

"What an exemplary member of society we have here," I snarled.

"Let me give you some advice." His tone was low and even.

"This ought to be good. Advice from a criminal. I'm waiting with bated breath."

He tightened his grip around my waist until my breasts pushed into his chest. "You're bound and blindfolded and at my mercy. Provoking the very person who holds your life in his hands is unwise."

"You've made it clear that there's nothing I can do to stop you from killing me, so if you're looking for some docile hostage, you picked the wrong girl."

A breath of air huffed out of Green's nose. Like he'd...*chuckled*?

"Your attitude is unnecessary." He sounded like a father reprimanding a child.

"Your existence is unnecessary."

He chuckled. Again.

Dammit.

I wanted to tear him apart psychologically until he left this room, whimpering with his tail between his legs.

I was going to escape. I was. It was that simple. I had however the hell long a robbery took to do so, and by God, I was going to succeed. And if I failed? Well, I'd scratch and bite and claw DNA from him, so he'd for sure get caught.

Speaking of biting...

I opened my mouth and chomped down on the skin in front of me, but his hand pressed against my forehead and jerked it back.

"Did you just *bite* me?" Amusement and shock battled for first place in his voice.

Not hard enough. Probably didn't even leave a mark, let alone lose a chunk of his body.

I twisted my head, trying to gain access to his wrist so I could tear open his radial artery with my front teeth, but he held it out of my reach.

Have it your way. I'd have to settle for my original target.

I bucked my knee fast and hard, but he twisted his hip, so I missed his groin.

Green tsked. "You're a feisty one, aren't you?"

"Untie me and see how feisty I really am."

He laughed—laughed!—and released his hand from my face. Based on his leaning and the subsequent metallic squeak, he picked up the chair and rolled it over to me.

"You're trying to be a lion." He pressed down on my shoulder until I flopped back into his chair. "But you're a kitten."

If ever there was justification for pulling a Lorena Bobbitt on his ass...

A chime sounded from across the room, and magically, Green's footsteps receded away. Not far enough to make a run for it, though.

I could hear him rifle through the backpack I'd arrived with.

Because he hadn't invaded my privacy enough by breaking in here and holding me hostage.

"If you're looking for money, you won't find any in there," I snapped.

I heard my cell phone clunk onto the desk as he shook my bag upside down.

"I'm not looking for money," he said flatly. "I heard a chime."

I bit down on my teeth.

"It's the alarm on my phone to remind Dad to take his pills," I snarled. "Why don't you make yourself useful and dial 911?"

I heard a small breath of air, as if he'd laughed.

Great. I show a brave act of defiance, and he's merely amused by it.

Through the crack in my blindfold, I leaned my head back to see his fingers power off the cell phone. Right. Wouldn't want cell towers picking up the location of wherever he dumped my body and belongings.

As soon as that thought came, another crashed right behind it.

If these guys were willing to commit murder, what if they were also willing to hurt me in other ways? What if death itself wasn't the only thing I needed to fear tonight?

My heart started to race so quickly, it felt like it was going to explode from my chest, and dizziness performed a hostile takeover of my mind. I felt like I was going to be sick.

If they were going to do that, part of me didn't want to know because knowing would be mental torture, listening to every footstep with sickening dread—wondering when they would violate me. But I couldn't stop myself from asking.

"Are you going to..." I swallowed, my throat so dry that my voice was a whisper. "Are you going to rape me?"

"What?" he snarled. "God, no."

The resolve in his voice made me believe him, but he was one of three.

"Will they?"

Green let out an angry breath. "No."

"How can you be sure?"

"They're thieves, not rapists."

"And if you're wrong?" My chin trembled.

"If they even tried it, I'd kill 'em."

My muscles relaxed slightly.

If he cared enough to stop me from being violated, maybe there was still hope to make him see me as human, to convince him to let me go. It failed before, but I had nothing to lose by trying again.

And meanwhile, I'd work a parallel play of wrestling my hands free from these bindings.

Later, he might leave the room to check on his accomplices or go to the bathroom, so there might be an opening to run.

There had to be.

And when it came? I'd be ready.

I pulled at the makeshift handcuffs, assessing them in more detail. A loop wrapped around each wrist individually and then another loop around them together. The fabric—a tie, I presumed—was silky, so maybe I could slide my hand out.

Trying to conceal my arm movements, I pulled my right wrist, but couldn't wiggle my thumb bone through the opening. I confronted the same failure with my left hand. In fact, he'd tied them so tightly that each time I pulled, the tie dug deeper into my skin.

I twisted my hands and wrists in every direction, stretching my fingers to try to reach the binding's knot. My right middle finger touched the lump, but the angle was off, so I couldn't pinch the fabric, let alone loosen it.

I bit back angry tears.

"Why do you need the ring so bad?" His tone was ambivalent, as if merely asking the question to satisfy his own boredom.

As much as I hated this criminal with every fiber of my being, I forced myself to clear the animosity out of my throat and answered his question. "We need the money."

"Anyone who lives in a place like this has money."

Had. Past tense.

"I told you, this is my dad's place, not mine. And we don't live here; we live in a six-hundred-square-foot townhouse. Rented."

I churned my hands behind my back, the skin on my wrists getting so raw that I wondered if it would start to bleed.

"Why?" Curiosity danced through his voice.

I didn't want to answer Green's question; talking about our

precarious financial situation wasn't something I liked to discuss with anyone, let alone this guy. But I couldn't let my ego block any avenue of possible escape.

"My dad defaulted on his mortgage, so the bank is doing a short sale. Even that won't fill the financial hole we're in, though, so I need to sell that ring to pay bills."

Green spoke, but this time, his voice was completely different. He sounded...empathetic. "Why haven't you pawned some of this furniture? Or TVs? This place is loaded."

"I've pawned what we're allowed to." I shrugged. "But the rest is tangled up in my dad's bankruptcy."

"Except the ring?"

"It's the only thing left that's legally mine."

Speaking of the ring, he'd walked in on me about to open the safe. Why hadn't he asked me what was inside it or tried to open it?

As he took another step forward, I noticed his footsteps had changed. Before, they'd been forceful. Now, they were soft.

"Didn't he have medical insurance?"

"He'd been laid off shortly before the accident. Failed to line up continuity insurance. Guess he assumed he'd have another job before there was a gap in coverage."

He assumed wrong.

When I met with a lawyer who tried to help me sort out my dad's paperwork, he told me you'd be surprised how many people making crazy-high incomes live paycheck to paycheck. You'd assume they'd squirrel away that extra income, but nope. A lot of them just increased their lifestyle with mortgages, and vacations, and toys, presuming the income will last forever.

"And now, you're supporting both of you," Green realized. Almost as if...this bothered him. "How long've you been doing that?"

"Eight months."

The sound of skin grating over skin made me wonder if he was scrubbing his face, and when he eventually spoke again, his voice was a whisper, as if he was speaking more to himself than me. "You had to step up and take care of someone, too."

Too? Too, as in he had taken or was currently taking care of someone?

Who was this guy? Was he just some guy who had stumbled onto a house for sale and saw it as an easy target? It made sense. Lots of people were hard up these days, and if I was a burglar—which I'd never be—I guess I might try to target houses that were vacant. Was that why he chose this place? Because he knew no one lived here?

My shoulders felt taut with my arms bound behind my back, and as I continued to twist and turn my hands as discreetly as I could, it stung like hell, and the pressure against my bone seemed on the verge of breaking it.

A new grim sound from the main area stole my attention—a drawer being opened in the kitchen, metal clanking against each other. I'd spent so much time talking with Green, I hadn't given much thought to how they'd kill me. But hearing what had to be knives clanking sent my heart into convulsions. Of all the ways to die, I didn't want to be stabbed.

Green sighed, and in a soft voice, he asked, "Are you cold?"

I blinked. "What?"

"You're shivering."

"I'm not cold. I'm scared." Admitting that left an awful taste in my mouth.

The taste lingered for five seconds before Green came over to me. I heard a zipper, followed by the rustling of fabric. Something warm draped over my shoulders. A jacket, I realized.

Beneath his coat, I could smell the faint hint of his sugary scent again. I tried to tell myself it didn't smell good or sexy for that matter because only a crackpot would think such a thing.

It sounded like Green walked back to the other side of the room while my mind—probably just looking for an escape from worrying about being stabbed to death—analyzed him. Trying to measure the undercurrents of his temperament, trying to figure out why he'd put the jacket on me.

What did it mean? Had I won him over?

"I'm sorry about the restraints," he said. "It's a precaution."

"They're tight." I was careful to keep my tone pleasant. "Too tight. They're hurting me. Is there any way you could loosen them a little?"

Silence eclipsed the beating of my heart.

"I can't do that, Zoey."

And just like that, I realized again there was nothing I could say to get him to help me. He hadn't given me his jacket because he was being nice, warming up to me. He put it on me to make my last moments on earth bearable. A small act of mercy.

I was sitting in my future coffin. Green knew it. I knew it. The only person who didn't know it yet was Dad.

The pain came at me like a wildfire washing over my body, as I pictured my dad sitting in his wheelchair tomorrow, looking out our front window, worrying what might have happened to me.

I bet these guys would move my body, and no one would ever find it. Not for a long time, at least. What if Dad thought I took off? Cracked under the weight of the never-ending responsibility of taking care of him?

Tears marched down my cheeks, and whimpers escaped my throat.

Green's feet advanced toward me in soft, slow strides, and beneath the sliver of sight my blindfold allotted, I saw his shins, then his knees. He squatted directly in front of my chair, close enough to feel the heat from his body.

"Hey," Green said, his tone adding, "*Don't cry*."

"I'm the only person my dad has to take care of him," I repeated, words tumbling out of my mouth at rapid speed. "He needs me. Please, don't kill me. Don't do this to my dad. Even after what he did to me, I'd never wish this on him, so please. Just let me go."

My tears left a salty river down my cheeks, my mind exhausted.

During the ensuing silence, my breath caught in my throat as he removed his glove, revealing tan and smooth skin on his hand.

When he brought his arm up, the flash of sudden movement caused me to flinch, shrinking my neck back under my shoulders. Which wasn't ideal since it divulged I could at least partially see.

But Green didn't hit me. Instead, he pressed his finger lightly against my cheek and brushed upward, toward my eye, wiping the line of tears away—a tender gesture he repeated on the other side. But what was even stranger than what he was doing was how it made me feel.

His touch felt...nice.

Did he feel this energy shift, too? Because he stilled, and we both existed in the silent space of quiet breathing.

The clock on my dad's desk ticked ten times before Green stood up, walked away, and crossed one boot over the other—presumably leaning against the desk.

What just happened? Was he feeling upset, finally understanding the extent of the damage he was going to cause when he killed me?

Minutes passed with silence. Minutes that felt like hours while I heard the other guys moving around in the living room. Were they almost done? Were they making enough unusual sounds to spark any questions from a neighbor? Because now that I thought about it, this place was always empty. Surely, that would tip someone off, would it not?

"I'm going to ask you something." Green's words flooded with authority. "And you're going to be honest with me."

I waited.

"Did you see anything tonight?"

I pursed my lips. "You mean when I was trying to open the safe and you accosted me from behind? No. I didn't see you. I would have kicked you in the groin and then broken your nose if I had."

The fact that he chuckled surprised me and gave me hope that maybe he didn't hate me as much as he did a bit ago. "There's no way you could do any real damage. You look like an overgrown porcelain doll."

Maybe he even liked this banter. "Then, untie me and see how small I really am."

The breath of air sounded like he'd laughed lightly, but whatever moment we'd just shared came to an abrupt halt with the appearance of another voice in the office.

"Orange needs your help with the surround system. Having trouble with the wires."

Green paused. "Can't he just yank them out?"

"And ruin 'em? We'd never get full price for it if he did that," Brown snapped. "Get over there and help him. I'll watch her until you get back."

The goose bumps came fast, the hairs on the back of my neck standing on end. Especially since it took Green several seconds to finally exit the office.

As if he didn't want to leave me alone with this guy.

5

Having time with Brown could be a positive thing, though. While I felt like I was getting somewhere with Green, I couldn't be sure that was true, and having a chance to plead my case with someone else doubled my chances of getting out of this nightmare.

"You really screwed things up." The irritation in Brown's voice blended with superiority.

"I haven't seen anything. Please, just let me go."

He laughed, a careless disregard for my life echoing through its tempo.

A blizzard of fear blew through my chest, gusting snow through the oxygen.

"My dad needs me."

"Like I give a shit. Where're the valuables?"

I paused. "What?"

Through the void beneath my blindfold, I saw his brown boots stalk closer. The chair jolted from his hands, which slammed into the armrests, his breath a putrid mix of cigarettes and menace.

"We haven't found any jewels or cash. Where are they?"

"My stepmom's the one that kept jewelry, but she took it with her when she left."

"Place like this always has stacks of emergency cash and jewels." The chair tilted when he leaned so close, the heat of his breath invaded my throat like vapor. "Tell. Me," he snarled, "Where. They. Are."

Frustration tangled my chest. "I am telling you. There's no—"

But I never finished my sentence. A blow thrust my head to the side, and a stinging pain soared through my cheekbone.

Instinctively, I recoiled, as if the extra inch of space between me and the guy who'd just slapped me afforded me some layer of protection.

"Tell me!" he yelled.

"We lost all our money. We don't have anything." I didn't know why I was lumping Dad and me into a we. *We* didn't lose our money; he lost his money, but those kinds of details weren't relevant right now. What was relevant was this guy expecting a mountain of cash.

"You're lying," he growled. "Tell me where the jewelry is, or I'll make your death slow and painful."

My heart attempted to jump through my ribs. "The money went to medical bills."

"Bullshit." He seized my neck. I gasped as his fingers stretched around my windpipe and tightened. "Tell me."

But I couldn't tell him anything because he was cutting off my air supply.

Something hit my temple with enough force to knock the chair over, spilling me onto the floor. My left ear rang with a high-pitched chime, and my right cheek pressed against the cold hardwood as pressure mounted in my ears.

Disoriented, I tasted metal, warm blood dripping from my nose, pooling over my lips and onto my chin. Something squeezed my upper arm and yanked so hard, a sharp pain tore through my shoulder as my body was tugged into a sitting position.

"The jewels and cash," he barked. "It's in the safe?"

I wanted the boat to stop rocking, or I might throw up. "Just one ring."

"You're lying." He grabbed my jaw.

It took me a moment to answer; my thoughts weren't coming quickly. "Open it," I said and told him the combination. Praying that when he discovered I was being honest, he wouldn't hurt me anymore.

He released his claws and, based on his footsteps, advanced toward the other side of the room. While the safe's dial clicked, I yanked my wrists with more desperate jerks, the fabric biting at my raw skin.

"What the..." Another voice emerged near me.

I pressed my hands against the ground behind me, using my feet to scoot on my butt until my back hit a wall, where I curled into a semi-ball, my knees up for protection.

Brown's demonic laugh bathed the space in misery as I cowered away from the new man, who squatted before me.

When his hand rose, I jerked my face away.

"What'd you do?" the man snapped.

That voice. I tilted my head until I could see his combat boots.

Green.

"She won't tell me where the jewels are."

"You didn't have to hurt her."

I could only guess a look was exchanged because the room grew silent. It was a full thirty seconds before the safe's wheel started to click again.

Green's fingertip lightly pressed beneath my jaw, guiding my face up toward the light, and then an angry breath rushed from his nose.

"There's no cash!" Brown sounded furious. "Only one fucking ring that looks like maybe a grand or two."

It made no rational sense that his anger made me even more nervous. Why would anyone feel even more afraid when they'd already signed my death warrant?

I suppose it was human nature—adrenaline reacting as the promise of death ticked closer with each second of the clock.

I needed to try something different; begging and trying to win Green over wasn't happening fast enough.

I'm going to make another run for it.

I'd have to time it right, and it was a long shot. No doubt. I could trip and fall on the way or stumble onto one of the burglars, and that didn't even include figuring out how I'd get to be alone in the first place. But so help me, I was going to run.

It quite literally might be the last thing I did.

"What a waste of time. Hold this," Brown snapped. I heard the clank of the ring hitting wood and saw Green's feet move toward the desk. "Watch her. I'm goin' back to help."

Brown stormed away, leaving me alone with Green, a bloody nose, a stinging cheek, and wrists as raw as uncooked meat.

6

Brown had quite the right hook. He damn near knocked me out with that punch, leaving my head on an imaginary Tilt-A-Whirl. Why was the room cold all of a sudden? *Oh.* Green's jacket came off me during my fall.

"Here." Green's palm brushed along the skin of my arm and squeezed gently.

You'd think me recoiling from his hand would've frustrated him, but he held my upper arm, quietly waiting for me to accept his help.

An uncomfortable taste of iron lingered in my throat. I hated how blood tasted. How it smelled. How it felt. The sensation was disgusting, the flow slowing as it trickled over my lips and onto my chin.

"I'm not going to hurt you." He wrapped his other hand around my waist and pulled me to my feet.

When I wobbled, Green's arm tightened around me, pulling me firmly against his rock-hard torso. His muscular chest rose and fell against my cheek with each breath he took, and snuggled against him, protected in his grip, I stopped shivering.

His body felt dangerously sweet, pressed against mine, peaceful after what just happened. A warm fire crackling near your skin after escaping a frigid rainstorm. His chest a sanctuary, his grip comforting as his fingers spread over my hip.

Strange how, when you're going through hell, you latch on to any sense of security because, right now, I longed to stay in his tranquil embrace just a little longer. To listen to the tempo of his heart beating beneath my ear and savor his sweet scent.

Rationally, I knew he was still my captor, holding me hostage. But right now, his tender touch reminded me more of a friend than an enemy, and in my desperation to extend this reprieve from fear, I nuzzled my face deeper into his chest.

Green's other hand came up to the side of my head, holding me, as if sensing I needed comfort, no matter who it came from.

I closed my eyes and pictured the staggered rocks of the Grand Canyon blanketed in orange, etched in shadows as gradients of blue and purple clouds stretched into the horizon. I could feel the warmth of the setting sun on my face and smell the fresh pine from nearby trees. I could even hear a lone bird singing as it soared above the valley.

"Come on," he whispered. "I'm going to clean you up."

If he took me out of this room, maybe I'd have a legitimate chance to escape. If I could wiggle my blindfold up another inch to see, I could make a run for the front door.

Green guided me forward carefully, his arm wrapped securely around me so I wouldn't fall.

Still, I was unsure of my steps and shuffled at an agonizingly slow speed. Green didn't rush me or yank me along, though. Instead, he was patient, adjusting his grip when he sensed I needed reassurance with my footing.

Beneath my blindfold, I saw that we exited the office, crossed the hallway, and went into the guest bathroom.

When Green released me, he took the fire's heat with him, sentencing my skin to a prison of ice. The striking temperature shift wasn't merely from the absence of his body's heat, however, but more so from the compassion of his caress. As if tenderness radiated from his skin.

How could I long for his embrace to return?

Because being in his arms was the only time you haven't felt terrified tonight.

I shut my eyes, willing the uninvited, inappropriate feeling to go away.

I must be delirious from shock. In the face of death, plagued with fear, grasping on to any semblance of compassion and humanity in my final moments of life.

Green isn't your ally, Zoey. Don't be fooled by his chivalrous act. He's lethal, and he's going to kill you.

A threat that transformed this place into an eerie set of a horror movie. Normally, this bathroom looked gorgeous with beige tumbled stone blanketing the floors and walls, black faucets, granite countertops, and a claw-foot tub against the far wall. But with my sight obstructed, the room was a hallway of darkness, cold and damp. The faucet drip, drip, dripped, its tiny splash echoing like a countdown to my death. In here, the only warmth came from my captor's body, which was so close that I could sense it towering over me. With my arms bound behind my back, I remained at his mercy, vulnerable to whatever he decided to do.

The living room is only fifteen feet away. Maybe I could kick Green between his legs and make it to the front door before he could stop me. My stomach came alive with flutters, and as the faucet turned on, I tried to block its noise, so I could listen to where the other guys were.

But when I heard them, my heart sank.

Brown's and Orange's voices permeated down the hall from the living room—the very room I needed to run through to escape. Getting away from Green was already a long shot, and making it past both of them was undoubtedly a death sentence.

My eyes stung from frustration.

"Hold still." Green softly gripped my chin between his thumb and finger and tilted my face up slightly.

A warm, wet towel brushed against the skin just below my nose. It smelled like the pomegranate soap Dad kept in this bathroom—sweet with a trace of cinnamon. I had to admit, it felt nice. The water washed away the tacky, iron-scented blood while Green—being as gentle as if he was treating a burn—glided the cloth back and forth until the skin no longer felt soiled.

As he brushed my face lightly, carefully working the blood off, I felt confused by his touch, for the very hands that would later end my life were being caring and tender. Even harder to comprehend, however, was the unexplainable desire that worked its way into my head. His strokes against my skin didn't feel like a simple act of cleaning. The way he caressed me somehow felt sensual, my lack of sight making me more sensitive to his touch.

A touch that stunned me. Not just because of *who* had sparked this reaction, but also because it was making me feel something I shouldn't.

"I'm sorry he hit you." Green's voice brimmed with...sorrow?

"That makes two of us."

"He needs to learn self-control."

"What he needs is a psychiatrist who isn't deterred by a lost cause."

I liked that I heard Green chuckle.

I swore his strokes lightened into a more suggestive, rhythmic manner, and his deep breaths slowed, his face mere inches from my own.

His cleansing ceased, and I breathed in and out two times before Green spoke again, his tone low and raspy. "Can you part your lips?"

After a small hesitation, I opened my mouth slightly.

The wet fabric caressed the corner of my mouth—an intimate spot few had ever touched. It ignited a blaze of fire that spread from my lips to my throat and down to my stomach. He took his time, gliding the wetness over my crevice, and as he did, I wondered what he was thinking right now because my thoughts jumbled into confusion.

I should've been appalled by his touch rather than liking it. I should've hated him standing this close to me rather than savoring it, and I should not have compared his gentle strokes to that of an artist painting a canvas. The fact that this moment felt seductive made me wonder if I was having some sort of mental breakdown.

The towel returned to my face, this time dry, soaking up the leftover water droplets. The cloth calmed my nerves like a massage, and when it abandoned my skin, my breaths hitched as I anticipated his next touch.

As the faucet dripped with each passing second, I wondered what he was thinking. Why was he just standing here, not doing anything? I could feel him looking at me. Did he feel this irrational flicker of chemistry, too?

The energy coming off his body was like a magnet drawing me to him, and I craved being nestled against his chest with his arms wrapped around me.

After an eternity of waiting, I felt his finger, gloveless, on my lower lip, gently eliminating the last water droplet. His skin was soft, warm, just like when he'd wiped away my tears, and I closed my eyes to appreciate this moment.

Surely, everything going on in my head was all some warped survival-denial thing that was happening to me, like an alternate reality to help me cope with imminent death. I never believed in those people who claimed temporary insanity as a defense. But for the first time, I sort of understood what it meant because his touch...

Lord, his touch.

There was absolutely no reason to revel in physical contact, let alone like the guy. So what if he was nice enough to clean the blood off? He was responsible for the blood being there in the first place even if he hadn't been the one to hit me. Any compassion I felt for him was a misdirected coping mechanism. Period.

And as for the empathy he was showing me? Probably fake. Probably just something to keep me from screaming. Make me less of a liability; that was probably his real job—to keep me quiet.

But if that were true...why did I have to keep reminding myself of it? As if my rationale was fighting to overpower the energy between us.

"That's why you look so familiar." Green sounded as if he had solved a mystery that had been bothering him this whole time. "We've met before."

I blinked, stunned. "We have?"

He hesitated. Admitting that he'd met me was a bad idea if he wanted to keep his identity hidden.

I quickly flipped through my mental Rolodex of people I had met in my life, wondering if I could place his face among the sea of Dad's health care workers, waiters, or who knew what else.

He'd said I'd looked familiar, but he must not have placed me until now, when he stood only inches away, studying every curve of my face as he cleaned it off.

"You remember walking along the lakefront three months ago? A guy on Rollerblades crashed into another guy?"

I did remember that...

Spring temperatures came early this year. Melted the snow and ice into puddles of mud and water standing on the grass near the lake that stretches out to the horizon. The air is still cold, but when you live in Chicago, you learn cold is relative. Fifty degrees in August is something people complain about. But that same fifty degrees in April? You'd think the city was having a national holiday or something, what with all the people swarming near the lakefront.

I hate it. I'd rather it be ice cold right now, so I could walk along the lake and think in peace. Clear my head in my favorite place. But no. People taking selfies, jogging, walking their dogs. They're everywhere.

Case in point? Some dude in Rollerblades is on his phone—who the hell blades and texts?—and crashes into a guy walking eight feet ahead of me, nearly knocking him over.

"Watch where the hell you're going," the guy snaps.

I can't help but smile, grateful I'm not the only one in the city annoyed by people.

The Rollerblader stares at the guy for a second before frowning and rolling away.

But Angry Guy continues walking, obviously not realizing that in the crash, his wallet fell to the ground. I know it's his because I happened to be looking at his butt when the wallet became dislodged. I wasn't gawking. It was just a split second of appreciating something that gorgeous right in my line of sight.

In my defense, his backside belongs in a museum, to be admired for generations to come.

I pick up the wallet and jog a few feet forward. "Excuse me!"

He doesn't turn around.

I tap his shoulder. "Sir?"

He turns around, and holy crap, my icy mood instantly melts. This guy is level-ten gorgeous. He's over six feet tall with tan skin and brown hair that's short on the sides and several inches longer on the top with caramel highlights. Same darker color as his eyebrows and facial stubble, framing piercing blue eyes that stare at me like they can see through my skull.

He has to be a model.

That would explain why it takes me several seconds to remember what the hell I was about to say, hypnotized not only by his beauty, but also by this sense of mystery radiating off him—coming from the intensity in his face and the long silence he allows to pass, staring at me while I struggle to act human in his energy field.

"Is this yours?" I hold the wallet toward him.

He looks down at it. Stacks of hundreds shuffled in the fall, so they stick out slightly.

"It fell out of your pocket when that guy crashed into you."

He eyes me skeptically for a second. "You see a wallet full of cash lying on the ground, and you give it back to the owner?"

Lord, even his voice is unfairly beautiful. He could do voice-over work and make panties melt with it.

"Of course."

His lips twitch slightly, and his dazzling eyes soften.

"I'd like to believe most people would give it back, too," I claim even though I don't fully believe it myself. Truth be told, my life has turned me into quite a cynic lately.

"I'd argue most people wouldn't," he says.

"If more people chose to do the right thing, it'd make life more bearable for the rest of us."

He raises his eyebrows slightly, which makes him even sexier.

My hormones seriously need to simmer. But no. They are F-ers, warming my inner thighs with each second I stare at his flawless face and body. Because, yeah, with his jacket open, I can tell he's ripped beneath that long-sleeved shirt. His muscles bulge against the fabric.

"And life isn't bearable?" he asks in a tone that's not playful or antagonistic. More like a deep curiosity, his gaze somehow stabbing even deeper into my brain.

"Not lately." I chew the inside of my cheek.

He studies me. Left eye, then my right, and he looks at my lips as he parts his own. This energy buzzing between us makes no sense. I've heard of strong chemical attractions to someone, which must be what this is, but Lord to hell, no one warns you it's as strong as the suction of an F3 tornado. And they don't warn you it goes beyond physical and into full-on curiosity zone, wondering who this guy is.

Where is he heading? Does he live in Chicago, or is he a tourist, visiting? And—shamefully—does he have a girlfriend?

I raise his wallet a little higher—has he forgotten I'm holding it?

He looks down at it again, but when he moves to take it, he halts his arm mid-swing, his eyes cutting to my hand. Which is wrapped in gauze.

His jaw moves to the side, and he licks his teeth in displeasure before his sapphire gaze snaps back to mine.

My cheeks warm under the heat of his sudden irritation. Irritation that I can tell isn't directed at me, but oddly, at the injury to my palm.

Last night, Dad had knocked his wheelchair into the end table, and his water glass had broken on the floor. I was careless enough to think I could pick up the bigger pieces without slicing my skin open. A one-inch gash in my palm proved me wrong.

The guy's gaze becomes so intense, it's like the entire city vanishes around us.

"Did someone hurt you?" he growls, and his gaze borders on a glare.

Of all the ways one could injure themselves, why would he assume that?

"Not my hand." My heart? Hell yes.

Based on the tightening of his jaw, he doesn't like my answer.

It looks like he's debating grilling me on this, so I wiggle the wallet again to change the subject.

When he reaches for it, his finger brushes mine. The warmth of his skin against the frosty air sends a wave of heat up my arm and into my lower belly, and I swear he feels it, too, because he stills for a moment. Stares at me before shoving the wallet into his back pocket.

He glances down at my bandage again. "Your hand is bleeding," he says, the edge still punching through his words.

I look. Sure enough, blood has breached the gauze on my palm. Just barely, though. How did he see that before me?

"How deep is the cut?" His tone is full of authority and concern.

I shrug. "I've had to change the bandage a few times."

"You should go to urgent care."

I purse my lips. "Yeah, maybe I will," I lie.

I swear, he must sense my deceit because he studies me, seemingly trying to unravel the hidden meaning behind why I won't go.

I'm thankful he doesn't press me on it because the reason is embarrassing.

"If you won't get it stitched up," he says, putting a hand into his pocket, "can I at least buy you a cup of coffee?"

I try not to smile. "You want to get me coffee?"

His tone borders on playful. "There's no need for you to be thirsty and *bleeding."*

I want to go with him and learn about him and see if his magnetic field ever weakens, but my life is so complicated right now, and I barely get five minutes to myself each week. Let alone have time to date.

Plus, I haven't felt butterflies like this in a very long time. I don't think I've ever had them this strong before, and their power intimidates me. Everything in my life feels out of control lately, and the prospect of adding gasoline to this pull overwhelms me. I'm not sure if I'm ready for that right now. Especially when Dad needs me so much.

So, I don't take him up on his offer. I don't even ask his name or offer him mine. I simply say, "Sorry. I can't."

I give him an apologetic smile and turn to walk away but quickly pivot to face him one more time before I do.

"You should be more careful." I don't know why I said it—protective instincts maybe—but the words came tumbling out of my mouth. "You shouldn't keep so much cash on you. This city can be dangerous."

To this, the corner of his mouth tugs up as if he's fighting back a grin, and cripes, the flutter Gods make him look even sexier for it.

He stares at me as I walk away.

After a few seconds, I look back over my shoulder, wondering if he's resumed walking. He hasn't. He's still staring at me. Only now, a hunger consumes his eyes, as if he wants to march over and claim me as his own.

It takes every ounce of willpower to turn around and leave him behind.

Later, when I go to bed, I find myself thinking of him. Of his spell-binding eyes and magnetic charm. There was something about the guy that pulled me in, leaving me gasping for more. It felt different from other guys. Other guys are easy to forget about, yet here I am, tossing and turning, wishing I hadn't turned down his offer to get coffee.

After thinking about it, I can't help but wonder if I'd panicked a little when he asked me out. I mean, maybe I was worried that it wasn't just one cup of coffee. Maybe I presumed it could easily lead to two or three. And maybe that scared me a little, letting myself get invested in someone. Especially since I hadn't dated anyone seriously since the death of my boyfriend.

Because now? I can't think of a single good reason to have said no. In fact, yes is the only answer that makes any sense, and I find myself wishing I could go back in time and change my decision.

As days pass, disappointment fills me that I have no way to reach him. My eyes search for him on the streets. I even walk back by the lake, hoping to see him like a junior high school girl with a crush.

I try to tell myself that's all this is. A crush.

And crushes fade fast.

BUT MINE DIDN'T. I NEVER GOT THAT WALLET GUY OUT OF MY MIND. WAS that guy Green? Or was he the Rollerblader? Or one of the other onlookers who'd seen it?

"Couldn't believe you didn't take any money for yourself," he said.

I heard a soft noise, as if Green was rubbing part of his face.

"Was that you?" I asked. "The guy that lost his wallet?"

That was the only way he would know there was no missing money, right?

Unless another guy was watching me when I picked up the wallet and returned it...

Green didn't answer right away. "Lotta people were there. Saw what happened."

Translation; he's not stupid enough to reveal what he looked like that day.

"I can't believe I didn't recognize you sooner." Any trace of anger or animosity from our earlier fighting had faded behind reverence. "Because I've thought of you every day since." His voice was like velvet, gliding over my skin.

"Why?" I whispered, surprised by how much I cared about his answer.

Green's tone lowered into a rumble. "You had this...mix of sweetness and salt that I'd never seen in anyone before. Kind enough to return a stranger's money, but you still had this edge to you. This... anger toward the world."

My belly came alive with flutters.

"I found it to be quite...intoxicating," he said.

Whoa. No matter who this guy was, this had to be good.

Work with this, Zoey.

Maybe he wouldn't reveal his ID, but he *had* revealed we'd met, and that was a big give. It gave me the chance to figure out who he was. Plus, he'd had the compassion to clean my face, had scolded Brown for hitting me, and evidently, had thought of me every day since.

Could I win him over now?

There was one way to test it, I decided, before blowing my last chance at begging for his mercy. I could ask him something that had been gnawing at me, forced to the back burner of my mind while the front burner had been focused on surviving. And see if he answered.

"Why'd you keep asking who knew I was coming tonight?"

Because when I'd assumed it was to cover his own ass, to learn what other hostages might be on their way, he'd said, "That's not why I'm asking."

So, why then?

Green ran the sink—rinsing the towel, I presumed—and then I lifted my chin and saw him grip the edge of the counter. Looking down or at himself in the mirror, I didn't know, but his knuckles whitened as he stood there for several seconds before pivoting his feet to face me.

"Zoey..." Green cleared his throat, and I heard his body move, running a hand through his hair perhaps. "Someone sent us to rob the place tonight. Someone who knew this place."

7

Beneath my blindfold, I blinked. "What are you talking about?"

He hesitated. "We shouldn't talk in here."

I was about to demand he answer me, but the bathroom was closer to the living room than the office, so his colleagues might overhear. If I had any hope of getting the truth, we needed to be somewhere farther away.

Green wrapped his arm around my waist, his fingers pressing into my hip as he pulled my body against his torso again. Even through the fabric between us, I could feel the firmness of his bicep and forearm and the heat radiating from his skin.

With a gentle nudge, he guided my feet forward, and like the last time, I moved slowly. I saw the tile give way to wood as we entered the hallway, and despite having a little bit of vision, my foot caught on the doorframe.

But Green's arm tightened around my hip and righted me before I could fall.

"You okay?" he asked softly.

I nodded, relieved by how much he really sounded as if he cared.

We slowly crossed through the hallway and back into the office, where his warm body vanished from my side. A squeak, followed by a light rumble, told me he'd picked up the chair from its fallen position and rolled it behind my legs, his hands gripping my shoulders, ensuring I didn't fall when I sat back down.

"Comfortable?" He slid his hands to my upper arms.

I released an exasperated breath.

"What?" he asked.

"I'm tied up with my arms yanked behind my back, and you're asking if I'm comfortable?"

A small pause.

"Do your arms hurt?" His tone was deep with seeds of sympathy sprouting.

"Yes."

He was silent for four breaths. "If I retie your hands in front of you, would that be more comfortable?"

My heartbeat spiked; I hadn't anticipated him giving me this option. With my hands in front, I'd have a much better chance at escaping. I could move my blindfold easily, defend myself, and open doors quickly. *This might be the moment that saves me.* "Yes."

Another pause.

"I'm trusting you not to run, Zoey." His tone seemed to add, *If you do, you won't like the consequences.*

But I had to run.

The second my hands were untied...

He pulled me by my shoulders back into a standing position, then seized my hips and twisted me around so my back faced his chest. The heat of his breath tickled the back of my neck, and his fingertips brushed my wrists as he worked the binding's knots, the fabric tugging at my pained skin as it loosened. Then vanished completely.

The relief was better than I'd expected. The cool air soothing what must be significant rug-like burns. Plus, my arms no longer ached from being pinned behind me.

I moaned, my shoulders rejoicing at their new freedom, the muscles aching from having pulled on them so hard earlier. I rubbed my wrists but regretted it immediately; the skin was raw, and when I touched it, the salt from my fingers made it sting.

My hands are free.

He grabbed my hips and turned me back around to face him.

This is it.

I'd only have *one* move before he caught on and reacted, so what would it be? Run? Or move the blindfold?

Run, I decided. Once I made it a few steps away from him, I'd remove the blindfold.

But that meant I needed a seriously good assessment of where he stood in relation to the door. Based on the number and direction of our steps from the hallway, I'd ballpark the door at ten feet forward, to my left, but I could be wrong.

I never realized how hard it was to lose your vision. How crippling it could be. Aside from the crevice at the bottom of my blindfold, all I could see was blackness.

With my heart pounding, my breathing quickened, drawing in Green's aroma of burnt sugar, a scent that—should I be asked later —I'd deny smelled sexy.

Right before my legs sprinted, something soft danced along my skin.

His fingertips, I realized. Tracing my wounded wrists.

"Does it hurt?" His voice was a near whisper.

I paused. "Yes."

He trailed a finger down my hand, over my knuckle. "I'm sorry. I wish I didn't have to put this back on."

Something told me to keep working this angle, that I was winning him over, but with a decent chance to flee, fear took control. Because what if I never had another chance like this? This whole night felt like a fatal version of chess with me having to anticipate all the scenarios that could play out, calculating my best odds of survival.

Green draped the fabric beneath my arms.

But I moved faster.

I jumped to my left like a quarterback avoiding a tackle and broke into a sprint.

But I hit a wall, my body jerking to a stop.

My palms flattened against pectorals, and my stomach pressed against his as Green caged me in with his arms.

"Zoey." His whisper glided across my skin. "You run out there, they'll kill you on the spot."

"I stay in here, I'm dead anyway."

"Zoey..."

"Give me a chance to live."

If it was possible for a heart to stop beating, I swore mine did, waiting for his verdict. I wanted to rip my blindfold off and look him in the eyes to plead with him, but if I did that, he'd have an even bigger reason to kill me.

A reason I couldn't take back.

I was in enough trouble already; he'd warned me not to run, and now that I'd broken that promise, I had no idea what horrible consequences he'd inflict.

I braced myself for a blow or a hand around my throat, but as he held me prisoner in his arms, nothing came.

He's not hurting me.

I broke my vow to him, and even then, he refuses to hurt me.

Did that mean the only true threat was from the other men?

Fear melted away, softening my muscles, and a warmth buzzed beneath my skin as I became conscious of his body. His broad chest, rising and falling beneath my palms, his heated breaths rolling across my face, his steely grip around my waist, and the contours of his tight stomach pushing into mine.

But mostly, I sensed him staring at me, his face mere inches from my own.

Even blinded, I was sucked into his gaze.

And then his fingertips skimmed my cheek as he tucked a fallen hair behind my ear. The gesture was tender, igniting a firestorm of flutters in my stomach.

Sixth senses couldn't be trusted evidently because, right now, mine was telling me the way he was holding me, staring at me, was as if he wanted to kiss me. Which was ludicrous. He must be furious with me for lying to him, for trying to escape. But even more absurd was the small part of me that wondered what his mouth would feel like.

I'm definitely having a mental breakdown. It's the only way to explain this insanity in my head.

"I'm going to sit you back down," Green whispered, the energy crackling between us. "And you're going to hold still while I tie your hands. Understand?"

Maybe the survivalist in me wanted to sense his kindness, to fool me into believing I still had a chance to survive. Maybe that was all this was.

Green walked me backward and lowered me into the chair.

On my left arm, he slid his grip down to my hand and turned my wrist until the palm was face up. His thumb brushed along the scar from where that glass had cut me.

"This doesn't look like it healed properly." Disapproval wrapped around his words.

That had to mean he was wallet guy, right? Then again, there had been plenty of people nearby who could have witnessed the bandage on my hand. Maybe even overheard wallet guy's suspicion that someone had hurt me.

"I couldn't afford stitches." While I had medical insurance for myself, my deductible meant I was on the hook for the first three grand of medical bills. Stitches would run me a few hundred, at least.

"You get hurt, and you couldn't even afford medical treatment." Green seemed to say it more to himself than me. "And yet you hand back a wallet full of cash."

Was that...admiration in his tone?

Green didn't say anything else for a minute, his thumb trailing up and down the white scar on my skin. And when he finally spoke, a growl of vengeance dragged through his voice. "Did someone do this to you, Zoey?"

I was surprised by his reaction. "No."

"Tell me the truth."

"What difference does it make?"

"A big one."

"And if someone did do this to me, what would you do?" *Let me go? Because you feel sorry for me?*

"I would ensure the culprit who hurt you regretted it. Immensely."

What. In the actual. Hell?

"And why would you do that?"

No answer.

"Is this a last wish sort of thing? Because need I remind you what your buddies are going to do to me?" It was far worse than damage to a palm.

I wished I could see his face. Gauge his temperament with something other than sound and touch.

"Give me a name." His voice scorched with anger.

"There is no name. I hurt it, cleaning up a broken glass."

He hesitated. "That true?"

"Yes. If you want to do something for me, let me go."

He sighed.

But he didn't say no...

Was it possible he was reconsidering? Maybe even starting to brainstorm ideas of how to help me out of here? Even if we couldn't act now, even if we had to wait until the coast was clear, might he help me?

After another long pause, the fabric wrapped back around my wrists and tightened into knots. But he made sure it didn't rub the sore spots.

Was I reading too much into the small act of kindness?

He draped his coat over my shoulders again, the warmth of the fabric eliminating my chills. In the crack of my blindfold, I saw Green's feet walk to the other side of the room and cross, as if leaning against the table.

I imagined I had been here for about twenty minutes now, but I couldn't be sure. It could have been an hour. Either way, Dad wouldn't be calling the police yet to report me missing. He had no idea I was being held hostage or that my captor had just admitted someone had orchestrated this robbery.

"Who ordered the job?" I clenched my fingers.

Green kept his voice low. "I don't know."

"What do you mean, you don't know? You said someone hired you guys to do this, so who was it?"

"Didn't meet the person. They used a middleman, who introduced them to a...colleague of mine."

"A middleman?"

"Person on the streets who knows how to get in touch with us," Green said.

"How would anyone even know they could do that?"

"Our group is...well known in Chicago." Green's tone sounded matter-of-fact. A professor educating a student.

"What in the hell does the tipster get out of it?"

"A cut of the take."

"Of course." I shook my head. "It's always about money."

"It's not uncommon to get tipped off about places. Most places are insured, so the homeowners don't lose any money." His patience gave way to worry. "Anyone you can think of that might've organized this?"

Organized a heist? Seriously? "No." I didn't even know that was a thing until a few seconds ago.

"Who would know this place was empty?"

"I don't know. Our realtor?" I shrugged.

Green cleared his throat. "Whoever it was knew details of what we'd find inside."

"They tell you you'd find cash and jewels?"

"No."

That's why Green wasn't going after the safe.

"Then, why was Brown such an asshole when I told him that?"

Green's voice wound with tension. "He's not part of my crew."

Green's crew. As in he was a leader?

"Well, I don't know then. I hate to say it, but maybe it was my dad's ex-wife. She left him as soon as the money train dried up, so she doesn't strike me as the most moral person."

"Would she still have a key to this place?" Green sounded bitter.

"They gave you a key?"

No answer.

"If it wasn't her, maybe a neighbor, a friend of my dad's. I have no clue who'd want to or know how to hire someone to rob the place. My dad's friends are all rich-ish, so I can't imagine them doing something like this, but then I can't imagine anyone doing it, so I have no idea."

"Who knew you'd be coming tonight?" Green growled.

"I already told you. No one."

"Not a single person?"

"Not really."

"Elaborate on *not really*."

Where was he going with this?

"A family friend knows I needed to get cash quickly. He knows I was planning to sell a ring, but I never told him that I'd be coming here to retrieve it."

"What's his name?"

"I'm not handing his name over to you."

"I'm trying to help you. Figure out if someone set you up."

Set me up? That was a stretch.

But *help* me? My hope grasped on to that word like a drowning person clinging to a life raft.

Was this guy capable of changing sides?

Who was Green? Based on what he'd told me, he was the leader of his own crew, which did not include Brown, who he clearly didn't like.

As if the org structure of his criminal enterprise wasn't confusing enough, Green implied he'd had to take care of someone, too. Who? Was he still taking care of them? And if he was responsible for caring for someone, why would he risk his freedom by robbing places?

"Can I ask you a question?" I tilted my body forward slightly.

"Depends on the question," he said.

"Why'd you become a burglar?"

8

"What difference does it make?" Green sounded confused.

"I'm curious."

"Why?"

"You seem..." *Nice?* "Not abysmal."

Green chuckled. "Well, if that's not a ringing endorsement."

"You're part of that gang they talk about on the news, aren't you? The ones they call the Robin Hood Thieves because, after each heist, anonymous donations appear to homeless shelters."

"Veto," Green said.

"What the hell does *veto* mean?"

"Means I'm not answering that."

"That's a yes."

"You'd be wise to stop trying to guess our identity."

Our. So, at least one of those guys out there was a member of his crew.

"Do you really make donations to homeless shelters after each burglary?" I couldn't hide my high-pitched surprise.

"Why?"

I shrugged. "Seems odd."

"Yeah? Why's that?" he asked dryly.

"Criminals don't help other people."

"Because we're too busy plotting evilness in our lair?" He sounded amused.

"Or holding unsuspecting women hostage."

I wondered if he rolled his eyes.

"So, if criminals did anything nice for someone," he said, "it would surprise you?"

"Surprise me? I'd be less surprised if a black hole sucked me out of the atmosphere at a thousand miles an hour."

A gust of air burst from his nose. And when he spoke, his tone flooded with amusement. "It's confusing you, isn't it?"

"What is?"

"That a *bad guy* might be capable of doing something good, too."

"People's actions speak volumes."

"Like your father's."

My lips curled. "What?"

"You said *even after what he did to you, you'd never wish this on him.* What did he do?"

I'd said that to him?

Right. When verbal diarrhea exploded from my mouth, begging for my life.

"You're changing the subject, so you don't have to answer my questions," I said sternly.

"Maybe," he said. "What did he do to you?"

"Veto."

"Did he hurt you?" A protective edge sliced through his words.

"Why do you care?" I tightened my forehead.

"I want to know about you."

Hope took flight in my chest. While I didn't want to talk about what went down with my dad, my captor had just expressed interest in me, which meant he was seeing me as a human being, not just his hostage. A human being that he cared enough about to scold his colleague for hitting, clean the blood off my face, and warm me with his jacket.

Telling him I was a caregiver hadn't been enough to sway him because, clearly, he was interested in *me*, not in whoever depended on me.

Perhaps opening up to him would finally make him let me go, but if I was going to run this play, I needed to do it now; the robbery would be done soon. And if I hadn't won Green over by then, I'd be dead.

Of all subjects to get into, I wished he hadn't pressed for such a painful one. But in the fight for my life and my dad's life, I would pull out all the stops to stay alive.

So, I sucked in a deep pull of oxygen and steadied my quivering heart.

"It started a few years ago."

9

I suppose the darker times wouldn't make sense without some context of what life was like before it all went to hell.

"I grew up in Illinois," I started. "With my brother, Anthony, two stable parents, and a white picket fence. The life where you think everything will stay peaceful forever..."

"Merry Christmas." Dad smiles as he hands me a three-inch cube wrapped in silver.

We're in our living room in Oak Brook. Outside the eight-foot window, snowflakes drift from the gray sky, joining the four inches of snow already blanketing the ground. Inside, the fireplace's logs crack, spitting embers as we sit around the Christmas tree, sipping hot chocolate with whipped cream, its sticky sweetness lingering above my lip.

I set my mug down and take the gift from my father, who slings an arm around his crooked knee, and smiles. Joy dancing through a father's heart as he waits for his only daughter to open his gift.

I tear open the paper and open a black jewelry box. And not just any jewelry box. It's from L&B Fine Jewelry, the fanciest jewelry store in town, the one that sells one-of-a-kind pieces to rich people. We don't wear jewelry like this in our family—we wear stuff from Target—so I look up at him, wide-eyed.

His grin reminds me of a kid. "Open it."

I comply and see the most gorgeous ring I've ever seen. A pear-shaped ruby, surrounded by diamonds, in a rose gold band.

"Dad..." I bring my hand to my chest.

"This is our last Christmas together before you leave for college, so I wanted to get you something special. Something you'll have for the rest of your life, to remind you of how much I love you."

My eyes sting.

"I'm incredibly proud of you, Zoey. Straight A's. Getting accepted into the University of Illinois. I don't know what I did to deserve a daughter like you."

It would be hard, leaving the only home I've ever known next fall. To no longer have breakfast every day with Dad—eggs, blueberries, and a bagel. Extra cream cheese. I cherish our mornings together. It's when we talk about life. I'm closer to my dad than I am to my mom, not that I don't have a bond with my mom. I do. She's fantastic. There's just something... magical between me and my dad. Pixie dust that's been there since I was a toddler, running into his arms when he'd gotten home from work.

"Love you, Zo," he says. "Never forget that."

He hugs me.

I DID NOT KNOW THAT, SOON, OUR HAPPY FAMILY WOULD BREAK APART.

The first fracture wasn't a fracture at all. It was an earthquake. Magnitude eight, at least, when I got that phone call in college.

I was particularly vulnerable at that time, not only because I was new to college and struggling to find my confidence, but also because my best friend from high school had basically stopped returning my calls and texts. We hadn't had a fight. She'd moved to Arizona for college, and we went from seeing each other daily in high school to talking every day, then every week, then texting only, and then, well...my texts went unanswered. Calls went straight to voice mail.

She'd been my best friend since fifth grade, and all of a sudden, it was like I didn't matter to her anymore. Like she'd found new friends and I was in her rearview mirror.

How could our friendship not matter to her as much as it did to me? Each text that went unreturned sliced another gash in my chest.

That was when Dad called me up one day, out of the blue, his voice foreboding.

"I NEED TO TALK TO YOU." HIS TONE IS OFF. AND WRONG. AND SCARING ME, and I can't go to school or focus, worrying about what's wrong.

Is he sick? Is Mom sick? Is Anthony okay?

I ask him all these things, of course, but all he says is, "We should wait to talk in person."

"Tell me now," I plead.

"Zoey."

"Are you dying?"

"No, it's nothing like that," he assures.

"But it's something terrible. Please, just say it."

"This isn't something to be discussed over the phone. How about I drive over on Friday—"

"Friday! You think I can go through classes until then? I won't be able to focus."

I've never heard him like this. Sad. Afraid even. He's never been afraid to tell me anything.

"I'll drive over. We can have dinner."

He's covering something up. Mom must be sick, or he's sick, or someone's dying. He's playing word games to avoid telling me the truth because whatever it is, it's so bad, he thinks I can only handle it in person.

"I don't want dinner. I want you to tell me what the hell is going on."

"And I will, on Friday."

"Tell me now, Dad."

"Zoey."

"Tell me, or I'll leave right now and come home, so we can talk. I'm not waiting until Friday."

A weird hesitation passes.

"You can't come to the house right now, Zoey."

Can't? *"Why?" I start pacing.*

"I'll explain when I see you."

Suddenly, my best friend abandoning me loses its significance because if someone in my family is dying, nothing else matters.

"I'm packing a bag." I grab my travel suitcase from my closet and throw it onto the floor.

"Zoey."

Desperation comes out like the blunt tip of a sharp knife. "I'm not waiting to talk, Dad, so last chance. Spit it out, or I'm on my way."

I can hear Dad sigh like he does when something isn't going the way he wanted it to.

I'm silent during the next several seconds until, finally, he says, "Zoey, I've...well..." Dad clears his throat. "The thing is...I've met someone."

I've. Met. Someone. *Three words that thrust a sword into my heart, puncturing it deeper with each stab.*

"I didn't mean for this to happen," he claims. "But we have a lot in common, and we fell in love."

"What exactly are you saying?" I demand, clenching my fists so tightly that my fingernails sting my palms.

"Zoey...I've moved out of your mother's house."

"So, it's Mom's house now? Not our house?"

"Zoey—"

"Who is she?"

"I...she's someone I met at work."

"Does she know you're married?"

He sighs. "She knows everything."

"What kind of person dates a guy who's married? With kids? And is willing to break up a family?"

"Zoey...it's not like that."

"That's exactly what it's like! How could you do this to Mom? To us?"

"I understand you're upset—"

"Upset? More like betrayed and disgusted! The father I know would never cheat on his wife and leave his family for some other woman!"

The dad that I know is the rock of the family, the man who lifts us up when we fall, and the person I turn to anytime I feel lost or overwhelmed. After talking with him, I'm always clear in the direction that I want to head with whatever I'm facing. To put it plainly, he is my North Star, and even though I love my mom and my brother, I suppose we all have that one person in our life that is the most influential with guiding us. And Dad is that special person to me, not only because of his wisdom, but because I look up to him as a human being. That is the dad that I know.

"I'm going to let you go, so you can calm down. I'm coming up on Friday. We'll talk about it then."

"So, you're going to drop a bomb like this and just hang up on me?"

"This conversation isn't productive. You're too upset to talk right now."

"More like you destroy our family and can't face the heat of our broken hearts."

"I'll be up on Friday." He tries to make his voice sound loving, but it sounds dismissive. And then he hangs up.

This has to be a sick joke. This cannot be real. Dad gave no hint that anything was wrong with their marriage, let alone something big enough to leave Mom. Maybe he got catfished online, and he's a victim of some swindler that's brainwashed him. Or worse, maybe he has a brain tumor —something causing a sudden personality shift. Because the man that would do everything for his family would never do any of this to us. To me.

And if he would? Then, that would mean the father that I thought I knew for all these years wasn't real. That he was a completely different person. Not the hero who I looked up to, but a villain willingly hurting those he supposedly loved the most.

Which is too painful to endure. It's pathetic, I know. People face far worse heartaches in their lives. Death of a child. Famine. Abuse. And here I am, pathetically unable to cope with Dad leaving his family.

I put my hand over my aching stomach.

This is like a mudslide. Standing on what you thought was a solid foundation, only to have it go out beneath you.

Days pass in a fog. Days when I call my mom and brother. Mom tries to hide the hurt in her voice, and she's being diplomatic about the whole thing, reminding me he's a great father even if he's not being the best husband right now. Her having the grace to take the high road when he's ripping her heart out makes me even angrier at my father.

He doesn't deserve Mom.

I can't wait until he comes because I have so many questions: How long has this been going on? What does she have that we don't? And so many other things to get off my chest.

The day before Dad's visit, I'm a nervous wreck. I feel like our entire relationship hangs in the balance of this weekend because I don't think I can ever get past this. I desperately need him to say something to help me understand, or I'll lose my father forever.

When my cell rings with his number, I assume he just wants to confirm that I'm actually going to show up.

But as soon as I answer, I can tell something's wrong based on his tone.

"Zoey"—his voice has notes of apology and assertiveness—"I'm afraid I'm going to have to reschedule."

I laugh, my body rigid with anger and disbelief. "You're kidding me, right?"

"She didn't know I'd made plans with you and surprised me with a trip."

"You're going on a trip? With that woman?"

"Zoey."

I close my eyes and grab the lifeline to my father. Tugging as hard as I can. "Dad, we need to talk right away." If we don't, this anger will fester until it's spread through my entire heart, damaging it beyond repair. Our only hope is to talk now.

And I shouldn't have to beg him to make the right decision. This is my father, someone who's supposed to prioritize me above the entire world.

I can't believe he's hesitating on the other end. Each beat of my heart that passes in silence widens the chasm between a father and daughter.

Which is selfish of my feelings—to grab the wheel and take over like this. The headline here is him leaving Mom for another woman, not how badly he's breaking my heart. And yet, my emotions grip the wheel tighter, putting his decision to come here on center stage because right now, it feels like the most defining moment of our relationship.

"You need to make a choice about what's more important this weekend, Dad. Her. Or me."

"This isn't about who's more important."

"It is now."

"And we will talk," Dad said, his voice bordering on aggravation. "Just not tomorrow. The tickets she bought are nonrefundable. It's just a few more days, and then I'll come over, okay?"

I hope he realizes what he just said has taken that sword he'd placed in my heart and twisted it. Then sliced until it hemorrhaged.

"Well, I guess you made your choice then."

"Zoey."

"No, you've made your priorities clear, Dad."

I hang up and can't stop myself from cracking in half and falling to my bed in a heap of sobs. I'm angry that I'm crying. He doesn't even care enough about me to come when he said he would. He's more worried about some nonrefundable ticket, a trip with his new girlfriend, than salvaging a relationship with his only daughter. And I'm angry that I'm so fixated on this stupid visit when I should only be focused on how he's hurting the entire family.

But I guess it's hard enough when your parents are splitting, but a thousand times more hurtful when your dad is rejecting you *in the process.*

I'm pathetic because I stare at my phone, willing it to ring. He's my dad, and he should fight with every breath in his body to talk to me, to beg me for forgiveness, no matter how angry I am. Of course I'm angry! He's married, and he's just walking out on Mom!

But five minutes pass, and my phone doesn't ring.

He must be pacing, thinking about what he wants to say.

Ten minutes pass.

He realizes how badly he's hurt me, and it means so much that he's taking the time to gather his thoughts.

Fifteen minutes pass.

He's telling his girlfriend that he's not going on that trip. He's packing a bag and coming straight here. Now.

Thirty minutes pass. Then an hour. Three hours later, I throw my phone across the room and bury my face in my pillow.

He's not calling back.

As it turns out, the blade of the sword cuts much deeper when the person wielding it is supposed to be your protector.

A CHILD WAS SUPPOSED TO BE THE FIRST PRIORITY OF THEIR PARENTS. FROM the moment I was born, Dad loved me with an unspoken promise that my importance to him would never diminish. But it did diminish. Severely.

After he never showed up that weekend, the next time we spoke, there was an undercurrent of frustration in my dad's tone. Which made me even angrier. It was like, even though he was the one in the wrong, he expected me to revert back to being a five-year-old and just accept his decision as final, no questions asked. Which led to even more distance between us, and the more distance there was, the less he tried to fix things.

I guess my pain was too much of a handful to bother with.

That's when I discovered a shattered heart can crumble into even smaller pieces until the only thing left is dust.

When you have the unconditional love of your father, the world is a sanctuary of optimism and peace, but when that love is revoked, when you become insignificant to the person who's supposed to love you above all others, your foundation cracks.

And you question if his love was ever there for you in the first place. And if his love could go away, how could I ever trust anyone else's love again?

Mom and Dad got a quick divorce, which Mom didn't fight him on. She was probably too humiliated to beg him to love her the way he'd promised he always would. Especially when he hired some big-shot lawyer and left Mom with nothing—nothing, not even child support since Anthony and I were of age.

As if that weren't bad enough, right before my last year in college, I got an email from my father, letting me know I was on my own financially for my senior year tuition. Which was due a month later. I almost had to drop out of college because of it. Thankfully, I scrambled with loans and two jobs. But the thing that hurt the worst was that it felt like a penalty, like his promise as a father was contingent upon me approving of his life choices. And if I didn't? He was willing to risk my college degree to punish me.

In the years that followed, I became blinded in life, unsure of my footing, particularly in my relationships. I was skeptical anyone actually cared about me. Convinced it was only a matter of time before they would hurt me, too.

I almost didn't even allow myself to build a new friendship with my college roommate, Jenna, but I supposed we had something big in common—she and I shared in the betrayal of a father leaving his family.

But even with that friendship and a slow build of others, my foundation never mended.

After Dad married that woman—I didn't attend the wedding—he started calling me and reaching out again, but I doubted it had anything to do with his love for me and more about him wanting me to meet my new *stepmom.*

Fat chance.

I refused repeatedly until, one day, Anthony guilt-tripped me into attending Thanksgiving with him. After my big brother graduated college, he took a job in Oregon—pretty much as far away from Chicago as you could get. He used to fly home every holiday, though, and was hard at work, trying to make a peace treaty between me and Dad. But it was easier for him to encourage a reconciliation; Anthony had earned a full ride to college with his grades and soccer, so he dodged the bullet of having a tuition crisis with Dad.

A tuition crisis with a brand-new development.

Two months before Thanksgiving, I'd discovered the first three years of college tuition—the tuition that Dad *had* covered—hadn't been paid off like Dad had told me it would be. Instead, the "temporary" student loans that he'd cosigned with me—the ones that were supposed to be paid off when I graduated college—had recently defaulted, destroying my credit score and leaving me with over $53,000 in loans I hadn't been expecting. Without so much as a heads-up.

Did I expect my parents to fund my college? No. In fact, I offered to pay for it myself by getting jobs, but Dad insisted —*insisted*—on funding my education. It was something he'd wanted to do my whole life, and even though we had fallen out, I guess I'd let him pay for two reasons. One, maybe part of it was an FU. You want to ditch me, destroy Mom, and ruin all our lives for some woman? Least you can do is fulfill the promise you'd made to me. And two, maybe the little weakling in me grasped on to the only proof I had that he still cared...until he stopped funding senior year, that is.

In any case, paperwork had been filed. With both our names on it. Loan paperwork, so Dad had a little flexibility with cash flow, given the timing of his bonuses each year. At least, that was what he told me.

But as it turned out, those monthly statements he'd arranged to only go to him had been ignored. He hadn't paid them and never bothered to tell me they'd been sent to collection.

My credit rating tanked, and I was sacked with the unexpected debt, which had accrued interest and penalties.

What a slap in the face.

To drag my credit score down without even telling me.

Not surprisingly, finding an apartment in Chicago willing to rent to a tenant with horrible credit was nearly impossible. Not to mention, drowning under unexpected financial weight was beyond stressful.

So, when my brother pushed me into Thanksgiving, I rolled up my sleeves, ready to confront my father about it all.

I arrive at Dad's place. A luxury condo that makes me seethe with anger.

Mom and Dad graduated college together without a penny to their name, and Dad worked his ass off, climbing the ranks of a sales executive until he finally made some serious bank. Just in time for this new woman to invade our lives and live in the lap of luxury.

It's not that I wanted the money or the lifestyle. It's just that it feels like another slap in the face. Another thing she took from Mom that was rightfully hers.

"Zoey." Dad smiles when we enter. "I'm so glad you came."

He must've practiced that fake-ass smile in the mirror. Like he gave a crap if I came. Like he gave a crap about me at all.

I twist the ring on my finger. The one he gave me that fateful Christmas Day, the last one we spent as a family before he let his dick make all his decisions. I don't know why I still wear it. Probably some last tiny string of hope that my dad will come back to me.

"This is Holly."

He ushers a tall woman, wearing a bright red dress, toward me. Her black hair looks like it has a thousand products in it to keep every strand in perfect waves, her makeup thick and elegant. Like a bride on her wedding day.

I, on the other hand, am wearing jeans and a black sweater. I chose black on purpose. Like, FU, Dad. I've been in mourning since the day you left.

But any thoughts of our outfits quickly fade when I see what's on her hand. Not her left hand—although her wedding ring is ten times nicer than the one Dad gave Mom. Another FU to our family. But her other hand. Because on it is the identical ring I am wearing.

Rose gold. Pear-shaped ruby. Diamonds.

Dad sees my gaze cut to it, and his eyes widen.

"You were screwing her back then?" I snap.

The handful of people at Thanksgiving stop talking and stare at the scene.

"Zoey."

"You gave her this ring, too?" I'm crying, and I'm furious that I'm crying because he doesn't deserve my tears. Back when he gifted me that ring, I was special to him, and that time in my life was all I had left of my dad.

But it, too, is gone. He'd been cheating on my mom back then. He'd given this woman the same ring he claimed was special, just for me. A tender moment between us ruined. A ring he claimed he wanted to remind me of his love.

What a crock of shit.

The ring once symbolized his unending love for me, but now, it symbolizes betrayal.

I take off the ring, and I throw it at my father's face.

I run out of his condo and out of his life.

I COULDN'T BRING MYSELF TO TALK ABOUT WHAT HAPPENED NEXT; IT WAS SO painful, it made me feel sick to my stomach.

As the silence ticked on, Green said nothing. In fact, he'd barely moved or made a noise.

"Are you still there?" I pretended I couldn't see his combat boots.

"Yes." His voice had changed. It was lower, as if pain anchored it down.

Another pause.

"Has something happened?" I bent my neck. "You went all quiet."

"No."

"You sound different." I wrinkled my forehead. And he did. He sounded like...sad or something...

He didn't respond.

"Are you okay?" I asked, my pitch higher.

"I'm fine."

"You don't sound fine."

He cleared his throat and seemed to take a second to calibrate his response. "You were mistreated by someone you trusted. Someone who should've protected you," he snarled. "At least what happened to me wasn't done to me by my own flesh and blood."

There was a lot to unpack there. What happened to him? And by whom? And more importantly, was this the moment I'd been hoping for, when his allegiance shifted to me?

But before I could ask, Green spoke again. "How'd you get stuck taking care of your dad? And why'd you bother after he'd treated you like that?"

It took me a second to stop wondering what Green's past was. "That's an even longer story," I hedged.

As much as I hated everything my dad did to me, nothing topped what I'd done to him.

"How long ago did he leave your family?" Green asked.

I squirmed. "Six and a half years ago. My sophomore year of college."

"So, you graduated, what, four years ago?"

I nodded.

The clock ticked three times.

"But the bank didn't tell you about the loans defaulting until now?"

"I found out about it last year. I can only assume minimum payments were made for a while before they finally stopped completely."

"And now, you're on the hook for them? Isn't he still on the hook, too?"

"Legally, he might be, but the reality is, my name is on them, and he can't pay. Most likely will never be able to. He was already in financial distress before the accident, and now, the hospital bills killed any hope of him avoiding bankruptcy. We started the process a couple months ago."

What an overwhelming crash course in how personal bankruptcy works. The different versions you can file, each with pros and cons. It didn't release the burden of the student loans, though.

"And your dad's ex won't help?"

"She left him right after the accident. Before he was even discharged from the hospital."

"That's why he came to your place when he was released?"

"She wasn't going to take care of him, and my brother lives too far away."

Green's voice lowered another octave and let out a huge sigh. "Taking care of someone's an expensive burden," he said. "And yet, you had that wallet in your hands, stuffed with money. And you didn't take any of it."

The admiration in his voice wrapped around my skin like silk.

"Stealing won't change what that guy did to my dad."

"You said it was a hit-and-run?"

I had to clench my eyes shut from the memories of not just how badly Dad had been injured, but also, everything else that came before it. "He left my dad without even checking if he was alive."

"Maybe he panicked."

To this, I tilted my head, both in offense and scrutiny. Because why would he say that?

"Did *you* hit someone?"

"No," Green assured. "And I don't know anyone that did, either. I'm just saying..." He was silent for a minute, and when he finally spoke, his voice was vulnerable. "Sometimes, good people are capable of bad things, Zoey."

Good people doing bad things, meaning what—something happened that caused him to become a thief?

"You never answered my question before." I leaned forward slightly.

"What question?"

"Why did you choose a life of crime?"

Green sighed in a way someone does when they're preparing to give a long answer.

But before Green said anything, I heard a thump.

Then another and another, in quick succession, and as Green's ankles stiffened, I realized someone was on their way down the hall.

Thump. Thump. Angry boots slamming against the wooden floor.

Green moved to the doorway, and the way he positioned his feet —half-forward, angled toward me—if I didn't know better, I'd swear he was frazzled. The footsteps grew louder, closer to me, and with Green blocking the doorway, I had nowhere to run.

There was only one reason a man would be coming toward us, and Green would be rigid.

The robbery was done, and it was time to kill me.

10

My body trembled, ready to take all one hundred fifteen pounds and turn it into a lethal weapon. With my hands in front, I could punch and claw and open the front door hella easier than when they'd been behind my back. It'd be easier if I could free them, though. As I twisted my right wrist, trying to pull it through the loop of confinement, Green's breathing quickened. Another step echoed through the hallway.

I'd have to act now. Jump up, move the blindfold, bulldoze my way past whoever was in the hall, and make it to the front door. Not ideal. Not probable I'd succeed, but what other choice did I have?

I braced my feet on the ground and prepared to strike.

But when the person took their next step, they were on a different surface. The carpet in the master bedroom, I realized.

Whoever it was wasn't coming into the office.

Not yet, anyway. But if they were finished with the main area already, it wouldn't be much longer until they were done.

I wasn't going to sit here and wait for a perfect shot because one wasn't coming. When Green shifted his position to come back near the desk, I decided it was now or never.

My heart pounded in my chest so hard, I felt dizzy as I assessed my senses. I could hear the padding of one set of footsteps in the master, which was twenty feet away, but I couldn't hear the other. Was he in the living room? Or maybe already starting to haul away stolen goods?

They must have a getaway van in the garage, which meant they might —probably did—have lookouts. I'd have to avoid the lobby in case they had them there, too.

Green stood to my right, fifteen feet from me, and the doorway was to my left. Maybe eight feet away.

Screw it.

I shot up out of the chair like a jack-in-the-box, sprinting to the doorway as I yanked the blindfold up and off my head.

Sight. A sense I'd taken for granted my whole life, but now that it was back, it afforded me the ability to see the hallway as I rounded the doorframe to the left and bolted four steps into the hall.

"The hell you think you're doing?!" Brown yelled. I recognized his growly voice behind me.

I hadn't seen him yet—hadn't seen anyone—and I didn't dare risk a glance behind me to give him another reason to kill me. I needed to stay focused on what lay ahead—the living room, which was only ten feet away.

But arms slammed around me like steel bars, squeezing my waist as he lifted me off the ground, pulling me back into the office, back into the nightmare. My hands flailed wildly for an anchor, finding the office door handle.

I held on to it with everything I had, kicking my feet, trying to break free of his grip. His smell—stale cigarettes smoldering in an ashtray—made my stomach roll.

"Brown." Green's voice was behind me now, too.

"Stupid bitch was trying to escape!" Brown snapped.

My ribs threatened to crack under the pressure of his arms, but I focused on the handle. On the only thing that kept me from going back into that prison.

Brown shifted his focus to my fingers, trying to pry them off. As it turned out, the groaning I heard was my own, my body crying in pain from Brown's death grip.

The wolf had caught his rabbit, but I'd try to thrash my way out of his trap.

He grabbed my fingertips and pulled backward, and though I fought it, my middle finger slid over the handle, and the rest of them followed suit.

Just like that, I was robbed of my escape, trapped back in my cage with a killer.

The vise around my body released, and my body flew like a rag doll until my head smashed into something. A sharp pain channeled up my spine as I crumpled to the ground while things pelted me from above. I threw my still-tied hands above my head out of instinct, protecting my head from further blows as something rained down on me. Books, I realized. Brown had thrown me against the office's bookshelf.

My sense of up or down had been compromised by the blow to my head, the room waving as if on a boat. Two more books hit my shoulder and my thigh, and then the noise stopped, and something smashed into my ribs with a searing burn. I shrieked, the sound almost inhuman, like an animal. Another blow slammed into my back. I buried my head into my arms even deeper, protecting it, when a third strike whacked my hip. My scream was bloodcurdling this time.

"Enough!" Green shouted.

The strikes stopped, but I remained cowering in the fetal position, arms covering my head, eyes still clenched shut. My body ached. My head was pounding, and my lower back was on fire from Brown's kicks.

The blindfold snaked around my eyes before I had a chance to see them—pain having a way of clamping your eyes shut. It took only a second, and I suspected it was Green who'd covered my eyes. If it were Brown, he'd have been rougher.

"Move," Brown ordered.

Peeking beneath the gap, I noticed Green's boots standing in front of me, facing Brown's feet.

"Go back down the hall," Green insisted.

"Move aside," Brown snarled.

A high-pitched metallic shrill pierced through the silence. It reminded me of silverware scraping together.

"What are you doing?" Green's voice rose in anger.

"Killing her," Brown explained in a resolute voice. "Before she has the chance to get away."

My stomach twisted. That was what that sound was—a knife, pulled from its sheath.

Green remained in what appeared to be a protective stance. "No."

"Move," Brown ordered.

"Finish the job first."

"She just tried to escape. Not gonna let that happen again. She dies now."

"I'm not going to get life in prison because you're impatient." Green took a step closer to him. "You kill her now, then we *leave now*."

"News flash: you don't call the shots. Move the hell out of my way," Brown said, his voice sinister. "Move."

At the sound of his footsteps advancing, I collapsed into my body again, my muscles clenching at the thought of the knife tearing into my flesh. I heard a crack and waited for the pain. When I heard another snap, I still didn't feel pain, and then the sounds of grunting and thuds gave me the courage to peek through the crevice of my blindfold again.

It took me a second to realize why their feet patterns were tangled and irregular—Brown and Green were fighting. Punches flying, they moved all over the room. Had they not been blocking my path to the door, I would have tried to jump up, no matter how badly Brown's beating had hurt. But I didn't dare get closer to the knife meant for me...

"Break it up!" Orange shouted, standing between the two men. "Green's right. We need to finish the job first."

The two men breathed heavy.

"Big mistake, attacking me like that, Green," Brown snarled.

So, it was Green that had thrown the first punch...

"Here," Orange said. I heard a small thump, as if something had been thrown and landed in someone's hand. "Tape her up, so she don't escape again. We're almost done. Let's just finish the damn job, and then we'll deal with her."

For a moment, things were silent.

"Fine," Brown finally agreed. "But I'm the one that tapes her up."

He marched past Green, who didn't stop him this time. My hair yanked back so hard, I was confident blood came with it, my hands instinctively grabbing Brown's wrists as he dragged me and shoved me into the chair.

The unmistakable sound of duct tape unwrapping from its spool preceded my ankles being slammed together. I could feel the anger coming through the tape, wrapping roughly around my feet. Over. And over. And over. Round and round the tape went, enough to go around the freaking Empire State Building. Brown shoved my shoulders back, wrapping tape around my torso a dozen times, binding me to the chair.

This tape—and my failed escape attempt—signed my death warrant. If I couldn't save myself, I refused to give him the satisfaction of seeing me cry.

"There," Brown snarled. "You ain't goin' anywhere now. Gonna come back for you, sweetheart." He made a kissing sound. "We'll have some fun before I kill you."

"Well then, it's a match made in heaven," I snapped. " 'Cause the only thing I'd want to do after sleeping with you is die."

Someone chuckled, and Brown slapped me, severely stinging my cheek.

A tearing sound preceded duct tape slamming over my lips.

"She gets away," Brown said in a warning tone, presumably to Green, "I'm holding you responsible."

His threat hung in the air for several moments before he and Orange left.

After a few seconds, Green's feet slowly advanced toward me. He must have been pissed that I tried to get away. That I got him in trouble with his accomplices. That I risked him going to prison by trying to escape...

When he squatted in front of me, I slinked my neck between my shoulders, waiting for his blow, for his revenge.

"Hold still." Green pulled the corner of the tape off my cheek, then gently peeled the rest of it off my mouth.

"I thought you said they were thieves, not rapists." I could taste the disgust in my throat.

"Brown's a loose cannon, but I've never heard of him touching a girl. He's probably just flexing."

"*Probably*? Well, let's file that under *not comforting at all.*"

"I won't let him touch you." Green's voice rumbled with protection. "But you really didn't need to provoke him."

"Yeah, well, he really didn't need to rob my house."

"Does your head hurt?" He pressed his fingers in my hair now. "You hit it pretty hard."

When his fingertips landed on a soft spot, I gasped.

"You're bleeding," he said, pulling his hand away.

He left, returned to the room, and pressed a towel to my head. I didn't mean to hiss, but the pain overcame my lips.

"Sorry." He applied pressure, his body close to me.

I didn't like being taped to this chair. Even if I couldn't get away, I felt like that girl on the railroad tracks in those old movies. Tied down, waiting for the train to run her over. I'd just rather it be over already.

"You need to be quiet," Green urged. "If you scream, they'll kill you, and there will be nothing I can do to stop them."

They.

Not him.

That one word shifted everything. It drew battle lines, them against me, with Green caught somewhere in the middle. When he'd saved me from being killed a moment ago, when he'd fought Brown, I couldn't be sure if it was for my sake or for Green's. If he'd done it because he wanted to wait until the end of the burglary to kill the hostage for his own protection. But that word. *Them.* Told me the fight was something more.

Or maybe I was wrong.

All he'd said was that if I screamed, there was nothing he could do to stop them from killing me. So, really, it was more of a threat than a warning.

Not to mention, he'd told them that they had to wait to kill me until the robbery was finished. Wait. That was all he'd pushed for. Waiting made sense, for his sake. You don't stick around a place with a murder victim inside. Maybe his saving me hadn't been a display of battle lines. Maybe it was self-preservation.

He was just trying to control me. Keep the hostage calm, so I didn't screw things up for them.

He probably didn't care at all if I lived or died.

If he did, he'd have helped me get out of here by now. He could see. He knew his colleagues and would know how long it took them to clear each room. If he really wanted to, he probably could have come up with some way to let me run without his colleagues knowing he'd let me escape. Yet he hadn't even tried.

The only thing he'd done was delay my killing.

"You're shivering again," Green said. As if he cared. As if it bothered him.

"Leave me alone, Green," I whispered over the lump in my throat. "Or whatever the hell your name is."

I wasn't going to talk to him anymore. I'd lost my chance at escape. I ruined everything by not timing this right, and now, I was screwed, and by default, my dad was screwed, too.

"Easton," he said in a quiet voice. His fingertips grazed gently along my forehead, sweeping a fallen patch of hair back into place.

I blinked. "What?"

"My name is Easton."

11

My adrenaline dispatched needles throughout my limbs. He'd told me information that I could use against him.

And when he spoke again, he kept his voice low to shield the sound from the other guys.

"This...new life, I guess you could call it, started when I was thirteen," Green—or, I guess *Easton*—said. "My brother and I returned home after having dinner at a friend's house. When we walked in the door, first thing I noticed was the glass tumbler broken on the kitchen floor and how its ice cubes were melting into little puddles. Like they were bleeding. Should've pulled my brother back outside and gone to a neighbor's, but my feet just..."

Apprehension spread over my skin.

"They were in the master bedroom. Both of my parents. Shot to death." He hesitated. "Dad still had the gun in his hand."

Oh God.

Why is he telling me this? Is he trying to keep me calm by distracting me? And why am I so interested that I'm tilting my head forward?

It must be morbid curiosity, same as a person who looks at a car accident as they drive by.

After all, finding out what makes a person rob houses is a captivating mystery, and I was a moth to its flame.

"Later, they ruled it a murder-suicide. Pieced together that they must've had an argument, and my dad was drunk when he shot my mom. Whether it was intentional or he was just trying to scare her and the gun went off, we'll never know. But once he shot her, he turned the gun on himself."

Easton stayed silent for ten heartbeats, and when he spoke, his voice darkened. "I've often wondered why I was sentenced to survive their deaths. What had I done that deserved the punishment of staying alive after that?"

My throat clenched.

"My little brother was ten at the time. I walked into the house before him, and I just...froze. If I hadn't, maybe I could've shielded him from seeing..."

I couldn't even imagine. Seeing your parents in a pool of blood and then the shock, realizing your life would never be the same.

"Both sets of grandparents were already dead, so they tried to locate an aunt on my mom's side and a distant uncle on my dad's. They told us they couldn't get in touch with them, but I suspect my relatives weren't willing to take on the burden of two kids. Neither relative was close to my parents, and that's a lot to take on."

A pang hit my chest. "Did they find anyone to take you in?"

"We went into the foster care system. First homes we went to, we got split up. Brother went to one family; I went to another. I stayed with a guy who was an alcoholic and liked to use my face as his punching bag when he'd had too much to drink. One night, he got so drunk, he burned the only things I had left of my parents in the firepit as a punishment."

Easton paused, his tone becoming even more somber. "I remember the way the flames seemed to grab the cloth and the pictures and pull them to the center of the heat. Eat them until they were ash."

When a stretch of silence elapsed, I wondered if he was fighting tears—especially when he had to clear his throat before speaking again.

"Anyway, didn't take long before someone noticed bruises, and I was taken out of that place. Second home I went to was worse. They fostered two other kids, who were a year older than me and had been through hell, so I was getting it from both the parents and the other kids. Beatings mostly."

Jeez. All while trying to process the sudden deaths of his parents.

A rush of unease skated up my spine as I listened to the predator's transformation back into prey.

"Then, finally, we got our first stroke of good luck, and my brother and I got put in the same home. Was the first time I felt hope since my parents died. At first, things felt almost too good to be true. Home-cooked dinners every night. Warm beds, trips to the Lego Store. The foster dad even bought us our very own bikes. But the way he looked at my brother, gave him more attention and treats than the other kids staying there...couldn't put my finger on it, but it gave me the creeps. Thought maybe I was just being paranoid, like after having so much shit happen, I was too messed up in the head to accept that we were safe and well cared for.

"But one night, I heard another foster kid's bedroom door squeak open and then latch shut. Kid was only ten or eleven, so I thought maybe he was having a bad night, missing his parents or something. Didn't want him to feel alone, so I went to check on him. His door was locked, and when I knocked, the kid told me to go away. But his voice sounded more scared than sad. I refused to go away, kept knocking, and eventually, the door opened. Out walked the foster dad, at two o'clock in the morning with his fly still open. Took a while to get it out of the kid, but he confirmed that the foster dad...*liked* little boys, if you know what I mean. And my ten-year-old brother was his favorite age."

Bile swirled in my gut.

"I wanted to tell our case worker, but if I did, we'd be separated again, and I wouldn't be able to protect my little brother. And that was assuming they'd get him away from that pedophile immediately, before it was too late. Decided our best option was to run away. Life on the streets was better than any other alternative we had at that point, and even though I didn't have a plan past escaping that house, I'd do whatever it took to keep my brother safe. I wasn't going to let that son of a bitch keep hurting other kids, though, so I reported him to the cops before I left."

The bile crept up my throat, threatening to erupt. "Where did you go?"

"The foster family lived in a condo on the east side, and luckily, it was relatively warm at the time. Above fifty. So, that first night, we found an awning in an alley, hidden from the main road behind a dumpster." Easton's voice darkened. "My brother wept for hours that night as I held him. Sounded like a puppy whimpering for his mother."

This was hard to listen to. I wasn't sure I could endure any more of it, picturing two children so hopeless and lost that sleeping behind a dumpster in an alley was the only place they felt safe. Yet I needed to hear what happened next.

This time, when Easton spoke, I could hear him fighting off an emotion. "My brother kept crying that all he wanted was Mom and Dad. Wanted to go home and finish building his Mandalorian Starfighter Lego with Dad and draw Chewbacca using sidewalk chalk with Mom."

Damn. Here I was, feeling sorry for myself for Dad's medical bills and how hard it was to take care of him, and these kids had endured hell on earth.

"After that first night, everything just turned into survival. And evasion. If cops or anyone found us, they would turn us back over to the foster care system. We didn't feel safe, going to a homeless shelter or anything. Figured they'd turn us in."

"And you started...robbing people to stay alive."

Easton cleared his throat.

"I got good at pickpocketing. Would get some cash to buy food that way. Last for a day or two, and I'd do it again. The first time I broke into someone's place was when I was sixteen. We were still living on the streets, but we'd managed to find the best places to stay, where it didn't seem so bad anymore." Easton's reflective tone became weighed down with sadness. "It's strange. When you're in a dire situation, how you get used to it, so it doesn't feel so dire anymore."

He let a small silence elapse.

"So, one day, I walked past this townhouse, and the guy left in such a hurry that when he slammed the door behind him, it bounced open. But he didn't turn back; he walked down the street and got into an Uber. Figured there must be someone inside, but out of curiosity, I went up and rang the doorbell. When no one answered, I looked around and realized I could get more than just a few bucks. Found a stash of cash in his sock drawer. Enough for a month of food. Found a couple of watches that I later pawned. And that night, I was able to buy a cheap hotel room for me and my brother. It was the first time we'd slept in a bed in years."

Years of sleeping on a dirty concrete floor. Outside. On the streets of Chicago, where violent beatings and killings unfortunately happened daily. Not to mention, the unforgiving winters with snow and ice.

"That's why you make donations to homeless shelters." My posture slouched. Because he knew how it felt to be vulnerable with no one there to help him.

The snake had gained his venom and used it to help unsuspecting prey.

"I didn't want my brother to have to go back to sleeping on asphalt, in subzero temperatures, so I came up with a plan. To rob my first house. I targeted the wealthy because I didn't want to take something from someone who really needed it."

I didn't want to take something from someone who really needed it.

I never expected to feel this rush of compassion.

"And you got away with it."

"With enough money to last three months," Easton said. "Rest is kind of history. Got it to the point where I could usually get a few hundred bucks to survive on in just a few minutes. Everything just escalated from there. I figured if I could do that, I could save and get our own place. Started putting crews together to help me."

What an awful way to live. Now, I understood why this guy had been drawn into a life of crime because, yes, these were things I took for granted: having food, a warm bed, safety. Even though my life had dealt a few tough blows, I didn't spend my childhood worrying about starving. Afraid of being abused. Terrified of dying on the dangerous streets. I didn't have to spend my youth plotting ways to get money just to survive. That was too much for an adult to handle, let alone a kid.

"Funny, what I was capable of doing once my brother's life was on the line. Before my parents died, I never broke rules."

It was in this moment that my feelings for Easton transcended beyond pity. Would I have had those same street skills to keep myself alive at that young age? Would I have had the balls to do what he did? Grow the fangs needed to survive?

"It's hard to imagine you as a rule follower."

I heard a burst of air from his nose.

"Yeah, when I was a kid, I never would've imagined my life going this way."

"What did you imagine?" I couldn't hide my curiosity. "Before everything happened with your family, what did you want to be when you grew up?"

"What does every young boy want to be? A professional baseball player."

I smiled.

"Wanted to play for the Cubs, of course. Starting pitcher. Future Hall of Famer."

"Naturally."

"What about you?" His pitch increased with interest. "What do you do for a living?"

"Marketing analyst. I do analytics to identify the most profitable ROIs on our clients' advertising campaigns and work with them to scale up their most effective ads." Which generated revenue for our company.

"You like it?"

"Honestly? No. I wish I had done something with animals. When I was a kid, I wanted to be an animal rescuer or something."

"Why didn't you?"

I shrugged. "I let myself get coached by my parents on the practicalities of life. Getting a degree in something that could earn decent money to support a future family. And now, I'm kind of stuck because I can't afford to give up the paycheck." Especially with the huge student loan debt and Dad's medical bills.

He grew silent, and I wondered if it was because he felt guilty that I wouldn't have a future family to support. Why did he want to know about me, anyway? And why did he share what had to be the most intimate moments of his life with a stranger?

"Why did you tell me all this?" I wondered.

"You asked why I became a thief."

True, but he could've just said he was homeless and needed the money. He didn't have to tell me about being abused and running away, trying to care for his brother.

He chose to share this with me. The lion wanting the lamb to understand the reason for her fate. A fate that might end in death, but didn't need to include torture.

"Is that why you saved me from Brown?" I shifted in my seat. "You feel bad for targeting someone who couldn't afford to lose stuff?"

A rubbing sound of skin on whiskers told me Easton must be scrubbing his jaw for several long seconds. "I'm sorry about this. If I could take it all back, I would. I'm sorry about your belongings, your dad's health, about everything. I wish we'd never come here tonight. You don't deserve this."

This. As in the end.

The rattlesnake raised his tail and began shaking it, offering a warning of what came next.

It still didn't feel real, the prospect of death—and I wasn't giving up on going home, no matter how abysmal it might seem—but I needed to cover my bases. Just in case.

"If tonight doesn't end well..."

Dad would suffer more pain than I'd wish on my worst enemy. But there was one pain even worse than your daughter dying—having her disappear and never knowing what happened to her. He'd spend the rest of his life hunting, holding on to a shred of hope that I was out there somewhere, alive. Or worse, he might think I'd left him, just like he'd left me.

"If I don't make it out of here"—I tried to hide the cracking in my voice—"will you please make sure my dad knows what happened to me?"

I was fully aware of how insanely bizarre this was—asking my captor to help ensure my body was found. Even contemplating the aftermath of my death felt akin to preparing a will. You don't want to think about your death, but you also feel a sense of responsibility to make sure those around you are protected from the subsequent fallout.

Easton remained silent, and then he blew out an angry huff. "I'll be right back."

He was gone in an instant. He must have been standing outside the doorway because Easton's voice was still loud when he commanded, "Orange. A word."

I'm alone.

I began jerking my body, trying to pry a crack in the layers of duct tape. Most likely a fruitless effort, but I had to at least try, so I twisted, and stretched, and jerked, and thrust my torso.

Orange's steps joined Easton's as they shuffled a few feet away from the doorway, but I could still hear the discussion.

"Listen to me." Easton kept his voice low. "I need you to distract Brown. Keep him occupied on the other end of this place."

"Why?"

Easton said nothing.

"No fucking way," Orange said in angry disbelief.

"He's going to kill her."

"I'm not going against Brown," Orange whispered in a high-octave panic. "You know what he'd do to us?"

"That's exactly why I never wanted to work with him! He's a fucking lunatic," Easton snarled. "An unpredictable loose cannon."

"You want to save the witness, talk to him. Not me."

"I don't trust him." Anger thrashed through each word.

"You don't trust anyone."

"Least of all him. I trusted *you*, though. You knew I refused to work with him," he barked. "And you blindsided me by bringing him anyway! Why?"

"He agreed to let me in on another heist if I let him in on this one. I didn't tell you because I knew you'd say no."

"So, what, you're going to work with *him* now?"

"He's forming a bigger crew. Plans on doing bigger heists. Tonight's a trial run. If he's pleased with how it goes, I have a chance to work my way into a leadership position in his organization. You know how much cash that would bring in?"

"That guy'll get you killed. I've spent every day of the last decade keeping you safe, and I'm not going to watch you throw it all away."

"Not your call." Orange sounded ambivalent about my death. "And I don't have time for this shit. We're already ten minutes past our end time."

Ten minutes *past* their estimated end time. I would have thought a robbery was a lot faster than this. A grab-and-go, frenzied type of thing. But this was methodical, calm. They clearly knew the house was empty, knew no one else would be showing up, and used that to their advantage.

"Let's just finish this job." Exasperation pulled Orange's tone lower.

Three footsteps clanked on the hardwood before Easton spoke again.

"Are you really going to go along with this? *Killing* someone?"

Orange said nothing back.

Just walked down the hall.

When Easton's steps returned into the room, I felt dizzy.

"They're really going to kill me, aren't they?" I clenched my stomach.

Why did this continue to feel shocking? I guess facing your own mortality comes in waves. You think you'll die. You hope you'll live. You plan in case you don't, but you still hope. And then you get another confirmation. *It's over.*

There's no way I'm making it out of here. I'd never watch another sunset. Or hear the birds sing to each other. I'd never feel the ocean's surf lapping at my feet. And I'd never get to tell Dad I was sorry for what I'd done to him.

I expected to start sobbing uncontrollably, like I had before, but all I felt was numb. Maybe it was exhaustion or the realization and acceptance that I couldn't change the outcome.

Not for *me*, at least. But Easton, on the other hand...

"You should leave," I said, defeated. "Put as much distance between what's about to happen and you as possible."

He squatted down and rested his hands on my armrests, his face, undoubtedly, only inches from mine.

"You want me to leave you alone? With *them*?"

"If you stay, you're going to get caught and spend the rest of your life in prison. Walk away while you still have the chance. I'm doomed, but you don't have to be."

Another loud noise made me jump.

It was a clap, followed by, "That's it," from one of the guys.

They were really done this time. No doubt about it, no more false alarms. The robbery had been completed.

Which meant, there was only one thing left to do.

Kill me...

12

"Go, Easton."

A huff escaped his nose.

"You shouldn't want to help someone like me, Zoey." The tone of his voice turned sullen and reflective with undercurrents of pain. "Trust me, I'm not a good person."

A metal scrape sliced through the room from what I presumed to be the blade of a knife drawn from its sheath.

Trembling, I cringed, clamping my eyes shut so I wouldn't see even a sliver of the coming carnage.

I love you, Dad. I wish I'd said I'm sorry when I still had the chance.

A tearing sound—like wet fabric ripping—preceded my torso loosening from the chair, then my legs.

"You know about the back staircase?" Easton whispered.

The emergency exit was next to the master bedroom, at the end of the hall.

"It's always locked," I said, crinkling my forehead. With a separate key I didn't bring. If I had, I'd have tried to make a run for it to that door already.

"We unlocked it when we got here." Of course they did. Methodical burglars would want a second escape route, just in case. "You've got fifty-five flights ahead of you. Go. I'll hold them off as long as I can."

My mind raced. I couldn't believe this was happening. As Easton cut away the rest of the duct tape and my wrists' bindings, I prepared myself to take the last chance I had to stay alive.

"You understand?"

I nodded. "What will they do to you if they realize you let me escape?"

He didn't answer. Instead, he lifted my wrists, and I felt his lips gently press against my injured skin.

I sucked in a breath because his kiss unleashed a wave of pleasure that surged up my arm and became a tsunami in my chest.

"I'm going to take your blindfold off, Zoey."

His hands moved to the back of my head, and his knuckles brushed my scalp as he loosened the knots.

And then the fabric lifted from my eyes.

I clenched them shut and lowered my head, assuming he'd want to disappear into another room before I could see him, but Easton's thumb and finger pressed my chin up until my face aligned with his.

He wants me to look at him.

I waited another second, just in case I was wrong, before slowly opening my eyes.

Holy crap. It was him. Wallet guy. Sexy, stunningly gorgeous, and seductive.

He still had dark brown hair with caramel highlights, longer on the top by several inches and so short on the sides that it was nearly a buzz cut. Matching facial stubble stretched down his jaw and around his pouty lips, which sat beneath a perfectly sculpted nose. But most distinguishing were his spellbinding eyes, which were the color of the Caribbean Sea.

Those same eyes had popped up in more than one fantasy since I'd seen them last...

He kept them locked on me as I quickly took in the rest of his appearance. His frame was even more muscular than I'd remembered, trying to break out of his long-sleeved ivory shirt, his jeans.

Inappropriately, my lower belly warmed just as it'd done the day I'd first met him. Especially now that he stared at my lips with an insatiable hunger.

And then never breaking that gaze, Easton lowered his face and gently pressed his mouth against mine.

A sane person wouldn't have a wave of sensual heat rush through her body when her captor's lips seized hers. She wouldn't find his lips warm, and gentle, and...utterly perfect. And her skin wouldn't erupt into thrilling goose bumps when the palm of his hand cupped her cheek.

It felt like time froze, and I existed in the confusing space of unexpected desire.

And then Easton pulled back, leaving me reeling.

He cupped both sides of my face with his hands. "I've been wanting to do that since the first moment I laid eyes on you."

That day at the lake, I'd wanted him to do that, too. Even though I wouldn't admit it to myself at the time.

He helped me stand up, grabbed my cell phone from the desk, handed it back to me, and watched me shove it into my back pocket.

He wants to ensure I can call for help.

When he spoke next, he tilted his head slightly to compensate for his height. "I'll keep them back as long as I can," he whispered. "But if they catch you..."

I nodded.

"When I give you the signal, you run, Zoey."

His eyes glided down my face, and then he went to the door, where he looked up and down the hallway. I could hear his colleagues in the living room, checking for anything they might have missed. The emergency exit, located by the master bedroom, would be to the right, in the opposite direction.

But I still had to go into the hallway and expose myself.

Easton looked at me again—his eyes swimming with trepidation—and then he stepped outside the office. His broad shoulders and tall frame provided some cover, allowing me to quietly step outside behind him. I could see the tension radiating across his muscles as he cast his azure eyes back to me.

Looking into his eyes was like looking into his soul, an intimate moment between the man who was risking everything—his freedom, retaliation from his colleagues—to save me.

Adrenaline surged through my muscles.

Easton nodded his head.

I kept my footsteps light, trying to shield their sound as I ran toward the end of the hall. It only stretched fifteen feet in front of me, yet it felt like one of those dreams where you're running and it keeps extending beyond your reach.

"The fuck!" a voice shouted.

I risked a quick glance over my shoulder and witnessed Easton tackle a guy to the ground. Orange, based on his Converse. As Easton and Orange exchanged blows, the third guy—a bald, tattoo-covered dude with a nose ring—locked his merciless eyes on mine. And charged me.

I opened the door and threw myself into an outside hallway, hearing the *thwap, thwap* of blows. I wanted to see if Easton was okay, hoping they were his punches, but I couldn't slow down.

I hurled myself through another door, into a stairwell, and down the first flight of steps. The beige stairwell was silent, only wide enough for three people, and I was going so fast, I lost my footing and missed the last step, having to grab the cold banister to save myself from falling. I spun to make the next fourteen steps when the door slammed open behind me.

As if someone had kicked it in.

And then thundered down the steps behind me.

My legs began to tremble with each step. I tried not to look back, but Brown was right there, taking two steps at a time, using the railing to balance himself.

He's only ten feet back. And gaining on me.

My dad's condo was on the 55th floor of this building. There was no way I could make it down another fifty floors without him catching me.

But every floor had its own emergency escape door leading to the other condominiums. With people. Witnesses. People who could hear my cries.

When I landed on the next platform, I threw open the door and launched myself into the hallway.

I screamed for help.

But I was too late.

My neck snapped back as he yanked a fistful of my hair and then kicked me to the ground. I rolled onto my back and tried to get up, but he jumped on top of me and pinned me down, straddling me with knees on each side of my hips. He pulled a knife from its holster and raised it above his head.

His eyes were dark, soulless, as he thrust the blade toward my body to stop my beating heart.

I threw my hands up and held his wrists, slowing the knife's descent.

The hair on his arms twisted beneath my fingers. His nostrils flared, and a drop of sweat pooled around his titanium nose ring as his tattooed muscles swelled with strain.

He growled. He wanted me dead, but I wanted to live more.

With the knife heading right for my throat, I bucked with all my might and managed to throw Brown off-balance.

It was enough to roll out from underneath him.

I kicked him right in his nose ring and then took off running.

Screaming.

"Help me! Help!"

Fifteen feet ahead, a door opened, and a middle-aged man emerged, his face contorted in confusion as he saw me running toward him.

I charged past him, and as I entered the guy's open apartment, I turned around and spotted my attacker's figure running in the opposite direction.

13

Sitting in the back of the open ambulance, I second-guessed my refusal to go to the hospital because dozens of pedestrians stood outside, staring at me. Or maybe it wasn't so much at me as it was the chaotic scene.

Six police cars hugged the curb. Uniformed officers came and went from the building's front entrance while an EMT treated a cut on the back of my head. He wore purple latex gloves that looked so tight around his knuckles, I wondered if they would tear.

The smell of disinfectant and the lingering taste of blood in my throat angered my already-unstable stomach, no matter how many deep breaths of fresh air I took. Earlier, it had been muggy out, but now, a chill draped around my shoulders, as if the nightmare refused to release its grip on my goose bump–lined skin while Dad's sixty-story building towered over me, looking down on me and my omissions.

All I wanted to do was get home, take a shower, and crawl under my covers.

But right now, a detective was interviewing me, taking notes in a royal-blue miniature notebook. He'd introduced himself as Detective Shane Hernandez of the Chicago Police Department and looked to be in his late twenties with black hair and thick eyebrows.

"I'm going to see if we can get you in with a sketch artist tomorrow." He scratched the side of his face while he looked at his notes. "In the meantime, can you think of any other details?" His eyes implored me to come up with something. "Anything at all that might help us identify these guys?"

His stare penetrated my body like he could see through my lies, uncovering my hidden deceits.

I twisted my hands together.

Why did this feel so confusing? It shouldn't be confusing. I was furious at myself for allowing apprehension to choke my words. I had told him every single detail that I could think of. How one of the burglars wasn't as aggressive as the others, the description of the man who had attacked me as I ran away. The timing, the weapons I had witnessed, the number of men, how they seemed to know that the place was going to be empty and seemed to be aware of what was inside.

I even told him how I'd heard one of them say they'd been tipped off to the heist.

I told him everything, except for a couple critical details—Easton's name and description, claiming I'd only gotten a good look at Brown. I also left out that Easton had kissed me—*because how the hell do you explain something like that to a trained interrogator when you don't even understand it yourself?*—and that Easton helped me escape. Worried it would make the detective suspicious that I was holding back.

Which, of course, I was.

What was wrong with me?

Yes, Easton had saved my life. Yes, he seemed different than the other ones, and something told me deep down that he was never going to participate or allow my death. But I couldn't be sure of that. My adrenaline was high, my thoughts incapable of being trusted.

I was being interviewed by an official law enforcement officer, who was here to help me and my dad. I needed to give them everything I could, so they could track down these sons of bitches and put them behind bars before they could hurt anybody else. That was what a good, moral person would do. And I, of all people, was on the extreme end of that moral scale of holding people accountable.

Tell him Easton's name. It was an unusual name—surely not a lot of Eastons in the city. Maybe he'd been arrested in the past, and they'd pick him up within the hour. And he'd spend the rest of his life behind bars. No matter what his circumstances were in the past, that was where he belonged, I reminded myself.

Why was I having to remind myself? Was this some sort of shock? Because I definitely felt like I was in shock. Traumatized, relieved to be alive. All of those things. But also uncertain what to do. Once I gave him Easton's name, I could never undo it.

"I think it might be the same group on the news." I watched his expression for any kind of reaction. "The one that's been robbing houses."

Hernandez kept his face neutral, but I swore a flare of newfound interest flickered in his eyes. "What makes you say that?"

"The guy that had to babysit me. I asked him, and he didn't deny it."

"Did he confirm it?" The detective licked his bottom lip.

"No. But he'd mentioned being homeless at one point in his life, and the news said homeless shelters get donations after the robberies, so I figured..." I shrugged.

The detective held his unblinking eyes on me. "He told you he'd been homeless." His tone contained undercurrents of...skepticism? "He tell you any other personal information?"

I bit my lip, trying to remember. Because honestly, with my head spinning, I couldn't think of anything. Except his name. Which just kept echoing in my mind like it was trying to break free.

"It's okay," Detective Hernandez assured. "You did good."

No, you didn't. Tell him, Zoey. Tell him now before it's too late. Before he walks away and you've left your interview, having withheld information from a police officer.

"If you think of anything else." The detective handed me a business card.

It was blue with a raised Chicago Police logo on the right side, Detective Hernandez's name on the left, embossed in white letters.

"I'm glad you're okay, Zoey." Detective Hernandez offered a sad smile.

"Detective," a cop with a stocky torso called out. "Condo's empty."

I tried not to flinch; I could feel the detective's eyes on me, gauging my reaction to this news. Cops were trained to detect liars, and I wasn't very practiced in the art of deceit.

But this meant Easton had survived the scuffle with his colleague, and somehow, they'd all made it out.

But is Easton hurt? Could they have killed him in the getaway car?

Worry pitted in my stomach, recalling the thump I'd heard when I ran. Easton had committed a cardinal sin; he'd sided with a hostage, and I could only assume that warranted a harsh punishment. A punishment that might have gotten interrupted in order to escape. But certainly, they'd resume carrying it out, right? Easton had to be in danger.

"It *was* the Robin Hood Thieves, wasn't it?"

Hernandez said nothing.

"The MO fits what I've seen on the news," I pressed. No denial. "Have you worked other burglaries by them?"

"More than I'd like to count," Hernandez said with an edge. "Nothing would give me greater satisfaction than taking them down."

"So, you *do* think it's them." I bent my head toward his.

"Too early to say." Hernandez rubbed his jaw. "But if they are? You're the first person who's seen their faces."

My mouth ran dry. "That a good thing or a bad thing?"

Hernandez tightened his lips. “I’d keep your doors locked if I were you. Just to be safe.”

14

The EMT finished cleaning me up, and then one of the uniformed officers drove me home. Walked me to the front door to make sure I got in safely and locked it.

Sitting in the living room in his wheelchair was Dad. Watching TV.

If I hadn't made it out, how long would he have sat here, waiting, before he realized I was never coming back?

"Dad."

I rushed to him, knelt, and wrapped my arms around his fragile shoulders, relishing the warmth of his hand on my back. He smelled like his spicy aftershave and like home.

I'd prayed for just five more minutes with him, and now, I'm holding him.

We hadn't held each other since before he'd left Mom. His accident had warned me not to take this for granted, and yet I had. I'd been selfish. At the time, I told myself it was only human to rebuild our fractured relationship slowly. But tonight? When I thought I was going to die? I realized that the larger truth was that I was afraid; letting myself feel his love for me this way made me vulnerable.

"What's going on?" he asked.

But the words failed to come. If I started talking about it, I might start sobbing, and then I wouldn't be able to stop. What I needed was a hug, a shower, and a good night's sleep because I was exhausted.

"Zoey?"

"I'm fine," I assured. Even though I felt anything but fine. It felt like my world had opened some sort of portal to another universe, one where you can walk through a wrong door and have your life taken. One where you can be robbed of the chance to apologize to your father for the terrible things you'd said to him.

If I had an ounce of energy left, I'd start having that long-overdue conversation now. But Dad deserved a thoughtful, deep apology from me. Not the ten percent version when he'd only be half-listening, trying to figure out what in the world happened tonight.

Dad pushed my shoulders back and scanned my bruised face with wide eyes. "What the hell happened to you?"

"I'm fine," I repeated.

"The hell you are."

I tried to pull away, but Dad held on to my arms. Firmly. "Tell me what the hell is going on."

I was so exhausted, I felt like I was about to fall over. The physical aspect of my ordeal was only part of it; the emotional toll it took was like swallowing an entire bottle of sleeping pills. The only thing prying my eyes open had been the last micro surge of adrenaline from seeing my father, but now, it was waning.

He wouldn't let me go to bed without at least a partial explanation, though.

"Why did a police officer walk you to the door?"

When he let me stand up, I looked down at him, wishing I didn't have to tell him something so upsetting. "Tonight, I went to your condo, and it got robbed."

"What?"

"Some guys held me hostage, but I escaped."

Dad's eyes were so wide, I could see the whites above his irises, and he gripped the wheels of his wheelchair so tightly, his knuckles turned white.

"What did they do to you?" Dad scanned my face.

"Turns out, burglars don't like to be interrupted. They prefer to have the place to themselves."

Dad licked his teeth, his voice seething. "Did they...Zoey, were you—"

"No."

A momentary relief relaxed his shoulders. But he kept his eyes on me, rage funneling through his thin body. Somewhere in the back of my mind, behind my exhaustion and shock, there was a piece of my heart that appreciated his protective edge. Because it reminded me of my dad before he had broken my heart.

"Who are they?" Dad demanded.

"Police are trying to figure it out."

"Why did you go to the condo?"

"To get my ring," I said, walking into the bathroom.

"Your ring? Why the hell..."

"Dad, I love you. I do. But please, I can't even keep my eyes open."

He looked like he was about to let it go for now and let me get some rest, but instead, he said, "Tell me everything that happened."

I pinched the bridge of my nose, blinking back exhausted tears. "Please, Dad?"

Dad pursed his lips and studied the bags under my eyes. And evidently decided my physical needs outweighed his emotional ones in this moment. Because rather than fire off his million questions, he sighed and thankfully allowed me to shower and climb into my bed without further interrogation.

I couldn't sleep, though. My mind flashing through memories of the night, no matter how hard I tried to stop it.

Not to mention, the weight of what almost happened invading every cell of my body.

I almost died before I'd resolved things with Dad.

After his accident, all our unresolved feelings had been swept under the carpet, daily survival taking center stage. Getting Dad well enough to get out of the ICU, then a normal hospital room, then home with me. Juggling the medical appointments, bills, and bankruptcy in addition to the paperwork for his divorce. All of it had taken priority, pushing our unspoken pain regarding our relationship deeper into the cracks of our foundation.

But now, I was again reminded we didn't have forever. Dad and I needed to have a conversation soon—to lift up the carpet and work through our pain. If we had any hope to reseal our bond, we needed to talk.

I pressed my fingers against my eyes. My head was spinning. I needed to stop my brain.

I couldn't though—until I took one of Dad's sleeping pills.

I closed my eyes and drifted to sleep like welcoming a current, floating through the silent waters of detachment, pulled deeper into the sea from the meds.

Suddenly, I sat up in my bed, acutely aware of footsteps headed toward my room, which was blanketed in candles, whose flames flickered against the shadows like they were dancing.

The footsteps grew louder, but I didn't tremble; I clenched the covers and leaned forward, watching the doorframe. Knowing who was coming for me.

Easton stalked into my bedroom like he owned it. Like he owned me.

He wore the same ivory shirt and pants from the robbery, only this time, they seemed to encase his body tighter, showcasing his rugged muscles.

"What are you doing here?" I whispered.

The soft glow of candlelight wrapped around him as he closed the distance between us and sat next to my hip, the bed shifting with his weight.

Easton's sapphire eyes stared into mine as he brought his hand up and cupped my chin.

I tilted my head, ready to surrender my lips to his, the heat of his breath rolling across my skin as he whispered, "Forgive me for stealing one more kiss."

My heart fluttered as he trailed his fingers down my neck, goose bumps erupting all over my body. He looked at my mouth and drew his body closer, inch by inch. I closed my eyes and felt his lips brush against mine so lightly, it tickled.

He didn't hold it there for long enough. He didn't deepen the kiss or let me taste his tongue, instead pulling away far too soon, leaving me silently begging for more.

When I opened my eyes, he was gone. The candles were gone. My phone's alarm singing a lovely melody.

I sat up in my bed and touched my fingers to my lips.

It was a dream.

Easton coming into my bedroom was a dream. But it had felt so real.

His touch, his fingertips, his lips. And most of all, how badly I'd craved him.

I shut off my alarm and sat there for a minute, stunned.

The dream meant nothing. It didn't mean I wanted Easton. It was probably nothing more than my brain's warped way of processing this entire situation. I mean, seriously, how many people were held hostage and kissed by their captor? It was only human for that to plant a seed deep in your psyche and mind-F you.

Not to mention, I'd taken sleeping pills, which could probably give you seriously weird dreams.

I probably dreamed about him because I was hella worried about what might have happened to him after he'd betrayed his colleagues.

Is he okay?

Sweat broke across my palms at the memory of him fighting Orange, wondering what happened after they'd left. I would never find out, would I? Unless Easton was arrested and his name made it into the news, I'd never know if he was alive. I swallowed over the lump in my throat, unsure how I'd endure the day, let alone the rest of my life, without knowing.

I forced myself to stand up, hissing when I stretched my body. The aftermath of being kicked and hit last night was no longer dulled by adrenaline, so my ribs, my back, even my neck ached. The paramedic didn't "think" my rib was broken, but all my bruises still hurt, so I'd need some Advil to get through the day.

I shuffled over to the window and opened the blinds. Light assaulted my eyes so severely, I had to turn away from it, and when I did, I noticed the sunlight reflecting off something shiny on my nightstand.

Something that hadn't been there yesterday.

I stepped closer to get a better look, and what I saw made me grin with my hand over my mouth.

My ring. The very ring I'd been hell-bent on getting last night.

There was only one person who had access to that ring, knew how much it meant to me, and had the skills to quietly sneak into my house and leave it here—Easton.

Easton was *in my room last night.* And while I knew the rest of it was just a dream—candles don't magically appear and disappear on romantic command—I wondered if any part of it had been real.

Had his fingertips touched me? Had he whispered in my ear? Had he grazed my lips with his? I wasn't sure, but one thing was certain—the ring meant he'd gotten away last night.

My smile widened.

He must have followed me home or something.

Where was he right now? I looked out the window, up and down the block, but saw nothing. I wondered how long he'd been here last night and if I would have heard him had I not taken sleeping pills.

Placing the ring on my nightstand meant he'd been only two feet from me.

A warmth rushed through my veins.

Followed by ice.

Because someone had gotten into my place and I didn't even

wake up. If Easton managed to get inside, did Brown and Orange know where I lived, too?

No. Orange and Brown were on the other end of the condo—too far to hear—when I'd given information to Easton, and Easton had protected me. Saved me, so he wouldn't be reckless enough to lead those men to my front door. They probably scattered from that building like the roaches they were.

I'd take precautions just in case—locking all the doors and windows, turning on the air conditioner against the oppressive heat, costs be damned. But deep in my soul, I trusted Easton to keep me safe.

No matter how irrational it sounded.

I hid the ring in my underwear drawer and emerged from my bedroom to get caffeine.

"Morning," Dad said. He rolled his wheelchair from the living room to the kitchen, where I began making coffee. "How'd you sleep?"

I hated the worried look on his face. Was that the way I'd looked at him when he'd first come home from the hospital?

"Fine," I lied.

Exhaustion weighed my body down like lead, and I had to keep snapping my eyes open. Ironic that when you want to sleep, you can't, and when you want to stay awake, your body wants to sleep.

It was going to take a seriously strong cup of coffee to get me through this day. Maybe a hundred.

I avoided his incredulous stare by starting the coffeepot and rooting around the cabinets, looking for anti-inflammatories, but as luck would have it, no Advil to be found.

Great.

I watched the machine start to spit its brew. It gurgled out dark liquid into an amber-stained pot, puddling the way my blood had last night on the hardwood.

"I think we should go down to the police station today," Dad announced.

"Why?"

"I want to find out if they've arrested the guys."

"I'm sure the police will keep us informed." And call me in when that sketch artist was ready.

"Zoey..."

I pressed my finger above my eyebrow, pinching off a growing migraine. "Dad, I spent forever talking to that detective last night. I'm sure they're doing everything in their power to find the guys, and by us monopolizing their time, we're taking them away from the investigation."

"Nonetheless, I want to know where they're at with it and, if they haven't arrested the guys, what they're doing to catch them."

My eyes stung.

Dad hadn't acted like my protective father in a long time. I'd almost forgotten what it felt like—to feel him fight for me like this. Demanding justice for me. That he wanted to ensure whoever had laid a finger on me would be put in prison.

Tragedy had a way of flipping things around sometimes.

"Maybe after work," I said.

"Work?" Dad choked. "You're thinking of going to work?"

"What I need and want more than anything is to have a normal day. To work and do my best to completely forget about last night by staying busy."

I yanked the coffeepot out long enough to pour myself a cup.

"Your face is bruised."

So was my body. My body, I could hide with clothes. My face...

"I have concealer." If I couldn't conceal my bruises well enough, I'd consider staying home, if only to avoid questions. But I hoped I could go. I needed last night to stop playing on repeat in my head.

I took a sip of bitter caffeine.

My dad's chest inflated slowly and then collapsed. I felt bad for him. I was sure it was gut-wrenching for a parent to sit back and not be able to actively fix what happened to your kid. And I was again warmed by his desire to help me, just like he would've done before he left our family.

"Why did you go there in the first place?" Dad rolled his wheelchair closer to me. "Why did you want your ring all of a sudden?"

A knock at the door thwarted my ability to answer. Thank God. I didn't want to get into our dire financial situation right now.

I looked through the peephole and opened the door, surprised to find him here.

"Alex?"

He wore his usual physical therapy polo and khaki pants, his trimmed blond hair polished with hair product that smelled like the ocean.

His grin quickly vanished. "What the hell happened to you?"

His eyes widened as he scanned my face, then my wrists.

"Are you okay?" he demanded.

"Yeah."

"What happened?"

"Long story." I motioned for him to come inside. "What are you doing here so early?"

Alex stepped into the living room and crossed his lean arms over his chest. I could tell he wasn't going to let the bruises go—he couldn't take his eyes off of them.

But he begrudgingly answered, "I had a client that requested the night spot, so I figured I'd come before my workday started."

This was the first time he'd ever come before work. Was it really because of a client's schedule? Or did he know that the robbery took place last night and wanted to check in?

I mentally chided myself. Alex had done nothing but help us in our time of need. What I'd just experienced was making me look at people and suspect the worst, and it wasn't fair to look at him with even an ounce of suspicion.

Was this what it was going to feel like from now on? Looking at everyone in my life with a skeptical eye, paranoia infecting my relationships?

No. I was just exhausted and overwhelmed. This would all go away.

It had to.

And in the meantime, I didn't have the energy to recount it again.

"My dad can fill you in." I slammed a giant chug of coffee and headed for my bedroom. "I have to get ready for work."

I escaped more questions, took a shower, and managed to cover up my bruised face fairly well. I changed into my favorite outfit—hoping it would incite confidence in addition to covering up my other injuries—and came back into the living room.

"You sure I can't talk you into staying home?" Worry etched into the crease between Dad's brows.

"Positive. Have a good day, boys." I made my way to the door.

"Zoey?" Dad called after me.

I turned around.

"I know you don't want to talk about this, but when your mom calls, I'd answer."

I pursed my lips. "You told her?"

He offered me a silent apology. Dad and Mom didn't talk to each other often. For him to make the effort to fill her in meant he was even more worried about me than he was letting on. Plus, it meant another person wanting to talk about the one subject I wanted to avoid.

"And Anthony?" I tensed.

"They're worried about you." Dad tugged his ear.

Ugh.

At the "L" platform by my house, I passed the usual group of guys who harassed women, but today, I looked at them and wondered, *Who do they work for?*

If people on the street knew how to hire Easton's crew, could these guys be associated with Easton? Oh God...what if they knew Brown? What if they were like his eyes and ears on the streets or something?

My heartbeat turned into a racehorse. I took a seat on the "L" and stared at them out the window. Surely, if they were part of Brown's crew, they'd follow me, right?

As I sat on the "L," I answered Mom's call. Her voice was high-pitched, and I could hear her pacing in her kitchen.

"This is all too much stress for you, honey. Let me make some calls. The last thing you need is to take care of Dad right now."

"I like him being here." I was surprised that I said it and even more surprised that I meant it. Because it meant I wouldn't be alone each night.

"I'm fine," I assured. "But I'm on my way to work right now. Maybe we can talk tomorrow?"

She sighed. "You're really okay?"

Mom wouldn't have anything to do with the burglary.

I know I'm going crazy when those ridiculous thoughts pop into my head.

"I'm okay, I promise."

I shut my eyes with relief when I hung up, but two seconds later, my phone rang again. This time from my brother.

"Anthony."

Now that he was married and had a baby, I barely saw him.

"You were held hostage?" His voice was as high-pitched as Mom's. It was only five thirty in the morning on the West Coast.

"How early did Dad call you?"

"I'm getting on the next flight."

"Don't."

"My little sister was robbed, and you think I'm not coming?"

"I appreciate it, but there's nothing left to do, except catch the guys. What I want right now more than anything is normalcy. My routine."

"Zoey..."

"Anthony, I swear I'm fine. You have a family you need to focus on. If you spend the money to fly all the way here, there's nothing you can do but stare at me. Let's save the trip for another time—when I'm up for a visit, okay?"

Anthony was silent for ten seconds. “When they catch those guys, I want five minutes alone in a room with them.”

Anthony had always been a good brother. Caring and protective. When someone stole my inline skates from our driveway when I was twelve, he scoured the neighborhood and found the girl who took them—a stranger two blocks over. Had it been a boy who’d stolen them, he’d have probably gotten a black eye out of it, too. When Dad left us, Anthony flew home and spent a few days with Mom and me. Truly, I was lucky to have him.

“Do they, uh,” he started, “have any suspects?”

I crinkled my forehead. “Suspects?”

“Dad said there weren’t any arrests last night.”

Oh. “Not that I know of,” I said.

“Did they know the place was empty or something?”

There was something in his question that made me pause.

Did he already know the answer to this?

Am I reading too much into his question?

“Yeah. They were definitely surprised to see me.”

In the background, a baby cried, and my heart ached, wishing I were there with my brother, doting on my new niece.

Among the many sacrifices we’d made financially, one of the hardest was that I hadn’t gotten to meet my brother’s baby yet. I always thought that when Anthony had children, I would be one of the first to the hospital. And while living on the other side of the country didn’t make getting there that fast realistic, I hadn’t expected this many weeks to pass without getting to meet his daughter. But leaving Dad wasn’t feasible, nor were airline fees. It was another joyful experience withheld because of all of this.

“How’s the baby?”

Anthony hesitated. I could picture him picking at his thumbnail, looking down at the floor. “She’s good. We’re good. I just...worry about you.”

“It’s over,” I assured.

“Not just about the robbery.” Anthony sighed. “I worry about everything you have on your shoulders with Dad. I wish I lived closer."

After the hit-and-run, Anthony kept asking if there was more he could do to help. But what could he do? He couldn't physically be here to help without quitting his job.

There were times I felt resentment toward him for being so far away, like, somehow, he left me holding the bag by taking care of Dad while he lived freely. Which wasn't fair. No one *expected* me to take care of Dad. Not even Dad himself.

"You're raising your family, Anthony, and no one ever makes decisions to move away, thinking their parent might get hit by a car."

"It's too much for you to handle alone. I wish I could do more."

"You send money every month. It helps more than you can imagine." Without it, we'd have probably been homeless already.

I didn't have the energy to get into all this again. When Anthony's guilt for living far away reared up, it normally took thirty minutes to talk him out of moving back. Moving back meant losing the job he loved, moving away from his wife's family, who provided free childcare. As much as I'd love to have him closer, Anthony deserved the little slice of heaven he'd carved out for himself.

Besides, like we'd talked about last time, by the time he sold his house, moved here, and found another job, Dad would be back on his feet. He'd have given up everything for nothing.

Was Dad's recovery going longer than originally planned? Yes. But he *was* recovering, and there was no point in allowing the damage from this whole situation to spread.

"I'll call you later, okay?" I smiled.

"Zoey?"

"Yeah?"

"I love you."

My throat swelled.

"I love you, too, Anthony."

As I walked the rest of the way to work, it surprised me how ordinary the city felt today. The steel buildings stretched so high, they cast me in their shadow, but even in the shade, the sweltering heat was as relentless as it had been the last few days. The businessman walking ahead of me already had a dark spot on the back of his blue shirt, and his iced coffee was sweating, a single drop splatting onto the sidewalk. The morning traffic jam on Wacker Drive was in full swing with bumper-to-bumper vehicles casting a symphony of impatient horns, infecting the space with the smell of car fumes. The routine of it all was almost eerie. How mundane any day can seem until it takes a tragic turn.

I kept walking and was suddenly overwhelmed by an ominous feeling of being watched. I looked around at the pedestrians, at the cars. The doors of the buildings opening and closing as people entered and exited, but nothing explained the chill skating across my skin.

I hustled quicker, and once I was safely inside my office building, I'd hoped I could put it all out of my mind and have a normal day. But as soon as I walked to my desk, my friend Emily—a gorgeous redhead with a curvy figure—saw me, and her eyes grew wide.

"Holy crap! What happened?" She grabbed my arms and scanned me head to toe.

Clearly, I hadn't covered up the bruises well enough, and I couldn't escape yet another interrogation.

As I sidestepped her questions, only revealing the bare minimum, I twisted my hands together so forcefully that it became painful. The only way I could get her to stand down was to promise to do drinks "soon" and tell her everything then.

"Did you call Jenna?"

I shook my head. "I'm not going to call her when she's home with a newborn."

My best friend had been through a lot, and the last thing I was going to do was steal her joy during her maternity leave with her second baby.

"If you need anything..." Emily's voice trailed off.

And then, thankfully, she walked away from my desk and let me work.

By the end of the day, she returned. "Do you want me to walk you home?"

"No." She'd ask me a thousand questions, and the "L" was safely public. "I'm fine. I promise."

And I *was* feeling better. It helped, getting lost in work. Taking phone calls, building spreadsheets, presentations. It was good for me to focus on anything other than the memories that kept flashing through my mind.

Some of them were disturbing. The violence. The promise of death.

Some of them were of Easton. The touch of his finger in the corner of my lip as he washed the blood away. The sound of his voice, rough, like life's hardships had manifested into sandpaper in his throat. And the look in his sapphire eyes after he'd gently removed my blindfold.

I felt like I was a prisoner trapped in my own thoughts, incapable of controlling them.

As I left work and walked toward the "L" station, I rounded the building's corner, and something prickled my spine.

I'm being watched.

I looked around at the city, crowded with bodies, trying to place where this sensation was coming from. Until my eyes landed on the source.

Standing on the other side of the road, staring directly at me, was Easton.

15

Easton stood with his hands in his jean pockets, a gray T-shirt strangling his lean muscles and flat stomach, his gaze firmly locked on me. His stillness—a statue among a stream of pedestrians—stood out like a rainbow in a black-and-white photo.

The gentle breeze blowing in this sticky weather seemed to penetrate my stomach's walls and swirled around inside. Jazz music from a nearby saxophone blended with the groans of vehicles crawling along Wacker Drive, flanked by seventy-story buildings, and the overheated asphalt smelled like fresh tar.

A smarter person would take off running in the opposite direction or call the police. But evidently, I wasn't very intelligent because after a few seconds of staring at him, I ambled through the crosswalk and closed the distance between us.

Based on the stern look on his face, I couldn't tell if the Easton standing before me was the captor who had held me hostage or the savior who had helped me get away.

He looked down at me with those ocean-colored gems, darkness locking his jaw and tightening his lips—a lip which was split, the only indication of his scuffle from last night. The peppering of caramel highlights in his hair looked brighter in the sun than they had in the condo, the texture richer with the deeper tones underneath.

It was impossible not to notice how incredibly sexy he was, his olive skin glistening with sweat beneath the base of his throat, his athletic frame standing nearly a foot above mine so he had to tilt his chin down to look at me. Even with a drop of sweat journeying down his temple and the ends of his hair damp against his forehead, Easton looked unfairly gorgeous. Like sweat was an accessory.

Easton tightened his lips when his eyes landed on my bruised cheek. It had been dark in my bedroom last night, so clearly, he hadn't seen it until now. And in the sun, the concealer didn't block it fully. He raised his hand and touched the skin just beneath the mark, tilting his head to get a better look.

"What did he do to you?" he growled.

I swallowed. "He caught up to me in the hallway and took me down. I got away, though." Obviously. What a stupid fact to clarify.

"Is it your ribs or your back?" His eyes snapped to my waist, then my shoulders.

"Is what my ribs or my back?"

"You were wincing in pain when you walked over."

He misses nothing.

"I'm fine. I just ran out of Advil," I hedged. There were more pressing issues than listing my injuries. Most notably, "Why are you here?"

And why did he feel so distant, compared to last night? Why did hostility seem to pulse outward from his body?

Easton ran a hand through his thick locks. Looked off to the sidewalk and furrowed his brows, then returned his attention to me.

He motioned with his chin to follow him into an alley, presumably where we could talk in private.

I froze. Yes, Easton had saved me, but he'd also held me hostage, broken into my house last night, and had clearly been following me.

Isolating myself with him wasn't wise, no matter how much my heart claimed he'd never hurt me.

I glanced around at the pedestrians, at the busy traffic.

It didn't feel safe to talk out here, where police or Brown's crew might spot us. But I wouldn't go too deep into the alley with him; I'd stay close enough, where people could see what was happening.

Just in case.

The narrow passage—which felt like a tunnel burrowing through steel skyscrapers—was a welcome ten degrees cooler than the sidewalk, thanks to the buildings blocking the sun, but I had to watch where I stepped. The asphalt ground was a spiderweb of cracks, so deep that they threatened to twist my ankle with one wrong move. As we stopped walking, I noticed an army of ants carrying off what appeared to be crumbs of food, marching in organized lines with their loot.

"Why didn't you give the police my name?" He tilted his head to the side.

"How do you know I didn't give them your name?"

"If you had, I'd be in jail by now."

"So, they know you, then."

"Petty theft. And Easton's not a common name."

When his gaze tightened and a crease cemented between his brows, I wondered, *Has anyone ever shown kindness to him before?*

"You saved me," I answered. "Didn't feel right to sic the cops on you for that."

He said nothing, as if still struggling to understand why I'd protect him.

"Is that why you're here?" I grabbed my elbow, holding my arms over my body. "To find out why I didn't turn you in?"

To this, Easton finally broke eye contact. Widened his stance as he looked down.

"My colleagues are furious I let you get away. In their eyes, you're a liability. A big one."

I gulped. That term, *liability*, was a thinly veiled threat. One that I couldn't tell if Easton was on board with. Was his rigid posture from being upset about what his colleagues had said? Or because they'd changed his mind and he now agreed with them?

"Do you see me as a liability?"

Easton's eyes cast over my face, and he took a deep breath.

"Brown's crew runs different than mine," he hedged. "You're an innocent. But to him, you're nothing more than a risk."

Brown had people on the street, too, didn't he? People that worked for him?

"Do you think Brown might've sent someone to find me?" I held my breath, waiting for his verdict.

Easton furrowed his brows. "What makes you ask that?"

"There were these guys hanging at the "L" stop by my house."

"What guys?"

"They're there every day, and they always give me a hard time, but, today, I wondered if maybe—"

"Give you a hard time how?"

"Like, what if they're part of his crew or something?"

"What do they look like?"

I shrugged. "Tattoos covering their arms, with, like, lightning or something extending down their hands? One of them wears a cross earring, and another has a missing lower tooth, like he's been in a fight or something."

"No," Easton said. "They're not Brown's crew."

"How can you be sure?"

"No one in his crew has tattoos like that. Or looks like that."

"And they aren't on your crew? The...middleman who someone contacted to arrange the heist?"

Easton's shoulders relaxed two inches. "No, not part of mine."

I let out a relieved breath.

Easton licked his teeth. "They give you a hard time?"

I shrugged. "They do it to every girl that walks past them."

"Do what?"

"Wolf whistle. Say crude things. Grab their crotch while they follow me for a few steps. The first few weeks it happened, I was terrified they were rapists. Started getting off at a different stop and taking a taxi the rest of the way, but I couldn't afford it, so I had to go back to walking past them."

Easton's glare became so intense, it could crack me open.

"They've never attacked, though," I assured.

But his expression didn't soften; the way he scrubbed his temple with an unfocused gaze looked like he was mentally trying to identify who they were.

"You're sure they're not part of Brown's crew?"

His jaw ticced. "No. But he's got a lot of dangerous minions at his disposal, ready to kill on command."

Well, that's comforting.

"So what, you're here to...convince me to retract my statement? So he never gets caught? Because he deserves to be in a prison cell for the rest of his life."

"But I don't?" Easton towered over me, his frame screaming power.

I looked down at my hands. "I owe you my life, Easton. If you hadn't helped me escape, I'd be dead right now. And I can't even think about what that would mean for my dad. Plus, I promised that if you let me go, I wouldn't turn you in."

If I were being honest, some other part of ratting him out felt wrong, too. Maybe it was some sort of chemical reaction. With the threat of death hanging over my head, he had been the warm comfort in the midst of it, the man who'd saved my life. That was what I tried to tell myself last night. But seeing him now, I knew that was a lie. It was something deeper. It wasn't rational, but something lured me into his intoxicating presence, and now, I wanted more. I wanted to know everything about him.

It felt like the second he walked out of this alley, he'd vanish forever.

"I was worried something happened to you last night," I admitted. "I couldn't fall asleep."

"You looked to be sleeping soundly when I saw you."

I snapped my eyes to his. I couldn't believe he'd just admitted to being in my room, but he couldn't deny it, could he? "How do you know where I live?"

"I followed you."

"Did you see me sitting in the ambulance?"

He nodded.

He was good; neither I nor the cop noticed him.

"How did you get in?"

To this, the corner of his mouth curled up slightly, like he found my innocence amusing. "You do know what I do for a living?"

Right.

I was consumed with disappointment because if I'd known he was there, I could have talked to him. Spent time with him without fear of Orange or Brown interrupting. And it stung that I'd been robbed of that opportunity.

"Why didn't you wake me?"

Easton moved a stray piece of hair away from my cheek, his fingertip leaving a blazing fire in its path. "You looked peaceful."

But I would have stayed up all night if I'd known he was there.

"I wish you had woken me," I managed.

Easton sucked me into his gaze, the city around us vanishing until nothing else existed, except me and him.

"You should stay as far away from me as you can, Zoey."

"Why?" I'd already lied to the police. What harm could it do if we spent time together and got to know each other?

Silence.

"I know you're a burglar, but..."

He pursed his lips, a profound depression casting his features in disdain. "If only that's all it was."

A panic settled into my bones, manifesting in anger. "If this is the last time we can ever talk to each other, at least tell me why."

More infuriating silence.

I lifted my chin. "I deserve to know what's going on."

To this, he looked down as he nodded and rubbed his cheek, some sort of internal debate waging in his head. It felt like an eternity before he finally looked back up at me, tucked his hands into his pockets, and cleared his throat.

"No good way to say this."

"So, just tell me."

His chest inflated. "I've been sent to kill you, Zoey."

His hardened voice grated across my skin and squeezed air out of my lungs.

Easton ran a thumb along his jawline. "They've given me one chance to make this right. Eliminate the witness that got away. Or I'll pay the price."

Instantly, I felt sick.

"If I don't do it soon, they'll send someone else for you."

Easton kept his eyes locked on me, like he was worried I'd faint.

Maybe I'd been wrong about him. Maybe when he was backed into a corner, he'd make a very different choice than the one he'd made last night.

After all, keeping a girl from being killed was one thing. But giving up your life to protect her was another.

Maybe he'd even think he was doing me a favor, being the one to end me so it would be as painless as possible.

His eyes stretched past me to the nearby pedestrians. Was he searching for a member of Brown's crew? Or possible witnesses to whatever he was about to do?

Instinctively, I took a couple steps back until my back hit the alley's wall, suppressing the hiss from bumping my bruise in the process.

Easton furrowed his brows and stalked closer until he was only a few inches away. "I'm not going to kill you, Zoey."

But he could. He very much could. He was a body carved of chiseled stone, and I had no doubt his fighting skills were crazy high for him to have survived on the streets as long as he had.

The hint of danger wrapped around me like a dark embrace.

"Why?" My words tripped over my dry throat. "Why would you risk your life for some girl you barely know?"

His spellbinding eyes warmed. "You saved my life"—his voice rumbled over my skin—"when you returned that wallet."

I blinked. "What are you talking about?"

Easton swiped his nose with this thumb. "My brother and I approach this lifestyle differently. I'm more, I guess you could say, methodical. Planning. Careful. He's more a wild card—after the easy cash, spending it faster than he can earn it. Whenever he gets money from a heist, he blows through it like water, which is not only risky—that kind of shit'll get you busted by the cops. It's also unsustainable. You still have to pay your rent and bills, but when you save nothing for that?"

Easton licked his lips. "Kept bailing his ass out of financial holes until I had nothing left in my own reserve. Once that happened, my brother went to a loan shark. The kind that collects in blood if you don't pay it back. He was going to get killed because he didn't have their money. So, I talked the guy into giving me one more week to come up with it, but to do it, I had to vouch for the debt. Which meant, if I didn't pay it, they'd kill my brother. *And* me."

My jaw fell open slightly.

"I barely scraped it together in time. I was on my way to pay it off when you found my wallet. And returned every dollar to me. If you hadn't..."

He didn't finish the sentence.

He didn't have to.

"That's why you protected me last night? Why you saved me?"

He placed his palms on the wall next to my head, tight lines of muscles twisting around his forearms, as if blocking himself from coming any closer.

"Even if you hadn't returned my wallet, I was never going to hurt you, Zoey. I was standing watch to figure out how to get you out of there."

Which had to feel impossible with how adamant Brown had been about killing me and his failed plea to Orange to let me go.

Orange. Easton had spoken to him in a familiar tone and had said he'd spent a decade protecting him.

"The other man, Orange, he's your brother, isn't he?"

Easton's lips pursed, but eventually, he gave a soft nod.

Why did I feel so safe around a man confessing he'd been ordered to kill me? Denial? Temporary insanity? Or a sixth sense that told me he would never harm a hair on my head?

That he was telling me the truth?

"Thank you"—I placed my palms on his chest—"for protecting me."

The muscles blanketing his torso rose and fell while his Caribbean eyes looked from my left eye to my right. Easton's Adam's apple bobbed, and his breaths grew quicker as he shifted his gaze to my mouth, studying it, as if fighting against urges that wouldn't lead to anything good. Kissing me would make this even more complicated and painful than it already was.

This crazy pull we had toward each other might be wrong, yet nothing ever felt so right.

I studied his mouth, remembering how it had felt on mine last night, but it had been so unexpected when it happened that I hadn't been able to savor it. His full lips taking mine between them.

I wanted to feel his warmth against me now, his hands in my hair. I wanted to taste his tongue, and I could tell he wanted it, too. Even if he was fighting the urge not to.

Unable to take it anymore, I reached up on tiptoe and gently brushed my lips against his.

That was all it took.

Easton groaned and crashed his mouth against mine. His tongue pressed through my lips, and I welcomed it, licking it, weaving my hands around his neck. Feeling it tighten as he pressed his body up against me.

Our kiss deepened, and I ran my hands down his shoulders,

down his tight bicep muscles, and back up again. His body was smooth and rock hard, ridges upon ridges of lean muscles bulging beneath his shirt. I traced my fingertips down his back, and my every touch incited a growl from him.

I wanted him. I wanted to feel his hands all over my body.

"Zoey," Easton managed.

He pressed his forehead against mine and panted, his hot breath bouncing off my lips. I tried to reach up, to feel our lips unite again, but he stepped back.

Balling both hands into fists as he stared at the ground.

"We can't be seen together." Despair washed through his tone. "It's not safe."

How could it hurt this much, him stopping anything before it even started? Him making it clear that he'd come here to tell me good-bye?

I shouldn't care.

At all.

And yet...my heart burned. Why?

Whatever the reason, I wanted to lose myself in the feeling even if only for a little while.

My cell phone interrupted my thoughts, though, ringing with a number I'd pre-saved into my Contacts.

It took me a second to digest what I was looking at, to break from the sensual fog and back into the crisp reality.

"It's the detective." I held the phone toward him. "He must want to ask me more questions." Maybe put me with that sketch artist. But what if I could give him something better than a description? "Do you know Brown's real name?"

He scratched his temple. "Yes."

"Let me give it to the police."

"You ratting him out will only put you in more danger."

"He already has a hit out on me. What more danger could there be?"

"You don't want to know."

I shivered.

"I'm going to give Brown a day or two to cool off." Easton stretched his fingers straight, then balled them into a fist again. "And then I'm going to talk to him. Try to convince him that hurting you will just bring more heat on him. Heat he doesn't need right now."

"But if you show up to that meeting without having"—killed me —"taken care of me already," I said, "will you walk out of that meeting alive?"

16

I stepped onto my front porch to catch the Lyft to the police station for my scheduled meeting with Detective Hernandez and almost tripped over a blue bag.

I froze in my tracks.

The mysterious plastic gift bag was the size of an index card.

What if it's a bomb?

It had been a day since I found out there was a hit on my life. In that time, I went through life shell-shocked, processing it, trying to figure out what to do about it.

Today, I called in sick to work. Dad assumed it was because I was tired, but after hearing about the threat, I didn't want to risk leaving the house. I drew all the blinds closed. I checked the locks on the windows and doors no less than thirty times, and I wanted to stay inside forever.

But Hernandez insisted on meeting today. *Insisted.*

And if Brown didn't listen to Easton, the only other thing that would eliminate the threat to my life was if Hernandez locked up Brown. ASAP. So, here I was, rushing out my front door toward a waiting Lyft.

A ride I couldn't even afford, but I was too scared to venture farther outside to get to the "L" or walk. The car was parked ten feet away, just a few steps from this possibly deadly bag at my feet.

With my heart galloping, I pulled up Hernandez's number, but just before I clicked the Call button, something else caught my eye—the tag on the handle.

It had a handwritten note and, on the bottom, a signature.

E.

I inched closer until I could read the rest.

Take four with food. Then another two when that wears off.

I moved even closer and pressed the tip of my finger on the edge, opening it slightly.

Inside was a bottle of Advil.

I let out a huge breath of relief that the bag wasn't some ploy by Brown to hurt me and looked around. Was Easton out there somewhere? Watching me? When did he leave this here? Didn't he realize how dangerous this was? Dad could have seen him or found the bag, or a million other things could've happened.

I scrubbed a hand over my face, reminding myself I needed to hurry. I quickly ripped the note into a million pieces so Dad would never be able to read it, shoved the Advil into my pocket, and discarded the bag and note remnants in my neighbor's trash can before getting into the waiting ride.

Fifteen minutes later, I arrived at the police station, praying Hernandez might have some good news about the investigation. But equally worrying he might have information on the one person I didn't want locked up. Because if they locked Easton up, I had no doubt Brown would hire someone else to kill me—someone who would never hesitate.

It was wrong to withhold information from the cops. I knew that. And I hated that I was doing this—again—because it went against every moral fiber in my being. But my first priority right now was to do what I needed to do in order to stay alive. Because it wasn't just me who'd pay the price if I was executed; Dad would, too.

The lobby of the police station had become all too familiar to me, from the many times I'd come here to press the detective assigned to my dad's case to keep searching for the criminal who had run him down. I'd always tried to be strong, coming here during those times, pretending my heart wasn't a hot mess, shuffling through haunting images of my dad's mangled body after the accident. The way doctors gave us that look of uncertainty about his future.

I walked up to the mahogany desk and gave the gray-haired woman my name, and then I stood back and waited in the open area, where a handful of chairs—all occupied—hugged the exterior wall. Blue-and-tan tiled flooring stretched beneath my tapping foot with the Chicago Police logo at its center. To my right, a staircase wide enough to fit a compact car led up to a landing, where a bulletin board housed perfectly aligned papers, before the stairs twisted to the right and ascended to the second floor. Above my head, lights illuminated the space in a soft white glow, and the air conditioner hummed, blasting cool air throughout the space. It smelled like rubber in here. And crime. Crime and rubber.

"Zoey." Detective Hernandez came from the first-floor hallway and motioned for me to follow him. "I appreciate you coming in today."

He led me to a conference room that was so small that when I pulled the chair from the wooden table, it hit the wall. I had to slide into it like someone had parked their car too close to me.

"I'm going to grab a water. Would you like one?" he asked.

"Sure." I hoped it would help wash down all this trepidation of what he was going to tell me.

My cell phone buzzed in my pocket. Maybe Dad needed me to pick up something on the way home.

But it wasn't Dad texting me; it was from an unknown number.

Be careful what you say at the station.

Ice surged through my limbs.

Me: Who is this?

We talked in the alley.

Easton.

My muscles relaxed.

Me: How did you get my number?

Looked it up on your Settings when you were...subdued.

Me: Why?

Because I couldn't imagine never getting to talk to you again.

My heart pathetically melted into a puddle of goo, but my army of suspicion quickly slapped my heart, warning against possible manipulation. After all, how convenient to have the phone number of the only witness who could land you in prison.

Me: If the police search your phone, they'll think you're trying to intimidate a witness.

I'm not trying to intimidate you, Zoey. I'm trying to protect you. And this is a burner.

I bit my nail.

Don't give him anything that will put you in more danger. Not until I can make sure you're safe.

Me: If he shows me a photo lineup and I recognize HIM, I'm going to point him out.

Then again...if I did that, would he turn Easton and his brother in, too? Surely, Brown wouldn't take the fall by himself.

Even so, the only way to protect myself was if Brown was locked up, right?

"Sorry about that," Detective Hernandez said.

A badge hung from the belt of his black pants, a navy button-down clung to his shoulders, and his dark hair complemented his eyebrows. Which sat atop blue eyes that looked at me as if he could see right through me.

He set down two bottles of water on the table, shut the door, and then—much more gracefully than I'd managed—took a seat opposite of me. Pen and paper in front of him.

"How are you holding up?" He scratched his eyebrow.

I shrugged and started to pick at my nail, watching my phone.

The chess pieces on the table had moved while he was gone, and I was trying to decide where to position my pawn.

"Have you made any headway on the case?"

"Nothing I'm at liberty to talk about." He frowned. "I'd like you to work with a sketch artist. She'll be here in a minute."

I nodded, the disappointment of not hearing, *We got him, Zoey. You're safe*, making my posture slump.

"You okay?"

My stomach felt like an empty pit.

"I think my life is in danger."

Detective Hernandez kept a poker face. He folded his hands on his lap and leaned back in his chair, studying me. "Has someone threatened you?"

I clenched my toes.

"Zoey?" Detective Hernandez pressed.

I forced myself to clear my throat. "They threatened me that night," I reminded him. "I saw that one guy's face, so he wanted me dead. He chased me down and attacked me, and I know he's going to come after me again. And if he does, what if my dad is there? If he won't leave one witness alive, surely, he won't leave another, and my dad's in a wheelchair and can't even fight back."

Hernandez said nothing. He studied me with tight eyes, as if he was cataloging my every word, analyzing it even. Maybe he sensed something had changed.

"This group"—I clenched my eyes shut for a moment before opening them again—"have they killed people before?"

He regarded me. "We're still trying to identify who 'they' are."

"I saw the news about that gang robbing wealthy houses. If it's them, have they killed before?"

"A lot of wealthy residences are targets. Unfortunately, they're not the only crew out there, hitting them."

"You're not answering my question."

"You're scared."

Maybe I could get something useful out of this meeting. Something to keep us safe. "Can you put a protective detail on my house?"

He leaned forward, picked up the pen, and twisted it around. "I can send a car to drive past your house every so often, but we don't have the manpower to put protective details on people. You only see that kind of thing in the movies."

I frowned.

"I'd like to go over your statement again." Hernandez glanced down at the paper in front of him.

"Why?"

"Standard procedure. After a couple days, you might've remembered something that you didn't at first."

My neck broke out into an instant sweat. Was that true? Or did he sense I'd lied?

I shifted in my seat, wincing from the back pain, where Brown had kicked me.

"You mentioned three men. Is that correct?" he asked.

"Yes. One guy, Brown, seemed to be the mastermind."

Hernandez nodded.

"I described the tattoos." I motioned toward his paper. "Wouldn't those be on file if he'd ever been arrested?"

"We're still working on that," Hernandez said flatly. "But it's possible he hasn't been apprehended. Or the tattoos are new."

Translation: It hadn't led to Brown's identity. So, either the tattoos took place after his last police bust, or maybe he'd never been busted. Maybe he wasn't in the system. Maybe he was scary good at evading cops because he'd do anything to not get caught.

"And you believe someone tipped them off to the heist." Hernandez raised his brows.

I nodded. "Someone who knew the place."

Hernandez stared at me and narrowed his lips, as if...what? He thought I was the one who'd tipped them off?

A flicker of panic sparked in my bones.

"It wasn't me," I clarified. "If I knew the place was getting robbed, I never would've gone there that night."

Hernandez nodded, but I couldn't tell if it was because he believed me. He then went through his routine follow-up questions. I told him everything all over again with the exception of the things I'd omitted before—Easton's name, the kiss, him helping me escape.

He didn't ask me if my captor broke into my house to return my ring or if he'd kissed me after warning me I was in danger. So, at least that was one less outright lie.

Funny how thin a moral fiber I was clinging to these days.

Throughout it all, Hernandez prodded me along with more detailed questions and follow-ups. His attention to detail gave me renewed hope that maybe, just maybe, the detective would be able to solve this case quickly. Maybe Brown could be locked up without risking our lives.

A redhead with her hair slicked back into a bun walked in. She smiled at me. "Ready?"

"Think I got all I need for now," Hernandez said. "But if you think of anything else, anything at all that can help us identify these guys... nothing would make me happier than getting you justice."

Justice. Would I get justice? It felt much more possible than it ever had with Dad's hit-and-run case because Hernandez was good. Thorough. Nothing like the detective currently working Dad's case.

Which gave me an idea.

Even though I was obsessed right now about the robbery case, I had an opportunity here—an opportunity that might close as soon as I walked out that door. Who knew if I'd be back here, talking to Hernandez again?

I cleared my throat. "I was wondering if you would consider taking over the investigation of my dad's hit-and-run."

Detective Hernandez stared at me.

"Someone hit my dad and got away with it, and I'm sure the detective assigned to his case is doing the best he can, but I think it's time for a fresh set of eyes to look at it."

"That's not how things work around here," the detective said tightly.

"Could you at least make some calls? See if you think that they've done everything they possibly can?"

Detective Hernandez rubbed his chin. He was silent for what felt like an eternity before offering me an empathetic hint of a smile. "I'll see what I can do."

Sweet optimism etched its way into my soul.

He left me alone with the sketch artist, and when I finished, I walked outside the building, staring at the app that warned me the nearest ride was forty-three minutes away. That long of a wait didn't happen often, but sometimes, the city traffic became so jammed, cars were trapped on the roads.

I looked up and down the street for a taxi, disappointed that none were in sight. I rubbed my arms and looked up at the "L" train platform a half-block away. It didn't feel safe, taking it. But it felt less safe, walking home.

I debated going back inside the station. Waiting for the ride there. But the ride was going to be another fifteen dollars I shouldn't spend, and what was I going to do? Spend thirty dollars a day or more to get to work or anywhere else I needed to go? The "L" was public, always packed with witnesses.

And a train was approaching.

F it.

I ran like a girl being chased in a bad horror movie—more than a few eyebrows arched at me, I was sure—and hopped on the thankfully crowded train.

I felt like I was in a fog on the ride home. So much so that when I reached my stop, I almost didn't notice the punks that normally harassed me. But this time, they didn't wolf whistle. They didn't shout profanities or say obscene things.

Instead, when I walked past them, their cocky grins fell, and their eyes rounded to the point of looking...afraid?

All three of them had black eyes. Fat lips. Not to mention, other bruises along their faces and necks. One of them had a white bandage where his forehead met his hairline, blood seeping through.

They only looked at me for a couple of seconds before turning around and putting as much distance between me and them as possible.

17

I pulled out my phone and texted the same phone number Easton had used earlier. I quickly added his name to it so I wouldn't do something stupid like accidentally text someone else something meant for him.

Me: I have a question for you.

His text back was swift.

Easton: Can't talk right now. On my way to meet...a *friend*.

I felt ill, worried about Easton walking into a dangerous conversation. Because I knew he was referring to Brown.

Me: Be careful.

Easton: Are you alone?

Me: Almost home. Why?

Easton: Because I don't want you to be alone until I know how this goes.

I held my hand to my stomach.

Me: Will you text me when you're done?

Easton: Yes.

Me: Promise?

Easton: Yes. I'll text you the second I'm able.

After jogging from the station to my house, I walked inside, needing to think in complete silence because the thought of Easton talking to Brown fired my nerves on all cylinders, and I seriously needed them to calm down before coping with normal life. But Dad didn't even wait for me to get my shoes off. He wheeled himself over to me, studying my face with such scrutiny that I wondered if he could see right through all my falsehoods.

"How'd it go?" he asked.

My shoulders slumped. "Fine."

"Did they have suspects for you to look at?"

I don't have it in me to go into this right now. Right now, Easton's life hangs in the balance of a conversation.

"No. But now, they have a sketch of one of them." I tried to do Orange, too, but I didn't recall enough details to make the sketch useful. I was hopeful that if I ever saw him again, I'd recognize him. I just didn't have a strong enough memory to create a sketch like I had with Brown.

"Have they had a development in the case?"

Please, Dad. Sense my need for space, allow me to talk about this later.

"If they have, they're not saying anything."

"What *did* they say?"

I pinched the bridge of my nose. I so did not have the energy to go through a play-by-play of all of this. I knew Dad meant well, and before, I'd appreciated his worry. But right now...couldn't anyone just give me five minutes without having to talk about it? Could I take my shoes off first? Could I have that one minute of sanity to myself?

How was anyone supposed to get over something traumatic when the police and your dad insist you go over it and over it? Making it feel like your entire life now centered around one awful night.

"We just went over the details again."

Based on my dad's tightened lips, that was unacceptable.

"Tell me everything they said," Dad insisted.

"There's nothing more to say." I didn't mean for the edge to slice through my words. Maybe my mood shift wasn't just from exhaustion; maybe it was from worry over Easton.

All I wanted to do was have some peace and quiet until I knew he was okay. But no. The universe wouldn't let that happen, would it?

"Zoey."

"Dad, even if I felt like getting into all this, Alex is on his way over."

My dad looked confused. "I already had my physical therapy this morning."

"I know." But he left while I was still in the shower, before we could chat. "I need to talk to him about something."

"About what?"

I took a deep breath, trying to calm my growing frustration. I didn't have the time or patience to get into this because I needed to focus on the task ahead of me—telling Alex that I didn't have the money I'd promised, hoping he'd still give Dad PT while I figured out a new plan.

It was selfish of me to beg him for another extension, but I was so desperate, I didn't know what else to do.

In the midst of all this drama with the robbery, life still moved forward. Bills still had to be paid, and Dad had to keep progressing with his PT and his medical appointments or else he would never get better.

The problem was, if I couldn't sell the ring Easton had returned —it was flagged as stolen by police, who were probably watching for it to turn up—I was running out of ideas on how to get extra money. The only thing I could think of was to try to get a second job. It would mean leaving Dad alone at night to wait tables or tend bar. That I'd have to figure out, but the bigger problem was that finding a job and getting paid would take time, so I prayed Alex would work with me.

It felt like a group of rubber bands had wrapped around my ribs, like everything in normal life was at the mercy of this upcoming conversation.

Normal life. Excluding a group of criminals who intended to end my life.

"Our bill," I said, and before he could ask another layer of questions, I cut him off at the pass. "I'm going to lie down for a minute because I'm beyond drained."

Then, after I got Alex's verdict and Easton's—God willing—good news, I'd take a warm bath and slip into bed to get some sleep. Because I didn't trust myself in this life-or-death game of chess when my mental gas tank was running on fumes.

I tried to walk into the hall, but Dad rolled in front of me.

I gritted my teeth at yet another blockage between me and what I needed.

How did Dad's concern go from feeling loving to suffocating?

"Where are they with the investigation?" Dad pushed.

I curled my fists tighter until my nails dug into my palms.

"If you're this curious, why don't you call them yourself?" I tried to massage the frustration out of my temples.

Dad flinched at my tone. "I did. They're not telling me anything, but you, they should tell you."

"I think they're not telling you anything because there's nothing to tell. They haven't caught whoever's done it yet."

"Which is bull. Why aren't they behind bars?"

"Why are you so angry?"

"Three violent criminals held my daughter hostage, beat her, and threatened her life, and you're asking me why am so angry?"

So, now, he was going to act like a good dad? The protective one?

I was pathetic because part of me relished him being the protective dad, the one extending affection that I'd desperately craved after he left us. But I was also angry because he lost the right to act like a good father—a good father doesn't leave you for another woman and doesn't subsequently blow you off at every turn, making it clear you are no longer a priority in his life. Sabotaging your finances in the process while he lived in the lap of luxury.

"I'm starting dinner." I walked around him.

"Those cops aren't doing enough," Dad growled.

"I really don't want to talk about this anymore."

"Do you know if they got any fingerprints or anything?"

"I don't know! If you wanna think about anything, maybe you should think about who all has a key to your condo."

"What?"

"They got into the condo, Dad. Maybe you should think about who could've gotten them in."

"What the hell is that supposed to mean?"

"It means, maybe the person had a key to get inside the condo."

"They think this is an inside job?"

"I swear they're even looking at me like I might've had something to do with it."

"That's preposterous," Dad said. "You'd never do anything like that." But then he stared at me with this look that I swore said...*Would you?*

Wow.

"Does Holly still have a key to the condo?" I tried to sound curious and not accusatory.

"Zoey..."

"If someone did set this up, it had to be her."

"I know you never liked her but—"

"She's always been obsessed with money, and when you got hit by that car, her lifestyle went up in smoke. She didn't get anything in the divorce. She's bitter, angry, and always acted entitled to your money. Stealing the last of your stuff fits her to a T."

"I know you didn't care for your stepmom—"

"Do *not* call her that."

"But she wouldn't rob me."

"So, in all your years together, you're telling me she never did anything that made you second-guess her character?"

His silence was all I needed to hear.

"Do not call her my stepmom. Ever again."

Dad studied me, picking up on the deeper meaning behind my words. "Do you have something you want to get off your chest? Because it certainly feels like you do. And we've never talked about everything."

"And you want to have that talk? Right *now*?" I crossed my arms over my chest.

Dad seemed to consider this and scrubbed his face. "No," he decided. "Talking things out is exceedingly overdue, but you and I have a long conversation ahead of us, and I'd prefer to wait a bit. You've been through a significant trauma and need time to heal from that first."

My eyes watered. Making me remember how desperate I'd been to work through our hurts when I was tied up. Shame on me for being mean to him. A lot of this anger probably wasn't even because of *him* right now. I was scared, and exhausted, and taking my frustrations out on my dad.

"I'm sorry for snapping at you," I said. "I'm overwhelmed with... this entire situation, and I'm exhausted."

"It's okay," Dad said gently. "Why don't you get some rest?"

"I will. As soon as I'm done talking to Alex."

18

"Hey," Alex said when I opened the door. Then, he noted the look on my face, and he looked past me toward my dad before returning his gaze to me. "You okay?"

"Yeah." I forced a smile. I checked my phone for the millionth time, willing Easton's call or text to arrive to let me know he was safe.

Alex looked from me to my dad again, perhaps sensing the tension. "Want to step outside for a second? Get some fresh air?"

My mouth ran dry. Getting fresh air and a moment to breathe from my father sounded like heaven. But I couldn't afford something as simple as stepping outside for some fresh air anymore, could I?

I clenched my teeth, looking at the glorious summer sky that I was missing out on.

"Are you afraid to come outside?" A crease formed between his brows.

I shrugged.

Alex's mouth curled into a line of frustration, no doubt because he could tell the robbery had stolen my sense of peace. "We could go inside?"

I didn't want to have this conversation about money in front of Dad.

"I have been staying inside," I said. "But even that doesn't make me feel safer. I keep thinking someone could just set fire to the place or shoot me through the window even if the blinds are closed. Or ignite a bomb or something. Staying in hasn't made me feel safe; it just makes me feel like a prisoner again."

Only this time, I was confined to my townhouse instead of that chair. This time, Brown didn't just inflict fear during the span of one burglary. Now, he'd infected every safe haven in my life—my home, my work, my bedroom.

And the problem was, even if it was safer to hide in my house, it wasn't sustainable. I couldn't miss another day of work without losing pay. We were out of groceries, Dad couldn't physically do the shopping, and I couldn't afford the hike in fees to have them delivered. Plus, I had to get to the pharmacy to get Dad's medication. Staying inside indefinitely wasn't an option. I had to figure out how to live my normal life amid this chaos.

"We could go around back?" Alex offered.

"No," I decided.

If I had to come out of hiding, then I just wanted to get the first time over with. I looked up and down the block twice before finally stepping my right foot outside. And then my left.

I took a huge breath of air.

Nothing bad happened.

I took another step.

And another.

No gunshot. No man appearing from around the corner or parked car.

I walked farther outside into the summer evening air and savored the way a light breeze danced across my cheeks. It was twilight, the sun having set not long ago, and in the near distance, the city's skyscrapers were aglow against darkening lavender clouds. Here, the beat of a rock song drifted from a few houses away, and the delicious scent of barbeque ribs puffed out of a neighbor's grill, making my stomach growl and my mouth water. I could almost taste the sweet mesquite flavor.

Alex's concern for my mental health was obvious through his tone. "You okay?"

No. But I need to be. Because I needed this conversation to go well. I needed a win. Without it, I felt like I would just crumple, and once I did, I wasn't sure I would get back up this time.

"Honestly?" I ran a hand through my hair. "I've been better."

Alex tucked his hands into his khaki pants pockets, his white polo shifting around his biceps. The freckles on his face had darkened in the summer's sun.

"I can't imagine what you must be going through. You talk about it with anyone yet?"

I shook my head.

Alex frowned. "You need to talk about it with someone, so you can process this. What about a therapist?"

"Can't afford one."

"Jenna?"

"Maternity leave."

"So, she's home then," Alex said.

"Not sleeping. Up all night with a newborn. Breastfeeding. I'm not dumping on her right now."

"Emily."

I sighed. He wasn't wrong; I could feel a level of tension winding inside me, ready to snap. Maybe I did need to talk about this with someone. And of all the people in my life, Emily was certainly the best candidate. I trusted Emily. I could be completely honest with her, including details I hadn't even told the police.

"Yeah," I allowed. "Maybe I'll talk to Emily."

But right now, I needed to focus on Alex.

"Listen, the reason I asked you over was to talk about the money."

"Zoey—"

"The ring I was planning to sell was in my dad's condo."

Alex tensed. The veins on his forearms bulged like little snakes beneath his skin, and his eyes tightened as they stared at me, unblinking.

"You were at the condo that night for the *ring*?" he asked. His angry tone cut through the air.

"I've been thinking a lot about this. And I think if I get, like, a second job, waiting tables or bartending, I can have the money to you within the month," I said. "Two at most."

"You kept that ring at your dad's place?" he asked.

"I feel awful, putting you in this position, asking for another extension, but I feel like I don't have any other option."

"*I'm* the reason you were there that night?"

I blinked. "What? No. I just mean, I have to figure out a different way to get the money."

Alex flexed his fingers straight, then tightened them into balls, and for some reason, the breeze that had been dancing across my skin chilled my shoulders until goose bumps erupted.

"Don't get a job," Alex said. Now, his voice was soft and low, and his shoulders sagged.

"Alex, the only way—"

"Let's not focus on the money right now. We'll figure that out later. For now, the important thing is that you're okay."

"But your rent—"

"I'll figure that out."

I opened my mouth to protest, but he held up his palm.

"I'm going to keep coming pro bono until we figure something out, together. Okay? You're not alone in this, Zoey."

I couldn't stop my lips from quivering. Relief—sweet relief washed over me like cold water putting out a fire. When Alex saw the look on my face, he reached out and pulled me against his chest and held me.

I leaned into his embrace, the sanctuary of his body calming my nerves.

"Why are you doing all this for me?" I asked.

"We're friends."

"Yeah, but this is a lot. Even for friends."

Alex was silent for a minute, and then he cleared his throat, his tone low and riddled with pain. "You remember junior year of high school," he said, "when things went to hell with me and my parents?"

Of course I did. I remembered the very first day I noticed something off—when his mom pulled into the driveway and didn't even look at Alex as she walked into the house. Same thing with his dad. At first, I'd figured Alex had gotten into trouble and they were pissed—normal teenage stuff—but it quickly became apparent there was something deeper going on. After that day, Alex's demeanor became sullen at school, and I'd see him climb out his second-story window onto the roof of his house and lie there for hours, looking at the stars, as if needing an escape.

Whatever was going on in that house was clearly painful, so my family and I stepped up and started to invite Alex over. A lot. He had dinners with us and even spent some holidays with us, but he never told us what was going on with his parents.

"You became my family, Zoey," Alex said, "when I didn't have one. And I've never forgotten it."

He hugged me tighter.

Would he ever tell me what went down with his family? He never mentioned them, so I could only assume they'd never repaired whatever fallout had happened.

My cell phone rang, and when I saw the number, I pulled away from the hug and walked a few feet away.

"Hello?"

"Zoey," Easton said.

I could tell by his tone that whatever he was about to say was bad.

"He's not letting you off the hook," I deduced.

"No. He's added some...motivation."

"Meaning?"

"If I don't follow through, it won't be just me who pays the price." Easton sounded exhausted. "My brother will, too."

19

"Holy crap." Emily perched at the edge of her seat, leaning her elbows on the small circular table, looking as gorgeous as ever with her auburn hair flowing around her unfairly perfect porcelain skin and wearing tight jeans and a red top that accentuated her curvy body. Around us, the bar was in full swing with a scattering of people ordering drinks from two bartenders, wearing teal polos, while rock music blasted through the speakers so loudly, the bass vibrated in my bones.

The entire space was lit up in blue lighting, making the walls look like ice, people's skin look purple—as if we were having drinks inside an ice castle. The salt along the edge of my margarita looked like snow, the liquid's sharp lime scent pricking my nose.

"Why did you leave your house tonight if there's a threat on your life?" Emily glanced around the place. "Should we leave?"

"No."

"Zoey—"

"Cowering in my bedroom for the rest of my life isn't an option."

"Coming to a club *is*. We could go to my place?"

"Your roommate won't leave."

"Your place, then."

"My dad's there. He keeps staring at me like I might crack, and I seriously need a break from that. Besides, I don't want him to hear any of this."

"We can sit on your front porch."

Two girls at night, alone?

"Out in the open? This place is safer. It's public, with a lot of witnesses."

Emily's lips pulled into a worried line. "That's a lot of deliberation just to have a drink with a friend. I can't even, like, fathom how stressful this is. Are you okay? Like, mentally?"

I laughed. "Probably not."

Maybe I *was* being reckless.

But I was done letting Brown control my life. How dare he threaten both Easton and his brother if Easton didn't obey his commands?

Hell, maybe this was my FU to him. I spent most of the robbery convinced I was going to die, and then I got lucky enough to escape, and he thought he could send me back into that chair, tied up, terrified?

No way, mother-F-er.

Tonight, I wanted to talk to my friend.

I *needed* to talk to my friend, so here I was, spilling everything to Emily.

Everything.

"I can't believe you kissed that guy."

"He rescued me."

"Still." Emily crinkled her nose. "He's, like, a criminal."

Criminal. Why did that word feel like a betrayal to Easton?

"He's not just a criminal."

To this, Emily sat back in her chair, head tilted.

"What?"

Emily took a long sip of her margarita before finally spitting it out. "Okay, so first of all, I don't think you're processing the robbery itself or even the almost-dying part. I think there's something else that you're working through that's even deeper than that."

I raised my eyebrows.

"If you think about it"—she traced her glass's rim with her glossy red fingernail—"this is, like, the first time that you've paused to consider someone's reasons behind their bad choices."

I blinked.

"This Easton guy opened that up for you."

Hearing his name roll off her tongue made me tense. I trusted Emily completely. But was it a mistake, telling her his name? A betrayal?

"Before this," she continued, "everything was, like, black and white. Like when your dad left your family, there was no explanation that could justify it."

"It wasn't just that he left," I reminded her. "It was *how* he left."

"I know. I'm just saying that you—understandably—only look at people's *actions* when you're forming an opinion of them. Easton is the first person that shifted that. He made you pause and wonder *why* he was doing the things he did. Part of you empathized with why he became a burglar. You started to see him as a flawed human, not just a list of choices he made."

Easton's words echoed through my ears. *"Sometimes, good people are capable of bad things, Zoey."*

"Most people probably would have just sat there and been victimized," I said. "But he took actions that most people wouldn't have the courage to take. What kid lives in an alley in Chicago when winters get below freezing and takes care of his little brother?"

Emily looked at me like I'd just admitted to eating caterpillars for protein. "When you said you guys kissed, I assumed it was like a momentary sexual-tension thing," she accused, her jaw dropping open. "But you *like* him."

"What? No, I don't."

I can't.

"You *do*." Her eyes grew so wide, her eyelashes nearly hit the roof of her forehead, and horror rolled across her features.

I took a sip of my drink.

"You can't like him. He's a *burglar*. He held you hostage and has been ordered to kill you."

"I'm aware."

"He might've helped you escape, but that does not mean he's a good person."

I said nothing.

"Any feelings you have for him is probably, like, that kidnapping disorder. What's it called? Stoke ham?"

Emily looked it up on her phone, then read from the screen. "Stockholm syndrome. When hostage victims have positive feelings toward an abuser or captor." She put her phone down. "That's got to be what this is."

"Yeah. Probably," I lied.

That's not all it is. I can't stop thinking about him, wondering where he is. How he's doing. Worried how much he's sacrificing just to keep me alive.

I took an uncomfortable sip of my margarita, avoiding Emily's accusing stare by glancing around the club, and when I did, my eyes landed on a familiar face. Who appeared to spot me the same moment I'd spotted her.

"Is that Willow?" Emily squinted.

Willow was a friend that I'd made at the University of Illinois. Jenna was friends with her, too. I just happened to be a lot closer to Jenna than anyone else in my life, but when Willow moved to Chicago, she came around our friendship circle enough to get to know Emily as well.

Willow waved at us and then started walking toward our table.

I plastered a smile onto my face and shot Emily a warning look that the conversation about the robbery was paused until we were alone. It wasn't that I didn't trust Willow; I could only stomach unraveling all this chaos to one person right now, and that person was currently Emily.

"I didn't know you girls were coming out tonight." Willow gave me a quick hug, then Emily.

"Last-minute thing," I hedged, not wanting Willow to feel excluded.

"Want to join us?" Emily motioned to one of two empty seats at our table.

"I was just leaving, actually." Willow waved to a friend who was standing by the door, in full flirtation mode with the bouncer. "Maybe we could get together soon? For dinner or something?"

I smiled, relieved. "Sounds great."

"Have a great night, ladies!" Willow walked off.

And thankfully, it was just Emily and me again. To resume Operation Dissect My Crisis.

"So, you think the person who hired the robbers was your stephag?" Emily leaned forward.

I shrugged. "She's the only one with the motive and the means to do it."

"Do you think you're letting your hatred for her cloud your judgment?"

"She texted my dad." I curled my lips. "The day after the robbery. Claimed she heard about it from the detectives who'd been by to see her. Guess they were following up with anyone who might've had a key to the place. Or a reason to rob it."

"And his cell phone caught fire?"

I smiled. See? This was why I was out tonight. Emily could pull me out of the heaviness and we could laugh at ourselves.

"She asked if I was okay and then got to the real reason for her text. She asked if, by any chance, I'd grabbed her necklace before escaping."

Emily's jaw almost bounced off the table. "She did not."

"I didn't even know she had a necklace there. Evidently, she'd kept it in the master bedroom."

"Why? I thought she moved out a while ago?"

"She did. Convenient, isn't it? She probably didn't leave it behind; if she did, she could've gotten it at any time. I bet she put it there, so she'd have something to lose in the robbery, too, so she'd be a victim. Diverting suspicion away from her."

"Or she could be lying about there even being a necklace, hoping to collect the insurance money," Emily added.

Also possible.

"She's just the gift that keeps on giving, isn't she?" Emily arched a brow.

I smiled. "Thank you for talking about all this with me. I feel a lot better."

"You sure you don't want to go?" Emily bit her lip.

"Positive." I nodded.

Alex was right. Getting all this off my chest to Emily made me feel lighter, and now, I wanted to try and feel like a normal person, if only for an hour or two.

"Let's just have some fun?" I suggested.

Her grin widened. "How about we find some cute guys to talk to?"

That was Emily's version of fun, not mine. "I'm not in the mood."

"Oh, come on. It's been forever since I've been kissed."

"I find that hard to believe."

Emily's dating life was active. She was a redheaded fox, and the only thing that kept guys away was intimidation by her beauty.

"Look." She nodded her chin toward the bar. "There're two super-cute guys staring at us."

"Let them stare. How about we dance?"

"With them?"

"With each other." I rolled my eyes. "Guys are the last thing I want to deal with right now."

"Well, that's too bad because they're walking over here." She grinned.

I groaned.

"That tall guy is so cute. At least let me talk to him for, like, a few minutes, okay?"

"Emily..."

"Please? I haven't had a date in over two months, and it's totally making me insecure."

I frowned at her puppy-dog eyes. Emily had been a really good friend to me tonight. The least I could do was give her a few minutes to see if she'd hit it off with this guy.

The two men sauntered over to our table like they were in a hottest-men-in-the-club competition. Spoiler alert: they'd probably win, but that made me like them even less. Hot guys weren't hot when they acted like their beauty was a gift to civilization.

"Good evening, ladies," the tall, thin guy said with a grin.

Even his grin was arrogant.

"I'm Henry," he said, flashing his super-white teeth to Emily.

"Emily." Emily nodded, already folding her shoulders into a flirtatious pose.

"I'm Thomas," the other guy said to me.

I forced myself to smile. "Zoey."

Thomas nodded with his chin to the dance floor. "Would you like to dance, Zoey?"

I'd rather go to my high school reunion, wearing my bra outside of my shirt.

"She'd love to!" Emily chirped.

I threw her a death glare, and she shot me a *pretty please* look. I sighed and reminded myself—again—that she'd been a good friend, coming out with me tonight despite all my baggage.

One dance. I could do one dance—for her.

"Stay where I can see you!" Emily insisted.

Thomas chuckled, probably thinking it was a sexual inuendo, but the look she flashed me said, *If you leave my sight, I'm going to assume you're being murdered and call the FBI.*

I followed Casanova to the dance floor.

The beat of the music vibrated my bones as overhead lights

transformed the room to a shade of purple. The air smelled like sweat from young couples wearing outfits that showed off their bodies—girls in dresses so short that their underwear was nearly exposed and guys in tight shirts with the top two buttons undone. Eyes raking over their partner's body, hands wandering, fingers touching. Sexual tension radiated through the club.

Thomas moved closer to me.

I glanced over at Emily and saw the huge smile on her face as she ran her fingers flirtatiously through her hair and then leaned forward on the table.

She likes him.

I wasn't going to ruin that; I'd give her a few minutes of fun—enough time to exchange numbers—before I politely sent Thomas on his way.

Dancing like a horny college boy, Thomas stepped into my personal space.

I took a step back, trying to keep a minimum of three feet between our bodies, but he didn't get the hint. Instead, he circled me, his eyes wandering over my body as he did a lap like some sort of mating ceremony. The dude reminded me of a peacock flaunting his feathers, like his mad dancing skills were supposed to make me want to drop my panties right here on the dance floor.

And he clearly flunked the course in reading someone's body language. Because mine was saying, *Back up, buddy,* but he didn't back up. He put his hands on my hips. I winced, less from the pain from where Brown had kicked me—my injuries were starting to feel better, and I'd taken Advil before coming here. It was more that his fingers felt like paws, grabbing at my torso like he had a right to me.

I was about to push him off and tell him that if he liked having unbroken fingers, he wouldn't lay a hand on me again without my permission.

But if I were being honest, my seriously foul mood had little to do with this guy. I think the whole situation just reminded me that Easton and I could never date, let alone anything past that.

And the guy was just dancing, for heaven's sake. Maybe spending time with another guy wasn't a horrible idea. My hormones had evidently imprinted onto Easton, and I needed to train them to become attracted to someone else—anyone else.

I put my hands on Thomas's shoulders and let him pull me to the beat of the music. I willed myself to feel a spark—any spark—with him. If ever there were a guy hot enough to feel a spark for, Thomas would be it with a tall frame and chocolate eyes that reminded me of Hershey's Kisses.

But nothing flickered between us, not even when he moved his hands up my back.

Suddenly, a tall figure appeared near my left shoulder.

"I'd like to cut in." He didn't state it like a question; his broody voice made it sound like an order that bordered on a warning, causing Thomas to look at me and then slink away.

He positioned himself in front of me. Dammit if he didn't look sexy as hell in a black T-shirt that showed off his muscles and flat stomach and jeans that stretched around his legs.

I crossed my arms over my chest. "What are you doing here?"

20

"What are *you* doing here?" Easton demanded. "You should be at home."

His voice was raised, but I couldn't tell if he was actually yelling at me or if it was just to compensate for the loud music, which, thankfully, provided a privacy shield around us. Around everyone. You were lucky to hear the person standing right in front of you, but that was about all you could hear over its beat.

"And what, wait in my tower until you tell me it's safe to let down my hair?"

"There's a hit on your life. You're being reckless."

"*I'm* being reckless? You're standing out in the open with the woman you've been ordered to kill. Pot. Kettle." I pointed with my finger between us. "How did you even know I was here? Are you stalking me?"

"*Stalking* is an unkind word."

"That's a yes."

"You shouldn't be here," he repeated.

"I'm just having a drink with a friend."

"Do you not understand the danger you're in? Honest to God,

Zoey." Easton ran a hand through his hair. "Do you have a death wish? How the hell am I supposed to keep you alive if you're this careless?"

"So, the hit man's going to lecture his target on staying alive?"

"I'm not a hit man." Easton stepped into my space. "You keep acting like this? I'm going to throw you over my shoulder and take you somewhere. Keep you there until I know you're safe."

Shame on my hormones for squealing, for acting like kids begging their parents for ice cream. *Please?*

"And when will we know I'm safe, Easton?"

"It's only been three days."

"It feels like a decade."

"I'm working on this," Easton said.

"Working on this? Didn't he threaten your brother?"

"He did. And you should know, I don't respond well to threats. Especially when it comes to those I care about."

I tightened my lips. "How are you going to convince him to not murder me?"

How peculiar my life had become for those words to make sense.

"Last time I talked to him, I made it all about you. About killing an innocent unnecessarily, on my heist. Next time, I'm going to make it all about him."

"What the hell does that mean?"

"Right now, the cops haven't made any arrests for the heist. So, there's a chance it'll blow over. But they kill the only living witness? All of a sudden, homicide's involved and up their ass so deep, they can't conduct business as usual. Financials suffer. People start getting pulled in for questioning. Risk people talking."

"And you think that'll change his mind?"

"Brown has his eye on a huge heist coming up, so he might focus on his new toy and let this go. But only if he doesn't feel the heat from the condo. Best thing we can do right now is let things cool down. Let the investigation fizzle out."

I didn't know why Emily's words suddenly echoed in my head.

"He might've helped you escape, but that does not mean he's a good person." But they began to mind-F me, making me question my judgment, question if I'd read this wrong, if Easton was the good person I thought he was.

"How can I be sure you're not actually working with Brown now? Trying to scare me? Maybe what you're really trying to do is intimidate me into not telling the cops your name."

Easton took a step closer to me. I held my ground and looked up into his angry eyes.

"If all I'm trying to do is manipulate and intimidate you, then why would I have returned the ring? Why would I have left you Advil on your front porch? Why would I be here tonight, watching over you? To keep you safe?"

I bit my lip, watching his eyes snap to my teeth.

"Let's say, for argument's sake, you can't convince Brown to let me live. What will you do?"

To this, Easton's eyebrows crunched in a disgusted line. "I would never hurt you, Zoey. And I *will* figure a way out of this—a way to keep both you and my brother safe. I'm asking you to trust me."

Trust him. Could I let go of my lingering reservations and trust Easton?

I'm scared the good side of you isn't the real you.

I studied his face, looking for any sign of deceit.

"You didn't have to scare off my dance partner to keep me safe," I reasoned.

Easton flexed his fingers at his sides, his jaw ticcing as he looked away before returning his gaze to me. "I can't stomach another man touching you."

I tried not to smile, and after a moment, the fast song ended, and a slow song started.

A sultry song.

Because the universe likes to torture my hormones.

Without taking his eyes off me, Easton stepped forward and gently grabbed my hips. And instantly, I no longer wanted to escape the dance floor. I drew my hands up, placing them on his rock-hard shoulders, and began to sway with him as his piercing blue eyes remained fixed on mine. That facial stubble framed his perfectly kissable lips, as if calling attention to how amazing they would feel, pressed against mine.

I was grateful the volume of this song was much lower than the last, so we didn't have to shout anymore. In fact, with us dancing this closely, we could talk much softer and still hear each other.

His eyes scanned my body. "Are you still sore?" His tone was full of angry concern, like he hated imagining me in pain.

"The Advil helped," I said. "Thank you."

He nodded, relief not fully consuming his features. He still had an edge of anger that I'd been hurt, but something else washed over him, too. Desire.

"So, this doesn't bother you?" He tightened his grip on my hips.

I shook my head, loving the way he was looking at me right now. Loving the feeling of his hands on my body.

"I keep reminding myself to stay away from you," Easton said. "But I can't seem to listen."

Could he see the flush in my cheeks?

"Why?"

"I tell myself it's to keep you safe."

"But that's not the only reason?"

"No." His gaze drifted to my lips. "That's not the only reason."

I had to focus on my next breath. "Weren't you just lecturing me on irresponsibility?"

He licked his bottom lip and then pulled it into his teeth.

I'm officially jealous of teeth.

"What if I told you I can't get you out of my head?" he growled. "That I haven't been able to get you out of my head since the moment I first laid eyes on you?"

I cherished the feeling of his knuckles brushing my temple.

"That day by the lake," Easton said, "the wallet wasn't the only thing you gave me."

I waited for him to explain.

He hesitated, though, like he was second-guessing going into whatever it was, but after a few moments, resolve cascaded over his features.

"The last decade of my life, my only purpose has been raising my brother, but now, he's a grown man. And while I'll still protect him, having that chapter of my life end..." Easton chewed on the inside of his cheek. "I'd been so fixated on raising him that I never built a full life of my own. Found myself feeling like there was something missing in my life."

Human connection.

"And then, that day by the lake, there you were. I'd never been so drawn to anyone before."

He cleared his throat.

"And the more I got to know you during the heist, the more captivated I was by you."

Easton pulled me closer until our chests were touching. I could feel the rise and fall of my breasts pressed against him, and the sexual haze he cast around me made me wonder if Emily was right.

If Easton was affecting me more than I wanted to admit.

"Emily thinks you're changing me."

Easton's delicious mouth curled up on one side, and he ran the backs of his knuckles down my neck, leaving a spark in their wake. "How so?"

It was hard to focus with him looking at me like I was the only person in this club, the only thing that deserved his attention.

"Making me rethink my point of view on some things," I managed.

Easton's gaze glided down to my lips. "Elaborate."

I took a deep breath and tried to think of how to explain this. "Ever since my dad left, I've believed that people's actions tell you everything you need to know about them."

"Actions speak louder than words," Easton said.

"Especially if those actions hurt you."

Easton's jaw tightened. "Like your father?"

"We're going to finally talk things out."

Easton evaluated me. "You don't look happy about it."

"I am." I scrunched my shoulders.

He waited, staring at me until I revealed the rest of the answer.

"But I'm also scared." I bit my lip. "Forgiving someone who's hurt you is like handing them back the loaded gun they shot you with. They've already shown what they will do with it."

He trailed his thumb along my collarbone. "So, you shut them out to protect yourself."

I tightened my grip on his shoulders, trying to focus on our words rather than my lower belly, which was warming. Begging me to kiss him. "Just like you left that home to protect you and your brother from being hurt."

Easton stared at me silently, our bodies swaying to the music.

"I think there's a difference, though." Easton brought his hand to my cheek, cupping the side of my head, inciting another riot from my hormones. The burnt-sugar smell of cologne on his wrist wasn't helping.

His touch, his smell, the way he looked at me—it was like he was flooding my body with an aphrodisiac.

"I left people who didn't give a shit about me." Easton's voice was low. "Some of the people you're pushing away are people you care about."

I ran my palms down his shoulders a few inches, my fingers falling into the folds of his arm muscles. "When someone's done something that hurt you, why would you give them another chance to hurt you again?"

"Because"—he stroked my cheek with his thumb—"you wouldn't worry about getting hurt if you didn't still love them. And if you love them, that's all that matters." Easton studied me. "It's easier to give up on people. It's harder to love them despite what they've done to hurt you. But some people are worth fighting for."

I thought about how Easton's brother had been pulling away

from him, and I wondered how badly that hurt and how vulnerable Easton must feel, never giving up on him.

"And here I thought you despised my dad for what he did to me." I slid my hands back up his shoulders.

"I despise anyone who causes you an ounce of pain," Easton said, his voice pulsing with vengeance. "But I also want what's best for you." He traced his thumb down my jaw. "And living in an ocean of isolation will only make you miserable."

I wrapped my arms around his neck, which pulled our bodies even tighter together. "You think I should forgive *your* actions?" I raised my brows.

To this, Easton looked at me carefully. "No." He frowned. "But I'd be lying if I said I didn't *want* you to."

I bit my bottom lip. A gesture that didn't go unnoticed by him. Easton glared at my mouth like it was the enemy he was trying to fight, a temptation he was trying to resist.

But I didn't want him to resist it. His kiss was something I hadn't been able to shake from my thoughts since he'd first pressed his mouth to mine.

Easton took my chin in his hand. "You should walk away from me," he said in a tone that implied he lacked the strength.

"Is that what you want?" I kept my lips parted.

Why did my heart feel like it was slowly being poisoned every moment it wasn't with him, the only relief coming in the moments we were together?

All the while, it felt like Easton was about to disappear, and I'd never see him again.

Easton studied my eyes, then my lips for three breaths. "What I want is you."

His gaze pinned my mouth, and it felt like my heart stopped beating as he slowly drew his face closer. And brushed his lips against mine.

Surrendering to our kiss, all the complications outside evaporated, if only in this moment.

Easton's tongue connected with mine, delicately at first, then with urgency. If we couldn't be together, it was like this kiss was his good-bye. And like the waves of the ocean, it started gently, then crashed to the shore more forcefully as the sea's waters darkened with the coming storm of us being separated.

I raked my hands through his hair. Silk tickling my fingers as I opened my mouth wider, pulled his neck so he kissed me harder, greedily taking the kiss he felt he didn't deserve. Easton put his hands in my hair, gently scratching my scalp with his nails. It sent a rush of goose bumps throughout my body, my lower belly pulsing with his touch.

In a sea of people, it was as if we were the only ones that existed. The only things that mattered right now were his hands on my body and his tongue dancing with mine. I ran my palms down his chest, feeling the ridges of his strength.

Easton growled against my mouth as I nibbled his bottom lip.

I could've kissed him forever, but every moment the kiss continued, my desire soared to have more of him. To do things we could never do with each other, let alone in this club. I sensed Easton struggling with the same urges when he pulled away from me, as if hoping it would curb his hormones.

Panting, he pressed his forehead against mine. "How will I ever endure the pain of seeing you in another man's arms?"

My stomach clenched. There was no way Easton and I would ever be free to date like two normal people, but for a fleeting moment, we'd existed in a heaven, pretending we could. Until he burst the bubble, the cold reality of our forced separation freezing every organ in my body. Did his comment imply he'd always be in the shadows, watching over me?

"I wish this wasn't so complicated," I said, clutching his arms tightly.

Easton separated his forehead from mine, and every inch of space was a raft floating farther out to sea. Threatening to never return.

"I should let you get back to your *date*."

I could tell that was the last thing Easton wanted, that he was once again trying to be noble after his jealousy had overcome him.

"He isn't my date. He's a guy I just met here."

I'd have thought Thomas's ego would be too bruised to want anything more to do with me, but he lingered by my table, obviously waiting for my return.

Easton glanced over at him, and instantly, all the romance evaporated from his eyes, his jaw tightening in disgusted anger.

"What?" I studied his face, puzzled.

His chest ballooned.

"What's wrong?" My voice hitched.

"They're a team." Easton's lips tightened.

"What? Who's a team?"

Never taking his eyes off Thomas, Easton let me go. "Don't drink anything. Tell your friend not to, either."

"What? Why? Where are you going?"

Easton kept his eyes fixed on Thomas as he marched across the bar toward him. As soon as Thomas spotted him, he pivoted and slithered away to the back of the club.

Easton didn't give up that easily; he pursued Thomas like a hunter locked on his prey.

I jogged over to Emily and whispered in her ear, "Don't drink anything."

Emily looked at me, confused. "What?"

I glared at her date, who put his hands in his pockets as he watched his "friend" vanish into the back hallway of the bar, followed by Easton. The fact that Henry asked no questions sealed my suspicion.

I now understood what Easton meant when he said they were a team.

"You guys work together," I accused.

Emily flashed me a puzzled look.

"The two of you separate the girls, so it's easier to spike the drinks. Easier to let the effects of the roofie kick in, and the longer you keep them apart, the easier it is for the girls to assume it's alcohol affecting their friend. Especially if that girl's drugged, too."

"The hell are you talking about?" Henry snarled.

"As soon as you and your buddy came over, you immediately split us up. Thomas took me to the dance floor while you stayed with Emily. Then, we were conveniently separated, so you guys could roofie us easier."

The guy's eyes hardened. "You're crazy."

I made eye contact with the bouncer and motioned for him to come over.

"Then, you'd have no problem drinking Emily's margarita." I held her glass up to him.

His lips curled. He did not take the glass or drink.

"That big a dose, eh? It'll knock you on your ass?"

"Everything okay?" The bouncer looked from Henry to us.

"No. This guy's drugging your female patrons."

The bouncer's eyes cut to the guy, then the glass in my hand. Took it. Sniffed it. "Empty your pockets."

"Go to hell," Henry snapped.

The bouncer shoved Henry against a nearby wall and searched his pants until he produced a baggie of capsules.

I looked at the back hallway, where Easton had disappeared, and as much as I wanted to witness this guy getting escorted out by his face, every second I stood here, Easton got farther away.

"I'll be right back," I said to Emily.

"What? Where are you going?"

"I think a friend of mine is about to do something reckless."

"After everything you just said, I'm not going to leave you alone."

"This place is packed, and I won't be alone. I can't explain this right now. I'll be right back." My tone was firm, leaving no room for arguments.

Emily pursed her lips and glanced around the very public, theoretically safe bar. "If you're not back soon..."

"I know." I nodded.

I offered her a reassuring smile and then made a beeline for the back of the bar, the last place I'd seen Thomas and Easton, but the hallway was empty.

The back door to the club was ajar.

I pushed it open.

The warmth of the outside air cascaded over my skin as I entered the alley. Twenty feet wide, it stretched a hundred feet long and swallowed everything in its shadows. The only lighting came from a single overhead bulb on the opposite building and from the reflections of headlights and taillights as they scurried past either side of it. But even with minimal lighting, I could make out a very distinct shape fifteen feet from me.

A man was hunched over another, fists swinging. Each strike landed with a thwap and a groan from the man on the ground, who tossed his arms up in a failed attempt to defend himself. The man on top, however, was in a primal predatory position. He threw another blow, and this time, it cracked the guy's face.

And he stopped moving.

This was the moment the assailant turned his head and spotted me. He was still nothing more than a silhouette, the only light coming from behind him.

"Easton." I marched up to him.

Clenching his fists, he looked nothing like the man who had rescued me from a hostage situation. This Easton looked dark. Dangerous with a tightened face and rigid muscles. Rage pumping through his eyes as he glared at the man on the ground.

Nearby car engines rumbled as the metallic squeak of the "L" train echoed off the buildings.

"You beat up those other guys, too," I said. "Didn't you?"

One Mississippi.

Two Mississippi.

Three Mississippi.

"You'll have to be more specific."

"The guys at the "L" station by my house. I told you they were giving me a hard time, and the next time I saw them, someone had beaten them up."

"You said they harass a lot of women. Probably make enemies out of a lot of men."

Why wouldn't he give me a direct answer? It made no sense...unless...

"You're denying it, so I have no knowledge of that crime," I accused. So, if I was ever questioned about it, I couldn't get into trouble for knowing about it.

Easton raised an impressed eyebrow. Looked down at the guy groaning on the ground. "Didn't intend for you to see this one, either."

"So, that's a yes."

"Whatever happened to them? Sounds like they had it coming. I'm sure they won't be bothering you anymore."

And something in the air shifted in that moment. All remnants of skepticism dissipated like the clouds after a storm, and the rainbow that came out was a moment of pure honesty.

Easton would never hurt me.

His every action had been one of protection. Helping me escape. Warning me about the hit. Risking his safety to try and talk Brown out of it and planning to do so again. Protecting me from the guy that'd slipped something into my drink. Roughing up the guys on the "L" who'd been harassing me.

His actions backed up his words.

Easton was my dark protector, hiding in the shadows of the city.

The ordered killer, risking his life to keep his target safe.

His eyes stabbed mine, then speared the man who was stumbling back up.

"Go back inside, Zoey." He gritted his teeth. "You don't want to see what I'm going to do to him."

21

"What's going on?" I froze.

Because when I walked into my townhouse, I'd clearly interrupted something. Something that I could tell Alex and Dad had not meant for me to see, based on their rounded eyes. I'd told Dad I'd be out later because I hadn't expected for Easton to show up at the bar.

Or beat up a guy who'd tried to hurt me.

Only beat up. I hadn't left that alley until Easton walked away from the man before killing him. Only then did I rejoin Emily and call it a night.

Alex stood by the kitchen table, where Dad sat in his wheelchair with papers splayed out in front of him. Copies of police reports, photos of my injuries from the night of the robbery. In the middle of it all was Dad's cell phone, currently on speaker.

"I'm gonna have to call you back." Dad's finger hovered over the End Call button.

"I have enough information to get started," the man on the other end of the line said in a voice so gruff, he might have been a smoker. "I'll be in touch."

"What's going on?" I repeated, unable to hide the alarm in my voice.

"Didn't expect you home so soon." Dad's mouth curled down slightly.

"Who was that guy?" I motioned to the phone.

"Did you and Emily have a nice time?"

I looked at the table. "Where did you get all these police reports? And these photos? Do police hand these out to anyone who asks?" Wasn't there some sort of privacy protection for something like this?

"I'm not anyone. I'm your father and the owner of the condo that was robbed."

"Who was that on the phone? Because it didn't sound like the police."

"Zoey."

"It was a private investigator." Alex turned his lips down, as if he knew I wouldn't like the answer.

Dad shot him a glower.

"A private investigator?" I put my hand over my stomach. "Why were you talking to a private investigator?"

Alex crossed his arms over his chest and couldn't hide the frustration in his tone. "We hired him to help find the assholes who hurt you."

"What?" I looked at Dad. Expecting him to tell me that Alex was wrong.

But Dad didn't say that. Instead, he just offered me an empathetic look.

"Why would you hire a private investigator? The Chicago Police Department is working this case."

"They've failed to arrest anyone."

I threw my hand in the air. "It's only been three days!"

"Most crimes need to be solved within forty-eight hours, or they go cold."

"I think that's for homicides, Dad."

"They're not moving fast enough. The longer this goes on, the harder it is to get justice."

"Dad," I started.

He slammed his fist onto the table. "Three men held you hostage and beat the hell out of you. And I'm not going to rest until they're behind bars."

This couldn't be happening. Easton was right; the best way for me to stay alive was if this entire investigation fizzled out. Because even if I could miraculously get Brown behind bars, I had no doubt that Brown would order his crew to eliminate the witness. No witness, no testimony, and he'd go free.

"Dad, having some guy poke around in an active investigation is probably going to get in the *way* of the police."

"This guy has come highly recommended to us. He's solved more crimes than most police detectives have in their entire careers."

My heart pounded so hard, I wondered if he could hear it. "How are you even paying for him?"

"I'm funding it." Alex scrubbed the side of his face.

I snapped my eyes to him. "Why?"

"Because you're like family to me, Zoey." Alex's voice was soft, as if it hurt him, that the answer wasn't obvious to me. "And someone hurt you."

My eyes stung. Alex had no idea how much it meant to me, him going this far out of his way to try and help. If only he'd put his big heart into something that wouldn't get me killed.

But as soon as that feeling came, a chill erupted through my ribs. Why would Alex take this big of an interest in the investigation? PIs couldn't be cheap, and he told me he was short on cash—his rent sucking him dry.

"I thought you needed money for rent," I said.

Alex crossed his arms over his chest again. "My Mastercard isn't maxed out yet."

"And when the bill comes?"

"You let me worry about that," Alex said.

I could see in his eyes there was no changing his mind, no matter how financially irresponsible he was being, so I returned my attention to my father.

"Dad, please don't do this."

"Why do you care if we hire a PI?" Dad looked at me with...suspicion?

Really? Did he seriously think I'd orchestrate the heist? And be stupid enough to show up when it went down? How insulting.

"These guys are dangerous." My legs felt weak. "If they find out you're poking around, trying to get them arrested? They might hurt you."

"They tied my daughter up, beat her, and planned to kill her. So long as there's a breath in my body, I'll hunt them down. And make them pay."

And in that instant, my fairy tale and nightmare collided. The fairy tale of Dad finally loving me so much that he put me above all else, to the point he'd risk his own life for me. And the nightmare that his good intention might cost me my life.

22

As flattering as it was that Dad was finally showing me the kind of love I'd been craving for years, why'd he have to pick now of all times to finally do it? Why couldn't he have done something when I was in college, pleading for him to come talk to me to salvage our relationship?

I had no right to be mad. I should only feel flattered and appreciative that he loved me this much. And I had no right to be angry because what I had said to him was far worse than anything he'd done to me. But there it was. Anger. Bubbling in my veins until it boiled over the surface.

"Dad, can I talk to you for a second?"

At the tone of my voice, Alex exchanged a look with my father. "I'll step outside for a minute."

I waited until Alex left and crossed my arms over my chest. "Maybe instead of solving who the strangers were involved in this robbery, you should look at your inner circle and figure out who set all of this in motion."

My dad's head tipped back. "What's that supposed to mean?"

"Someone hired these burglars, and *they* need to be found, too."

"If anyone else was involved, the PI will figure it out. But in the meantime, those three criminals need to be locked up, and I will not rest until that happens."

If only the yellow countertops could somehow disperse cheer into the room. Because right now, all the hurts that I had swallowed over the past few years unraveled in my chest, firing a mixture of anger and resentment through my veins.

Where was *this* dad—this protective, loving dad—all those years he'd basically abandoned us? Why did he show up now all of a sudden? And why so dramatically?

Was this whole thing because I'd taken him in and he felt some sort of obligation because of that? Or was this his way of pacifying his guilt for having been a bad father to me?

"Solving this robbery isn't going to undo everything that you did to me, Dad."

I could tell by the jerk of his head that my comment had taken him by surprise.

It took me by surprise, too, especially since we agreed to wait to air our grievances until this robbery was behind us.

But that's the thing about emotions. Sometimes, they escape when you least want them to.

Dad folded his thin hands on his lap. "I know that, Zoey."

"No, you don't."

He couldn't expect this Band-Aid would heal his third-degree burns.

"Leaving Mom was bad enough, but you abandoned *me*."

"You were angry. I was trying to respect that and give you your space."

I didn't appreciate his tone of voice. He should be begging for forgiveness, not annoyed with me right now.

"And when I thought I'd given you enough time, I did try." Dad's cheeks reddened. "But you wouldn't let me in."

"Because it was too late! You broke my heart, and you broke my trust, not just in you, but in humanity. Because when the foundation of your world crumbles beneath you and your dad is the one holding the bulldozer that destroyed it, the rest of the world feels like a pretty unsafe place. And after that, you look at everybody with a skeptical eye, looking for any clue that they might hurt you, just like your dad did. And if you see any red flags, you immediately walk away."

I hated that I was crying. I hated that I was standing here, looking down at the father I had once looked up to, and I hated that I was finally having this out at a time when his body was physically so vulnerable. The whole thing made me feel like an awful human being, unworthy of his or anyone else's love. And yet, I couldn't stop the waterfall of words from finally breaking from their dam.

"You're the reason that when somebody does something wrong, I walk away from them and write them off. You're the reason I don't know how much slack to give people for their mistakes or their bad choices. The only thing I've learned from you is to protect my heart because you broke it so badly, it can't withstand another break."

Dad ran both hands over his face. His shoulder bones rose and fell with a deep breath, and his long fingers interlocked again on his lap as he regarded me. "I'm glad you're finally being honest with me."

"I'm finally being honest? You never gave me an opportunity to be honest! You left us without so much as a single conversation with me face-to-face. You went off with that woman on your trip and your holidays, and you left me like I was disposable. It's one thing for you to stop loving Mom, but when did you decide to stop loving me?"

"I never stopped loving you."

"Your actions said otherwise. We were your disposable family. The second some new, shiny car came along, you threw us in the junkyard and never looked back."

Dad shook his head. "There are some things I've never told you, Zoey. If you understood the circumstances around everything, I think you would be less critical of me."

"I wanted to understand. Desperately. With every fiber of my being, the only thing I wanted to hear was some words that would make sense out of nonsense, that would have the power to unbreak my heart. But you no-showed. Again and again. And that's when I decided it didn't matter what you said. The only thing that mattered was what you did."

And that was why I'd judged everyone based on their actions, never listening to their justifications.

"I'm not saying I didn't make mistakes," Dad replied. "I did. Gigantic ones. I should never have gone on that trip the weekend I was supposed to come to your college to talk, and I realize now that space was the opposite of what you needed. That lapse in judgment is something that I can never forgive myself for. But as far as leaving your mother for this other woman, you need to trust me that there was more to it than meets the eye."

"So, this is the part where you tell me Mom was a bad wife or you were unhappy in your marriage or she wasn't giving you enough attention or whatever? Because none of that is going to fly with me. You took an oath for better or for worse, so long as you both shall live, and you tossed it aside."

"Why did you take me in then?" Dad snapped. It was the first time he had shown anger toward me since his accident. "If I'm such an awful human being, why are you helping me?"

"Because you're still my dad!" I wiped a tear. "What am I supposed to do? Anthony's raising his own family on the other side of the country, so he's not here to help. You destroyed Mom and left her, so she's not going to help you. And the woman that you broke all our hearts to marry? Left you the second times got tough. So, what am I supposed to do, Dad? Leave you to rot in some homeless shelter? I could never turn my back on you—on family—regardless of how much I've been hurt. I'd like to think I'm better than that" —*than you*—"even if you don't deserve it."

Dad stared at me as his body slowly deflated, drained of every morsel of energy in its cells. His mouth turned down as he gave a slow, disbelieving head shake.

"And here I thought it was because I was getting a second chance with you."

Dad turned his wheelchair around, rolled into his bedroom, and slammed the door.

And all my anger burst, replaced with suffocating guilt that I'd just broken my dad's heart.

23

I slammed the door and stepped outside our townhouse, into the dark summer night, wiping tears from my cheeks. The sticky humidity had cooled slightly with a gentle breeze frosting the bands of sweat on my neck. The front porch's wooden planks vibrated to the bass of music—a party nearby in full swing with laughter cracking through a hum of voices. What did that feel like, to be young and carefree? How had my life become so complicated?

My cell phone buzzed with a text.

Easton: You okay?

I scanned my street, looking for Easton, wondering where he was.

Me: No. I just had a huge fight with my dad.

Easton: Did he hurt you again? Because if he did, so help me...

Me: No. But we have a problem with the case.

Easton: I don't care about the case right now, Zoey. I care about you.

Tension began to loosen in my muscles, and my heart warmed.

Easton: Do you want me to pick you up?

My insides quivered.

I wanted Easton to pick me up. I wanted to talk to him about all of this. I wanted to spend time with him, just me and him without a bar full of people, without anything around us. Without distractions or complications. But if I left right now, I'd probably hurt Dad even worse than I just did.

Yet I did need to talk to Easton. It felt like every second that this private investigator had a head start risked Dad's life exponentially. Dad and Alex were sticking their necks out with this private investigator, and if they ID'd Brown and Brown found out Dad and Alex were responsible for putting him behind bars? Revenge city. I needed to protect them.

Maybe Easton would know how to ensure the PI didn't find anything that could make Brown do something reckless.

Three dots appeared on my screen, indicating Easton was texting me again.

Before he finished, though, Alex appeared.

"Hey."

I looked out at the street, at the shadowed row of townhouses, at the road, with its trickle of traffic lumbering along, at the sidewalks. Blue-and-silver beer cans pooled along the base of my neighbor's broken chain-link fence, and the smell of freshly cut grass floated through the air.

"You're crying." Alex placed his hand on my upper arm.

"I appreciate you checking on me, but I just want to be alone." I looked down at my cell. The three dots had vanished.

"What happened?"

"I don't want to talk about it."

Alex rubbed his jaw, evaluated me. I recognized that stubborn look in his eyes. He'd had it many times in the past when everything had gone down with my dad and I'd come home from college for visits. Alex would sometimes sit silently next to me on the front porch of my home for hours. And I could tell he was gearing up to do the same thing when he took a seat on the stairs, inches from my hip.

"I don't mean to be rude." I pinched the bridge of my nose. "But I really do want to be by myself."

"I'm not going to leave you alone when you're upset."

He rested his elbows on his thighs and stared at my tears, as if debating wiping them away. I did it myself before he had the chance.

"Everything will be okay," Alex cooed.

Somehow, his empty promise made me cry harder. Because it was starting to feel like nothing would ever be okay again. Each time I found a glimmer of hope that things might get better in my life, it got obliterated. Finally carving a path of independence after college? Boom. Dad gets hit by a car. Finally have a way to pay off the physical therapy? Boom. We get robbed. Finally escape the robbery? Boom. A hit's put on your life. Easton comes up with a solid plan to appeal to Brown's goals—a plan that'll only work if the investigation stays quiet? Boom. PI enters the picture.

But worse than all of that combined? Was that look on my dad's face as he'd rolled away from me.

My lips quivered. "I broke my dad's heart."

As it turned out, being the person wielding the sword hurt worse than suffering its sharp blade.

Alex rubbed my back. "He broke yours first."

I looked at my phone again, but it was still empty of texts.

"That doesn't make it okay." I wiped my dripping nose. "Plus, as it turns out, I'm a judgmental hag."

Alex tried to cough back a laugh. "You are not."

"I am. I never listen to people's words. I just write them off the second I disagree with something they did. Like I'm so perfect."

"You're being too hard on yourself."

"You wouldn't be saying that if you knew what I did to him," I said.

Alex regarded me. "What did you do?"

I wiped a tear. “I said the worst thing a person can say to someone.”

He looked at me. “Which was?”

I let out a huge breath. “It’s so bad, I can’t even repeat it.” I still couldn’t believe I’d ever said it in the first place. “I feel like...like I used to be a good person. But when my dad and I fell out, I became this bitter, resentful version of myself.” I pushed down the pain. “I feel like I became a bad person.”

“You’re the furthest thing from a bad person, Zoey.”

That wasn’t true. Alex didn’t know that bubbling beneath the stress of taking care of Dad, resentment had planted its seeds and spread its roots over everything that was on my shoulders. A good daughter would never feel resentful, no matter how overwhelmed she might feel. She’d only feel grateful that he’d survived and gotten a second chance at life.

And that didn’t even include how critical I was of people now.

“I changed into someone I don’t like.” I bit my lip. “I just want to be the good person I was before everything happened.” A person I was proud of.

“You are a good person, Zoey. It’s only human to put your guard up after someone hurts you.”

I thought cutting people out of my life would hurt less than handing them the knife and waiting for their slash. But years of hardening my skin into an impenetrable shield had done nothing more than pump loneliness through my blood, poisoning my happiness.

“Why did you team up with him?” I asked. “I thought you were angry at him for what he’d done to us?”

Helping him learn to walk again was one thing, but becoming his BFF detective buddy was another.

“I told you, you’re like family to me, Zoey, and whoever did this needs to pay. That trumps anything I had against your dad.”

Alex put his arm over my shoulders, and when he pulled me in for a hug, an ominous question echoed through my ears. What if

Alex had organized the robbery as a way to get back at my dad for hurting me? And what if the real reason Alex had inserted himself was to stay close to the investigation? If he was the one funding the PI, maybe he could push the PI in certain directions? Away from himself?

Or at the very least, get a heads-up if any suspicion was about to fall onto his shoulders from the police.

You're being paranoid again. You know who did this. Holly, not Alex, who'd been nothing but kind and generous to us.

Yes, we owed him a lot of money, and he knew about Dad's stuff —like his collector's items. And, yes, someone else in his position might feel entitled to get some of that money before Dad's things were sold and we had nothing left to pay him. But still, this was Alex.

I trusted him, and even if I didn't, Alex didn't have a key to Dad's old place and couldn't root around for one without Dad noticing.

Besides, Alex was like family to me, too, and not just because he'd been there for me through hard times; we'd bonded when the mystery drama went down with him in high school.

"Can I ask you a question?" I said.

Alex waited.

"Is the reason you never told me what happened with you and your parents because you thought I'd judge your family?"

Alex picked at a crack in the wooden plank. "No," he said. "I didn't tell you because it's freaking embarrassing."

"I thought maybe you didn't feel close enough to tell me."

He'd only lived across the street from us for what, two years before it went down? At the time, him not telling me wasn't shocking, but I was curious why he'd never told me in the years that followed.

"If anything," Alex said, "what happened with my family made me feel even closer to you. Because I know what it feels like to have a parent choose someone over you."

I scrunched my face in confusion because, as far as I knew, his parents were still married. So, his dad didn't walk out on them the way my dad did. Did he?

"When I was seventeen," Alex started, obviously seeing the questions in my eyes, "I walked home from school early because I'd gotten hit with the stomach flu right before lunch. I walked in on my mom with another guy."

My jaw fell open.

"She begged me not to tell my father, said it would break up the family, but I couldn't live in a house of lies. My dad deserved to know what was going on, and I wasn't going to get sucked into her affair. Especially when I'd lost all respect for her. So, I told him, and we had this huge family blowout over it, and I lost my cool. Called her some names that I shouldn't have and tossed all her shit into suitcases and told her to get the hell out. Told her she was the biggest freaking hypocrite, going to church and holding everyone else to a high standard when, the whole time, she was banging some guy. My dad was furious with her, but he told me not to disrespect my mother like that. Said this was between him and his wife and I was to honor my mother. I told him I'd never honor her again after what she'd done."

Alex chipped a dry piece of wood off the plank and kept his eyes down.

"Things just escalated after that. I wasn't speaking to my mom, and she stopped speaking to me. Dad started drinking, and of course, he and my mom were fighting every night, but he still tucked away enough anger at me for falling out with her." Alex cleared his throat. "Shit just became toxic."

"I thought they were still married," I said.

"They are." Alex shook his head. "He decided to stick it out and work through it, but it was years before we started to talk like normal again."

"You guys are talking now?"

"A little," Alex said. "It's a work in progress, but we're finally trying, and it's headed in the right direction."

I nodded. "I'm sorry you went through that."

He shrugged. "Felt like she chose that other dude over us, you know? That's the part that hurt the worst, so when your dad left, I knew what it felt like."

That was why he felt so close to us. First because we'd taken him under our wing when he was evidently in a toxic home and then when we went through something similar.

We sat in silence with the wind breezing through my hair, understanding settling around us.

"You've always been there for me, Zoey, more than anyone in my life, and I'm not going to stop until I find who hurt you."

My stomach dropped.

Alex shifted his gaze down to my face. "You're like a sister to me, you know that?"

He leaned down and kissed my cheek.

And when he did, I heard the cracking of a tree branch from across the street.

24

It had been four days since Alex kissed my cheek. A kiss that Easton must've witnessed and misunderstood, given his abrupt drop-off in communication. I knew it probably looked romantic, but if Easton would talk to me, I could explain that Alex was like a sibling, not a love interest. I almost tried to explain that via text since he wasn't answering my calls, but I got paranoid that maybe I was full of myself or wrong that the kiss had anything to do with him blowing me off. And then I got angry that he wouldn't tell me *why* he cut me off.

He didn't completely ghost me. Doing so would make me think something bad had happened to him, and I guess he cared enough to not put me through that. But with each unanswered communication, I felt Easton drifting further away from me.

I stared at our string of texts.

Four days ago, when I wanted to tell him about the PI.

Me: I need to talk to you about something.

Easton: I can't today.

His abrupt change in tone alarmed me. And hurt. From *did your dad hurt you* to *I don't have time for you.*

Me: It's important.

No response.

Me: I'd rather not do this over text. Can we meet?

No response.

Me: Easton?

No response.

Me: There's something you need to be aware of.

No response.

Then, three days ago.

Me: Are you okay? Because you're starting to scare me.

Easton: I'm fine. Just busy.

Me: Can we talk?

No answer.

Me: Are you there?

No answer.

Two days ago.

Me: Are you safe? I'm getting worried.

Easton: I'm safe.

Me: Why are you avoiding me?

It took him ten minutes to answer.

Easton: I'm sorry, Zoey. I don't think it's a good idea for us to talk anymore.

My stomach caved in on itself in pain. I put my hand over it, pacing as I tried to call him.

But he didn't answer.

Me: Can you tell me why?

No answer.

The hurt from his rejection consumed me, but I didn't bother texting him yesterday; my pride took the steering wheel. If he wanted nothing to do with me, I wasn't going to chase him. I wished I could tell him Alex's kiss on the cheek meant nothing, but if he wouldn't listen to me, if he'd write me off this easily, then maybe he didn't care as much about me as I thought.

And if that was true...if he wanted nothing to do with me anymore, did that mean his oath to keep me alive was also broken?

A growing pit had implanted itself into my stomach walls, and now, its tentacles reached into my chest and pulled.

My silent suffering was disrupted by my cell phone's ring, which, pathetically, I hoped was Easton.

"Hello?"

"Zoey, it's Detective Hernandez. Catch you at a bad time?"

My heart deflated. And then it galloped as I wondered if the detective was about to tell me they'd locked up Brown. After all, it was late—Dad was already in bed—so why call at such an odd hour?

I began pacing. "No. Not at all. What's up?"

"I just wanted to keep you posted. I might have something on your dad's hit-and-run."

Adrenaline tingled my fingers. *This isn't about the robbery.*

"You do?"

"I *might*," he caveated. "Made some calls. Day of the accident, a witness got a partial plate number. At the time, it didn't yield anything, but I bounced it against traffic violations that've taken place since the accident and got several new hits."

"You did?"

"Doesn't mean any of them will be the car that hit your father, but I wanted to keep you posted. Might be a step forward."

I nodded even though he couldn't see me. "Thank you, Detective Hernandez. Seriously. Thank you."

Finally, some good news.

I opened my phone and was about to text Easton about it.

It's funny how for a split second, you can forget someone's rejection.

Whatever his reasons, Easton was pulling away from me just like Dad had when I was in college. And Easton wouldn't even explain why.

What is it about me that makes it so easy for people to walk away?

Maybe I repelled them. Everyone had flaws, but maybe mine

were so off-putting, people couldn't stand to be around me after a while.

No. I would not let my self-esteem spiral; I was stronger than this. I shouldn't even care about Easton's aloofness. It was stupid, this ache in my chest.

I set my phone on the counter with more force than necessary.

Maybe cleaning would help my mind from spinning about Easton. It was late; I'd have to be quiet.

I padded into the kitchen and unloaded the dishwasher, straightened the counters, and stared at the holy-mother-of-God-that-stinks trash. I'd forgotten to take it out after dinner, and now, the smell of decomposing food was going through some sort of biological transformation, infecting every ounce of air with its exponentially stinky smell.

I pulled the trash bag out of the bin—gagging in the process—and tied knots as tightly as possible, setting it by the back door. Hopefully, it would contain most of the smell until morning. I moved into the living room, straightening the pillows, picking up our water glasses and fallen food crumbs Dad had dropped.

But that damn trash. The smell had already doubled in the span of five minutes, and even though the outside can was only a few feet from the back door, I wasn't about to go outside at ten thirty at night. Not when there was a hit on my life and my protector had abandoned me.

Maybe even turned on me.

My traitorous lips quivered. I shut it down by scrubbing the bathroom counters, the sink, the back of the toilet.

By the time I went back into the main area, a nuclear bomb of a smell had blown up.

I gagged and noticed the bag had a small tear in it, and a teaspoon of liquid oozed out of the bottom.

Son of a...

I considered attempting to tape it, but the smell would just get worse with each passing hour. Dad was going to be stuck inside all day tomorrow, and I wasn't about to let him open windows when I wasn't here to protect him.

This was infuriating. I was sick and tired of overanalyzing something as benign as quickly throwing a trash bag outside.

I grabbed the bag and looked out the back window. The trash can was nestled against the exterior wall, resting on a concrete passage, riddled with two-inch-wide cracks and black engine oil stains—which you could sometimes still smell on particularly hot days. I studied the space for several beats, making sure there was no sign of activity.

Then, I unlatched the lock and swung the door open. It betrayed me by squeaking hella loud, and when I stepped outside, the city traffic seemed suspiciously quiet, too, like the universe was making my footsteps as loud as humanly possible.

It only took two seconds to make it to the exterior can and pry the lid open.

The attack came from the front.

It was so sudden; all I saw was a flash of dark lunge toward me and hit my chest. The asphalt drive slammed into my back, and the next thing I knew, screams echoed off the building's bricks. My screams, I realized. Bloodcurdling as my mind raced to process what was happening.

The person attacking me was small.

And...fuzzy?

"Zoey!" a deep voice bellowed from a distance.

When the assailant jumped off my chest, I shot up to my feet, my eyes straining in the dark to see my attacker.

And when it scuffled back up into the trash, I stopped screaming.

Because as it turned out, my murderer was a freaking raccoon.

"Zoey?"

The silhouette of a man appeared between me and the porch light. A man whose hands clenched my shoulders as he tilted his head down, staring at me, chest chugging like a train picking up steam.

"Easton?" I jerked my head back.

"I thought someone was fucking killing you!" He let go of my shoulders and shoved an angry hand through his hair.

"What are you doing here?"

"Do you always scream like that when you see a damn animal?"

"You just cut me off!"

"You're lucky I didn't pull my gun!"

"Stopped returning my texts."

"One shot, and I could've blown your head off!"

"Without even explaining why!" I hated that my voice was shaking.

"Over what? A fucking rat?" Easton extended his arm toward the trash can.

"It was a raccoon." I gestured toward the scene of the attack.

Glowering at my unwelcome correction, Easton put his hands on his hips and began to pace, a pair of dark shorts hanging beneath perfectly sculpted abs.

Exposed abs, because he had no shirt on.

Where would he even put a gun?

"Have you been here the whole night?"

"Zoey?" Dad shouted.

I held up a finger. "So help me, if you run off, I will go off into the dark and roam around, looking for you."

Easton stopped pacing and glared at me.

I glared right back.

I jogged inside and explained to my dad that a raccoon had scared me and I was cleaning up a garbage mess. I told him it was a big mess to buy myself some time to talk to Easton. Thankfully, Dad appeared to buy it, his eyelids already heavy again as I left his bedroom.

When I went back outside, I half-expected Easton would be gone, but I guess he believed me that I would go hunting for him, so he stood there. Looking as pissed as ever.

"You've been here all along, haven't you?" I accused. "Watching me."

"Protecting you."

"Blowing me off." I pointed at him.

"We can't be friends, Zoey. You know that."

My traitorous heart burst into flames. If that was how he felt, he could have acted like that from day one instead of inviting me in, dancing with me, making me feel something for him, just to yank it away.

Making me question his motives.

"When you refused to talk to me, I thought maybe you turned on me. Maybe you changed your mind and you were going to follow through with your order."

I'd never seen such an intense mixture of disgust and anger contort someone's face like this.

"I told you, I would never hurt you, Zoey," he snarled.

"You did hurt me. You shut me out, just like my dad when he left me."

Easton's eyes rounded slightly, and the line between his brows deepened.

I tried to storm past him, but he grabbed my arm. I looked at his hand and then up into his sapphire eyes, a foot from my own.

"I'm sorry," he whispered. "I never meant to abandon you." He searched my gaze for understanding. "I'm trying to do right by you, Zoey. Whatever's going on between us can't continue."

"If that's how you feel, why are you out here right now?"

"You know why."

"If you want nothing to do with me? Then, no, I don't understand why you'd watch me at all hours to ensure Brown doesn't send someone else for me."

Easton flexed the fingers of his free hand and then balled them into a fist. "You think just because I won't allow myself to be with you, I'm going to stand back and let you get killed?"

Allow himself.

Allow.

That one word redefined this whole argument. My anger washed from my veins, replaced with the longing I could see him fighting as his eyes stole glances at my lips.

"I'm not going to let anything happen to you," he growled.

"Alex didn't kiss my cheek in a romantic way," I said. "I'm like a sister to him. And he's like a brother to me."

Relief extinguished the jealousy in his eyes. But pain followed. Because it obviously didn't change his stance.

"We can't be together, Zoey."

Easton needed to understand that my feelings for him wasn't just some survival thing with the robbery. That even if Alex, or anyone, *had* kissed me romantically, it wouldn't change how I felt.

Standing inches from me, his eyes hardened as they roamed over my face, and he licked his lip with a greedy want he wouldn't allow himself to have.

"When this blows over—" I started.

"You deserve someone better. Someone uncomplicated. Who doesn't have colleagues who want you dead."

"What about what I want?"

He released my arm. "I won't let you throw away your life on me."

My eyes burned. "That's what this is about. You think you don't deserve me."

"You don't know the things I've done."

Goose bumps erupted on my arms.

No, I didn't. But I wanted to know every detail of his life's story.

"Have you killed before?" My heart caught in my throat, seemingly stilling until he finally answered.

"No." He looked from my left eye to my right. "But I would in a heartbeat, if anyone ever hurt you."

The air chilled over my skin. A good person would feel appalled by that confession. Disgusted maybe. But I felt the opposite.

"You're a good person." My chin quivered.

"I'm not." His gaze lowered to the ground. "I haven't been for a very long time."

"Easton..."

"You paint me as a good monster, but there is no such thing. After I'd lived on the streets for a few years, I could have tried to go mainstream. Get a normal job. I didn't."

"You were trying to survive the only way you knew how."

"Maybe I liked who I became. From victim to ruler. Powerless to powerful." He stared at my mouth, his breathing near panting, as if his willpower had begun to fray at the edges. "You deserve the prince, Zoey. Not the villain."

Was that how he saw Alex? A better fit for me?

I stared at Easton's mouth, remembering how his tongue had played so perfectly with mine.

"Want to know what I think?" I turned my body, so I faced him head-on, watching his eyes for any sign he'd stop me. I placed my hands on his bare chest. "I think you haven't felt unconditional love since you were a kid. I think you focused on money because money made you feel safe. And powerful. But deep down, those don't fulfill you. They never will. Not the way love will."

He hadn't let anyone in since he was a kid. And it scared the hell out of him.

In the distance, the "L" train cast its high-pitched metallic screech as it roared nearby, and a fire truck's wail pierced the air. The summer heat caused sweat to dampen my lower back and gloss the skin across Easton's chest, making his muscles look even more defined.

"You should avoid me." Easton's jaw shifted.

Should. I was making progress.

I stepped even closer.

The exterior auburn light draped over Easton's shirtless body like an artwork's spotlight, highlighting the curves of his chest and arms —ripped muscles clenching one another like bands of iron. His body was exquisite, perfection, save for scars that peppered his skin in various shades and shapes.

"I believe you," I whispered. "That you're protecting me. That you'd never hurt me."

"That doesn't mean I'm a safe person to be around, Zoey."

The threat of danger when I was near him—danger from his associates, his lifestyle—glided across my bones.

Maybe a smart person would heed his warnings and never talk to him again, but all the rational reasons I should never talk to him evaporated in his presence, and the only thing that existed was this persistent fear that he would walk away and I would never see him again.

That I would never get to learn every part of his life's story, like where all these scars came from. I wanted to inventory them, catalog them, uncover every piece of his puzzle.

Visible imperfections—a symbol to remind us no one is perfect.

I watched his eyes as I reached up and touched a six-inch jagged white line with my fingertip. "What's it from?"

He was silent at first, but in a low growl, he said, "Foster dad number two. Broken beer bottle."

He had three others just like it. I traced each one—on his right shoulder, along the base of his abs, and the one on his ribs.

"Same?" I whispered.

Easton gave a nod.

My eyes prickled, and I wondered how many times he'd been hurt before being removed from that home.

No wonder he'd assumed the cut on my palm was from someone hurting me.

I moved my hand to his bicep, where three crimson dots peppered his skin.

"And this?"

"Foster dad number one. Cigarettes."

I swallowed. I wouldn't cry in front of him.

"And this?" I traced what looked like a clean surgery scar.

"Foster dad number three. Box cutter."

I swallowed. There were probably thousands of excellent foster parents in this country. What were the odds that this one kid would get the exception multiple times? No wonder he was so desperate to save his brother from what must have felt like certain hell. And that didn't even include that new abuse his brother was about to endure...

I wouldn't go as far as saying I forgave Easton for choosing to rob the condo, but I would say I understood how he'd fallen into an unsavory lifestyle. And that despite his choices, something in my heart had opened up to him.

I respected his fierce protectiveness. To know that all this time, he'd been steps away from me. Keeping me safe, even when he thought I was asleep in my bed.

Tracing my hand up his iron torso, I locked eyes with him as I slowly reached up on tiptoe.

A war raged inside his eyes as I inched closer to his mouth. I could tell by the quickening of his breaths that he wanted to kiss me, but he grasped on to the thread of resistance.

Six inches separated us. Then four.

His warm breath bounced off my skin, my heart pumping against my ribs as the summer night seemed to vanish around me. The only thing that existed was him and me.

Two inches.

Easton's brows pulled together as his resolve unraveled.

One inch.

And then...I grazed my lips against his like a whisper, and the dark notes of his primal instincts unraveled. He groaned and crashed his lips against mine.

Hard.

Easton grabbed my waist and pushed my back up against the wall, just as he slipped his tongue into my mouth. I accepted it with a moan of my own, my hands roaming up his arms, his rounded shoulders.

I nibbled at his lip.

He growled and slipped his hand under the hem of my shirt, cupping my chest.

I wanted his hands all over me. I wanted him to pin me against this wall and rip my clothes off.

Like his mouth, his hand was rough, full of pent-up sexual frustration that clenched my skin until I moaned.

"When you stopped answering my texts, I thought maybe..." I panted, my lips still hostage to his. "I thought you didn't want me."

Easton pressed his waist against me, silently proving me wrong. "I've never wanted a woman more in my life."

He moved his hips back a couple of inches to give his hand room to slide down my stomach, beneath the fabric of my cotton shorts, lower and lower until...

I grabbed his shoulders as he kissed me and moved his hand with perfection. He knew my body. Knew the spots to caress. If this felt incredible, what would it feel like with him on top of me?

Easton slipped his tongue into my mouth again, and my muscles began to tense. Feeling the rise from his hand's magic.

"I've wanted you since the moment I first saw you." Easton licked my lower lip.

That was all it took. My release consumed me, and he pressed his mouth tighter against mine, like he wanted to eat my moan. Swallow it. Devour it. And only when my last tremble subsided did he pull his hand back and stop his kiss.

But it wasn't enough. I needed more. Wanted more. Had to have more.

He cupped my cheek, stroking my lower lip with this thumb.

"Good night, Zoey," he whispered.

He offered one last kiss—a soft, gentle movement—before staring at me for three more seconds and turning to walk away.

"Wait," I said.

I couldn't let him leave without telling him why I'd been so desperate to get ahold of him these last few days.

“A private investigator is looking into the heist.”

Easton said nothing. Didn’t move.

“I can’t imagine he’ll be able to find anything that cops won’t.” I fidgeted my footing. “But another person poking around, trying to solve it, isn’t going to help Brown calm down.”

Easton ran a hand along the back of his neck. “No.” He pursed his lips. “Especially since he’s planning something big. Last thing he’ll tolerate is someone poking around.”

25

A week had passed since that kiss with Easton outside my townhouse with no complications developing.

Nothing had come of the case yet. No updates from the PI or cops, and while that might have been bad news to Dad, it was good news to me. No update meant leads might be dwindling, and that was my best shot at staying alive, the best shot for Brown to give up and move on. The best shot at finally getting my life back.

I was about to start making dinner for Dad and Alex when a knock came. I looked through the peephole and seriously considered not answering, but her incessant knocking drew Dad's attention.

I opened the door and found my dad's ex staring back at me.

"Holly," I said with a clipped tone. "I didn't know you had our address."

"Holly?" Dad wheeled himself closer, the shock of her unprecedented pop-in written all over his face.

"What are you doing here?" I demanded.

I looked over her shoulder, across the street, where Easton stepped out into the early evening light, hands shoved into jean pockets, watching me, his hackles raised from the distress in my tone.

"May I come in?" Holly smiled.

I licked my bottom teeth when she walked past me, as though my nonanswer held no weight.

As soon as she came inside, she noticed the dining room table, which was blanketed with papers and photographs and notebooks filled with little scribbles. Alex and Dad had been at it every night this week, working the case.

Which I totally didn't understand. I mean, why hire a private investigator if you're just gonna turn into an amateur sleuth? What a waste of money. I tried to tell them that repeatedly, but they wouldn't listen.

"What's all this?" Holly arched one of her penciled-in eyebrows.

I still stood in the doorway with it wide open, and Easton stared at me with guarded eyes.

He mouthed something to me, which I was pretty sure was, *Are you okay?*

I nodded.

And reluctantly shut the door.

"We're trying to find the guys that hurt Zoey." Sitting at the table, Alex fidgeted with a pen, glancing from the awful woman to me, then back to her.

"It was such a shock to hear about the robbery," she claimed.

"Was it?" I crossed my arms over my chest.

I wanted to tell Holly off and tell her what a repulsive human being she was. But I tried to calm myself down because, hell, if I'd learned anything from Easton, it was that even if she had orchestrated the burglary, maybe she had a story of her own—a desperate reason for having done it.

But what I could not get past was how awful she treated my father.

Holly put her hand on her collarbone. "To think, I was just at the condo the week before. It could've been me in there!"

"Why were you in the condo the week before? It's Dad's condo, not yours."

"Zoey," Dad said. Outwardly, he appeared respectable—expecting me to act that way, too, I guess—but I could see from the way he clutched his wheelchair tightly that he didn't want her here either.

"No, it's fine." Holly smiled, but it didn't reach her eyes. "When I moved out, I had forgotten that I had stored some of my Manolo Blahniks in your father's closet."

Because Holly's closet—the master suite had his and her closets—was overflowing with her crap.

"Why did you stop by, Holly?" Dad cocked his head.

Seriously, why? I'd rather sit on a beehive than have this woman in our home. And clearly, she wasn't here out of the goodness of her heart; she'd never checked up on my father in the eight months since the accident.

"Just say whatever the hell it is you came to say and leave." I gestured for her to get on with it.

"Zoey." Dad flashed me a *be polite* look.

"No, it's okay." Holly held up her palm to him, as if she was going to be the bigger person here and deal with the unruly toddler in front of her. "I guess I'll get right to the point." She raised her blood-red lipstick-stained lips up in the corners.

Alex leaned forward in his seat, studying her.

"I'm waiting." I tossed my palm in the air.

"I'm afraid I left a necklace behind in the condo."

"You already texted Dad that," I said. "Pretty odd that you made sure you got every last thing you could get your hands on, and yet you left behind some expensive necklace."

She traced her collarbone with her perfectly manicured crimson nail. "I don't know what you're insinuating."

"I think you do."

Holly's lips pursed into a bitchy line. "As I told the police, I had no involvement in that awful burglary."

Yeah, right.

Even if Easton had taught me to consider why someone might have robbed Dad's place, she had some balls, coming here like this. Putting Dad's emotions through the wringer. For what? One of her bazillion pieces of jewelry?

"We don't have your necklace," I spat. "So, if that's why you came here, there's the door."

"Zoey," Dad said.

"What? She never even checked on you once after you were almost killed!"

Alex looked from Holly, to Dad, then back to me.

"I didn't come here to get into all this," Holly said. "I came here to ask if the police are letting you inside the condo. Because they won't let me inside and I want to know if the thieves got the necklace. If they didn't, I would really appreciate getting it back."

A chuckle of disbelief erupted from my throat.

"You have some nerve." I went to the front door and opened it, noting Easton was gone. "Get out."

"Zoey!" Dad chided.

"This is my townhouse, and you are officially trespassing. Leave, or I'll call the cops."

Holly glared at me.

Seriously? Getting her precious jewelry back was more important to her than asking a single question about how Dad was recovering? This was the first time she had seen him since the accident, and she didn't even seem to notice, let alone care, that he was in a wheelchair and had lost almost half his body weight. I bet the police wouldn't let her inside the condo because they suspected her and didn't want her fingerprints to get inside and destroy evidence that could be used against her.

Once she stormed out and I shut the door, I turned to my dad.

"You know she wasn't just coming here to ask about a necklace, right? She was trying to establish her alibi for having been in the apartment days before the heist. I bet her fingerprints are all over things that they shouldn't be."

I bet she cataloged everything of value in that apartment.

"Zoey, Holly's made a lot of mistakes, but—"

"Don't tell me she's not capable of it, Dad."

Before my dad could argue further, his cell phone rang.

"It's the PI." Dad's surprised eyes met Alex's.

I immediately tensed.

"Hello?" Dad answered it on speaker, probably so Alex could hear, too.

"Turn on the television right now. NBC. Evening news," the PI said.

Dad and Alex exchanged a look, and then Alex jumped up and dashed to the TV in the living room. Turning it on. Dad ended the call and rolled his wheelchair in front of it as Alex flipped around until he got to the top story on the evening news.

Curiosity lured my steps closer, and my eyes landed on the news anchor sporting a blonde bob with not a hair out of place.

"Two weeks ago, a robbery took place in the Loop. Police say three men broke into a home, where a young woman interrupted the robbery."

An electric volt shocked my limbs.

"Live with the latest is our own James McGey."

The shot cut to a young blond man. "That's right, Jules. It was here"—the reporter pointed toward Dad's old building—"that police say three armed men broke into a luxury condominium, and now, law enforcement is looking for tips that will lead to their arrests."

The shot cut over to a prerecorded message by Detective Hernandez. "We encourage anyone with information to call the police hotline. The number is on your screen."

Ten digits appeared in the lower part of the television.

Hernandez looked right into the camera. "We are offering a

twenty-thousand-dollar reward for any tip that leads to the arrests and subsequent prosecution of these suspects."

The electric shock ran through the rest of my body while my head took on the characteristics of a helium balloon.

Dad's worried eyes remained locked on me, as if he was waiting for me to say something.

Incapable of calming my erratic heartbeat, I managed to utter some syllables that sounded like words. "It's been two weeks. Why put it on the news now?"

"The PI said he put pressure on them."

"Police didn't need pressure, Dad. They have every motivation to solve cases without someone else pounding their fist on their desk."

"Two weeks. No arrests. Someone needed to turn up the heat on the investigation before it grows even colder, and now, anyone who has any information will be motivated to turn in that band of thieves."

Nausea swirled in my stomach.

My life depended on the investigation fizzling out, but now, it was front-page news with a bounty on Brown's head.

26

I pried open my heavy eyelids and looked at the digital numbers on my iPhone—1:53 AM. I sighed, wishing I'd slept a lot longer. After that news story last night, the only way I'd silenced my inner anxiety was by, once again, taking a sleeping pill. But evidently, it wasn't enough because here I was, already waking up with a bundle of nerves.

I rolled onto my left side and tucked my hands in a prayer position beneath my ear.

And froze.

I'm not alone.

The shadowed figure of a man sat in the corner chair, his head tilted at an awkward angle to his side.

Instantly, adrenaline became my caffeine, pumping energy through my heart and my muscles.

He isn't moving.

Is he asleep?

Could it be Easton? He'd gotten into my room before to return the ring. It had to be him, right?

But the shape didn't look like him. Easton was bigger. And the angle of the nose looked different.

Then again, it was dark, so maybe his size and angle did match Easton?

No. Easton wouldn't scare the shit out of me by breaking into my home. He'd call, or text, or even knock. He wouldn't just break into my bedroom like this and not wake me up.

Even if he'd seen the news story and assumed I'd be scared.

That news story...

Whoever this was must have come with a mission to hurt me.

Why did he sit down so long that he fell asleep? Was it because Dad had been staying up late these days, reading police reports, and the hired killer was quietly waiting for Dad to fall asleep, so he didn't get caught? Why wouldn't he have just killed Dad outright?

I wasn't sure, but thank God it meant Dad must still be alive.

For now. I needed to act before this intruder woke up.

I looked at my nightstand for any kind of a weapon. My cell phone, a lamp, and a book. The lamp was plugged into the wall behind the nightstand, which I'd have to move to unplug it. Too noisy. My only weapons were my cell phone and my library book.

A hardcover, at least.

I kept my eye on the guy as I slowly reached out and lifted the book. My shaking hand held it tightly, sweating as I watched the criminal.

The man made no move, no sound, his head still at that awkward angle over his shoulder.

I dangled my feet off the side of the bed and pushed up on my elbow an inch at a time until I was finally sitting. I grabbed my phone and looked at him again.

He still hasn't moved.

I scooted forward onto my tiptoes, then the balls of my feet, then they fully met the carpet, and I quietly began shifting my weight onto them.

The figure didn't flinch.

What if he's faking being asleep? Knowing I have to walk by him, no matter which route I take?

What is my best escape route? The window? No. The blinds would make too much noise. I need to get out the door, go into Dad's room, and call 911.

I wish I didn't have to get within strangling distance to get past him.

I took the first step on the ball of my foot, and I swore my lungs squished into a tiny knot in my ribs. I gripped the hardcover book tighter, its glossy cover cool against my now-sweating skin.

I took a second, then a third step, rounding the corner of my bed.

Now only four feet from him, I strained to get a closer look at the guy, but the only light came from the moon's glow via a cracked blind. Nothing to illuminate his face—*is it Brown?*—or his eyes to warn me if they were open or closed.

My mouth ran dry as I tiptoed through the three-foot gap between him and the bed. If he opened his eyes, I was standing right in front of him within punching distance. He could reach up and choke me before I could ever make a sound.

A creak on the floorboard beneath the carpet sounded like a cannon.

I froze, and his head moved.

He's awake.

As he tilted his chin up, I slammed the hardcover down onto his head as hard as I could. Corner first.

His head snapped back, and I ran for the door.

"Motherfuck!" he said, bringing his hand to his head.

I stilled. *I know that voice.*

"Easton?" I whispered.

He groaned and sat up straighter in the chair. Hand still clutching where I'd smashed him with my weapon of mass destruction.

"What the hell did you hit me with?" he asked.

I flipped on the light switch.

It is *Easton.*

"What the hell are you doing here?" I whisper-shouted.

"Why the hell did you hit me?"

"Why the hell are you in my bedroom? You can't keep breaking into my house in the middle of the night. What if my dad caught you breaking in and called the police?"

"I think you dented my skull." He pulled his hand away, which now had blood on it.

Who knew a book could do so much damage?

"Did you climb in through the window?"

"You're going to need to get me a towel or something, or I'll bleed all over your chair."

I hesitated. "Don't move," I demanded.

I tiptoed out into the hallway and risked opening Dad's door a crack.

He's still asleep. Thank the Lord.

I went into our tiny bathroom, retrieved hydrogen peroxide and a washcloth, but I couldn't find our Band-Aids. Not without rifling through the drawers at a decibel level of one thousand.

I returned to the bedroom and shut the door, so Dad wouldn't spot Easton if he woke up.

Easton still sat in the chair, one elbow on his knee, the other holding the side of his head that I had bashed. He wore black running shorts with a black T-shirt that stretched around his muscular arms. His hair looked tousled, like he'd been stressed and running his hands through it, but his eyes were still slightly puffy—still half-asleep.

"Here." I drizzled some hydrogen peroxide onto the washcloth and brought it up to the side of his head.

He hissed.

Luckily, it wasn't bleeding that bad.

"Why are you here?" My shock made my voice almost sound shrill.

"We need to talk."

"Normal people knock at the front door, between the hours of eight in the morning and nine at night. Or call. Or text."

"We have a problem." Easton's eyes darkened.

"No shit."

"You saw the news story?"

"Pretty sure half of Chicago saw the news story."

"This changes everything. Brown's not going to listen to reason now. He's not going to risk his freedom over one witness. He wants you dead now more than ever."

"Feeling's mutual."

I pulled the washcloth away, folded it in half, and put some more hydrogen peroxide on it. I pressed it against his head, and Easton looked up at me.

"Is that why you're here? To watch over me?" I dabbed his wound.

A sadness etched into Easton's eyes, and his tone strained with anguish, as if he knew I wouldn't like this. "Zoey, I need you to tell me exactly what you told the police. Word for word."

I pulled the washcloth away from his head and didn't like the look in his eyes.

"Why?"

"Because we need to get our story straight."

"Our *story*?"

He pursed his lips. "You withheld my name. You lied to the police about an ongoing investigation. You've aided a wanted felon. I need to know what you told them so that I can align my facts to what you said. So that I don't get you into trouble."

"Meaning what? You're going to talk to the police?"

"I won't contradict anything you've said."

"You're going to turn Brown in," I realized.

"No." Easton touched his head, pulled his fingers back to see if there was any blood on them. There wasn't. "You are. So he'll get locked up and you can collect the twenty thousand dollar reward."

"What?"

"First thing in the morning, you're going to tell them the news story sparked a memory. That you'd heard one guy call out *Easton*. You're going to play it off like you're not sure if it's a real name. They have no reason to doubt you, a witness who barely escaped with her life. They'll bring me in. I'll flip on Brown, and you'll collect the money. You can use it to get back on your feet."

"You'd go to prison." My jaw went slack in horror. "Possibly for good, if they add on kidnapping or other charges."

He said nothing.

My eyes watered. "I don't want you to go to prison."

"Keeping you safe is the only thing that matters."

"No." I shook my head.

"Tell me what you told them in the initial reports."

"No." I walked away.

"Zoey, if you don't turn me in, I will. Only difference is, no one will get the twenty grand."

"You said if you were in jail, he'd get to me faster."

"Not if I put him in jail, too. And not if I become a bigger problem to him."

"Why won't you just give me Brown's name? I'll come up with an explanation for knowing his name and turn him in."

"I'm not going to have you be the person who *names* Brown and gets him locked up."

"Me going to the cops will lead to his arrest anyway, so what's the difference?"

"A big one in his eyes. The person that actually *names* him is a hell of a lot different than moving the investigation in a direction that finds him. I'm not going to let you do that."

"If you snitch on him, he'll kill *you*."

"If he does, he'll face a murder charge."

"No! That's not an acceptable solution," I said. "And it wouldn't work anyway. He would probably just hire some minion to take me out."

"If you're the key witness against an organized crime ring, you could get protective custody."

"You don't know that for sure, and what about your brother? If you turn Brown in and yourself, there's no way your brother won't get tangled up and arrested. You've spent your whole life protecting him. Are you really okay with him being behind bars?"

"If I don't do something, my brother's going to cross the line and become an accomplice to murder. That's not a line he can uncross. Ever. Maybe some time away will be the pause he needs to find himself again. But even if it's not, I can't stand by and let him turn into a killer."

"I'm not turning you in."

"Zoey."

"They wouldn't give me the money anyway; I lied to the police."

"There's a reason they say *anyone* with information is eligible for that reward money. They start cherry-picking who they think *deserves* the reward money? The incentive system crumbles. Next time they need help, no one would come forward, and they know that. You'd be surprised what kind of people land rewards, Zoey. Trust me. They have to follow through; you'll get the reward money."

"Answer's still no."

Easton walked up to me. I could feel the heat coming off his body as he stared down at me for several long seconds before bringing his hand up to my face. He brushed the backs of his knuckles along my cheekbone.

"This isn't just about you. You have to keep your dad safe, too."

My lips trembled, and my eyes watered. I pressed my forehead against Easton's chest and allowed his arms to wrap around me. There had to be another way out of this nightmare. One that kept us all safe and didn't include Easton sitting behind bars when it might not even lead to anything good.

But there was no other option, was there? He was probably right, no matter how much I wanted him to be wrong.

My heart felt like it wept in my chest.

How come every time I find happiness, it gets taken away?

I shouldn't be focused on my feelings right now, though; I should focus on how badly this would hurt Easton and what I could do to make things right.

"If I go there," I whispered, "I'm going to tell them everything. Including how I lied to the police."

"Zoey—"

I looked up into his sapphire eyes. "I'm not going to rat you out for the stuff you did wrong without coming clean myself."

He tucked a hair behind my ear.

"You withheld my name to protect me." The corners of his mouth turned down. I wasn't sure if it was the lighting or if his eyes were growing glassy, but when he spoke again, his voice sounded almost hoarse. "No one has protected me for a very long time."

On top of everything he'd been through—abuse, homelessness, running from police—he'd never had anyone in his corner, watching out for him. Making him feel loved and safe. Easton was the big brother, but no one had done that for him.

What did it feel like to have your sanctuary ripped from you at such a young age? To know no one would ever fight for you again? I couldn't imagine how hollow and alone Easton must have felt all these years. Living in the outskirts of society like an unwanted stain.

He stroked my cheek with his thumb, his skin brushing against it so gently that it was like the whisper of a breeze before a storm. Charged with electricity.

"If ever there was a person worth sacrificing the rest of my life for, you are that person, Zoey."

I wiped a tear from my cheek. Easton had a way of making me feel like I was his everything, that I was all that mattered to him. His heart was bigger than most people's I'd ever met, and this whole thing didn't seem right.

"I don't want you to go to prison."

"It's where I belong."

But it didn't feel that way.

Yes, factually speaking, he was a criminal. And perhaps an honorable person wouldn't feel like her heart was collapsing into itself at the thought of him in an eight-foot cell. But he'd opened my damaged heart up like a flower's petals, and the thought of him rotting in a jail made me sick.

"In the morning, I'll escort you to the police station," Easton said. "I'll watch to make sure you get in the building safely, but I won't walk inside with you. Doing so would get you in a lot of trouble."

"And then?" If I went along with his crazy plan?

His tone dropped a painful octave. "It'll be the last time you'll ever see me."

My eyes stung like they'd been hit with a hostile cloud of tear gas.

Easton going to prison would mean him leaving me, too, that he was choosing to leave me, just like my dad had.

"No."

"Zoey."

"I won't do it."

"There's no other way."

"There has to be. We just have to think about it."

"You have to take care of your dad. You can't do that if you're dead."

I was full-on crying now. There had to be an out we weren't thinking of. "Maybe an anonymous tip."

Easton wiped a tear from my cheek. "With no proof, it'll just give them his name from someone who isn't a witness and can't corroborate he's the burglar. And if cops start watching him, Brown will move quicker to remove you from the equation."

"We'll think of something."

"Zoey"—Easton stepped even closer to me—"this is the best way to keep you and your dad alive, and deep down, you know it. Even if you won't admit it to yourself yet."

There had to be another way to get Brown locked up without risking my dad becoming collateral damage. How did it even come to this anyway? Feeling like I had to choose between Easton's life or Dad's?

Easton going to prison didn't feel fair. He'd lived in a form of prison since he was a child, and he deserved to feel free for the first time, not have life deteriorate even further, forced to live like a caged animal, confined to a concrete cell for decades. The little boy who'd once dreamed of becoming a baseball player deserved to feel some semblance of happiness.

To get his happily ever after.

But as I stood there, staring up into his eyes, I could see his resolve. He was going to do this whether I helped him or not. He was going to turn himself in and accept the consequences of his actions, and there was nothing I could do to stop it.

Maybe it was time to realize that I couldn't control Easton's choices—or anyone's for that matter. The only thing I could control was how I reacted to their actions and how I would deal with the fallout.

Clearly, I couldn't talk him out of taking responsibility for his crimes. But if he thought I was going to walk away from him, he had another thing coming.

"I'm not giving up on you, Easton."

Because that was what this was about, too, wasn't it? Him not being worthy of my affection.

I placed my hand on his chest. "So long as your heart is beating, I'll fight for you. Even if you do wind up in jail, this won't be the last time you see me."

Easton brushed his knuckles down my jaw, staring at me like I was the eighth wonder of the world.

I wish the kindness I've shown him weren't so foreign to him.

Easton's forehead crinkled as he brushed his fingers down my jaw, my neck, and then he traced my collarbone with his thumb. His touch was a match, igniting the flames of desire now pumping through my veins. I licked my lower lip, watching his pupils dilate with my movement.

Far too slowly for my greedy desire, he inched his face closer to mine. I parted my lips, anticipating the fullness of his, the taste of his tongue. And then, finally, he brushed his mouth against mine.

For this one glorious moment, I wanted to live in the present with just me and him, alone. Our bodies touching, our lips connecting. After this moment would be tears and heartbreak and sadness. But not right now.

Right now, I pulled his face harder against mine, willing our burning passion to create a rainbow from this hurricane.

Easton brought his hand to the back of my head and twisted his fingers in my hair, opening his mouth to invite my tongue inside. I accepted his invitation and slipped my tongue past his teeth, treasuring his moan. His left hand cupped my cheek as our kiss deepened, our mouths opening and closing in perfect rhythm.

A greedy need pulsed in my lower belly as our kiss gained momentum.

But a kiss was not going to satisfy me. Not tonight. Not if this was the last night I might ever have with Easton. The last night of his freedom.

I still couldn't process everything he'd said to me, especially now that my body was exclusively focused on only one thing—needing him to touch me everywhere.

I let my hands roam down his shoulders, down his arms, feeling the ridges of power beneath his skin. I traced my hand down his stomach.

His hands began to roam, too, and when he briefly pulled his mouth from mine, his eyes raked over my sleeping attire—a white T-shirt and a pair of pink lace panties.

Easton tugged at the hem of my shirt. I lifted up my arms as the fabric glided up my skin and over my head, a whisper of cooler air dancing across my chest, which instantly perked under the weight of Easton's eyes.

His gaze continued its journey down my stomach, my legs, and back up to my face.

"You're even more gorgeous than I imagined," he whispered.

Imagined. He's thought of me like this.

Everything warmed. I wished we were somewhere else, where we didn't have to worry about time or the need to be quiet.

I tugged his shirt up and marveled at how effortlessly he pulled it off over his head.

Damn, he was sexy. Skin wrapped tightly over lean bands of muscles. Arched shoulders cut into rounded biceps. Wide chest, narrowing to a flat, washboard stomach. And on top of it all, the scars that spoke of his strength. Survival.

I grazed my hands along his chest until he kissed me again, licking my tongue, opening his mouth wider and wider. But it wasn't enough. Nothing would ever be enough. I needed him now. All of him. Every inch of his body.

Easton walked me backward until my legs hit the bed, and then he gently lowered me down and climbed on top of me. His weight sank gloriously into my thighs as his lips trailed along my neck and down my chest.

Where he cupped me so hard, it made me gasp. I ran my hand through his hair, feeling the air dance across my freshly wet skin, where his tongue had licked me—across my chest, down my stomach, and then to my thighs. His fingers skimmed beneath my panties and slowly pulled them off.

Followed by his own shorts.

A while back, when I'd had a love life, I'd kept supplies. Supplies that, when I'd recently cleaned out my drawers, I'd discovered hadn't expired yet. I reached over, pulled one out, and handed it to him.

Easton kept his eyes locked on mine as he ripped open the foil packet and slowly shielded himself—agonizingly slow. How a man could make something like that seductive was beyond me, but I loved every second of it.

Every. Single. Second.

I worshipped the wanton look in his eyes—him knowing what he was about to do. The way he seemed to drag it out and make me wait for it, heightening the anticipation.

And then, finally, he leaned back down.

I arched my back as he trailed kisses up my stomach, my chest, up my neck, and back to my mouth. And then I felt him positioning himself between my thighs.

He pressed his hips down one inch at a time.

I grabbed the back of his shoulders as he filled me more and more. When his hips had completed their journey, he crushed his lips to mine, slipping his tongue past my teeth while his hand cupped my chest.

And then he began to move.

Oh my word. Never in my life had I felt something this...sensual. The weight of his body, his desire filling me, his greedy mouth roaming all over my skin. I wanted to explore every inch of him forever.

I wrapped my legs around his waist, linking my ankles together.

And, man, he knew how to move. He knew how to hit my pleasure points, varying his pressure as he moved his body, his lips wandering down my throat to my chest again. His every touch was magic, radiating sensual energy throughout my body, making me curl my toes in pleasure.

As our bodies worked against each other, I could tell he was trying to be quiet, but it was becoming exceedingly difficult for both of us. I began to move my hips with the rhythm of his, and the only way to silence my cries was to bite his shoulder.

Inciting a soft groan from his lips.

He sensed my rising wave and watched my eyes as he moved methodically until, finally, I tightened my legs around his waist and gripped his arms.

"Zoey," he growled.

And then he really began to move.

I had held my breath through my release, and just as I took my first pull of oxygen, Easton moaned into my neck. And stilled on top of me.

27

When my morning alarm played on my phone, something felt different. My pillow was warmer and firmer than usual, and some sort of rhythmic metronome beat beneath my ear. The soft sunlight that warmed my eyelids meant it was after sunrise, after five thirty in the morning.

I slowly stretched out my legs and arched my back, groaning as I tried to free myself from the grip of deep sleep.

"Morning," a gruff voice said.

My eyes snapped open. Easton was lying on my bed, the covers draped over his nude body, and I was lying next to him, my head on his chest. Last night came flooding back to me. The news story, Easton, our talk, our...lovemaking.

I bolted to a sitting position and shut off the alarm.

"Crap." I flung the covers off of me. "Get up!"

"What's the matter?" Easton asked.

I grabbed the T-shirt and panties I'd been wearing before Easton and his magnetism had stripped them from my body and began to throw them back on.

"My dad gets up soon," I whispered. "And you need to be gone before he does because if we go along with your plan…" And that was a big freaking *if*. I seriously needed at least three cups of coffee and a hella lot more consideration before I could commit. Not to mention, I had some things to say to him before it was too late. "There'd be no way to explain how or why the guy in the defendant's chair had been in my bed."

Lord, what had I turned into? A liar, rushing around to cover her tracks?

I'd own up to all of this. I would. I needed to come clean to the police about withholding information, but right now? Dad was seething with rage against the men who'd held me captive. Letting him see the very man he was hunting walk out of my bedroom? Was like pulling the pin of a grenade and waiting for it to explode.

"Get dressed!" I demanded.

I wished we'd woken up sooner and had time to talk because it felt like we had so much to say to each other, but right now, I had to focus on getting him out of my bedroom without being spotted.

Maybe he should go out the window. I opened up the blinds and peeked outside.

"Shit," I whispered.

Parked out front of our house was a police cruiser with an officer inside. A cruiser with a full view of my bedroom window. Seeing a man climb out of it? That'd be pretty damn suspicious. Inviting him to come investigate.

"Why is there a cop here?"

Of course there was a cop here. Was it here when I'd *wanted* one to keep me and my dad safe? When I'd stayed in like a hermit, convinced someone was outside, waiting to get me? Oh no. *Let's wait until your captor-slash-lover is trying to sneak out of your bedroom. Then, we'll put a cop outside.*

I seriously deserved this level of karma, but I was too flustered to soak up the irony.

Easton risked a glance outside the window. "Probably doing extra patrols now that the news story broke."

I let out a huge sigh of stress. "Maybe we should just go outside together," I said. "If the whole goal is to identify you as the burglar, what difference does it make?"

"It's the difference of you turning from a witness to an accomplice."

"I *am* an accomplice," I said. "I withheld your name from the police."

"We both know that's not how this is going to look," Easton said. "If you come clean about withholding my name, you do it the right way. In an interview with the detective. Not getting caught red-handed, helping a burglar sneak out of your house."

He was right. That would look a thousand times worse in the police's eyes, and it was already pretty bad. I was ashamed of myself for being the type of person that was dodging police right now.

"Besides, the point is to protect you from Brown."

I wanted to argue, but we had no time.

"I'll take you out the back door." I'd have to figure out the rest later. "Come on. We need to be quiet."

Easton threw his clothes on, and I opened my bedroom door, looking across the hall. Thankfully, Dad's bedroom door was still closed.

I put my finger over my lips and motioned for Easton to follow me. Quietly. We walked down the hallway, and just as I entered the common area—the kitchen to my right, dining room table in front, living room to my left—I saw movement.

Too late to do anything about it.

Dad was wheeling himself from the living room toward the kitchen when he stopped abruptly, eyes narrowing as the grenade's pin came out.

Boom. We're dead.

Forget Brown. I'll be murdered by my own father, right after he slaughters Easton.

"Zoey?" Dad's lips narrowed as he glared at Easton. "Who's this?"

No worries, Dad. He's just the guy you've been hunting day and night. He broke into our house last night and made sweet, sweet love to me.

"Uh..." I risked a glance at Easton, who silently implored me to not answer the question. "This is my friend."

And then, because this wasn't awkward enough, Alex stepped out of the living room. As he looked from me to Easton, his eyes narrowed like a protective older brother who'd caught a man banging his little sister.

I hadn't had sex in forever. Of course the first time I do, I have not one, but *two* witnesses to catch me. The worst two.

"Alex"—my voice quivered slightly—"what are you doing here so early?"

Very early. Before Dad even normally got up in the morning.

Alex didn't answer me. He was too busy condemning Easton with his eyes.

Something Easton obviously didn't appreciate, what with the way he was now glaring at Alex and flexing his fingers at his sides.

I needed to get Easton out. Now.

"He was just leaving," I explained and tried to take a step.

But Dad didn't move out of our way.

Just past his shoulder, on the dining room table, was a stack of police reports and photographs of my injuries and whatever the hell else he and Alex had accumulated in their investigation.

I willed Easton's eyes to not look over there because, if he did, I wasn't sure how he'd react.

I tried to pretend like my breathing hadn't become erratic. I tried to look as innocent as possible because while the truth would come out eventually, now was not the time.

"Detective Hernandez called." Dad's gaze hardened. "He wants us to come down to the station."

My mouth ran dry. "Right now?"

"Right now. Was just about to wake you up."

Holy handbags, that would have been a thousand times more

awkward than this already is. If awkward were a bomb, that would be the nuclear one.

"Why does he want us to come down to the station?" I asked.

Dad glowered at Easton, then looked back at me. "Because he has somebody in custody."

Instantly, I felt dizzy. But I couldn't faint; I couldn't leave the boys unsupervised.

Did the cops lock up Brown? Orange?

"And he wants me to do a lineup?" I clarified.

"He didn't say, but I can only assume so," Dad said.

"Why'd he call you and not me?"

No answer.

Either way, that news story clearly worked. It only took a few hours before $20,000 had motivated someone to turn one of the burglars in.

"Is that why Alex is here?"

"I invited him to come along." Right. Co–armchair detective and all. "Say good-bye to your *friend* and get dressed," Dad demanded. "You're coming with us."

I didn't appreciate the authoritative animosity in his tone—I was a grown woman, and he was staying at my house, not the other way around—but I wasn't about to pick a fight with him right now.

Dad wheeled out of the way, so I could walk Easton to the front door. Which felt like a terrible idea with that cop parked outside, but there was no way to explain taking him to the back door at this point.

"Remember what we discussed," Easton whispered. He gave me a severe gaze, and then he slipped outside and walked down the sidewalk with his back to the police cruiser.

While I got ready to face Hernandez and whoever he had in custody.

28

It took forty-five minutes to get to the police station. Twenty minutes getting ready, calling off work, and waiting for the wheelchair-accessible van to show up, so my dad could come. Another twenty-five minutes battling rush-hour traffic.

When the van pulled into the parking lot of the police station, I forced myself to focus on the bigger priority—the robbery investigation and the possibility that whoever they had in custody might not be the only one sleeping in a jail cell tonight.

I might be as well, for having lied to the police in an active investigation. No matter what Easton said, I had to take accountability for my mistakes.

I double-checked that my license and credit card hadn't fallen out during the ride—I'd shoved them in my back pocket because I wanted to travel light in case I got arrested. I opened the van door, helped roll Dad up the concrete walkway, and as I turned him around to pull the back wheels of his chair over the slight lip of the doorjamb, a chill crawled up my ribs.

I looked around, trying to identify the source of my internal red flag going up.

This police station—Chicago had several peppered in and around the city—was on the west side, blocks away from the skyscrapers. Here, buildings stood only a few stories tall, and the station sat at an intersection managed with a traffic light. A parking lot wrapped around the building on all sides, and police cruisers lined up like a white-and-blue barricade along the left side of the building while out front, a row of identical buildings nestled across the street with a café a half-block down—likely the source of the coffee smell that floated through the sunny air. A gray pigeon sat on top of a steel pole, where an American flag fluttered against the morning's breeze. Aside from a Boston cream donut twenty feet away that had fallen victim to a tire, nothing seemed out of place.

"Zoey?" Dad's tone became worried.

I didn't realize I had frozen.

"Sorry." I jerked the wheelchair backward while Alex held the door open. And as I glided the wheels over the lip, my eyesight's radar finally hit its target.

Across the street—tucked between two buildings—a man leaned against the exterior wall with his shoulder, his right hand in his jean pocket, his left drawing a cigarette from his mouth.

He's staring right at me.

The guy threw his cigarette to the ground and watched me as he stubbed it out, then disappeared behind the building.

If he wanted to watch me, he wouldn't have walked away, though.

Right?

Alex must have misconstrued my delay as a lack of upper body strength because his hands replaced mine, pulling the wheelchair backward into the lobby.

Where Hernandez was already waiting for us. Wearing black trousers and a gray button-down, his badge hanging from his belt, he said his hellos, introducing himself to Alex, and motioned for us to follow him down a hallway, up an elevator, down another hallway, and into some sort of conference room.

He gestured for us to sit down.

Alex rolled Dad's legs under the table and let me have the chair directly across from Hernandez.

As the detective leaned back in his seat and pressed his fingers into a steeple, I wondered if he could smell my guilt like a canine could sniff drugs—if it would overpower the scent of stale coffee and bagels. I wondered if he had already pieced everything together and had called me in here to arrest me.

He gave nothing away. Not with his sapphire eyes, not in the way he carried his tall, muscular frame that stretched his wrinkle-free shirt.

"As I explained to Zoey," Hernandez started, "day of the accident, we obtained a partial license plate from the vehicle that struck you, Mr. Williams. And while it didn't help us find the vehicle at the time, we bounced that partial against traffic violations that took place *after* the accident."

I blinked. "This is about my dad's hit-and-run?"

Hernandez looked from me to Dad. "That's why I called your father."

"After that news conference last night, I assumed this was about the robbery," I said.

"So did I," Dad agreed, annoyance ringing through his words.

"I should've been clear when I called. I know this has been a long road, Mr. Williams, looking for justice. I thought you'd want to come in and see the person responsible."

"You have him?" I asked.

"Yes."

"Here?"

"Yes."

"And you're sure he's the one that hit my dad?"

Hernandez rubbed his jaw. "After bringing him in for questioning, the guy confessed."

Finally, something was going right for the first time in forever! For months, I had dreamed of the day that I would walk into this police station and look at the person who had done this to my dad. And finally have justice tip in our favor.

"Can we see him?"

"It would be helpful if Mr. Williams could identify him," Hernandez said.

"I don't really remember what the driver looks like," Dad reminded him. Dad didn't remember much about the accident, courtesy of his concussion.

"It might be a long shot. But sometimes, a witness's memories can get triggered when they see the perpetrator in a lineup. Witness identification would help, just in case he withdraws his confession."

Hernandez spent the next couple of minutes walking my dad through the process and then led us into another room with a large two-way glass. On the other side of it, six men stood beneath the numbers one through six. All of them looked similar. Thin, short, jet-black hair. And young.

Younger than I expected.

Dad was able to see through the glass despite his lower height in the wheelchair. His eyes swept through the men, one by one, and then they landed on man number five. Dad gripped the armrests of his wheelchair tightly.

"Take your time." Hernandez stood next to my father while Alex and I stood in the corner of the room.

"Number five," Dad said. "I can't be sure. But I think it's number five."

Hernandez's lips curled up on one side.

That's the guy that confessed.

I stepped closer to the glass and studied the suspect's chubby cheeks and round, childlike eyes.

This whole time, I had no idea what the person looked like who had destroyed my father's life. I didn't know what I expected, but as I stared at the face of the boogeyman that had haunted our lives, he looked nothing like the evil monster I imagined him to be.

"He's just a kid," I said in disbelief.

He couldn't be more than sixteen.

"Texting and driving," Hernandez said. "That's why he didn't slow down. He wasn't paying attention, and once he realized he hit somebody, he panicked."

That was all this was? I never truly believed that what happened to my dad was some diabolical murder for hire or anything, but somehow, this explanation was incredibly empty. Unsatisfying even.

When someone has taken almost everything from you, I guess you expect the explanation behind it to match the size of its damage.

But he was just a kid. A human being who made a horrendous split-second error in judgment.

"What's going to happen to him?" I asked.

"He'll be tried as an adult. Face a jury on multiple felony counts."

"So, he'll go to prison."

"Most likely," Hernandez said.

Why did I feel so hollow inside? This was everything I ever wanted. Finding the person that hurt my dad and putting him behind bars. Here the guy was, wrapped up in a red bow, in the express lane for justice.

I didn't expect to feel this...emptiness, where I thought only celebration would be.

I thought this moment would feel different, but when we left here, nothing would change for my dad. He'd still be in his wheelchair, fighting to regain his mobility, fighting to reclaim his financial independence. Arresting this guy didn't magically give my dad his old life back.

I paused to examine the kid for another moment. "Does intention get taken into account during sentencing?"

Hernandez regarded me. "What do you mean?"

I shrugged. "I don't know. He's just a kid who panicked."

"He almost killed a man and never turned himself in."

True. But who was I to judge him? Look at my behavior. Over the past couple of weeks, I had lied to my dad and Alex. I committed a crime by withholding information from the police, and I protected a wanted criminal. I had my reasons, but if I were friends with someone like me during all this? I would have left her.

Before, I would've judged her actions and cast her out of my life.

But today? After everything that had transpired over the past couple of weeks? Maybe I would have stopped and listened to her before shutting her out. Because, yes, some people were probably inherently bad. Some people made inherently bad decisions with a callous disregard to the trauma they caused others. Like Brown, who'd gladly murder an innocent person to save his own ass. But he was the exception. The rest of us? We were flawed humans.

Maybe that was why I met Easton—to pull me out of my judgmental funk and force me to see people past their missteps.

"You guys are free to go." Hernandez gestured toward the door.

But I couldn't go.

I needed to tell him everything. And come clean about all the mistakes I had made in the process. I didn't want Easton to go to prison, but that was out of my hands. We had all made our mistakes, and we all had to answer for them, just like this kid had to answer for his.

I followed Alex and Dad down the hallway, down the elevator, and to the lobby.

"You guys go ahead." I opened the door for them. "I'm gonna stay and talk to Detective Hernandez."

"About the burglary?" A crease appeared between Dad's eyebrows.

I nodded. "I feel like we should talk after that news story."

"I can stay." Dad's expression softened.

"Me, too," Alex said.

"No," I said. "That's not necessary. I won't be too much longer."

Unless I wind up in handcuffs.

Dad pressed his lips together. "You'll come right home when you're done?"

"Right home," I assured.

"You'll get a taxi, not walk alone?"

"No walking."

"Good. Because I have some questions about your *friend*."

Alex flashed me a look that said, *So do I.*

With one last glance, Alex wheeled Dad down the ramp and into the waiting van. I watched to make sure he got loaded safely, and then when the van drove away, I walked back into the lobby and asked to see Detective Hernandez again.

It didn't take him long to greet me.

"Zoey?" He furrowed his brows. "Everything okay?"

"Can we talk?"

Hernandez looked at his watch. "Is it quick?"

I shook my head.

"I'm running late to a few meetings."

We were supposed to be here twenty minutes earlier, but traffic. Mobility van waiting.

"Why don't we schedule something for tomorrow?"

"It can't wait until tomorrow."

Hernandez hesitated, and then he pulled out his phone, glancing at the screen. "How about six o'clock?"

"Can you do it any sooner?"

He studied me, must've measured the severity of my gaze.

"I can line up another officer if you—"

"No." I picked at my nail. "I prefer to talk to you."

"Is it an emergency? Because I can—"

"No," I assured. It wasn't, was it? It was urgent. But not an emergency. "I just...what's the soonest you can meet?"

Hernandez stared at me, then frowned at his phone. "I can move some things around and make four o'clock work. Can you come back then?"

It wasn't even seven thirty in the morning. I guess that would give me a few hours to talk things out with Easton and say our goodbyes.

"Four o'clock," I agreed.

I turned to walk out the door.

"Wait." Hernandez's tone had a sense of worried urgency to it.

I pivoted and looked at him.

He sighed. And motioned for me to follow him.

29

The interrogation room was dark, save for one light centered above a rectangle table, with two metal chairs on opposing sides. The mossy-green walls showcased no artwork—only two mirrors on each side of the room, undoubtedly two-way glass, and a door occupying the third wall. The space, which smelled like stale coffee, was eerily quiet, tucked in the back of the hallway so the person left here would be alone with their thoughts.

I rubbed my hands along the outsides of my arms, willing the goose bumps to die down as Hernandez stared at me with those knowing eyes, like he could see past all my lies.

"I'd like to make a deal." I folded my hands, trying to look confident.

He leaned back. Held a pen between his fingers. "Have you done something wrong?"

"Yes. But the deal isn't for me. I have some important information about the burglary that can lead to the identities of the burglars you're looking for. Before we get started, I need some assurances."

Hernandez kept his eyes guarded. "Assurances." He folded his hands together and placed them on the table, his eyes revealing nothing about his mood. "What kind of assurances?"

I swallowed and tried to muster the confidence of someone capable of striking a deal.

"I know the name of one of the burglars."

Hernandez held perfectly still for several seconds, as if he knew my heartbeat needed time to come back down. "How do you know the name of one of the burglars?"

"I'll explain all of that, but before I say anything, I need a pledge that he won't be charged."

Hernandez kept his face completely neutral. "You want one of the burglars to get immunity?"

I nodded.

Hernandez leaned back in his chair and steepled his fingers together, staring at me for several seconds. "You know the name of one of the people that robbed your father's condo. Held you hostage. And you want to protect that person," he clarified.

I nodded.

"Why?"

"Like I said, I'll get into that, but first..."

"*When* did you uncover the guy's name?" Hernandez asked sharply.

"I'll explain all of that, but I need to know—"

"Zoey, were you involved in the burglary?"

I blanched. "What? No."

"Then, do you care to explain to me why you withheld the name of a wanted criminal who supposedly held you hostage?"

Shit.

"He saved my life. If I give you his name without assurances, he'll go to jail, probably forever, for doing the right thing. I can't sentence him to that."

"That's not how this works. This is an active criminal investigation, and you're required to be transparent about the facts of the case."

I couldn't rat on Easton, not without protecting him. No matter what Easton said, it didn't feel right. I needed to take responsibility for my mistakes, but I couldn't look at myself in the mirror if I took down the one person who'd saved my life in the process.

"Zoey..." Hernandez cleared his throat. I sensed him swallowing down his frustration as he kept his voice low and steady. "If you have knowledge of someone who has committed a crime and withhold that information with intent to help that person avoid arrest or punishment, you can be charged with accessory after the fact. Meaning you could face charges related to that robbery, maybe even the other string of robberies that took place after, if they prove they're connected. You have to tell me his name."

I opened my mouth, but words failed me. I should've thought through this better. We had come here in such a rush, and it just felt like everything was spiraling out of control.

"Did you lie to me, Zoey?" Hernandez pressed his fingers together tighter. "When I asked you if you had any other information that could help with the robbery, were you withholding something?"

I bit my lip. And nodded.

"Lying to a police officer during an ongoing investigation is a crime. You could be charged with obstruction of justice."

"I'm sorry."

Hernandez ran a hand through his hair. "Why did you protect him?"

"He saved my life. I told you everything I knew about the other two men, I swear. I just didn't tell you the name and description of the man who saved my life. He risked his own to do it, and I guess I was scared that in the eyes of the law, he'd be treated equal to the other two. It didn't seem fair."

"That wasn't your place to sort out. I specifically asked you if there was anything else you knew."

"I know."

"And you lied."

"I'm sorry. But I want to state for the record that he risked his own life to save mine."

Hernandez frowned.

"Look, my goal of coming here today was to give you his name. So, I'm not intending to help him avoid arrest. I just don't think he should be treated like the other two burglars who beat me and intended to kill me."

"What's his name?"

How could something so right feel so wrong? No matter what Easton said, this felt like betraying him.

"Easton," I said. "I just know his first name is Easton."

I guess it would have been too suspicious for Easton to tell me his last name.

Hernandez scrutinized me. "You had nothing to do with the robbery?"

"I would never do that. And I would never put myself in a position where I might get killed. My dad needs me."

I couldn't tell if Hernandez believed me or not, but all the fight inside of me evaporated.

In hindsight, this whole time, I'd been trying to control the outcome of everything. Control the outcome for Easton, for me, for Dad. But I had let things spin out of control, and now, whatever happened was completely out of my hands.

"Are you going to arrest me?" I deserved it.

Hernandez scrubbed his hands over his face and let out a huge breath. When he looked at me, his chest inflated, and I got the sense that he believed me.

"Do you know how many man hours we've spent on this case?"

I hadn't thought about that, all that time and money.

"I wasn't sure only a first name would help." I lowered my head and stared at my hands. "But I was probably just trying to rationalize away my bad decision."

Hernandez rubbed his fingers along his upper lip, tugged his ear, and then straightened his chair.

"Are you going to arrest me?"

He cleared his throat, looking as though part of him really *wanted* to put me in cuffs. Maybe all of him did, actually. "Unfortunately, it's not uncommon for victims to be less than forthcoming after suffering a traumatic ordeal. Arresting victims anytime they aren't entirely forthcoming would widely reduce the rate at which they report. And that rate is already damn low."

I twisted my hands together.

"Don't pull that crap again, Zoey," Hernandez said. "This Easton guy might've saved your life, but he's a dangerous criminal."

"He's the only person that can give the names of the other burglars."

Based on the hardening of his eyes, this seriously seemed to annoy Hernandez.

"I can't speak to what the prosecution might be willing to do for him."

I bounced my leg under the table, feeling like I'd failed Easton. I'd screwed this up, giving up his name without a written agreement stating that he wouldn't be charged. And while I trusted Hernandez would try, there was no assurance he'd protect Easton at all.

"You know any other details that could lead me to the names of the other burglars?"

"One of them is Easton's brother." I hoped Easton was okay that I'd said that.

A pause.

"Anything else?"

I shook my head, feeling like a child in a principal's office, who'd been caught cheating.

Hernandez stared at me. "He's dangerous, Zoey."

My cheeks warmed.

The detective stood up so slowly, he almost made a show of it. "You're free to leave."

I blinked. "I am?"

"Like I said, don't pull that crap again."

I wanted to ask him how long it would be before he might have Easton in cuffs. But I seriously didn't want to piss him off further.

What I wanted to do was talk to Easton one last time. Because I had some things to say to him that I might never get the chance to again. Not without being able to hug him after, at least. From this day forward, we might be separated by bars or plexiglass.

I needed to find him.

Fast.

30

Hernandez escorted me through the lobby and out the front door of the police station. It was there, as Hernandez was about to walk away, that ice prickled the back of my neck and flashed down my spine. I looked across the street, searching for the source of my sudden unease, and spotted a man.

That's the same guy who was staring at me earlier.

His grim gaze fastened onto me, and then he shook his head. Like I'd just made a lethal mistake.

"That guy"—I pointed—"I saw him out here earlier."

But the guy was crazy fast; he dipped behind the building before Hernandez's eyes drifted across the street.

"Where?" Hernandez asked.

"He was just there." I pointed again. "I saw him before I came into the police station, and I just saw him again. I think he's following me."

"Did you recognize him?"

"No. But he was staring right at me with this...*look*. Like I just made a mistake, coming to the police station."

Hernandez squinted, scanning across the street for any indication of a person. Then, he hollered, "Deputy."

A thin police officer with a mustache diverted his original path to the front door to join us.

"I need you to take Ms. Williams home."

"Sure." The officer's tone was like a student wanting approval from a teacher.

"I'll be right back," Hernandez said.

I followed the deputy as he led me to his car, but my eyes stayed fixed on Hernandez as he jogged across the street and looked around.

I sat down in the passenger seat of the cruiser, and as the police officer started the engine, Hernandez jogged back over and leaned into the now-open window.

"Whoever it was is gone."

"What if he follows me home?"

Hernandez shifted his gaze to the officer. "Keep your eyes open. If you see anything suspicious, bring her back here."

The officer nodded.

With nerves twisting my stomach into knots, I watched Hernandez grow smaller as the cruiser pulled away. With no further sign of the mysterious guy.

I looked at the cruiser's dashboard with its computer screen and keyboard positioned directly below it. Right now, the screen illuminated a digital map, but with the click of a button, it would undoubtedly have access to names and addresses and all sorts of information. So much information and so much power, harnessed in this mobile vehicle, and yet the people that you really wanted to find felt like they could hide from that screen.

"Do you think it's safe for me to go home?" I asked the officer.

"If I know Hernandez, he'll send officers to perform a more thorough sweep. If someone's out there, they'll find him."

I wished I shared the same confidence that the officer did, but any fragment of hope that the bad guys were not actively hunting me just went up in flames. It felt like it was just a matter of time before they unearthed my identity, my location, or both.

In the race between the bad guys and the good guys, I could feel the hourglass's sand draining faster and faster to the bottom with no clarity on who would win.

I had no clue how any of this would unfold, and worse, it felt like there was nothing more I could do to influence the outcome. I had laid all the cards on the table for the police, and now, all I could do was wait.

It was overwhelming. And beneath my nervousness and my fear was guilt. Guilt for lying to Dad about Easton. Guilt for all the things that came before that—most notably, the massive fight Dad and I had gotten into the day of the accident.

The guilt over what I'd said to him had been lurking in the shadows of my heart ever since, veiled behind judgment and criticism of others, infecting my body like a cancerous growth. And now, my time to apologize might be running out.

Time was running out even faster to talk to Easton. Any second, he'd get arrested and locked in some jail cell, possibly forever.

I worried he might give up mentally—what hope did he have, facing decades in prison?—and without his physical freedom, his mind and heart were all he'd have in his hollow concrete cell. In the decades he'd spend there, he might sink deeper into the abyss of self-hatred. Easton saw himself as a villain, doing nothing but bad things in this world. A cancer to our society that I, and everyone, would be better off without. And without hope of ever breaking free physically, without seeing anything good about himself, he might eventually lose the desire to keep himself safe from other violent prisoners. Because he'd think he deserved whatever came to him.

But he needed to know that he'd done a tremendous amount of good in my life, that he was my prince, rescuing me from my own demons. And that he wasn't a monster; he was a beautiful human being.

And he needed to hear it now; otherwise, he might think I was just trying to cheer him up when the undercurrent of depression dragged him down in prison. This would be the last time I could get through to him.

As the police officer silently pulled onto another road, methodically scanning the side and rearview mirrors for any sign of trouble, I pulled out my cell phone and texted Easton.

Me: Where are you?

His response was immediate. Thank goodness. That meant he probably wasn't in custody yet.

Easton: At home. Making it easy for the cops to find me and arrest me. The sooner the cops get me, the sooner I can give them Brown's name, and the sooner he's behind bars. Are you okay?

Me: No. I need to talk to you before that happens. And now, I'm not even sure you sacrificing yourself will help to protect me.

Easton: What are you talking about?

Me: There was this creepy guy staring at me. I can only assume he's part of Brown's crew, and if I'm right, he probably thinks I just gave some important information to the cops.

Easton: Where was he? What did he look like?

Me: He was standing across the street from the police station.

Easton: Fuck. Brown must've assigned a detail to watch the station. Are you still there?

Me: No. A police officer is escorting me home, making sure we're not being followed.

Easton: When you get there, lock all the doors and windows. I'm going to head to the station and look for him.

What?

Me: No! He could be dangerous. And the police are canvassing that area right now, looking for the guy. If you go there, they'll arrest you right now, and I need to talk to you before that happens. Can we meet?

Easton didn't text back for five seconds.

Easton: Lock the doors. Stay inside. Do NOT open the door until I'm on the other side of it. I'm coming right over.

31

The officer walked me to the door and waited to leave until I'd gone inside and locked up.

I double-checked all the window and door locks and drew the blinds closed. Just to be safe.

I'm sure that guy didn't follow me here.

The officer had kept his guard up. Looked around. Hernandez had probably found him already, had him at the station.

Still, I rubbed my arms, praying these walls wouldn't become my and Dad's tomb.

"We need to talk." Dad appeared out of his bedroom.

"Dad, I know you have a lot of questions about the guy staying over—"

"I did." Dad wheeled himself into the living room and folded his pale, bony hands onto his lap. "I was going to give you the third degree over that guy, but then I reminded myself about something."

Dad's expression was firm—tight lips, resolute eyes.

"It's none of my business. You're a young woman, Zoey, in the prime of your life. And you shouldn't have to worry about your dad intruding on your personal business."

Why did this feel like something deeper than letting me off the hook with an explanation about Easton? It was in his eyes, I thought, in the way Dad stared at me, alerting me that he was about to say something important.

"I called your mother." Dad brushed nonexistent wrinkles out of his pants. "She's going to make up the couch for me."

"What? Why?" And why now?

"I should never have stayed as long as I did. It was selfish of me."

"It's not selfish. You were in a horrible accident and need help."

"But I should never have put you in the position of being the person to help me. Candidly, a lot of these decisions were made when I was still in extensive pain. Maybe if I hadn't been, I wouldn't have burdened you with this. But if I'm being honest with myself, I think the reason I let you take me in was because I wanted to reconcile with you. All that time we'd spent apart had broken me, and the opportunity to be with you? Every day? Was something I didn't have the strength to turn down."

My eyes stung so badly; Dad's face blurred with my tears.

"But you and Mom are divorced. She shouldn't—"

"We might be divorced, but we both agree on one thing—the priority right now is giving you your life back. Your mother wants to take me in because it will help you. I don't like the thought of leaving you right now because I want to protect you, but being wheelchair-bound makes me more of a liability than a help."

"Dad, I swear I did not mean to make you feel like a burden. I'm sorry." I wiped a tear from my cheek.

"Zoey, you've gone far above and beyond anything that I deserved, ensuring I made all of my doctor's appointments, arranging physical therapy, working with bill collectors and the bankruptcy attorneys. You're a young woman; you shouldn't have to deal with any of this."

I wiped the stream of tears from my face.

"But I've seen the toll it's taking on you. I know the reason you went to the house that night was to get a ring. To pay bills that you can't afford."

I looked down, ashamed I hadn't been able to keep that secret from him. "How did you find out?"

"I know which drawer you hide the bills in. And I know how expensive health care is. It wasn't hard to piece together." Dad's voice sounded like it was being stabbed in self-loathing. "That burglary, the reason you were there, was like shining a big spotlight on the damage I'm causing to your life. And it's all I've been able to think about since."

"Dad, it wasn't your fault."

"It's time that I move out. It'll take a couple weeks, and I'll want to work with police to tighten up the locks of this place, put a game plan together to keep you safe, but it's time for me to go." Dad squared his shoulders, resolute in his decision. "This is something that I should've done a long time ago."

I knew he was trying to be noble, but it didn't lessen the throbbing from his blade.

"So, that's it?" My lips trembled. "You're just going to leave me? *Again*?"

He sighed. Wiped his face with his palm. "Zoey, it's long overdue for us to discuss what I did to you in college."

"I'm not just talking about that." I stepped closer. "On Thanksgiving, you almost left me forever."

Before he got hit by the car, I took for granted that my dad was there and that whenever I was finally ready to reconcile with him, I'd have that chance.

But with the squealing of tires and a thump that had since haunted my dreams, I was nearly robbed of that opportunity. And then it turned into life-saving measures, conversations with the ICU team, working to get him healthy enough for a regular room, then rehab, then home, then medical bills and paperwork and finances, and now, here we were.

Having never worked through our pain.

"On Thanksgiving, you almost left me again. Forever," I repeated. My eyes burned, and tears cascaded down my cheeks. "If you had died, we wouldn't have had the chance to fix things. I'd have been so angry; there would have been no way to move past that. I would have hated you forever for taking that chance from me! I would have hated myself!"

Dad's shoulders shrank three inches, and his eyes shimmered, heartbreaking understanding washing over him. He tugged my arm and pulled me onto his lap.

"I don't want to hurt you," I whispered, realizing I meant more than just the weight of my body on his frail legs.

"And I never meant to hurt *you*, Zoey."

He held me for a minute as I cried on his shoulder. I could feel him crying, too, with the jerking of his chest and the sound of his sniffles.

"I have something I need to say to you," Dad said.

I lifted my head up, and Dad motioned with his hand toward the couch. Whatever it was, it must be too long for me to continue cutting off the blood supply to his legs.

I looked at the front door, wondering how long I had before Easton would show up. I wanted to come clean with Dad about Easton, about my lies, about it all, and I wanted to give Dad the time he needed to get whatever he was about to say off his chest.

I walked over, took a seat, and watched Dad position himself in front of me.

Taking several seconds before finally speaking.

"We never had that talk when you were at college." Dad folded his hands together. "The day I told you I'd left your mother."

My scalp prickled, and my stomach grew queasy. I could tell by looking into Dad's chocolate eyes that he was about to finally unveil all his ugly truths as to why my family had unraveled.

The old me would never sit here and willingly listen to explanations, would write them off as nothing more than excuses. But

Easton had shown me I should listen to people fully, to hear everything Dad was about to say to me.

Even though it was long overdue, I wasn't sure I was strong enough to hear it, though. It was like having a deep, festering wound, and the doctor informs you he needs to open it and scrape it out. You know the pain will be unimaginable, but you also know you can't heal if he doesn't do it. You dread the experience in front of you.

Plus, hearing him out, in a strange way, scared me because once we broke the last shackles of resentment, once I allowed him back into my heart fully, I'd have even more to lose if something ever happened to him.

Six feet separated our bodies, yet the space between our hearts was the length of a football field. My heart, at least. I twisted my hands on my lap—a gesture that did not go unnoticed by my father, who looked at my fingers and then looked up at my face.

"I've been thinking a lot about what you said the other day." Dad folded his hands in his lap. "I should've had this conversation with you a long time ago. But the truth is, the more time that passed, the angrier you were, and the harder it became for me to get the courage to talk to you."

He scratched his jaw.

"I suppose the first place to start is back before I left your mother. There's something that we kept from you kids because we didn't want to worry you. I'd had a bit of a"—Dad stretched his fingers—"medical scare. I'll spare you the graphic details, but I'll just say, many men of a certain age have uncomfortable preventative exams, and sometimes, those exams uncover things that need to be looked at closer. The doctor that had done the procedure sent the samples off for testing, but he warned me that based on the appearance and his experience, it was most likely cancer."

My breathing quickened.

"It took about three weeks for the test results to return. Three weeks of staring down the barrel of a terminal illness, you can't help but take a step back and examine your life. I had this remarkable family and comfortable home."

I stared at his lips, eager for his next words.

"But I also saw all the unfulfilled dreams I'd had for my life. When I was a kid, we struggled financially. I had this dream to build a high-end executive career with the financial windfall that came with it. The beautiful condo in downtown Chicago, luxury cars, charity function invitations. But most of all, I vowed to create a new family legacy. When I was a kid, it felt like everyone was running a race in the game of life, and for some of us, the starting line was a lot further back than others. I wanted to set you and your brother up with a starting line that was much more advanced than mine so that you and your kids would have a better head start than I did."

I didn't know his career aspirations stemmed from that.

"Then, I met your mom. And I fell madly in love, and I became what a lot of people become. A father, a husband, and I never pursued my dream because it came with a price tag of long hours and relocations—things that didn't fit in with our family. I don't regret it," he clarified. "But when that doctor told me that I might be dying, instead of focusing on everything that I *did* accomplish, I became fixated on what I *hadn't* accomplished for my family."

Dad leaned his head back and looked up at the ceiling. "For three weeks, this was all I could think about, and then I got the news—it was a false alarm. The lab tests confirmed there was no cancer. And I felt like I had been given a second chance. This cancer scare was a wake-up call that life was short and I needed to go after these dreams. That's when I started buckling down and getting much more serious about my career and the dream for my family that I'd pushed aside."

I remembered Dad working longer hours. I remembered him starting to miss family functions. In hindsight, they were the first cracks in the facade of our perfect family.

"Your mom was understanding at first, but at the time, I don't think I understood that going after my dreams meant changing hers.

She was completely fulfilled with her family and had no desire for it to change."

Mom had been so happy back then. I missed the way her smile used to reach her eyes.

"So, when I started to work longer hours, reaching for my aspirations, it started to cause friction between us. She said this was nothing more than a midlife crisis that would pass, and I thought she was trying to hold me back from building the life that I really wanted. She thought I was being selfish and putting my career ahead of our family. I thought she was being naive, not understanding that I was doing this for our family."

I'd always wondered what happened between Mom and Dad before he left us; it wasn't something I dared to ask Mom, and Anthony and I could never figure it out, no matter how hard we tried to speculate. Hearing about the start of their problems was surprising in a way. Because it was so...understandable.

"You can see the back-and-forth snowball that began as a result of all of this," Dad continued. "Your mom and I became distant, emotionally separated, even though around you guys, we made it seem like we weren't."

They did a good job; I had no idea.

"I think if we had worked at it," Dad said, "maybe gone to counseling, we might've been okay, but I don't think either of us realized just how big the crack between us had grown."

This was hard to hear because maybe there was a chance our family's destruction could have been avoided if we'd seen the signs the same way that doctors saw red flags for cancer.

Dad stared at his hands, locking his fingers together. "It was around that time that Holly started in our office. And a friendship started. She was encouraging of my career, encouraging of all my dreams."

And yet, she didn't care about him giving up his biggest dream of all—his happy family.

"As time went on, subconsciously, I felt Holly had become the supportive good guy and your mom had become the unsupportive bad guy, who was trying to hold me back."

What a perfect role for Holly to play. The encouraging "friend."

Dad scrubbed his face. "When I got a promotion, Holly came in with a gift bag, a thoughtful card, and a congratulations. Your mother crossed her arms over her chest and asked how many more hours this would mean in the office."

Of course Mom would feel like that. She'd gotten her happily ever after, and he was changing that. Maybe she even sensed something was going on at the office.

"Things just escalated from there. Our marriage fell apart, and I fell into the arms of Holly."

I tightened my stomach muscles to fend off the ache. I understood better what had happened behind the scenes. I did, but it still hurt, hearing about when he'd left us all.

"You and Anthony were out of the house by that time, so I told myself what was happening was just between me and your mother. Clearly, I underestimated how this would make you and your brother feel, walking out on your mom. I wasn't just walking out on her. I just didn't realize that until a couple years later. I think that's one of the reasons I didn't come visit you in college that weekend. If I'm being honest, when I called you on the phone and heard how hurt you were, I was nervous to see you face-to-face."

"You should have made more of an effort," I said.

He rubbed his forehead. "I know. I kept telling myself to give you just a few more days to cool down because you and I couldn't seem to get through a phone call without—"

"Fighting," I said.

And we couldn't stop fighting long enough to have a meaningful conversation.

As much as I blamed him for leaving and as much as I still believed he should have tried harder, I couldn't discount how hard I'd made it for him to talk to me back then.

Dad shook his head. "There's no excuse for my not coming. You deserved better. Your mom deserved better, too."

The tentacles of resentment began to unwind in my ribs.

When someone has hurt you deeply, having them acknowledge that hurt and acknowledge that you deserved better is incredibly healing.

"It took a while before I realized Holly wasn't the ride-or-die wife I thought she'd be. Holly chose to stay at home to free me up, so I could focus on my career. So, she took care of everything—cooking, shopping, errands. Even our finances. I was relieved to have the help, so I could focus on my career goals without distractions."

Dad rubbed the side of his face. "At first, it was incredible. She'd have a hot dinner waiting for me every night, kept the fridge stocked with my favorite foods. Took care of the administrative part of paying all our bills. It wasn't until years later that I discovered she was terrible with money. I would have noticed a lot sooner if I hadn't handed everything over to her with no oversight, but I'd been too blindly trusting."

Now, I felt guilty for how many times in those early days I'd hoped Dad's relationship with Holly would combust. Because hearing the beginning of its end made me realize that Dad was someone looking for happiness.

Like we all do.

Even if he looked for it in the wrong person.

Like many of us do.

"Holly spent money faster than it came in, and by the time I figured it out, my savings was gone. And that wasn't the worst of it. Those student loans were supposed to be paid off in full from my bonuses. But when Holly got control of the bills, it turns out, she didn't pay them off. Worse, she dug us in such a bad financial hole that she stopped making payments on them altogether. She's the one that sent you an email from my account about not paying for senior year. I didn't find out until shortly before that Thanksgiving when...well, you know."

He didn't cut off my college money? She did? He didn't even know?

"This was the last straw. I already knew I'd made a mistake, being with her, but I could no longer allow Holly to destroy more of my life. We had a huge fight about it. She claimed it was her poor financial skills that got us into that mess, but I started to wonder if there was more to it. She'd always been insecure about my relationship with you kids. In particular with you since you and I were struggling."

He scratched his cheek. "I wondered if she'd intentionally not paid that bill. And hidden it from me to drive a wedge between us. Finding out she'd sent that email to you made it pretty damn clear she didn't care about my relationship with you."

And that she'd stolen my college money. And if she was capable of doing that, she was certainly capable of stealing from Dad's condo.

He shook his head. "I held on to that relationship longer than I should have because if we didn't work out, I felt like I'd blown up our family for nothing."

I clenched my eyes shut for a moment, so tears wouldn't spill, at the thought of Dad forcing himself to stay with someone who made him miserable.

"I'd made a huge mistake in marrying Holly," Dad whispered. The tone of his voice made a rope twist around the inside of my rib cage. "I'd taken my family for granted, hurt my relationships with my children, I had broken your mom's heart, and I was ashamed of myself."

Dad played with the bare spot on his ring finger, where his wedding band once sat. "All I wanted was my family back, in whatever capacity you guys would allow. I didn't deserve you. But I was prepared to do whatever it took to make amends. That's why I begged Anthony to bring you to Thanksgiving. I wanted to apologize for it all and finally beg for your forgiveness."

Dad stopped fiddling with his finger and rested his hands on his chair's wheels. "Humans are capable of making mistakes," he said. "Enormous ones. But it's not because they're evil. Sometimes, we just...don't make good decisions."

My heart immediately thought of Easton.

"Mistakes can become learning moments, though. They can remind us of who we are and inspire us to be a better person."

Dad rolled his wheelchair forward, closer to me. "How I treated you was unacceptable. I was your father. Nothing and no one should have come between me and my daughter, and I allowed my panic over a health scare to cloud my judgment. I convinced myself I was doing this for a greater good, but I wasn't. All I was doing was neglecting the family that had loved me and supported me."

He looked down for a moment. "After the accident, it was weeks before I was well enough to have the conversation with you I needed to have, and by then, you were taking care of me, and I didn't want you to think I was only apologizing because you were helping me. I needed you to know it was sincere.

"I'm sorry it took me this long to apologize to you, Zoey. I don't expect you to forgive me. But you deserve an apology. I swear to you, throughout all of this, I never stopped loving you, not even a little. I love you more than you can imagine."

I reached out and hugged my dad, putting my chin atop his bony shoulder as I cried. His chest shook just as intensely as mine as we mourned the loss of the life we could have had together.

I now realized why I had been so nervous about hearing his explanation. Hating the version of Dad that made his bad decisions was easier, keeping that part of our relationship black and white. In that version of Dad, he was the villain, and all my nasty behavior that followed—the years of treating him with disdain and disgust—wasn't just understandable; it was justifiable. Because he *deserved* it.

But if Dad explained his actions in a way that made me understand, it wouldn't be black and white anymore. It would be gray, and that would mean all my awful, hurtful behavior wasn't defensible at all. The moment I'd accepted that as reality, I'd feel every ounce of pain I'd inflicted on him, and that hurt would be a hundred times worse than any pain anyone could ever cause me.

This whole time, I thought I needed to forgive my father. But the real person I needed to forgive was myself. No matter what he did, no matter how hurt I might have been, I had a choice in how I treated him, and I was the one that had turned into the awful person. I was the one that threw the ring in his face and said things I could never take back.

"I forgive you, Dad." I wept. "But I'm the one who should be asking for *your* forgiveness. I'm really, really sorry for what I said to you that day..."

Those words were forever lodged in my heart.

I could still picture the door flinging open as I ran through it.

"Zoey, wait! It's not what you think!" High-pitched panic pierces Dad's voice.

But I don't listen. If I'd wanted to talk to him, I wouldn't have thrown that damn ring in his face and stormed out of his condo's building and into the city's congestion.

He made his choices. He gave her that ring when it was supposedly some heartfelt gift for his only daughter. A special gift, the last Christmas before I left for college. How dare he rob me of that memory, too!

No, not just a memory. A version of my father that wasn't real. The version that made me feel special and wanted, like I mattered. He had no right to become the selfish, lying, cheating scumbag that he is.

"Zoey!"

"Leave me the hell alone!"

"Zoey, do not walk away from me!"

I turn around, so I can look at his face, so he can for sure hear what the hell I'm about to say. "You don't care at all about me!"

"That's not true."

"Six years!" I shouted. "You've had six years to make things right, and now that your life is perfect, now that the life you left us for is satisfactory,

now, you make time for me by inviting me to Thanksgiving? Fuck off! I'll make this really easy for you. You don't have to make time for me because I will never make time for you again."

"I know you're angry."

"Angry? No. I'm not angry." I sweep my arms up. "I don't care anymore, Dad. I give up on you. I give up on wanting you to be the man I thought you were because you're not. You're a pathetic asshole excuse of a father who chose another woman over his family. Don't bother inviting me to anything else because I won't show up. I won't even come to your funeral."

In that instant, I know I don't mean what I said. I know what I said is the worst, most hurtful thing you can say to someone, let alone your own father. The man who gave you life. The man you should respect. But my pain didn't care about any of that. It had been bottled up, poisoning me from the inside out until it finally exploded.

I guess sometimes, when people are hurting, they can say terrible things that they don't mean.

The difference? Most of us get the chance to apologize and take it back.

But when I run through a crosswalk and hear the awful thump behind me, I turn to see my father lying on the ground, bleeding.

Our chance to make amends hemorrhaging.

I scream and run to his side, looking into my father's terrified eyes.

I'm about to say, I'm sorry. I didn't mean it. I love you.

But his eyes close before I can utter a syllable.

A thin trail of crimson streams away from his head and pools into the uneven asphalt, like it's forging its own creek, while a screech of tires slices through the gathering crowd of voices.

"Dad," I cry. "Don't leave me yet." Not until I can apologize. Not until we've made up. I can't spend the rest of my life having this fight be the last thing we ever have together. "Please," I beg. "Please don't leave me."

And I sit there, sobbing, wishing I could take it all back. Wishing I had another chance with him.

• • •

"I'm so sorry, Dad. For the way I treated you and the awful things I said to you that day."

"I forgave you the second those words left your mouth." Dad tried to hide the quivering of his chin.

"I've always felt the accident was my fault," I whispered.

Dad's brows furrowed in shock. "It was never your fault."

If only that were true.

His eyes glistened. "I've always felt like I deserved to be hit."

His confession made my breath catch, my throat swelling.

"That's why you never pushed harder to find the driver," I realized.

Because he felt the man responsible for it all was sitting in a wheelchair in this townhouse.

"You never deserved it, Dad."

When he rubbed the side of his face, I couldn't tell if he agreed with me or not.

"There's one more thing I want you to know," he said.

I waited.

"The ring was special, Zoey. I never gave it to Holly."

I felt the air still in my lungs.

"She saw the ring in a picture of you one time. Told me she wanted one, and I explained that it was a special gift from me to you. Which seemed to only make her want it more. When she pressed me on it three more times, I got angry and made it clear there was only one person in my life who would wear that ring. And that person was you."

Dad bit his lip angrily. "That was the first time I saw how nasty she could be. You would think that anyone who had seen the love a man had for his daughter would be viewed as a good thing, but she took it as a threat. To her existence maybe? Her position in my life? I'm not quite sure, but it was the first time I actually saw her true colors come out, and I started to question if she was the person I thought she was."

It was sad that so much damage had been done to his family by then.

"At Thanksgiving, when you showed up," Dad said, "you saw that ring at the same time I did; Holly must have gone to the jeweler and bought it herself."

My jaw went slack.

"By that point, to say our marriage was on the rocks was an understatement, so I can't help but wonder if she thought causing a huge fight between me and you would send me running back into her arms." Dad pinched the bridge of his nose. "Who knows, but her buying that ring? I can't imagine a more self-centered, narcissistic thing to do."

That was why Dad looked shocked when he saw the ring; that was why he kept begging me to let him explain as he ran after me that day. All the way out of his apartment and into the crosswalk.

If I'd listened to him, he'd never have been in that intersection, too focused on me to spot the car coming.

I hugged my father's brittle shoulders as we both cried our shared guilt for that fateful day. It felt good to cry it out, a river of tears cleansing our past and washing a path to our future.

I was grateful for the fresh start that we now had. I felt like I had grown internally more in the past few weeks than the last several years combined. I wanted to tell him that I truly did not want him to move out, that I wanted to take care of him for as long as he needed. And I needed to tell him about Easton, his role in the robbery, before he got arrested. But before I could start, a knock came at the front door.

I reluctantly let go of my father—savoring one last look we shared between us—and ambled toward the front door, emotionally shell-shocked from what I had just gone through. And yet, I knew I had another deep conversation ahead of me with Easton.

32

I looked through the peephole, surprised to see who was on the other side.

"It's Alex," I said.

"He ran out to get us bagels and coffee," Dad said.

Alex had accompanied us to the police station, but...

"Doesn't he have to get to work?"

I grabbed the latch of the door lock and hesitated. Easton said not to open the door for *anyone* but him, and for reasons I couldn't pinpoint, having Alex here didn't provide the comfort I expected.

"Zoey, open the door."

"I don't know if that's such a good idea to let *anyone* in." Except Easton. How would I explain that?

Dad pulled his head back. "You don't trust Alex all of a sudden?"

"I...I just..."

"Alex has been a family friend for years, Zoey. He's just trying to help."

I pulled my lips between my teeth and shut my eyes as my fingers clenched the silver lock, the two-inch piece of metal that protected us. And then I flipped it and opened the door.

Alex gave me a crooked smile and walked inside, carrying breakfast into the dining room, where Dad and his empty stomach followed.

A few seconds later, another knock at the front door, this time Easton.

I opened the door long enough for Easton to slip inside.

Easton's eyes were wide with worry, his rough palms brushing my upper arms as he studied my eyes and asked the question that had clearly haunted him the entire drive over. "Are you okay?"

"I'm fine."

"What did—" Easton stopped when he realized we weren't alone.

Dad abandoned his bagel in favor of wheeling over and staring at Easton. He was trying to hide the glower, but I could see it in Dad's eyes; I might be a grown woman, but this was still a guy who'd slept with his daughter.

"Sir." Easton nodded a hello to my father and quickly returned his attention to me, a silent question pulsing through his eyes. *Does he know?*

I shook my head.

"Can I steal you for a minute?" Easton asked, nodding his chin toward the front door.

I was surprised he'd want to step outside, but when he turned slightly, I noticed a subtle line sticking out of his waistband. I wanted to hurry and tell Dad who Easton was before he got arrested, but I didn't want to do it with Easton here. I didn't know what Dad might be capable of with all his pent-up anger toward my captors.

After a brief pause, I followed Easton toward the door, feeling awful for, once again, delaying coming clean with my father. And also feeling awful for leaving my dad's side, however briefly, when there might be some stalker out there somewhere.

"Will you stay with my dad until I come back?" I asked Alex. "Make sure the doors are locked."

Alex thinned his lips. "Sure, Zoey."

I didn't have time to deal with his big-brother-like disapproval—no man would ever be good enough for me in Alex's eyes and certainly not one who spent the night before even meeting my dad.

"Thank you." I offered a weak smile and waited until I heard the front door lock behind me before following Easton across the street and into the black BMW.

The inside was pristine, like it had just been driven off the car dealership's lot. The white-and-blue BMW logo shining in the center of the steering wheel, cream-colored leather seats, digital screen so crisp that I wondered if it was 4K, a shiny gearshift, and what looked to be a high-end speaker system. It still had the new-car smell.

"Please tell me this car isn't stolen."

Easton furrowed his brows. And smirked. "No. It's not stolen. But the funds used to acquire it weren't from legal sources."

I frowned.

"I need to talk to you about something." I picked at my nail.

"You can talk on the way."

"On the way to where? I thought we were just going to sit in here and talk?"

"Put your seat belt on," he demanded.

"What?"

Easton started the engine and pulled out into traffic. He darted in and out of cars, and when a green light turned yellow, he gunned it, blazing through the intersection, narrowly escaping getting clipped.

"Seat belt. On," he repeated.

"What are you doing?" I gripped the edge of my seat tightly.

Without taking his eyes off the road, Easton reached all the way across my shoulders, yanked the belt down, and poked around until it clicked into place.

"You said he was standing across the street?"

I blinked. "You're going to the police station?"

Easton snapped his eyes to me. "Some guy was stalking you, and you think I'm not going to find out who it was?"

"There's no way the guy would've stuck around. The cop told me

Hernandez was probably canvassing the place, so best case, the guy is gone; worst case, the place is crawling with cops, and they'll arrest you before I can ever talk to you."

"If the guy is part of Brown's crew, I need to find out what he knows. Because if he already has your name, we're screwed."

"Screwed as in..."

He flashed me a look.

As in I'll be killed.

33

"Turn around." A flush of adrenaline rushed through my body.

Easton's knuckles whitened with his grip on the wheel, his eyes fixed on the road in front of us as our vehicle careened through traffic.

"What good can come of confronting this guy?"

"I need to find out if they've figured out who you are." His chest inflated. "Because I'm not turning myself in until I ensure you're safe."

"That place is across from the police station," I reminded him. "If they've put your face with your name by now and you go there, a cop will see you."

"Not if I'm careful."

"Unless you've summoned the power of invisibility, you're playing with fire."

Easton glowered at me.

"You're not thinking this through."

But he kept driving. Racing, really. A red Toyota Camry with a dented right fender blazed its horn when Easton gunned it through a yellow light. As we tunneled through the six-story buildings, I gripped the edge of the seat for balance, rocking from side to side as Easton wove in and out of traffic, the groaning of the engine rising in pitch as he accelerated.

"We don't know who this guy is or what he's capable of. If you confront him, it's just gonna make things so much worse! You could get hurt, and if he sees you with me? Brown's crew will figure out you've been helping me all along."

Easton pressed the accelerator harder.

"He might not even be alone! He could have buddies nearby."

"I don't care about *me*, Zoey," Easton growled. "I care about you. Only you."

The thought of Easton rotting in prison cut me open and left my soul bleeding, but the thought of him getting killed obliterated the remaining fragments of my heart into dust.

This can't be happening. Would the landscape of my life once again repaint, this time with Easton in a coffin?

No. That couldn't be how this ended.

And yet, there was clearly no way to talk him out of this. I'd never seen anyone's eyes like that before. Rounded with a hardened edge of vengeance that demanded reckoning.

And as if this weren't bad enough, there was no way to have the deeply personal conversation with him that I'd desperately longed for. I could tell he'd never truly listen to *anything* I had to say, no matter how hard I tried. It would be like talking to someone with earphones in, where the music was cranked up so high that it would drown it all out.

All too soon, Easton parked a block away from the police station, out of view.

Theoretically.

"Please don't do this." I put my hand on his knee.

But he got out of the car, opened my door, and grabbed my hand.

I got up only because I didn't want him to go into the alley alone.

But I didn't cease my pleas to stop this, even as he began walking toward the row of buildings across from the station.

"One cop sees you, and it's over." I looked around.

But I could see my words were bouncing right off of him; his eyes darted around the pedestrians, looking for any sign of danger.

Danger that dripped through the musk-scented air with the humidity of a coming storm. Bands of charcoal streaks crawled beneath dense clouds, cloaking the six-story buildings in its shadow, motivating many vehicles to turn on their headlights.

"Show me where you saw him."

"I don't remember," I claimed. "Please, let's just go back to the car—"

"Show me," Easton demanded.

I licked my lips.

I nodded my chin toward the building, and Easton tugged me by my hand as he walked across the street, down a half-block, and into the pedestrian path behind the building. All out of eyesight from the police station.

Again, in theory.

I thought for sure we would stumble across the police, but they must have already completed canvassing the area. Because when we emerged between the two buildings where I had seen the man standing, there was no one. Not a single person.

Maybe the police picked him up already.

"You sure this is where he was?"

I nodded, relieved. I didn't want Easton to confront this guy, and it looked like the universe had finally tipped the scales in my favor to keep him safe from himself.

"Can we go?"

"What did he look like?"

"Dark hair, jeans, black T-shirt. I was too far away to get his eye color or height."

Easton frowned. "Let's look around," he said, tugging me by the hand to move.

"Easton—"

"I can't leave you in the car, unprotected."

"Let's just go. He's not here so—"

But my words were immediately cut off because when we made a right turn down the pedestrian walk, a man blocked our path.

Not just any man.

The man.

The one that had been staring at me.

34

Tendrils of fear coiled around my muscles, urging me to run, but caught in the headlights of a villain, I became a doe. Frozen in place, staring at the man who'd evaded police earlier.

His dark eyes felt like weapons as they assessed me and then Easton, whose hand tightened protectively around mine.

"Easton." The guy's raspy tone rang through the air with echoes of warning.

I didn't like how Easton's body tensed. I didn't like how Easton's gaze fell to the man's waistband, as if looking for a gun, or the way Easton's fingers twitched toward his weapon. I didn't like that my sixth sense said whoever this guy was, he was powerful.

He wasn't the guy who had chased me the night of the burglary, but everything about him fired off sinister shots. The ghost of a smirk on his thin lips, as if he'd caught his prey. The callous indifference in his too-relaxed posture when facing a man more muscular than him. And the way he flicked the nail of his middle finger with his thumb, flick, flick, flicking a countdown to something.

"Why the hell are you here?" Easton demanded.

The guy scrutinized Easton.

"Assumed it was 'cause *you* couldn't find the witness." His eyes fell to our clasped hands. "Clearly, that was a lie."

His use of the word witness *must mean they don't know my name yet. Right?*

"How did you know she would be here?" Easton's eyes didn't blink.

"At the police station?" he asked as if it were a stupid question. "The day after the police put that parade on the news? Call it a hunch that they'd bring her in for questions."

So, he was watching the place then. A spider waiting in his web for the unsuspecting insect to walk into his trap.

"You're going to have to come with me, sweetheart," he said firmly, like his command was final.

"Over my dead body." Easton stood in front of me. "You so much as lay a finger on her, I'll end you."

Again, Easton's fingers flexed toward his waistband.

"You brought her here." The guy smirked. "What did you think was going to happen?"

Before Easton had the chance to pull his own pistol, the guy yanked a gun from the back of his waistband and pointed it at Easton's forehead.

"Come with me." He nodded his chin. "You and I need to go for a little drive."

I quickly assessed my options. Running was out. I couldn't make it around the corner fast enough when Easton's life was a squeeze away from ending. If I tried to pull Easton's gun and failed, Easton would die, too. If I screamed, would he pull the trigger? Or would police get here fast enough to stop what was happening?

"Now!" the guy snapped.

But when he grabbed my arm, everything changed.

Easton slammed his left palm into the assailant's wrist, knocking the aim of the barrel to the side, then grabbed the weapon with his right hand and kneed the guy in the balls. Even in obvious pain, the guy tried to fight for control over the gun, but Easton spun around, grabbed the guy's arm, and cracked it over his shoulder.

The snapping of the bone preceded his howl.

Easton smothered the guy's scream with his hand.

"Take this," he said, putting the weapon into my hand.

I was relieved that he handed me the gun because I assumed it meant the fight wouldn't escalate to death. But then I realized the gun was simply too loud to use this close to the police station.

Easton locked eyes with me for a heartbeat, his infuriated gaze plagued with the same warning he gave when he beat up that guy in the alley. The one that said, *Don't look, Zoey. I don't want you to see what I'm going to do to him.*

Easton had told me a few days ago that he would kill for me. In that moment, I knew with the cascading freeze to my bones that Easton was about to honor that promise. He was my dark protector, an unimaginable blend of kindness and danger, a man capable of violence, yet I knew with certainty that he'd never harm a hair on my head. Only those that wished me harm had reason to fear his form of justice.

Justice that could turn lethal.

"Let's just go," I pleaded.

But it was too late. Easton unleashed his tsunami of rage with his clenched fists against the man's face. Over and over. Cracks and thwaps echoed off the building's walls as blood splattered across Easton's face with each blow.

If I didn't stop him, he was going to kill him.

I wedged myself between Easton and the man, causing Easton's arm to halt mid-swing.

Panting, Easton stared into my eyes as I pressed my palm against his massive chest, feeling the thumping of his erratic heartbeat.

Knowing each beat was for me.

Easton was powerful, but with that one gentle move, I halted all the power coming from him and silently convinced him to stop. He looked down at the guy, who was unconscious but still breathing.

Easton clenched his jaw. Spat on the man's torso, took the guy's gun back—shoving it into his waistband next to the other—and led me by my hand down the abandoned alley toward the car.

35

"Easton," I whispered as we walked toward the sidewalk peppered with people.

He stopped walking and followed my gaze to his bloodstained shirt.

No way we could get to his car without someone seeing that. Not if we left the protection of the alley.

"You need to wipe your face, too."

Easton's jaw ticced, but he acted swiftly. Releasing my hand, he yanked the shirt up and over his head, turned it inside out, and wiped his face clean.

As clean as he could, anyway. Traces of blood still lingered in the hairs of his eyebrows, in the crevice of his right ear. He wadded the shirt into a ball, jogged to a dumpster, and threw the shirt inside.

Only then did he take my hand and lead me all the way back to the car.

"I can see the tops of the gun handles sticking out of your waistband," I warned.

Easton shoved them down further, protecting the exposed parts with his arm. Once we were safely inside, he stuck them in the center console.

"Who was that guy?"

Easton rumbled the engine to a start and pulled out into traffic. "Brown's right-hand man."

"He saw you holding my hand."

Easton blew through a yellow light so fast, I thought he was going to clip a red pickup truck.

"I'm taking you home," Easton declared. "What I just did will enrage Brown. I'm not leaving you alone, unprotected, until I can think of a way to keep you safe."

With that one violent episode, the pendulum of danger swung away from me and over to Easton. A witness was one thing—a risk of operations, so to speak. But another crew member betraying Brown like this? Surely wouldn't go without severe repercussions.

It felt like the air became trapped in the lower part of my lungs, and I had to focus on my breaths, so I wouldn't pass out. I couldn't lose Easton. Not now.

"We need to stick with the original plan now more than ever," I disagreed. "We need to get Brown behind bars because after what you just did? They're going to come after you."

"I don't care about me."

"Well, I do." But I could see I needed to appeal to what Easton cared about. "If they go after you, how are you gonna protect me then?"

Easton clenched the steering wheel.

"Turning yourself in is the best chance we have to stay alive, and you know it. You're a pivotal witness to an important prosecution, so maybe they'll have protective custody or something."

Guaranteed safety didn't exist. All we could do was evaluate the options in front of us and pick the safest bet.

"They could get to you while I'm being interviewed," he said.

I was making progress.

"So, I'll go in with you, then. I'll sit in the safety of the police station the entire time you're being interviewed."

As lightning began to flash in the distance, Easton gripped the steering wheel tighter, staring out the windshield, clearly willing a better scenario to present itself. But what other choice did we have? Even if I had the financial means to run, it physically wasn't a possibility with Dad's medical situation. Dad said it would take a couple weeks or so before he'd be able to move in with Mom, and even then, they might identify his name and come after him. I wasn't about to leave my dad behind and risk him becoming collateral damage. Plus, Easton would be a wanted criminal wherever he went. Now that the police had his name, it was only a question of *when* he would be brought in. Not if.

We could either try to get in front of this with the police or give Brown and his crew another advantage.

Easton was silent for several seconds. I could see the wheels spinning in his mind as the sky darkened even more, warning of the perilous storm brewing.

While our own hurricane intensified in strength.

"I need to get cleaned up first," Easton allowed.

Ten minutes later, Easton parked in an underground parking structure and held my hand so tightly, he cut off blood supply to my fingers, his eyes darting around the empty space as he pulled me into an elevator, then into a hallway.

He unlocked a door, ushered me inside, and immediately relocked it, glancing out the peephole for any sign that we'd been followed.

I took in my new surroundings. An open space with a kitchenette only three steps from a living room/bedroom containing a two-seater couch, a bed, and a dresser. Along the far wall, a six-foot window's white blinds were drawn closed, the sounds of the city—the roar of car engines, the high-pitched metal scraping of the "L" train, a distant fire truck's wail, and the rumbling thunder of the coming storm—muffled through their panes of glass. And in here, the air conditioner sputtered through rattling vents, flooding the cool air with the scent of someone's laundry soap.

In the midst of surreal chaos, it was remarkable, getting to see a piece of him like this.

"Is this where you live?" I wondered aloud.

Easton flipped a light switch on in the next room, the only other room in this small space—a bathroom.

"No," he said as he yanked off his jeans. "It's a studio apartment I keep off the books. Use it to hide out when things get too hot."

Stripping to a pair of boxers, Easton turned the shower's water on.

"So, we're safe here?" I touched my throat. "Brown doesn't know where it is?"

"Brown doesn't know where it is, but, no," Easton said, dropping his boxers, "I don't feel you're safe anywhere right now. Give me two minutes to rinse off, and then we'll head to the station."

Easton stepped into the shower and vanished behind a black curtain.

I was overwhelmed with a cascading sequence of emotions radiating through me. Anytime now, Brown would find out what Easton had just done, and though I talked a good game to Easton, deep down, I was terrified that the police might not be able to protect Easton from Brown's vengeance. It was Easton's best shot at staying alive, but it was by no means foolproof.

Nor was it foolproof that Easton would be able to get leniency from the DA.

How long would he be facing in prison?

I quickly googled *prison time for armed robbery*, and when the search results appeared, I felt sick. Up to twenty-five years in prison. And that didn't include the other charges on the table, charges they might slap on everyone involved that night—kidnapping, assault and battery. Easton might really spend the rest of his life in prison.

My stomach clenched.

A smarter person would stay focused and not let this heartbreak consume her right now. There were much bigger priorities, but my heart didn't seem to care about any of that. It was too busy crumbling, imagining the next thirty years without Easton.

Without the man who, after all my years imprisoned in judgment, had freed me. Had saved me, both physically and emotionally. I needed to tell him the impact he'd had on my life.

When the shower's water stopped, Easton emerged from the bathroom, wearing nothing but a towel fastened around his hips.

He locked his eyes on me and walked up to me with urgency, as if he'd worried something might've happened to me while I was out of his sight.

"You okay?" He planted his warm palm against my cheek.

I nodded and leaned into his touch. He released it far too soon and threw on a pair of fresh boxer shorts he retrieved from the dresser.

"I need to tell you something." Butterflies took flight in my stomach.

Easton pulled a new pair of jeans from his drawer but paused at my tone.

I swallowed. I had so much to say, yet my words jumbled in my head.

An avalanche of sadness swallowed every other emotion and its path.

"This might be the last time we see each other for a long time," I realized.

And this time, it wasn't hypothetical or in the future. It was right now. In a matter of minutes, we'd be driving to the police station, and then we'd have no control over when or if we could see each other.

Easton stepped closer and traced my cheek with his thumb. I could see in the curve of his lips that as he stared at me, he was trying to memorize every inch of my face, perhaps so he could call it up at will in his darkest days in prison. And then a hurt washed through his gaze.

"It *will* be the last time we see each other," he said. "*Ever.*"

I stilled from shock.

"I won't let you throw your life away, waiting for me."

My eyes stung. "That's not your call to make."

"We both know I'm going away for a long time."

"You could get a deal."

"Even if I do, I'm looking at years behind bars, Zoey. I'm not going to ruin your life even more than I already have."

"You didn't ruin my life." My eyes welled, and my lips quivered at him seeing himself as nothing but destructive to me. He needed to see that he wasn't the hurricane; he was the rainbow. "You saved it."

The crease between his brows deepened.

"Before I met you, I'd write anyone off that did something I didn't agree with. I've been so closed off, particularly after my dad left us, but you opened my eyes. You made me realize that behind every action lies a motivation, and it's equally important to understand both, to never presume to know why someone is making the choices they are.

"You changed me, Easton. Emily was right; you're the first person who made me stop and listen to *why* someone is making the choices they make. Before you came along, I never listened, but now, I'm trying to hear people out instead of jumping to my own conclusions. It helped me have a better conversation with my father than I would have before, but this won't stop with my father. It'll strengthen every relationship I have with people from now on. You've made me into a better person, and I don't ever want you to forget that."

Easton stood before me, wearing nothing but a pair of boxers, the jeans still clutched in his hand. His skin smelled of fresh soap, his hair still wet after being towel-dried. He looked at me beneath thick eyebrows as I placed both of my hands on his chest and looked up into his eyes.

Easton traced my cheek with this fingertip. With the slow breath escaping his lungs, I could see the battle raging in his heart, his feelings for me wanting to take the steering wheel, wanting to embrace my love, but his honor fighting it.

"You would pick me, even after everything I've done?"

"Without question."

Something shifted in his eyes, and instantly, I needed to know something.

Does he feel as strongly for me as I do him?

"If you weren't facing prison...what is it you'd want, Easton?"

Easton stroked my cheekbone with the backs of his fingers, his touch igniting sparks in my heart.

He pierced me with his gaze and was silent for several agonizing seconds.

"I want you," he said in a low rumble.

I allowed myself to have a silent gasp, savoring his answer. Relishing that in this moment, I got to hear what he really longed for even if it could never come true.

"If I weren't going away, I'd want to give you every desire you could possibly imagine. You want ecstasy? I'd sink to my knees to pleasure you. You want protection? I'd annihilate anyone who ever hurts you. You want to be worshipped? You'd be my altar."

I swallowed as he cupped my chin in his hand.

"I've lived the last decade in a prison of my own making, but you broke me out, Zoey. You gave me purpose, and now, every drop of blood in my body belongs to you. You asked me what I'd want if I wasn't going away." He pinned me with those piercing blue eyes and held the side of my face. "I'd want to be anything to you that you'd allow me to be."

A hungry desire pulsed in my lower belly, and the need to feel him overwhelmed me. He stared at me as if needing to memorize my every feature while my hands tried to memorize the contours of his skin.

Every other rational thought faded along with every sound, every smell. He was the only thing in my world right now.

His profession wrapped around my heart like a warm blanket

after a thunderstorm, and the need to make a profession of my own surged up my chest, to the tip of my tongue.

"I know this sounds crazy, illogical, and much too soon," I said. But after everything that happened in my life, including the robbery, I learned that life is too short to hold back from saying something that's truly in your heart. "But I'm falling in love with you."

Easton's lips curled as if my declaration healed the last remnants of his wounded soul. "I think I've already fallen."

My heart hiccuped at his words, watching his lips as he lowered his face.

When his lips finally grazed mine, I groaned and wrapped my arms around his neck as his tongue swept into my mouth. There was no way I could spend the next thirty years without being with him one last time. I let my hands roam down his chest, down his stomach.

"Zoey—" he warned.

"Once we walk out that door, we might never get to touch each other again."

I skimmed my fingertips down the ridges of his abs, sensing his resolve wavering with the quickening of his breaths.

"I need one more memory of us to cling to," I said. "Every night you're not in my bed."

As I skimmed my palm along his stomach, Easton's body remained frozen, but with each inch of skin I touched, his breathing quickened until one tug of his waistband made him lose all control.

He yanked my shirt over my head and almost tore my bra, taking it off. Then my pants. Feverish movements as he walked me backward, kissing my jaw. My neck.

And then he shoved me down.

I landed on his bed with a bounce, staring up at him as he stood over me, pulling his boxers off.

"If this is the last time I get to touch you..." He grabbed my legs, yanked me to the bottom of his bed, pulled my panties off. And knelt. "I'm going to make it memorable," Easton promised.

He trailed kisses up along my inner thigh, repeating the same agonizing tease on the other side until he pressed his tongue to my center. I gasped. When I moved my hips, he held down my thighs so forcefully, his hands pinched my skin.

I existed in a slice of ecstasy that I never wanted to end. He kissed me like a hungry man, like he'd been fantasizing about this moment since he'd first laid eyes on me, and now that it was here, he couldn't get enough. I'd never felt anything this sensual, this intimate before, and with him, I didn't feel shy at all. He was a sensual extension of my body, someone with whom I could live out my wildest desires without feeling self-conscious. When I began to squirm, feeling the rise, he held my thighs tighter. Until I called out his name.

He waited until every last aftershock rippled through my body before he stood up and grabbed a small plastic wrapper from his wallet.

"Turn over," he growled as he ripped a foil packet and slipped on protection.

I gladly obeyed and crawled up higher on the bed, feeling it sink behind me with the weight of his knees as he positioned himself behind me.

And then joined our bodies.

I bit his pillow as he began to move.

I loved every growl that escaped his throat. Every whimper that came from mine. He moved with perfect rhythm, as if knowing my body's tempo. And then, never breaking our bodies, he pulled my torso back, resting on his heels.

He grabbed my chest as he twisted my head around so he could kiss me. Slipped his tongue against mine as I rocked my hips on top of him, feeling another release coming. And when his hand found my center, it triggered my collapse, my mouth gaping.

"Easton," I cried out.

Once every tremble subsided, he pulled away, flipped me onto my back, and sank his body back to mine.

How was it possible that every position felt better than the last?

As good as it felt with him behind me, there was nothing like the weight of his hips pressing into my thighs, his arms on either side of my head, his lips trailing kisses along my jaw. There was nothing like getting to grab his shoulder muscles as he controlled his body in perfect sync with my own.

He kissed me again and moved his body with mine harder and harder until he felt another rise of mine coming. I grabbed his back.

"Don't stop," I whimpered.

I looked up into his azure eyes as he worked his body against mine, and he watched my release.

"Easton..."

Easton growled and slammed his body into mine until he stilled on top of me, cupping my face. His majestic blue eyes searched mine for the happiness we both wished we could hold on to forever, but I watched as his happiness receded behind a curtain of despair.

"I *have* fallen in love with you," he said.

I didn't like the hurt in his voice or the way his shoulders sagged slightly. Nor did I like how he traced my lip with his finger, pain radiating from his eyes as he gathered himself to say what came next.

"But I meant what I said, Zoey. I don't want you to wait for me."

It felt like my heart burst into flames, spreading its inferno to my bones.

"You spent the last year putting your life on hold to take care of your dad." He shook his head. "I'm not going to allow you to put your life on hold for me."

Instantly, the oxygen didn't come fast enough; my lungs inflated at a rapid pace, searching for relief that wouldn't come.

"You are my life." I clasped his arms tightly, as if holding on to him could make him stay here with me.

But with the distress on his face and his gaze falling from my eyes, I could feel him slipping through my grasp as he climbed off the bed and put his pants on.

I didn't know what to say, how to shift the cold front that had moved through the room so fast that I didn't see it coming.

He wouldn't look at me anymore.

I sat up and pulled the covers up to my chest, too raw to feel this hurt in the nude. I rocked slightly, clutching my knees, my mind racing.

I didn't know a lot about prisons, but I was fairly certain that if an inmate refused to see someone, there would be nothing I could do. And as painful as the years ahead of me would feel without him by my side, that pain was nothing compared to never getting to see him again. Feeling him cut himself out of my life like a cancerous tumor, unaware that doing so sliced my heart open, causing it to hemorrhage.

I couldn't let him walk in the police station without him promising me he'd never turn me away.

I opened my mouth to plead my case, but suddenly, the front door burst open.

A dark-haired guy, wearing a black T-shirt and jeans with tattoos of skulls wrapping up both arms, stormed inside and cut his eyes to me.

I tightened the bedsheet across my chest and stared into the dark eyes that made my body tremble. The guy's chest inflated, his fists clenched, as he turned his attention to Easton, who glared at the intruder.

"You fucking kidding me?" The guy gestured to me.

And that was when the ice in my bones chilled into an arctic freeze because I recognized that voice, and I remembered that face from the brief glimpse I caught on the night of the robbery.

It was Orange.

36

"You're screwing the witness you're supposed to eliminate?" Orange snapped.

Wearing nothing but a pair of jeans, Easton walked to the door, poked his head out, and looked up and down the hall before shutting and locking it.

"Thought Victor's guy had to be mistaken, that you were with some other chick, not her," Orange snarled.

"How did you find me?" Easton asked over a tightened jaw.

Orange looked at me with disgust, his face pinched, as if my very presence sickened him. "Weren't at your place, so I figured after what you did to Victor's guy, you might be here."

"Is anyone else with you?" Easton demanded.

"No." Orange glared at me. "Thought you'd be alone, too, after the stunt you pulled." He reached into his waistband and pulled a gun out. Pointed it at me.

I tensed.

Easton jumped between the barrel and me.

"Gavin." Easton's vein bulged from his neck.

"You know what Victor's going to do to you when he finds out about this?"

"You take your orders from Victor now?"

"He's making sure we don't get busted."

"He's reckless and violent," Easton barked.

"He's protecting himself and his crew. Including me."

The night of the robbery, Orange/Gavin said the heist was a test, that if it went well, Brown/Victor would offer him a job. The heist went sideways, so why invite him to the team? Was Gavin really in as good of graces as he thought?

Or was Victor using him?

"You think he gives two shits about you?" Easton snapped. "I'm your brother. I've always protected you and had your back."

"I know you have." Gavin dropped his arm slightly, the gun now angled lower, but by no means were we out of danger. "That's why I want you in on this opportunity. Victor has a bigger crew, bigger heists. We can be kings in this city. You always told me, 'We have enough cash. No one owns us.' He's offering us more money than we ever dreamed of."

"He's going to kill you, Gavin. He told me if I don't find the witness, he'll kill me and then you."

"Victor wouldn't kill me."

"Have I ever lied to you?"

"Yeah. When you left out that you're screwing the one person who can put us behind bars."

Gavin stepped to his right and raised the aim of the barrel again, but Easton matched his movement, taking up a protective stance, shielding me.

"Gavin, don't do this," Easton said.

"Step aside."

"You want to kill her, you'll have to kill me first."

"You fucking crazy?" Gavin demanded.

"Put the gun down."

"She's just some girl!"

"You're not a killer, Gavin."

Easton had a lot more faith in his brother than I did because the tone in Gavin's voice seemed pretty damn murderous to me.

I wanted to run, but exposing myself past Easton would get me killed.

"Look, it don't have to go down this way." Gavin's voice lowered with sympathy. "You come with me now, I'll tell him you lured her here, okay? That you were the one that took care of her."

The silence was earsplitting.

"You really plan to kill her," Easton said in disbelief, as if only now, it was finally sinking in.

"She could put us in prison for the rest of our lives." Gavin's face pinched.

Easton took a step closer to his brother. "If you spend the next however many years pulling off heists, you think you won't stumble across other witnesses? You gonna kill them all, too?"

Gavin said nothing.

"This isn't who you are," Easton insisted.

"And who am I?" His voice lowered.

But the thing was, Gavin didn't ask it in a biting, win-an-argument tone. He asked it as if truly seeking the answer.

The old me would see him as nothing more than an awful human, but like Easton, Gavin had a story, a reason for how he was acting, and my heart bled for him. For this human who'd been plucked from happiness, lost his parents to violence, and lived on the dangerous streets with none of the usual connections and guidance the rest of us had. Teachers. Structure. Friends. Sleepovers. Birthday parties. He probably didn't even remember what living in a non-fight-or-flight moment felt like. Knowing if he'd be able to eat again or if a gang would kill his brother, leaving him completely alone.

What is a human capable of when suffering from that much trauma?

He might be making terrible choices right now, but if Easton could change, maybe Gavin could, too.

"You're my brother," Easton said. "Who I would do anything for. I mean, shit, Gavin! What's this all been for if you go off the deep end and turn into some lowlife who'll kill people? I did all this to try to save you."

"You thought a life of crime on the streets would save me? You raised me in an alley! You ripped me from heat and food and a warm bed and made me sleep on concrete."

Easton's body tensed. "I yanked you out before a pedophile got his hands on you. I sacrificed everything for you, and this is how you repay me? Going against me for some guy who's willing to kill us and anyone else who gets in his way?"

"We've been stealing and lying since we were kids, and now, you grow some conscience and draw a line in the sand of what's an acceptable crime and what's not?"

Easton grabbed the back of his neck.

"We could rule this city," Gavin repeated. "Take whatever the hell we want, when we want it, and no one'll be able to do anything about it."

With his every word, I could see in the sag of his shoulders that Easton's heart was closing in on itself.

That was what this was about to Gavin; it wasn't the money. Like Easton, this life of crime was about the power. Going from powerless to powerful. Feeling afraid for years must be a heavy burden that leaves behind battle scars. And the desire to never feel vulnerable again clearly was a drug too tempting to pass up.

"I can't let you do this, Gavin."

"You've always protected me." Gavin flexed his fingers on his free hand. "Why won't you do it now?"

"I *am* protecting you," Easton said, his tone a mixture of anger and disappointment. "Even if you can't see it."

Easton charged Gavin, causing the gun to drop from his grip. Gavin grunted as he fell to the floor. He lay there for a few seconds before charging Easton's knees.

As Easton and his brother rolled around, swinging fists at each other, I hopped up with a bedsheet around my body and grabbed the weapon.

"Get off him." I pointed the gun at Gavin.

The men froze, eyeing me. But after a few seconds, Gavin and Easton both stood up.

"Get out," I ordered.

I held my arm out as intimidatingly as possible, unsure if I would have the courage to pull the trigger even if he came at me. Gavin looked from me to his brother in absolute disgust and then began straightening his shirt.

As if unfazed by my threat.

"You made a big mistake, brother." Gavin's face flushed red.

"I said, get out!"

Easton stepped closer to me in a protective stance while Gavin picked up his wallet, which must have fallen out of his jean pocket in the scuffle.

"Victor's going to come for you," Gavin warned.

And then his eyes caught something else on the ground. Something that clearly sparked his interest based on the slight widening of his eyes. My driver's license poking out of my jean pocket.

No.

Easton lunged for it, but Gavin kicked him in the ribs, sending Easton to the floor as he grabbed it.

"*Zoey Williams*," Gavin read.

My blood thinned.

"This your current address?"

Easton wobbled, holding the side of his ribs, but by the time he stood up, it was too late.

Gavin was in the doorway. "We'll be seeing you soon, Zoey."

And then he was gone.

37

"Zoey?" Dad answered on the first ring.

Thank God.

Easton made a left turn so fast, my body pressed into the passenger door. After Gavin left with my ID, Easton ran after him, but Gavin had vanished. I threw my clothes on, and Easton and I ran to his car, where I quickly pulled out my cell.

I was glad the storm wasn't producing rain yet; rain would make it harder to drive fast.

"Where the hell have you been?" Dad demanded. "I thought you stepped out to talk to your boyfriend, and you just vanished! Do you know how worried I've been?"

"Dad," I said, "listen to me very carefully. Do not open the door for anybody. I'm calling the cops, and I'm coming to pick you up."

"What's going on?"

"I'll explain everything as soon as I get there, but right now, I need to call the police. Do not answer the door. Do you understand me? And if you hear or see anything, call 911."

Easton wove in and out of traffic so quickly, I feared we'd crash.

"Are you okay? Are you in danger?" Dad's words fired as fast as bullets.

"The burglars have our address."

Easton turned right and nearly clipped a blue Ford pickup.

"What? How did they find out—"

"I'll explain everything, I promise. But right now, do not answer the door."

The light in front of us turned from green to yellow, but Easton pressed the accelerator, grinding the engine as we launched into the intersection seconds after the light had turned red. A cement truck coming eastbound nearly crashed into Easton's side, both vehicles swerving to avoid a collision.

Our back tires lost traction and fishtailed, but Easton regained control and changed lanes to get around a slow sedan in front of us.

His apartment was only a few minutes from mine, but with the men who wanted me dead now having my address, it might as well have been light years away.

"I'll be there in a couple of minutes," I said.

"Zoey," Dad started.

"I love you, Dad. Don't open the door. I'll be there in a minute."

I hated ending it with him like that, but I needed to call the police. They needed to send the full cavalry to my apartment to protect my dad. I quickly looked up Hernandez's phone number and dialed his extension. It rang three agonizing times before he picked up.

"Hernandez."

"Detective Hernandez!"

"Zoey?" His voice was tense. "What's wrong?"

"One of the burglars took my ID, which means he has my name and address."

"What makes you think he has your ID?"

"I saw him. He could be on his way to my house right now!"

"You saw him?" Hernandez echoed with angry confusion.

"Yes."

"Where?"

"And now, my dad could be in danger. He's home all alone with no way to defend himself."

"Zoey, I need you to calm down. Come to the station, and we'll discuss this further."

"I'm not leaving my dad at my townhouse alone! Not when they could come looking for me there at any time now. I'm going home. Can you send some of your men right away?"

"If one of them has your address, your house is the last place you should go. Come to the station."

"I'm not coming there until I get my dad! Can't you send a car?"

"Manpower's light at the moment. It'll take longer than usual for them to get to your place, so you need to come straight here."

"Why is manpower light?"

"Anonymous call about a robbery in progress."

"You think it's real?"

"I don't have confirmation one way or the other yet." Hernandez didn't hide the skepticism in his tone. Or the worry. "Worst case, it could be a diversion to lure manpower elsewhere while they try to come after you. So, you need to come to the station right now."

"And what about my dad?" I yelled.

"I'll send someone for him, but *you're* the witness. You're the one that's in danger."

"Right now, my dad's a sitting duck. I'm not risking my dad's life. I'm going to pick him up and bring him with me."

How I'd do that with Dad in a wheelchair, I wasn't sure. But I'd carry him myself if I had to.

"I'll be there as soon as I can." I ended the call.

Easton rounded the last corner and slammed the car into park so fast, I jolted forward.

With our eyes darting around the neighborhood—at the sedans parked along both sides of the road, one littered with orange tickets beneath its windshield wiper; at the passages between townhouses that could easily conceal someone's hiding position—we jumped out. I kicked an empty beer bottle out of my way as we rushed to the front door, Easton keeping a protective hand on my lower back.

I fished the key out of my pocket, unlocked the dead bolt, slipped inside with Easton, and immediately locked up again.

Inside, Dad and Alex were at the dining room table. My relief that they were okay lasted for only a moment before I saw what was splayed out on the table in front of them. Case files, police reports, and enlarged photographs.

They must have been working the case after breakfast since the lineup hadn't been about the robbery.

"What's going on?" Dad demanded of me.

Like a moth to the flame, Easton approached the table.

"You've been trying to solve the case?" An anchor dragged Easton's voice down.

Alex puffed up his chest, offense washing over him, like anyone that truly cared about me would be trying to solve this mystery. "Those scumbags won't get away with what they did to Zoey."

As Dad rolled himself closer to me, I was about to tell him to grab his stuff, that we needed to hustle into Easton's car and get the hell out of here.

But Easton eyed the pictures splayed across the table. Pictures of my mutilated wrists. Close-up shots of my bruises and scrapes, mascara dripping down my puffy eyes. And as he did, his lips curled down into a sickened expression.

Outside, a storm that had been brewing intensified with blowing winds and lightning.

Inside, a different storm raged on. One where Easton looked at Alex, then my dad. And after seeing the photos of what his life of crime had caused me, he must have decided jail or death by Brown wasn't enough punishment. Evidently, he felt like he also deserved a father's wrath, too.

Because he looked at Dad dead in the eyes and said, "I'm one of the men you're looking for, sir. I robbed your condo."

38

"You what?" Dad snapped. I thought he was going to jump out of his chair and strangle Easton.

Alex beat him to it, lunging and punching Easton across the face so hard that he wobbled back a step.

"Stop!" I shrieked, but Alex pounded his fists into Easton's face repeatedly, pushing Easton deeper into the living room with each hit—but Easton didn't even attempt to fight back. His hair bounced with each undefended jab.

Dad watched the brawl from the confines of his chair, making no effort to tell them to stop. If anything, I wondered if he was living vicariously through Alex's fists as Alex tackled Easton to the ground.

"Stop!" I climbed onto Alex's back, but he flung me off and continued to hit Easton's stomach, chest, and face.

I tried again to pull Alex off, but one of his blows accidentally landed on my ribs, knocking me to the ground with a sharp stab of pain to my right hip.

This was the only time I saw Easton's arm move. With one swift motion, he nailed Alex in the head, sending him flying backward into the couch.

"You ever touch her again..." Easton warned.

Finally, I was able to wedge myself between them, palms on each of their chests. I could feel their thundering hearts pulsing beneath my hands.

Easton clenched his hands into balls, glaring at Alex, who glared right back.

"We don't have time for this." I gave them both a gentle shove. "We have to go. Now."

Alex and Easton breathed heavily, perhaps contemplating fighting to the death. Alex wiped a drop of blood from the corner of his mouth while Easton looked...well, a little disheveled but otherwise fine.

"I'm not going anywhere until you explain what in the hell is going on," Dad snarled.

"I'll explain on the way to the station, but right now, we have to go. One of the other burglars got my ID. They know my name and address and could be headed here right now!"

"Zoey, tell me what the hell is going on!" Dad demanded.

"Dad!"

"Did you try to kill my daughter?" Dad growled at Easton.

"No, sir."

"Easton saved me that night, and he's been trying to protect me ever since."

Dad's accusing eyes met mine, full of anger that I lied to him, that I'd slept with one of my captors.

"Look, we *have* to get to the station, so we're safe. Once we're there, I'll answer any other questions you have, but if we don't leave right now, they'll kill me, Dad, and they might kill you, too."

Finally, the stubbornness in Dad's face took a backseat to his concern for my safety.

"Fine." Dad rolled his wheelchair a few inches closer. "But this conversation is *not* over."

Animosity wrapped around us as Alex and Dad followed me and Easton out the front door.

Easton held a protective hand around my waist while he looked up and down the street, scrutinizing all the cars and pedestrians, looking for any sign of trouble. Once he was satisfied we could make it the forty feet to his car, he ushered me forward, and Alex wheeled my dad behind us.

It was clunky, thumping his wheelchair down the first curb, crossing the road, and jerking it up the second curb to reach Easton's passenger door.

To most people, transferring someone from a wheelchair to another chair probably sounded simple, but the angle was off. The door didn't open wide enough for the chair to pull up alongside the seat, and Dad didn't have enough strength to move himself.

"I'll grab his shoulders," Alex offered.

"I can try to stand." Dad pushed his arms up on his armrests.

I wanted to help but felt it was safer with two strong men helping my father. I held the wheelchair steady as Alex grabbed my dad underneath his armpits from behind and Easton grabbed my dad's waist. They pulled my dad into a standing position, and while they began to shift him toward the seat, I quickly wheeled the chair to the back and opened the trunk.

As I folded and lifted the chair, tires screeched to my left.

A pop exploded in my ears and left them ringing.

It took my brain what felt like an eternity to process the scene unfolding around me. Easton had dropped my father and now stood hunched over, both hands grabbing his stomach, which leaked crimson. Alex must have tried to catch my dad's fall because both he and Dad were lying on the sidewalk with Alex's arm pinned beneath my father's back. A white van with a cartoon cockroach logo on the side stopped right next to us, and two men grabbed Easton while another grabbed me. Smothered my mouth and dragged us inside.

Where three men dressed in black threw us to the ground, slammed the van's side door shut, and then a fourth man gunned the engine, squealing away.

39

The back of the van had no seats, just a metal floor with a tarp that smelled like bug spray. The air was stale and hot, like neither air-conditioning nor an open window had seen the inside of this place for months.

"Easton!" I shrieked. "Are you okay?"

Easton slumped along the far corner of the van, his hand pressing against his bleeding abdomen. His muscles drooped, and as one guy held him down to take the gun from Easton's waistband, he groaned in pain.

Before Easton could answer me, one of the guys—who had a gap in his teeth wide enough to stick a pencil through—duct-taped my hands together and then did the same to Easton, who growled in pain from the movement. I didn't recognize Tooth-Gap Guy or the one with a tattoo of a spiderweb on his cheek. But the other guy...

The other guy was Gavin, Easton's brother.

Gavin shoved his fingers through his hair, staring at Easton's bullet wound with wild eyes. "Look what you made me do," Gavin said. "This is all your fault. If you had gotten rid of the girl like Victor told you to, it'd have never come to this."

"You don't have to do this," Easton mumbled through gritted teeth.

"Don't you get it?" Gavin snapped. Anger mixed with heartbreak in his tone, his voice trailing off as he said, "It's already done."

The finality thickened the oxygen in the van until it was almost unbreathable.

I glanced at Easton, whose grimaced face stared at his only blood relative with a look of betrayal. Knowing the very brother that he had sacrificed everything to protect was going to become his executioner.

Gavin scrubbed his face for several seconds before glaring at Easton with a fresh question.

"What the hell was that wheelchair dude doing with her?" Gavin snapped. "You never told me you talked to him."

I exchanged a look with Easton, whose narrowed eyes looked just as confused as mine.

The van made a sharp turn, sliding me into one of my captors' thighs.

"Answer me!" he demanded.

But Easton didn't answer him; instead, he grunted words through his pain. "Gavin, don't do this."

"Answer me!" Gavin kicked me in the ribs. "Or I'll beat the shit out of your girlfriend."

Easton tried to crawl to me, but one of the guys held him down.

"I'm calling Victor." Gavin jerked his phone from his pocket.

Gavin turned his body toward the side of the van as it careened through traffic, taking us God knew where. He punched a button, and after a few seconds, he said, "Hey, it's me. Yeah, we got 'em, but, dude, I think we have a problem. Remember that guy I told you about? The one in the wheelchair? He was with them." Silence. "I don't know, man. We grabbed them and drove off."

Gavin must have met my father at some point, but when? Had he come to the house after the robbery, trying to find me, and Dad had answered the door? If that were true, he would've known my address before he got my ID, and he wouldn't be so confused as to how I knew him.

I had no idea how he seemed to know my dad, but I didn't have time to speculate; I needed to tear my bindings, so I had a chance to protect Easton.

I pulled at my wrists. The duct tape had been wrapped twice around it.

"You want us to do it, or you want—" Gavin stopped talking. Nodded. "Okay, we'll bring 'em to you."

Gavin ended the call and shouted to the driver, "Change of plans. We're bringing 'em to the tunnels first."

First...

Gavin leaned in so close, I could smell the cigarettes and rage on his breath. He grabbed my jaw and looked at Easton. "You two love-birds are going to answer all our questions, or we're going to cut each of her fingers off, one by one. Keep going until she's nothing but a stack of flesh."

Easton looked sickened by his brother's vile threat.

I quivered, but the guy didn't ask me anything, obviously waiting until we were at the new location.

Even though the bumpy drive only lasted a few minutes, it felt like a year because the entire time, I was tugging at the duct tape, trying to free myself while simultaneously evaluating my options. Assessing the threat levels, trying to gauge who was armed with what. And if I managed to break free, how I'd ensure Easton was saved, too.

The van stopped, and the driver jumped out while one of my captors opened the van door and yanked me out. Then Easton. The bloodstain on his shirt was now the size of a softball, and his shoulders sagged, his body droopy.

I tried to get my bearings as to our location. If I could figure out where we were, maybe I could remember where the closest hospital was. We were parked in an alley littered with empty beer bottles, only wide enough to fit the van, the surrounding buildings at least thirty stories high.

Still in Chicago, then. But what area?

They pushed us, forcing us to walk down a small concrete staircase and through a metal door, where more stairs took us deeper underneath the city.

It was only after descending all the steps that I realized where we were—the underground tunnels of Chicago. Many school kids in Chicago knew about these tunnels because we had to study them in tenth grade.

Constructed in the late 1800s and early 1900s, the rails were constructed for hauling large spools of cables and other supplies through the city, but by 1909, the construction costs had bankrupted the Illinois Tunnel Company. By 1959, the tunnels were abandoned and closed off to the public.

But here we were, walking through them.

Tooth-Gap Guy held me by my elbow while the other three walked us deeper into the abyss. Portable lights broke up the darkness of the twenty-foot-high arched concrete ceilings, which rested above a cylindrical-shaped passage with two iron tracks. It smelled like water had once accumulated and then slowly dripped away from its stained concrete, leaving mildew and mold behind—along with a metallic taste pricking my tongue. And the place was cold. With no air circulation, the chill of being underground blanketed my skin and penetrated my muscles, making me shiver as our footsteps echoed off the hollow chambers.

I glanced at Easton, who didn't even have the strength to walk by himself; two men—Spiderweb Tattoo Face and the van's driver with long, oily hair—had an arm under each of Easton's armpits, pulling him forward as his semi-limp body sagged more with each step. He locked remorseful eyes with me as our captors drew us closer to our doom.

I love you, I mouthed. No matter what happened, I wanted him to know that.

I love you, he mouthed back.

But I knew that if I didn't do something drastic, that'd be the last time he could ever say those words to me.

The tunnel forked into two different directions, and we were pulled right.

Right, I repeated in my head. I needed to memorize our path, so I could find my way back to the door if we broke free.

But we didn't have much time. Easton was barely able to walk; he didn't look like he'd be conscious much longer.

After walking for a couple of minutes, we came to a clearing that must have been where the city had once stored extra train cars. Two tracks were covered with engine-sized wooden boxes that appeared to be man-made, and standing in front of them, staring at his phone, was the man who'd chased me the night of the burglary.

Brown. Also known as Victor.

He looked up from his screen, and when he saw us approach, he crossed his arms.

He regarded us with a sinister smirk. "We meet again."

I gritted my teeth. A smarter person would probably sink to her knees and beg for his mercy, but I knew there was nothing I could say to convince him to let us go. Our only hope was to escape. And that evil little smirk incited a rage inside of me. He stared at me like I was a pathetic weakling, one who was obviously stupid to ever think she could outsmart him.

"Victor—" Easton started, his voice weak.

"Shut the fuck up." Victor looked at Gavin. "You sure it was him?"

"Positive."

"Couldn't have mistaken him for some other cripple?"

Cripple. So help me, if I had the chance, I would knee him in the balls for using that offensive word.

"It was him," Gavin declared.

As Victor began to pace and his goons spaced out from us, I locked eyes with Easton, who stood ten feet to my left. His stomach was bleeding even more, causing his body to sway, as if about to fall at any second.

I looked past Victor. Where the tunnel extended into nothing but blackness, no lights illuminating the path. Could I run past him? And make it?

Not with Easton in his condition.

"The man in the wheelchair"—Victor's arm twitched—"how do you know him?"

Again, Easton flashed me a confused look.

I had no clue who they thought my dad was, but I could tell this string of questions was the only thing keeping us alive.

"How do you know him?" Victor repeated with an impatient edge.

And in that instant, something changed inside of me. It was my turn to protect Easton.

I was done with Brown/Victor making me feel afraid. For once, I wanted to make him feel afraid while I waited for my opening to get out of this mess. Bonus if I got to mind-F the hell out of him in the process.

A fresh rush of adrenaline coursed through my veins and sparked my mind to work on overdrive, firing on all cylinders. It was as if the adrenaline acted as a focal drug, my mind flooding with ideas—clear, crisp, and coming together with something that might rattle him enough to get us out of this mess.

"I'm an undercover, moron," I started. "We set you up, let you take me. It was a trap. So they could follow you to your stupid lair and take you down. Right now? Three dozen of Chicago's finest are surrounding all exits of this tunnel. You're screwed, asshole."

I relished that flinch in his face.

Victor stopped pacing.

"You do anything to me or him," I said, "you'll have a rock-solid murder charge to add to the mix. And you can spend the rest of your life getting raped in the showers."

"You ain't no cop."

"No? Why do you think the cops put a twenty-thousand-dollar bounty on your head? For an average civilian?"

Victor's dark eyes darted to his minions, then back to me. "You're lying."

"Why do you think you went to that condo?" I asked. "Kind of odd, don't you think? That someone set up that heist where an undercover agent just happened to walk in?"

"If you were undercover, you would've arrested us that night."

"You ran away like a little bitch out of a different exit than we'd anticipated. But we learned our lesson. Case in point, here we are." I looked around. "Fitting that you run your operation in this sewer."

"This isn't a sewer," Oily Hair said in offense.

"Shut up!" Victor snapped at him.

"I'm guessing we'll find a lot of stolen goods in those crates." I curled my lip slightly. "So, like I said, game. Set. Match."

"I'll kill you and any other cop that gets in my way." Victor tried to sound confident, but his breathing had quickened.

I couldn't contain my smirk. "You're outgunned. You kill even one of us? You'll be locked up before breakfast for the rest of your life. And the DA? Doesn't take too kindly to cop killers. He'll pull his weight to send you to a prison that makes Alcatraz look like a kindergarten camp."

Victor stomped up to me.

"Your choice. You let us go, I put in a good word for you with the DA. You kill us? You'll be in rat-infested solitary for the rest of your days." I looked at the hired guns. "Your buddies, too."

His subordinates looked at their leader with an obvious question in their eyes. *She telling the truth?*

"Look outside." Victor took a few angry steps away and began pacing. "See if you can spot any cops."

"Please do." I raised a brow. "Make sure you *don't* put your hands up. I want to hear what your brain sounds like, splatting against the wall."

Oily Hair looked nervously to Victor.

"Go! Look!" Victor demanded.

My mouth ran dry.

Oily Hair jogged down the tunnel, the clomp-clomp-clomp of his echoing footsteps growing quieter the farther he ran.

As he waited, Victor walked over to Gavin and grabbed a fistful of his shirt. "I find out the guy that hired you to rob the condo was a cop? I'll fucking kill you."

My blood ran cold, and vile pulsed through my stomach, inching up my esophagus at the shock of what he'd just said.

I couldn't have heard that right—*the guy that hired you.* There was no way it could be true.

Victor had to be either lying or mistaken. Dad would never have any contact with these people, let alone arrange for anyone to rob his condo.

After all, what did he have to gain? Money? There was no way Dad was that desperate. I mean, yeah, as it turned out, he'd seen the financial undercurrent that was pulling us under, he saw how much I was struggling to make ends meet. But he would never cross the line and do something illegal.

Right?

But why make up a story? These guys didn't even know how I was connected to Dad. Or maybe they did. Maybe *he* was playing mind games with me?

Why bother if their goal was to kill us?

None of it made sense.

My mind raced, looking for the missing piece to the puzzle that felt like it was just within my grasp. I quickly replayed our abduction and Gavin's confusion, seeing my dad. His nervousness over it.

When nothing clicked, I went back in time, sifting through the last few months to prove they were lying. But as I did, a sickening new lens came into focus.

I thought about the time Dad found out Anthony was helping pay for medication and how Dad had said, "If I could just get my hands on some money to help..."

And then some of his other words flashed back to me.

"I'd do anything to help, Zoey. Anything. This isn't fair to you, the burden I've become."

And...

"Why did you go to the condo?" he'd asked in a tone that bordered on panic.

My stomach twisted into knot after knot, growing sicker with each layer of realization. That it wasn't as impossible as I wanted to believe.

Dad knew everything that would be in that condo, save for Holly's necklace and the ring since Holly had put the ring in the safe *after* the accident—when Dad had been in the hospital. Dad knew the place was empty. He'd been watching those news stories religiously about the robberies and how they helped homeless shelters after. Perhaps willing to gamble on trusting them to help him. Dad was alone all day, every day while I was at work and had the means to roll up and down the blocks, getting to know people that worked the streets. People who could introduce him to Gavin. Dad had insisted we pay the insurance premium that recently came due on that condo despite how financially underwater we were.

All of it lined up to one sickening conclusion.

Dad must have been the one that hired them.

40

It didn't seem real. Felt like my world's foundation rocked beneath me, the landscape before me once again repainting a different reality. A different father figure.

If he'd done such a thing, why wouldn't he have come clean with me about it when we'd had our big talk? We'd put everything else on the table, and he kept this?

My chest tightened, wanting, demanding all the answers to my questions. But those answers would have to wait. Right now, I needed to focus on staying alive and figure out how in the hell to get Easton and me out of here.

I quickly assessed my surroundings, trying to identify any other paths out of here than the one behind us. One that might take them off guard. The arched concrete tunnel was thirty feet wide, twenty feet tall, with no doorways or staircases within view. Two iron tracks rounded a bend and came to rest behind Victor, where a flat man-made-looking train car stored ten wooden barrels. Far too big to pick up, but if I could get behind one, if they weren't filled with anything, maybe I'd have the strength to kick one and send it rolling over Victor. Or maybe I could turn the lights into a weapon. Three light bulbs with blue cables, connected to a car battery, rested on tripods, casting a wide spotlight in the otherwise blackened space, which smelled of stale water. Maybe there was a puddle out of sight, something I could use to electrocute these douchebags.

No. All of that was too far-fetched. My best shot was to run. And figure out how to take Easton with me, who was fading by the second. His eyes were barely open now, making my heart flutter in panicked beats.

But the goons. Tooth-Gap Guy was off to the left, leaning against the wall, Spiderweb Tattoo Face to my right, arms crossed over his chest. While Gavin—who stood in front—gave one last look of apprehension to his brother before facing Victor.

"No cops," Oily Hair declared, jogging back into sight after checking outside.

My heart became a racehorse.

Victor smirked at me.

"They're there," I claimed.

But I could tell by the narrowing of his eyes that he suspected I was lying. And judging by the clenching of his jaw, he was pissed he'd been tricked.

He picked dirt out of his thumbnail, then glared at Gavin. "The guy in the wheelchair. Why didn't you bring him?"

Gavin snapped his head back. "Why would I?"

Victor stopped picking his nail. "A witness who could *identify* you, and you're asking me why?"

"You told me to get her and Easton, and that's exactly what I did."

"I sent you to pick up the witness and the traitor. People who could turn us in. And you didn't think to grab the cripple? You fucking stupid?"

"I'm the one that got her ID. I found her and Easton."

Victor took two steps forward. "And you left a loose end behind."

"We had seconds to grab two people without being seen. That

guy wasn't moving; if we'd grabbed him, these two mighta gotten away, or the cops mighta seen us."

"You're filled with excuses. Have a PhD in 'em. You never leave a witness behind. You grab them. It's not rocket science."

Gavin's fingers flexed. "*I'm* the one that found that heist in the first place. *I'm* the one that organized it. Easton is the one that screwed this up, not me."

I cringed. Even with death hanging over our heads, it still had to hurt Easton, having his brother turn on him like this. Not even caring that Easton was dying. The only indication Easton was still coherent was his fingernail scraping at the tape on his wrists.

My throat burned, seeing him so helpless. He didn't deserve to die like this, handed over by his very own brother to his executioner.

I needed to save him.

"You never had what it took to be part of my crew," Victor declared. "Let alone one of my commanders."

Victor raised his hand and fired a shot, making me jump. In the condensed space of concrete, the blast was so loud, my eardrums rang. Gavin stood with his eyes wide, a crimson hole appearing in his stomach, before his body thumped to the ground.

"No!" Easton growled.

"Dump him in the sewer." Victor didn't even look at his fallen frame. "Let the rats feed on him."

Easton's eyes darkened as he stared at Victor.

"I'm going to take care of the cripple," Victor announced, ambling back the way we came in. "Kill them both and dump them in the sewer, too."

Victor's figure got swallowed by the tunnel's shadows.

Spiderweb Tattoo Face walked up to me and pulled the weapon from his waistband, but I slammed my leg into his crotch. He collapsed to his knees, but he didn't drop the weapon. I grabbed the gun, fighting to push his finger off the trigger and replace it with my own.

He was stronger than me; I couldn't get the shot lined up to his head, but I did manage to thrust it toward his torso.

I pulled the trigger.

But it missed him and fired into the wall, sending a chip of stone splintering through the air, backlit by one of the portable lights. It stunned the guy for a moment, though, affording me time to line up another shot.

Meanwhile, Easton bolted to his feet. He'd managed to free his hands, and now, with Tooth-Gap Guy raising a semiautomatic, Easton charged him. And knocked him to the ground.

As Easton wrestled with the guy on the concrete, Oily Hair walked toward me. I pressed my finger on the trigger and aimed my barrel at him, but it wasn't easy. Especially with Spiderweb Tattoo Face still fighting for the weapon, but I didn't need to be precise. I just needed to maim.

When Oily Hair took another step and raised his arm, I pulled my trigger.

Oily Hair jerked, his hip spewing blood as he screamed.

"Zoey!" Easton shouted.

Spiderweb Tattoo Face knocked me down, jumped on top of me, wrapped his hands around my neck, and squeezed.

I pressed against his wrists, thrashed my body. Wiggling it, twisting it. I tried to bring my knees up, my ankles, but it was fruitless. The guy's lips curled over his teeth as he looked down at me and squeezed my neck tighter, pressure mounting in my head.

As I stared into the eyes of my killer, my only hope was that everyone else would make it out alive. That Easton would overpower the other men, that Dad would have made it to the police station before Victor found him. That Alex wouldn't be anywhere near the danger, either.

The concrete walls around me began to darken, the sound of Easton screaming my name fading.

Suddenly, my throat opened, and a flood of air rushed into my lungs so violently, I choked on it. A deep, barking cough so rough that I gagged.

My attacker was on the ground, and Easton was on top of him, punching the guy's nose, his cheek, his temple.

While Tooth-Gap Guy, the one Easton had been fighting, lay motionless twenty feet away. Dead or unconscious, I couldn't be sure. But Oily Hair, with his bloody hip, dragged himself into an army crawl toward his fallen gun, leaving a streak of blood painted along the concrete floor behind him like an artist had brushed a canvas.

My lungs burned, and my throat laced with metallic-tasting blood. I felt dizzy and light-headed, but I could not allow Oily Hair to reach the weapon. His eyes were trained on Easton, who continued to beat the hell out of the guy who'd tried to kill me.

I pushed my torso up and wobbled as I stood. Oily Hair was four feet away from the weapon and closing. The gun rested on the floor like it was sleeping peacefully, unaware that whoever grabbed it would likely win this battle and the others would lose their lives.

I took a step forward, hearing the flesh-on-flesh smacks and groans happening behind me as I stumbled closer to the injured man.

The floor rocked, but this time, I leaned into the fall and landed on Oily Hair's head. The sound of a turkey's wishbone cracking in half marked his nose breaking on the concrete.

He roared, but I leaned my shoulder into his neck more.

Out of the corner of my eye, I saw Easton stand up. With his fists covered in blood, he marched over to me and pulled me up.

"You okay?" Easton panted, his right eye already swelling and his lip bloody from the battle.

I nodded.

Easton grabbed Oily Hair's gun and tucked it into his waistband before the goon could reach it.

Spiderweb Tattoo Face and Tooth-Gap Guy remained lifeless on the ground, their weapons lying along the railroad track thirty feet away.

"I thought you were dying." Just the thought of it made me cry. "You were limp."

"The more injured I appeared, the more they'd let their guard down."

Easton bit into the edge of my tape and then ripped it open, unraveling the rest.

"So, you're okay?" I touched his arm.

"If it hit an organ, I'd be dead by now."

Tentative relief flooded my system.

But his brother wasn't okay; he lay on the ground, bleeding.

"Do you have your cell on you?" A rising wave of alarm rose through my core.

"No. They tossed it when they threw me in the van."

"We need to get Gavin help. And we need to get to my dad before Victor does."

Easton unleashed those ocean-colored eyes on me, scanning my body and then locking his gaze with mine until he seemed satisfied that I was as okay as I claimed.

But Gavin wouldn't be okay much longer. Easton and I rushed to where he'd fallen. He lay on his back, his breaths labored as blood oozed out of the bullet wound in his stomach.

I pressed my left palm against his wound, feeling his warm blood pool beneath my skin. I added my right hand on top, so I could press harder, but the blood merely slowed.

"Hold on, Gavin." I tried to sound strong, but time felt like an enemy, flying by too fast to save him.

Gavin's rounded eyes locked with mine as crimson stained the concrete beneath him. "Why are you helping me?" His voice was weak.

"You're Easton's brother."

A crease appeared between Gavin's brows. "But I turned you over to Victor."

No matter what mistakes Gavin made... "You're the only family Easton has, and I won't let him lose you."

Like Gavin, Dad had strayed and made choices that had hurt those he loved. He'd almost died before we could make amends, but he'd survived, giving us the time we needed to finally talk things out, mend our wounds, and start a new chapter in our relationship.

Easton deserved that same opportunity with his brother—to get him back and heal their hurts.

I couldn't let Gavin die before they had that chance.

Gavin's chest rose and fell quicker.

"Go get help," I said to Easton.

"I'm not leaving you alone down here." Easton eyed the darkened tunnels.

"I need to keep pressure on the wound."

"*I'll* put pressure on it."

But before either of us said anything else, a sound silenced us.

Footsteps, echoing off the murky tunnel. The steps of a single person were slow and methodical, almost as if they knew we could hear them approaching and wanted to drag it out.

I wanted to believe it could be a police officer coming down here to rescue us. After all, surely, my dad had called the police by now, and maybe they'd tracked down the van, found it parked outside that door. But my instincts told me the steps didn't belong to an ally.

Whoever was down here with us wasn't here to help.

"Zoey, run," Easton whispered.

But before I could process his demand, a silhouette emerged into the light.

Pointing a semiautomatic at us.

"Don't move."

41

Victor glanced at his fallen men before turning his attention back on us.

Easton positioned his body in front of mine.

"We could've made one hell of a team." Irritation laced Victor's words, making me wonder if anyone had ever turned him down before.

"I would never team up with you," Easton growled.

"You rob places for a living. You really think a complication wouldn't come up eventually?"

"That's the difference between me and you," Easton said in disgust. "I don't view people as complications."

Victor licked his teeth. "You never had the balls to be on my crew."

"I never had any interest in joining your crew. My brother fell for your lies, but I didn't."

Victor's gaze fell to Gavin, whose breaths were so light that I feared he'd die at any second.

"He saw my vision. Bigger heists. More money. I don't let things like witnesses or cops scare me out of taking what I want."

I could only pray that if we didn't make it out of here alive, Hernandez would not stop hunting until he found Victor and locked him up forever. Because Victor was willing to kill whoever was in his way. And someday, a witness might not just be any innocent person; it might be a child.

Victor shrank the distance between us to fifteen feet, and when he pointed his gun at me, Easton lunged and knocked Victor to the ground. The gun scraped across the concrete as it slid away while Easton punched Victor in his jaw. Which cracked like a twig. Victor bucked Easton off of him and kicked Easton's bloodstained stomach. Right where he'd been shot.

Easton howled and grabbed his abdomen as he crumpled to the ground, where Victor began beating him.

"Help him," Gavin pleaded.

I glanced at the gun, which was a few feet away, then back at Gavin. A bloodstain the size of a pumpkin pooled beneath him. I'd finally gotten the hemorrhaging to slow down, but if I let go, the faucet would turn back on, and I had to assume any further bleeding would be fatal.

If I didn't go for the gun, though, Victor would kill Easton.

"Help him," Gavin repeated.

My eyes stung. I said it out loud to make sure he understood what he was asking me to do. "If I let go, you'll probably die."

Victor punched Easton in the ear so hard, his head swiveled and his eyes started to roll into the back of his head.

Gavin locked his fading eyes with mine. "Save my brother," he pleaded.

I glanced at Gavin for one more second before jumping up.

I bolted to the gun, grabbed it, took aim, and pulled the trigger.

The gun didn't fire.

As Victor continued to whap Easton's temple, I looked at the gun, trying to figure out why it wasn't shooting. The trigger itself gave no indication. The gun didn't look damaged.

Maybe it was out of bullets. It was one of those guns that packed the bullets in a magazine, and I didn't know how to release it to check the bullet count.

With Victor's cracking fists making Easton's eyes close, I frantically glanced at the weapon in my hands.

A little silver lever sat at the base of the barrel. A safety?

I pushed the lever.

Lined up my shot at Victor's head again.

And pulled the trigger.

Another blast echoed off the concrete as Victor stilled, then fell to his right.

"Easton!" I screamed and ran to his side.

But his eyes didn't open.

42

Easton has a heartbeat. Thank God.

I raced to Gavin's side, tears streaming down my cheeks as I pressed my hands against his wound again. Gavin groaned, but he lost so much blood, his skin was vampire-level pale. I needed to get him medical attention, but if I let go of his wound, by the time I ran out into the street and flagged down help and came back, I was confident he would be dead.

Easton might be, too.

I'm alone in a darkened hell beneath the city and watching the love of my life die right in front of my eyes.

"Hold on." I pressed my trembling hands down as hard as I could.

Gavin's eyes locked with mine again. Only this time, his eyes looked like his soul was connected to a dimmer, fading.

"I'm sorry," he whispered.

His eyelids slowly descended. I willed them to stop, to not close, for if they closed, they might never open again. And I couldn't tell Easton his only family was gone.

Gavin's eyes did close though, and he stopped moving, just as a new sound appeared.

The sound of hope.

As a symphony of footsteps grew louder, I couldn't tell if his chest was moving up or down anymore.

"Police!" a voice barked from the end of the tunnel I'd come in through.

"Over here!" I shouted. "We need help!"

A few seconds later, three police officers, wearing bulletproof vests, advanced toward me with their guns drawn atop powerful flashlights that swept the area for any sign of danger.

While the other two officers kicked the fallen weapons further to the side, one of the officers approached me and put his gun back into its holster.

Hernandez.

"Got a 10-52," Hernandez shouted to the end of the tunnel. Then, he walked to Easton, put his fingers on his neck.

What if it had stopped beating?

Hernandez was silent as his fingers felt for the heartbeat that was connected to my own.

"Is he okay?" I yelped.

"He's alive," Hernandez said.

I blew out a breath. But that didn't mean Easton was out of the woods. Blunt force trauma to the head, bullet wound to the stomach, and who knew what was going on inside his body?

One of the officers came to me and took over putting pressure on the wound, allowing me to rush to Easton's side. I wanted to cup his face but was terrified to move him, worried one wrong bump could damage his spinal cord or something.

His skin was pale, making me fear that he'd bled more than I realized. Possibly internally. And parts of his face were beginning to swell and darken from the assault.

If he hadn't fought Victor, I'd be dead. Easton had taken this beating to save my life.

And it might have cost him his own.

He was a protector for those he loved. A protector of his brother, of me, willing to lay down his life for us.

How many people would literally die to protect someone? How many would do it *after* that person had hurt them the way Gavin had?

Hernandez moved around to the other fallen men, checking their pulses. "This one's gone," he said, referring to Victor. "The others have a pulse."

"My dad. Victor was going to kill him. Is he—"

"He's at the station," Hernandez said. "Safe. So is Alex. Your dad called it in right away. Was smart enough to get the plate number. Put out an APB. Didn't take long for an officer to spot the van parked outside the tunnel entrance."

"He's really okay? Because when they shot Easton, my dad fell—"

"He's fine," Hernandez assured. "But we'd better get these guys to the hospital."

43

I stared at the crimson remnants on the tips of Easton's hair. The nurses had done an excellent job, cleaning the rest of the blood off, but dried fragments remained on some of his longer pieces. The skin around Easton's right eye was so swollen that only a millimeter of his sapphire iris was exposed, and his cheeks and jaw were covered in purple, as if someone had dabbed his face with a violet paintbrush.

Easton lay on a white hospital bed after undergoing surgery while a jumble of voices blended into the background of beeps and sneakers on the linoleum floor. It smelled like bleach. And fear.

"Hey," I whispered, taking Easton's hand when he stirred. "The doctor said you're going to be just fine."

Easton's medicated gaze landed on my face, inciting a smile. Which made him grimace from the pain. And then he frowned with concern.

After I'd been examined in the ER, I'd washed the blood off my skin, but I still had it on my clothes.

"Are you okay?" His voice was scratchy, like the beating must have roughed up his throat.

"I'm fine. But you seriously scared me," I said. "You weren't moving."

Easton looked down at his hospital gown, at the medical equipment surrounding him. "Fill me in on what happened. Last thing I remember, I was fighting Victor."

I squeezed his hand and picked up where his concussion had left off, Easton absorbing every word.

"My brother's alive?" Easton's face pinched in relieved disbelief.

"He was when they brought him in, but he lost a lot of blood. They took him up to surgery, too, but his is taking a lot longer. They said the doctor will be down soon to give us an update."

Easton's azure eyes looked down, a line appearing between his eyebrows. He cleared his throat and then held my gaze again.

"You saved my brother," he said. His tone was tight, as if fighting back tears. "Why? He was trying to get you killed."

"He's the only family you have." My chin quivered. "He may or may not continue to make terrible choices, but if he lives, at least he has the chance to turn his life around. The chance to love you again, the way you deserve to be loved by him, before it's too late."

Everyone deserves a chance to atone for their mistakes. Do they not?

Easton let out an incredulous breath, and he looked at me with a ghost of a smile.

"Just when I thought I couldn't admire you more," he whispered with a slight shake to his head.

Meeting Easton taught me that there are many different layers to people. Some good, some bad. Which is why it's so important to peel back all those layers to see what is truly underneath before we hastily rush to judgment.

We are not the sum total of our mistakes, but a sum total of what's in our hearts. We are all just a complicated array of good and bad choices, and I learned the importance of looking beyond our human frailties.

"You were worried that the lightness inside of Gavin was gone." I held his stare. "But when he saw you were losing the fight with

Victor, do you know what Gavin did?" I asked. "He told me to let him go. Even though keeping pressure on his wound was the only thing keeping him alive, he said, 'Save my brother.' "

Easton's eyes welled with tears.

"No matter what he did before then, in that moment, he was willing to sacrifice his own life to save you." That was the layer I wanted Easton to hold on to.

Easton's lips quivered, and he cleared his throat. As he looked down at the floor, I wondered if he was replaying the erosion of Gavin's love for him, only to realize it had been there all along, buried beneath his bad choices.

A doctor emerged from the hallway. She had short red hair that swept up a little higher in the front and vintage brown-rimmed glasses. "Easton Wells?"

Easton nodded.

"I'm Doctor Morrison." She rubbed her hands together, as if they were cold. "I performed surgery on your brother."

"Is he..."

"He's in recovery," she said. "We removed a .22 caliber bullet from his abdominal cavity, repaired a perforation of his small bowel, and gave him a blood transfusion."

"Is he going to be okay?" Easton's voice rose with hope.

"He got lucky. If he'd lost more blood..." She paused. "His vitals are stable. At this point, the biggest risk for him is a post-op inter-abdominal abscess. It only happens in about 3 percent of patients, though, so I'm optimistic he'll make a full recovery."

Easton's chest deflated in relief. "Can I see him?"

"Once he's out of recovery, he'll be moved into a room. Medically, he'll be cleared for visitors, but you'll have to ask law enforcement."

Right. Gavin was a wanted criminal, now in custody.

So was Easton, who looked down at his right hand, which was cuffed to the bed's rail.

"I'll keep you posted on your brother." The doctor offered a sympathetic smile.

And then she left us alone.

With Easton staring at the handcuff, each second that passed, all the hope he'd felt appeared to drain from his body as reality grew unwanted weeds over his heart.

Easton didn't look at me as he spoke in a pained voice. "I really wish you'd listen to me; I don't want you to wait for me while I'm in prison. I don't want you to throw your life away on me."

"You *are* my life."

"Zoey—"

"And I'm not going to let you take that away from me."

"Zoey—"

"I've accepted your choices, Easton. And now, you need to accept mine."

He pursed his lips together.

"I'll wait for you, no matter what you say or do about it. I'll visit you every chance I get even if you refuse to see me. And the day that you get released? I'll be there to drive you home."

I could see by the furrowing of Easton's brows and the tears that broke over his battered cheeks that Easton never allowed himself to imagine a future with me in it.

"I've never had anyone love me like this before," he whispered.

I tried to act like his declaration hadn't bruised my soul.

Easton squeezed my hand. "You saved me, Zoey. In every way a man can be saved."

I stood up and leaned over his bed so my face dangled in front of his. And then I slowly and incredibly gently pressed my lips against his.

My growing love for Easton was as if every cell in my body had been awakened from a deep hibernation, emerging into the light of a forest.

I kept my lips on his for several seconds before pulling back and staring at the sapphire speckles in his eyes. They were darker on the outside and grew lighter toward the iris in a gorgeous gradient of blues and greens.

"Is your dad okay?" Easton brushed my cheek with the backs of his fingers.

I nodded. "He's in the waiting room."

Easton looked from my left eye to my right. "Do you think they were telling the truth? That your dad organized the heist?"

I took a deep breath and ran a hand through my hair. "I don't know. But I need to talk to him."

44

"Hey." I walked up to my dad in the waiting room.

He'd parked his chair next to Alex, who'd come here to make sure I was okay.

"How is he?" Dad's voice was tense, like his concern for Easton only existed because Easton mattered to me.

"Easton's okay. They think his brother will be okay, too."

Dad nodded.

"Can we talk?" I asked him.

Alex looked from me to my dad. "I think I'll head home." He stood up and stared at me for a long moment. "I'm glad you're okay, Zoey."

All his earlier anger dissipated with the softening of his shoulders. I was sure he didn't understand how I could fall for a criminal who'd held me hostage, but Alex had been friends with me long enough to know there was a reason. He might not agree with it, might forever hold on to the belief Easton was a terrible person, but based on the soft smile he gave, clearly, he wasn't going to stay mad at me over it.

Something I greatly appreciated.

"Thank you, Alex. For everything. Seriously, you're a really good friend, and I don't know what we would have done without you."

I felt bad for having ever suspected him of being involved in the robbery. He really had hired the PI to help find who did this to me.

Alex offered me another weak smile and then ambled out the front doors to give me and my father some privacy.

The waiting room was busy, though. The conversation I wanted to have with him wasn't something I cared to do in public.

"Let's go for a walk," I suggested, "so we can talk in private."

Dad followed me outside the automatic doors and wheeled himself next to me as I lumbered down the sidewalk.

It was twilight, just after the sunset, and skyscrapers already had their lights on, bracing for the coming darkness that would soon swallow the city. The storm had passed a bit ago, and the pavement was still glistening from its brief rain. Vehicles hummed along the road in a stream of white headlights and red taillights while a scattering of pedestrians walked along the sidewalks. A light breeze blew my hair into my face as I looked down at my father.

"I'm sorry for keeping Easton's identity a secret from you." I looked away, a pang hitting my ribs.

Dad's wheelchair bumped over a sidewalk crack. "Wish you had been honest with me."

"It was complicated."

Dad pursed his lips. "Complicated?"

"I didn't think you'd understand." I shrugged. "But there's no excuse for lying. I'm sorry."

A block away, the metallic scraping pierced the air as the "L" train tunneled through the buildings.

"Dad, when they'd grabbed me and put me in the van, they recognized you."

Dad clenched his eyes shut and stopped rolling his wheelchair. An ambulance's siren wailed somewhere close by.

"So, it's true, then."

Dad blew out a breath so deep, he must've been holding it in since before the robbery.

"You hired them," I said through blurry eyes. "Why?"

Dad pinched the bridge of his nose. "Zoey..."

The ambulance came around the corner, its siren so loud that it stabbed my ears, and then it parked outside the doors of the hospital. Thankfully turning off the siren.

"I need to hear you say it. Because otherwise, it doesn't feel real."

Dad regarded me, his rounded eyes full of sorrow. "I couldn't watch you suffer the financial burden of taking care of me anymore. I spent weeks making phone calls, trying to get myself into an inpatient rehab, trying to apply for government assistance to get out of your way so you could have a normal life, but none of it panned out. I had even called friends, distant relatives, asking for help."

I put my hand over my aching stomach.

"And in the meantime," he continued, "I would see you come home so stressed over money, no matter how much you tried to hide it. And it was just getting worse." Dad shook his head. "I failed to get out of your hair."

Out of my hair. The ache spread up to my ribs.

"But I swear, sometimes, it's like once you're down on your luck, you're a plague that no one wants to touch. They don't want to get involved, like they're worried your bad luck will rub off on them. Or maybe they assume that once they open that door, I'll just keep walking through it, asking for more, and you know what?"

Dad scrubbed the side of his face. "It's not their responsibility to save me," he said. "But it's not your responsibility, either. This entire situation spiraled out of control. When you first took me in, I thought it would be for a few weeks. I never imagined that all the bills would be put onto your shoulders. It's not right. I'm the parent; you're the child. I'm supposed to enrich your life, not poison it."

Up ahead, a father and his little girl walked down the sidewalk, holding hands, while she licked an ice cream cone. The sight of it made my chest clench at the innocence of it all.

"I felt helpless, Zoey. You were drowning in financial pressure, and I couldn't work, and none of the government assistance was coming through, and hospitals and rehab places wouldn't touch me with a ten-foot pole because I had filed for bankruptcy. I could go on and on about all the other things I tried to do to help, but I didn't care what it took. I was going to find a way to help you, come hell or high water."

The farther we got from the hospital, the stronger the smell of fried pastries grew. Somewhere nearby must be a sweet shop of baked goods.

"But a robbery? Dad, you've never broken the law before."

"The robberies were all over the news. And I saw how they would target affluent houses when no one was home. When you would go to work, I started taking rolls through the neighborhood. Started talking to people on the streets and asking questions. Wasn't long before a guy introduced me to another guy who could arrange the whole thing."

The guy had introduced him to Gavin.

"Did they know it was your condo?"

"Just told them it was empty." Dad pinched his nose again. "If I'd had any idea you were ever planning to go back to that condo, I never would've done it, Zoey. I thought you wouldn't go back until it sold."

The traffic on the road slowed down as a stoplight turned red.

"Why didn't you tell me after?" I demanded, anger and betrayal boiling my blood.

"At first, I was in shock. I couldn't believe you had gone there that night and had almost been killed. The guilt ate me alive. I was disgusted with myself that I had once again found a way to hurt you."

My throat stung.

"Seemed like the harder I tried to help you, the more I hurt you, and I was so angry with myself, I couldn't bear admitting what I had done. It was pathetic and weak, but I was scared, too. I was afraid if you found out, you would never forgive me."

Dad looked down in shame. "And yet, I couldn't let it go, either. As angry as I was at myself, I was seething at the men who'd laid their hands on you. I was promised that no one would ever get hurt. They were willing to kill you over this, and I was not about to let that go."

He looked at me again. "That's why I was so obsessive in finding out who had done this. When you'd go to work, I would go back and try to find the original man I had talked to, but he was nowhere to be found."

I wonder if Victor took care of him.

"So, you hired a private investigator." I rubbed my forehead. "And when you found them, what were you going to do?"

Dad looked up at the sky before looking back to me. "I told myself I was going to turn them into the police. But I don't know if I would've had the willpower to do that. I might have taken justice into my own hands."

This was too much to process. Dad and I had finally reached a place where we were moving forward with our relationship. And that whole time? He knew that there was this big secret that he was keeping from me.

I thought the biggest thing I had to get past was Easton's prior offenses, but now, my dad's behavior confronted me. It felt like the universe was testing me, to see if I'd really get over my biases and forgive people for their bad choices.

"Why didn't you tell me about this sooner?" I clenched my hand. "We had that heart-to-heart, and you never even mentioned any of this."

"I was scared it would put you in more danger. I was concerned that if they found out you were the daughter of the man that had hired them, they'd try even harder to eliminate you because I could ID one of them. I was going to tell you once they were behind bars. I just wasn't going to do it when it might put you in danger, Zoey. I'm sorry."

This was unreal.

A man on a cell phone walked around us on the sidewalk. I waited until he was for sure out of earshot before I spoke again.

"And the police? They know what you did?"

"I confessed right after the heist. I was fully transparent and gave Hernandez every piece of information I had. What the middleman and the burglar he connected me with looked like, where I met them, everything. I turned over every piece of information, so they could try to find these people."

"And you didn't get arrested?"

"Was told charges would be forthcoming, but at the time, they were trying to find the suspects, and I think they were hoping the burglars might try to contact me. Maybe to find out who you were."

"And the police didn't think I had a right to know this?"

"I pleaded with them not to tell you until this was all over. You had been through a tremendous trauma, and the last thing you needed was more heartbreak." He dropped his tone lower. "I'm so sorry, Zoey. I hope you can find it in your heart to forgive me."

I looked at the father walking with his little girl up ahead. She was crying, staring at her ice cream cone, which had fallen on the sidewalk, while the dad knelt before her, wiping away her tears.

It would take time for my anger and disappointment to subside, but I wasn't going to turn my back on Dad. Because even though I was upset right now, he needed to know that, "I do forgive you, Dad. But you have to promise me that from now on, we'll always talk everything out. And no matter what happens, you'll never do something like this again."

"I can't believe I did it in the first place." He shook his head and pursed his lips. "I wish I could go back in time and take it all back."

I scrubbed my face with my hands. "I don't want you to move out, Dad. Not until you're physically and financially independent."

"Zoey—"

"This is my life, and I get to make the decisions for myself. And I want to help my father get back on his feet. And I want time with you, too, Dad. To have that second chance with each other that we've both wanted."

Dad's lower lip quivered, and a sadness cut through his eyes. It took him several seconds to find his voice. "How could you want to help me after what I've done?"

"Because you're my father. And what you did was really stupid, but I still love you. And I always will. And there's nothing you could ever do to make me love you any less."

Dad's Adam's apple bobbed.

"I might be going to jail." He cast his eyes down.

"Then, I'll visit you there. Someone's got to make sure you're doing your PT."

A ghost of a grin stretched over his lips.

"Maybe you'll share a cell with Easton."

Dad's smile fell, and he looked back up at me. "Suppose you wouldn't listen to me if I said you deserve better?"

"You kind of lost the upper hand, Dad. Besides, you both orchestrated that robbery."

Dad frowned. I could see his eyes searching for the building blocks of an argument of how his sins weren't as bad as Easton's, but he must have seen the determination in my posture and knew it was a lost cause. Leaving him with two options: alienate his daughter after all of this or accept her choices. Even if he didn't agree with them.

"Come on." I nodded toward the hospital. "You guys never had a formal introduction."

"You want me to meet the criminal that held you hostage?" Dad licked his teeth. "And not kill him?"

"I want you to meet my boyfriend. And, yes, non-murder would be great."

45

Dad wheeled himself over to the side of Easton's hospital bed. Gave him the don't-mess-with-my-daughter glare.

"Sir." Easton straightened himself up.

"You're a criminal."

"Dad..."

"Was," Easton said. "I'm giving up that lifestyle."

"You're dating my daughter."

"Yes, sir."

"She deserves better."

"Dad!"

Dad pursed his lips. Clearly, accepting my choices was harder for him than he imagined.

"You're right." Easton broke eye contact. "I've told her repeatedly to let me go, but Zoey's..."

"Stubborn?" I arched a brow.

"Headstrong." Easton's mouth curled slightly on one side. "And after everything she's been through, I won't break her heart by cutting her out of my life unless that's what she wants."

"And if she changes her mind? And does want you out of her life?"

"I'll support that one hundred percent. And be here for her in whatever capacity she desires."

Dad's chest inflated, but I could still see him struggling with this. "Why are...*were*," he corrected, "you a burglar?"

Easton explained his life story to my father—his parents dying, living on the street, stealing at first to stay alive and then allowing it to escalate from there. What I loved about it was that Easton made no excuses for his choices. He simply laid out the sequence of events and decisions he had made that brought him to this point.

"The condo burglary changed everything," Easton continued.

"Why?" my dad pressed.

Easton exchanged a quick look with me and then cleared his throat. "Ever since my parents died, my life had gone on this crooked track, heading toward a cliff. But then Zoey was like an electrical surge that jolted the train and made me look up for the first time."

My dad folded his hands in his lap.

"For years, I've been merely existing. Going on that broken track. Waking up each day and never thinking beyond it. Never having a reason to change. But then I met Zoey, and she made me realize how much more my life could be."

My throat swelled.

"After that, my only focus was protecting Zoey. And things just... evolved from there."

My dad rubbed his cheek. "You'll be going to prison," Dad grumbled.

"I told Zoey I didn't want her to wait for me."

"And I reminded him no one controls my decisions, except me."

Dad gave me a look with tight eyes, like he was about to go into the whole why-would-you-wait-for-him-while-he's-in-prison debate. But I shot him the I'm-a-grown-woman-and-this-is-my-decision look that shut it down.

After a few more seconds, Dad returned his stare to Easton.

"Even if you don't spend an eternity in prison, how can I trust you won't go back to breaking the law?"

"I'll never do anything that could bring her harm."

"If you ever hurt my daughter—" Dad flexed his fingers.

"I'd never."

Dad blew out an exasperated breath. I could tell he didn't like this. A felon wasn't his dream match for his daughter. But he also knew this wasn't his call to make. I was an adult, and Easton had my heart. In time, I trusted Dad would grow to love Easton as much as I did. Or at least not despise him.

"Some people are not bad in nature, Dad. They just make mistakes."

46

TWO YEARS, SIX MONTHS, AND THIRTEEN DAYS LATER

I jumped out of bed and looked at the clock, then danced to the shower.

I loved my new bathroom with the tiled floor that looked like wood, the white vanity, and the updated trim. But then I loved everything about my new apartment, especially its location. I loved that it was closer to the heart of Chicago and that it was only one block from the "L" train, so getting to work was super quick. I loved that I had my own balcony, where I could sit and watch the stars at night. But most of all, I loved that it was mine.

I missed living with Dad, but it was a wonderful new chapter for both of us when he'd moved out a couple years ago. Besides, he visited me. A lot. And we'd become closer than ever.

I hummed the entire time I washed my hair, the hot water cascading over my skin. I sang as I put my makeup on and glanced at the framed photograph hanging on the wall. Taken a year ago, the photo was me, sitting on the South Rim of the Grand Canyon, watching the sun set.

One moment of that trip stood out above the rest.

I hold up the dandelions I picked in honor of my deceased boyfriend.

I'd read that the dandelion is a symbol of resilience, hope, and the rebirth of life. The dandelion is able to survive in some of the harshest conditions, and can bounce back from adversity, and continue to grow. The bright yellow petals represent joy, and the black seeds carry wishes for new beginnings with them as they fly into the air.

I have a mixture of yellow ones and some that have already turned into white puffballs.

"It took me a while to get here," I say. "And I still miss you every single day. I always will. But from this moment on, I vow I will never break my promise to you again. I finally found the happiness I promised you I would, and this time, I'll never let it go."

I blow the little white puff balls off their base and watch them float off into the pastel sky.

And inside my heart, the past finally releases and floats into my future.

I glanced at the smaller picture that I'd hung on the side wall—of me holding Anthony's baby for the first time—and my heart warmed with memories from that day, when he'd flown to Chicago and Dad and I got to meet my niece.

I continued smiling as I got dressed, irrationally looking at the clock every two minutes.

I would not be late. Not for this. I wanted to hit the road within the next twenty minutes.

A knock on my front door made me grin.

I opened it, and there, standing on the other side—yep, standing—was Dad. He'd made a full recovery.

"I brought bagels." He held up a brown bag.

Dad gave me a quick kiss on the cheek as he walked inside and set breakfast down on my kitchen table. "Alex sends his regards."

"How does he like his new clinic?"

"Loves it. We'll have to go out to celebrate," Dad said.

We had a lot to celebrate these days. Including my much-improved financial situation. I never collected the reward money. Even if they would have given it to me, when I found out my brother had put a second mortgage on his house to fund it, I refused to take it.

Instead, I got a second job tending bar, collected a tidy little bonus from my primary job after another year of outperforming my targets, and slowly climbed out of that hole. I'd have to say, though, the biggest financial swing came when Dad's situation rebounded and that financial burden evaporated.

It allowed me to start classes at college to pursue my degree in veterinarian science. Would it take a while to get the degree? Yep. But time was going to pass anyway, so why not pursue a job working with animals, like I'd always wanted?

Dad pleaded guilty to conspiracy to commit burglary. He avoided more serious charges, thanks to his immediate confession and cooperation with the case. I also suspected that his physical condition and mental state at the time of the burglary played a role in the DA agreeing to lowering the charges and commuting his sentence, but I couldn't be sure. In any case, Dad was only sentenced to thirty days in jail with two years of probation and two hundred hours of community service.

Meanwhile, before and after Dad's stint in jail, Alex continued giving my dad physical therapy at a majorly discounted rate and let me pay off my debt to him over time. He kept fighting me on taking the money, but I insisted. Dad regained his independence, moved into his own apartment, and started his own company.

I didn't think starting his own company was his original goal, but getting hired back into his old position with a criminal record hadn't panned out, so he opened up a consulting agency. Without start-up capital, he built it on his sweat equity, slowly building it from the ground up. He was still doing corporate strategy work, but not for one company. Rather many different companies, on his own terms, charging his own rates, freelance.

It would take him several years before he was pocketing more than basic living expenses, but he was on the road to financial freedom and was thrilled about it.

The best part was seeing how happy he was. He and I had never been closer, and his independence had eradicated the remaining sadness inside of him.

These days, we hung out at least two times a week. Sometimes, we'd go out to dinner or take in a museum. Sometimes, we'd just sit and talk. To put a word on it, it was...wonderful. A fresh new chapter, full of joy.

Joy that was about to get a hella lot bigger.

"You nervous?" Dad met my gaze.

"Excited."

"Sure you don't want me to drive with you?"

"Positive. I want it to be just him and me on the drive home."

Dad took out a bagel, spread cream cheese on it, and took a bite.

"You worried it'll be different now that you'll be with him all the time?"

I checked myself out in the mirror, wanting to look perfect today. I kept my hair long, in waves, and had a brand-new white T-shirt and jeans on.

"I've visited him every week for the past two and a half years. We talk on the phone every single day, and we write letters to each other every day, too, so, no, I'm not nervous. I'm excited."

Beyond excited.

If a child had to wait ten years for Christmas? That was what this felt like, times a thousand.

Dad cream-cheesed a bagel for me and set it on the table. "Eat."

"I'm too excited."

"Eat. Your blood sugar might fall. Last thing you need to do is faint when you see him."

I sighed heavily, pretending to be annoyed, but he had a point.

I begrudgingly downed half a bagel and looked at the clock again.

"It's time."

I smiled so wide, I thought my lips might crack.

I kissed my dad on the cheek. "Lock up when you leave, yeah?"

"I'm heading out, too. I didn't take the day off work like you did."

"So, your offer to drive with me was kind of rhetorical then." I smiled.

Dad rolled his eyes.

"Drive safe, and, Zoey?" Dad paused. "He'd better be worth the wait."

I almost skipped all the way to my car—yep, I had my very own car now!—waving at Dad as he pulled away in his own. I blasted pop music all the way to the prison, and when I parked, my hands were shaking.

I wish Easton had let me come inside, but he'd insisted I stay out here.

"God knows how long they are going to take, and I don't want you getting exposed to something when I'm not there to protect you," he'd said.

I didn't fight much because honestly, it didn't matter to me where we reunited. Just that we did.

I chewed on my thumbnail, pacing near my car. It was cold out today. A fresh inch of snow blanketed the parking lot, and my breath came out in puffs of white clouds as the icy wind stabbed my cheeks. But I didn't care. I had my coat, I had my gloves, and my heart kept me warm.

I glanced at the time on my phone. Easton was supposed to be released twenty minutes ago. He'd warned me not to worry if it was a little late, but I was officially worrying. What if they'd somehow retracted his plea deal? The one that allowed him to only be convicted for five years, only serving half for good behavior?

If they did that, it would be complete bullshit. Easton followed through with every one of his conditions. He'd avoided kidnapping and attempted murder charges with my testimony that Easton never went along with the plan to kill me—in fact, he'd helped me escape and protected me from Victor and his crew. I mean, yeah, it got a little dicey there for a moment, given that Easton was the leader of those Robin Hood Thieves burglaries, but no one had been hurt in them. And Easton's information allowed police to take down Victor's crew, who'd moved here from Philly—where, evidently, their burglaries often resulted in murders.

Easton even convinced his brother, Gavin, to accept a plea deal in exchange for more information for the investigation. His brother had another few years to serve, thanks to some of his more serious charges, but the point was, Easton did everything they'd asked, and his testimony had been vital to keeping people safe from Victor's crew.

The officers stopped all the burglaries and publicly claimed a victory in front of the city. It would be a really crappy thing to do to wait until the last day of his sentence and take back his plea deal. And it would look really bad to do that.

Plus, I didn't think that was legal. But I chewed another millimeter off my thumbnail, wondering if it was possible.

No. Hernandez would have called me if that happened. Right? He'd been a fantastic detective, staying in touch with me the entire time.

I paced left, then right, staring at the prison for any sign of life. Barbed wire rested along the top of the beige stone walls, a 360° lookout tower positioned only twenty feet from the iron gate, whose copper coloring had faded through the years.

A gate that still hadn't opened.

Thirty minutes late.

I pulled my cell phone out to call the prison to confirm nothing had delayed Easton's release when a metallic groan alerted me to movement.

The gate slid open slowly, sounding like an ancient garage door struggling to maintain control.

Easton emerged in a white shirt and jeans, his brown jacket open in the front despite the frigid air.

Damn, he looked fine.

It felt like he walked toward me in slow motion, his brown hair with caramel highlights swaying in the breeze. With his fists shoved inside his coat pockets, Easton scanned his surroundings, searching for me. And when he found me, he smiled so wide, I could see his teeth.

I froze. I'd dreamed of this moment every night, and here I was, not running and jumping into his body, wrapping my legs around him like I thought I would. It was as if all the happiness I felt had paralyzed me.

Closing the distance between us, Easton kept his eyes fixed on mine with such severe focus that a car could've hit him and he'd have still kept his gaze on me. A hungry determination, patience losing its last edge, flashed through his stare as he finally reached me. Grabbed my waist and slammed his lips against mine.

We hadn't kissed for over two and a half years, and I swore it was like a drug exploding passion through my entire body. I had fantasized about having his lips on mine so many times, but this was more intensely better than I had ever imagined.

Easton's hands were in my hair, and mine were around his neck, pulling his ripped body against mine. We kissed and kissed and groped until we realized we could do more—so much more—as soon as we got home. Only the promise of *more* gave us the power to pause.

"I love you." He looked down at me with his sapphire eyes.

"I love you." I grinned. "Now, let's go home."

Easton smiled and opened my car door for me.

As we drove away from the prison, I knew that we could handle whatever life threw our way after everything we'd overcome.

Two lost souls leaving the ugly past behind and embracing the beauty of the future.

EPILOGUE

WILLOW

I did not have a sixth sense that something dark and twisted was about to happen. Or that I'd soon be fighting for my life. I was simply focused on grabbing a quick drink with some friends at a nearby restaurant.

As I walked over to the table where Zoey, Emily, and Jenna were already seated, I reminded myself not to stare at the scar slashed across Jenna's face. My friends were with another woman who I struggled to place.

"Willow!" Zoey jumped up and gave me a hug, then motioned toward the unfamiliar face. "Have you met Fallon?"

"I don't think so," I said.

"Fallon and I used to work out at the same gym," Zoey explained. "Before it burned to the ground, that is."

Right. The fire. Zoey had seriously been through the wringer.

"Good to meet you." Fallon shook my hand. "I hope you don't mind me crashing. I was just finishing up dinner with a friend and saw Zoey here. Thought I'd say hi."

"It's always nice to meet someone new." I smiled.

That was when I spotted him.

Shane Hernandez.

Walking toward the front of the restaurant from the men's room, he didn't seem to notice all the women's eyes in the place being pulled in his direction. He didn't seem to notice them salivating over his ripped body that tried to break free of his emerald button-down shirt and deliciously tight black pants. His black hair looked effortlessly styled, complementing the olive skin that stretched across his stubbled jaw—a jaw I'd fantasized kissing on more than one occasion.

I wondered if he ever sensed my attraction to him. It had been there since the moment he moved into the apartment next door to mine, but maybe he just saw me as a friend. A person he held the building's door open for, a person he exchanged mail with whenever the mailman swapped some parcels in the wrong box, and on a really great day, a person he stopped and talked to.

Maybe *friend* was even too generous of a term.

After all, he knew very little about me.

But that was all about to change.

Because as a detective, he'd soon work my case, determined to uncover the secret of how I'd fallen from a bridge into the deadly river below.

Was it an accident? Was I thrown? If so, who would want me dead?

And would they try again?

Working to uncover the shocking truth about that fateful evening, we had no idea what was about to happen to us both...

* * *

. . .

WHEN A HOPELESS ROMANTIC SURVIVES A FALL FROM A BRIDGE, SHE MUST uncover the secret of what happened that night. Was it an accident? Was she thrown? If so, who would want her dead? Will they try again? As she works with a handsome detective investigating the case, she can't fight her growing feelings. Nor can she fight the shocking truth about that fateful evening... or what's about to happen to them both... Don't miss it. **One click now** or order from your favorite retailer at KathyLockheart.com.

WHAT **SHOCKING PLAN DID EASTON HAVE AS HE WALKED ALONG THE lakefront the fateful day he met Zoey?** As a THANK YOU TO READERS, delve into this **exclusive FREE chapter from Easton's POV** (www.KathyLockheart.com/EastonPOV). It will leave you breathless...

FINALLY, IF YOU LOVED THIS NOVEL, I WOULD GREATLY APPRECIATE A **QUICK REVIEW** (even just two words!) on Amazon.

* * *

HAVEN'T READ THE REST OF THE SECRETS AND THE CITY SERIES? CATCH UP with all the interconnected characters now!

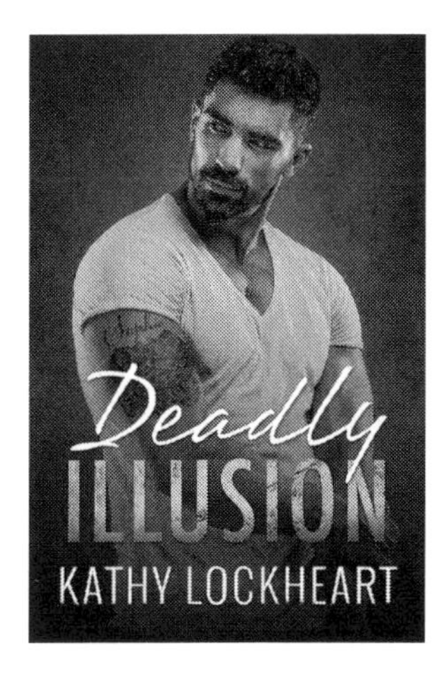

DEADLY ILLUSION: She was able to hide the bruises from everyone...until an MMA fighter came along. Now he'll die to protect her. Maybe even kill...

Characters from Lethal Justice in Deadly Illusion: Zoey & Emily

FATAL CURE: A DEA agent has no idea that the criminal kingpin she's hunting...is her boyfriend...

Characters from Lethal Justice in Fatal Cure: Shane

ACKNOWLEDGMENTS

First, **I'd like to thank you, the reader.** Your time is incredibly valuable, and I strive to give you an immersive reading experience that you will love. You have a ton of options when it comes to books, and you gave me and my books a chance. THANK YOU. Readers mean the world to me, and I'd love to connect with you. Please find my social media links at www.KathyLockheart.com.

Thank you to my husband for believing in me more than I believe in myself. We celebrated a milestone anniversary during the writing of this, and I love you more than you will ever understand.

Thank you to my children for bringing immense joy into my life. Getting to be with you and watch you as you grow is the most rewarding, wonderful experience of my life. I don't know how I got so lucky to have you both. I love you.

To my family for loving and encouraging me every step of the way. For my mother, who is a walking embodiment of kindness, your spirit has inspired me to be the best version of myself possible. To my dad, watching your inspirational fight to reclaim your life motivates me to keep pushing, even when times are hard. And to my sister, your love and kindness are felt more than you know.

To the rest of my family, thank you for cheering me on and being such a vital part of my life! Your love is the fuel that keeps me going on the hard days.

To my friends, Kristin and Sharon, for your incredible support. For cheering me on when I was taking a huge swing in life, and never showing a trace of doubt along the way. You guys are amazing, and I'm so blessed to have you in my life.

To my official beta readers and early ARC readers: Amy, Kristen, Katy, Alyson, Kayla, Terry, and Tracey! Thank you for reading this long before it was done and for all your valuable insights that made Lethal Justice even better!

To my editors—Susan Staudinger. Your brainstorming sessions and multiple rounds of editing made this story remarkably better than it would have been without you! And Jovana Shirley with Unforeseen Editing, and Judy's Proofreading—who ensured this novel was in fantastic shape. To my cover artist, Hang Le, for bringing such beauty to this novel!

To all the people who bring kindness and joy into the world. Thank you for making this world a better place!

LET'S CONNECT!

The easiest way to connect with me is to go to my website, www.KathyLockheart.com, and find my social media links. I interact with readers, so don't be surprised if you see me reply to your post or invite you to join a reader team!

Xoxo

Kathy

amazon.com/Kathy-Lockheart/e/B08XY5F2XG
bookbub.com/profile/kathy-lockheart
facebook.com/KathyLockheartAuthor
tiktok.com/@kathylockheart_author
instagram.com/kathy_lockheart
twitter.com/Kathy_Lockheart
pinterest.com/kathylockheart

Printed in Great Britain
by Amazon